SHADOWRUN

PREYING FOR KEEPS

Mel Odom

A ROC BOOK

ROC
Published by the Penguin Group
Penguin Books USA Inc., 375 Hudson Street,
New York, New York 10014, U.S.A.
Penguin Books Ltd, 27 Wrights Lane,
London W8 5TZ, England
Penguin Books Australia Ltd, Ringwood,
Victoria, Australia
Penguin Books Canada Ltd, 10 Alcorn Avenue,
Toronto, Ontario, Canada M4V 3B2
Penguin Books (N.Z.) Ltd, 182–190 Wairau Road,
Auckland 10, New Zealand

Penguin Books Ltd, Registered Offices:
Harmondsworth, Middlesex, England

First published by Roc, an imprint of Dutton Signet,
a division of Penguin Books USA Inc.

First Printing, July, 1996
10 9 8 7 6 5 4 3 2 1

Series Editor: Donna Ippolito
Cover art by: Carl Galian

Printed in the United States of America

SOMETHING TOLD SKATER THIS WAS MAGIC,

but before he could fire his gun, a whirling mass of shimmering hot air came at him from one corner of the room.

The flaming creature knocked his arm aside, making the bullet go wide of its intended target. More than two meters high and the color and consistency of orange clay, the body was roughly humanoid but definitely lizard-like. Fire clung to it like gossamer webs. Its eyes looked like they'd been poked into its head with a dull stick, and it had a crooked slash for a mouth. The thing had to be a fire elemental.

Skater yanked a pole from the second-floor hallway railing and swung it at the elemental. He'd been told that madmen had the best chance against elementals on the physical plane because they became obsessed.

The pole collided with the elemental's face hard enough to jar the thing's head. Flaming yellow blood trickled down its snout.

With a ragged howl of rage, the elemental filled one hand with a spinning ball of flaming plasma and threw it at Skater. The ball grew as it passed through the air. . . .

This book is for Darrel Madden.

For years you've been my friend, stood by me when the times were bad, sheared my ego down to size when things were going too well. You've been there to help me build dreams, and offered a hand to pull me out of the rubble of the ones that fell.

You've changed diapers on my kids, put up with inane jokes that only second-graders know how to tell terribly, and given doorknob wedgies to the children who really deserved it. Plus you play killer Super-Mario Kart.

Since I've known you, I've never had to wonder if I was ever without a friend, never had to question if my back was covered when we were in situations that looked tense. I knew you were there.

Sometimes family doesn't just come from flesh and blood, and I'm glad you and I are family.

Acknowledgments

My thanks to agent Ethan Ellenberg, who steered me in this direction.

Thanks to Donna Ippolito and Jodie at FASA Corporation, who gave me permission to play in their world, then a map to go with it. I couldn't have done it without you keeping me on track. Your energy and enthusiasm and patience are deeply appreciated. See you next year at GenCon!

To the folks at DarkCon here in Oklahoma who talked with me about the game.

And to my wife, Sherry, who put up with trolls and orks and magical nasties during the writing of this book, as well as our four children. Matthew Lane, Matthew Dain, Montana, and Shiloh, my kids. (They like to see their names in books, and it gives them something for show-n-tell day.) Also, they kept me inspired by looking through the sourcebooks I had scattered everywhere, going, "Cool! Hey, Dad, did you see this really neat monster? You should put it in your book!"

And to you readers: Run the shadows with skill and luck and nerve, chummers. Enjoy!

1

Buckled into the open cargo bay of the Fiat-Fokker Cloud Nine, Jack Skater felt the cool night air whip around him, carrying the wet taste of the approaching storm front. He trained his low-light binoculars on their prey. "How's it look, Wheeler? You got a positive lock?"

"Ninety-two percent probability of a hit," the dwarf rigger called from the cockpit where he was jacked into the controls of the amphibian plane. "Targeting computer says that's the best you're gonna get."

Peering through the binoculars, Skater saw the name *Sapphire Seahawk* emblazoned on the freighter's stern in English and Sperethiel and that she flew the flag of the elven nation of Tir Tairngire. Both would have been nearly invisible in the crawling dark of the storm, but the ship was running some lights, however minimal.

Pocketing the binox, Skater grabbed the lip of the cargo bay and hoisted himself back inside the plane. He unbuckled the safety harness and let it drop. At twenty-five, he was dark and slim, something under two meters, with high cheekbones, dusky skin, and thick, close-cropped black hair that showed the influence of Salish blood. He lived in Seattle now, and had since 2049, but he'd grown up in the Salish-Shidhe Council lands surrounding that outpost of the United Canadian and American States that was the Seattle sprawl.

Dressed in black and wearing combat gear that supported a shoulder-holstered Ares Predator II, a monofilament sword sheathed down his back, and a variety of other weapons, Skater looked more like he should be running the streets than riding the night skies over the Pacific.

"How far?" he asked.

"About a minute and we'll be within range."

Skater looked up at Elvis. "You done?"

The troll samurai had been connecting the Conner grapple gun to the firmpoint under the belly of the amphibian through the access port. Also wearing black, he was nearly two and a half meters of hard muscle and broad mien. The flat features showed a cruel history, reflected in a silver-crowned tusk and a twisted left horn. "You betcha," he rumbled in deep bass.

Sliding his hands over his gear in one final inventory, Skater glanced over at Wheeler. "Ten seconds, then fire at will."

"You got it."

Skater turned next to Quint Duran. "Keep bloodshed to a minimum," he said, not softening his tone though the ork had a good ten years on him. "Those fragging elves hold a grudge as long as god."

Duran scowled, his face a map of past violence. Silver tainted his bushy dark hair, and gold hoop earrings dangled from his elongated ears. His synthleathered armor was as scarred and war-worn as his face, and he held a pump-action Franchi SPAS-22 combat shotgun in one gnarled fist. "I read you."

Skater nodded and walked back to the cargo bay to check on Wheeler. His brain cybernetically linked to the controls, the rigger had heeled the amphib over and was gliding down for the kill like a swooping hawk. Squat and broad, with an immense nose and slightly pointed ears, Wheeler Iron-Nerve worn his hair braided into a single length, its dirty chestnut color only slightly lighter than his full, bushy beard.

The uneven planes of the ocean rushed up at the Fiat-Fokker, which was now just meters above the water, racing along in the same northeasterly direction the *Sapphire Seahawk* was taking to Seattle. They'd planned the operation well, choosing to attack where the freighter was most vulnerable—here at this point about equidistant from both Seattle and its home in the Tir. Certain aspects of the run were tricky, but once aboard the freighter, all they really had to do was lift some files from its computer system. And they had the magic, the muscle, and the decker to do it.

"How you holding up, Trey?" Skater asked.

The mage stood against the bulkhead on the other side of the cargo bay. All in black like the rest, he wore form-fitting body armor and a heavy Kevlar cape with high collar that was almost roguish on his slender, intense build. Thin beads of gleaming perspiration, ignited by stray strands of moonlight spilling through the amphibian's windows, dotted Cullen Trey's handsome face. "Making this bird invisible to either organic or technological detection isn't my idea of a slotting good time, chummer."

Skater unclipped the D-ring from his combat rigging while leaving the other end secured, and leaned out the cargo bay. Lowering himself outside the door, fighting the wind, he clung to the plane, tripped the light-enhancement circuitry in his eyes and watched as the grapple gun spun on its turret, locking on target. The charge of compressed air fired the grappling hook toward the *Sapphire Seahawk,* the wire spilling out behind it, whirring in a high-pitched scream.

Skater watched the line go taut, managed by a computer-assisted tension governor built into the gun.

"Locked on," Wheeler crowed triumphantly.

Reaching out, Skater attached the D-ring and let go of the amphibian. The governor allowed just enough slack to send him sliding toward the *Sapphire Seahawk* three hundred meters away. Even with the Cloud Nine throttled down, it was rapidly overtaking the ship. Accessing his Commlink IV, Skater tripped the Crypto Circuit HD to scramble all transmissions along the two radio and two telephone channels provided. The rest of the team carried the matching circuits on their headware. All except Trey, who used an external setup. Cybertech was commonplace in the Awakened world of 2057, but new rules existed ever since the return of magic. One of the firmest was that a mage and cyberware didn't mix.

"Count off," Skater called out. He shot across the open expanse of water, shedding altitude as he dropped toward the freighter. The line could hold only three people per hundred meters without snapping, so the five members of the team had staggered their approach accordingly. By the time Skater reached the *Sapphire Seahawk,* the D-ring was smoking and glowing cherry-red from the friction.

"You're made, kid," came Duran's gruff warning.

Scarcely forty meters out from the freighter's starboard side, Skater saw the shadows pull free of the deck and advance toward him. If there'd been any way to return to the amphibian, he'd have done it.

The sailors were dressed in the ship's yellow and red, and these elves obviously had no compunction about shooting first and asking questions later. Bullets sliced through the air around him, some of them phosphorus tracers burning past in purple blurs.

Two of the elves raced for the grappling hook buried in the wooden coaming of the upper deck while others prepared to meet Skater and friends.

"Skater," Wheeler called out, "you're running out of wire."

Just as he reached the freighter's side, Skater kicked in his boosted reflexes and unclipped the D-ring. His momentum carried him over the heads of the elves as he fell to the deck. "I'm on."

He pushed himself to his feet as hands reached for him. Computer-augmented reflexes honed by a lifetime of fighting for his own took over. He grabbed an outstretched hand and twisted it viciously, snapping the elbow behind it with an audible crack. An agonized moan followed immediately. No bloodshed didn't mean no maiming.

Slipping past two awkward blows aimed at his face as the press of elves swarmed around him, Skater kicked another sailor in the groin with enough force to double the man over. Bullets chopped into the wooden wall behind him with thunderous explosions.

"I'm on," Elvis roared.

Skater saw some of the elves break from him, moving to take on the troll. Knowing others were closing on the grappling hook imbedded overhead, he took two quick steps and sprang off the elf he'd dropped, using the body as a footstool to leap up and grab the coaming above him. He arched his body and flipped, landing on his feet in a squatting position just as one of the sailors advanced on the grappling line with a sword.

Pushing himself up and forward, Skater reached over his shoulder and ripped his monofilament sword free of its scabbard. The second elf shouted a warning in Sperethiel and then launched himself at Skater.

There wasn't much room to maneuver on the lip, but Skater managed to grab the leaping man's hair in his free hand while bringing his knee up into the elf's face. Bone crunched. He dropped his unconscious foe and lunged over him.

The first elf lashed his sword toward the cable with enough force to sever it easily, but not before Skater's sword sheared through the metal near the haft, leaving the elf with only a stub fronting the ornate basket hilt. The blade went spiraling loosely and clattered to the deck.

"You scrod-scarfing brainwipe," the elf snarled. He reached for the pistol at his hip.

Skater flicked his blade once, then stepped forward and gave the elf a mouthful of the sword's knuckle bow. Squalling in pain and anger, the elf went backward and over the lip of the deck, crashing down among the crowd attempting to stop Elvis. The troll was a rolling dreadnought of Arnie-Awesome cyberware unleashed in full frenzy.

"I'm on." Quint Duran dropped into an easy standing position only a few steps from the sailors. Without hesitation, he waded into the thick of the battle, triggering the SPAS-22 in a wide circle. His years as a merc had made him one chill opponent in combat. Elves scattered in all directions.

Trey was next to drop from the grappling line to the freighter's deck, a shimmering wave spewing from his hands. Wherever it touched, elven sailors collapsed in crumpled heaps.

Not all of them went down, however, but Duran and Elvis were making short work of the survivors.

"I'm on." Shiva, flame-haired and also dressed in skintight black, was just hitting the deck. More than two meters tall and possessing skillsofts and vat muscle, she immediately began to wreak havoc with a collapsible fighting staff. Once a bounty hunter, Shiva was as devastating as Duran when the drek hit the fan.

Trey meanwhile had whipped out his polished wooden walking stick. Among other nasty little surprises, the cane also powered up as a stun baton. He parried a sword thrust, then brought the stick up into his opponent's crotch and triggered the stun charge. Visible electric current sizzled blue-white veins through the air. The elf went down like he'd been poleaxed. Trey moved on, gripping his cape in one hand. He hadn't been born to street-fighting, but he had a natural aptitude.

"Drek, the line ran out," Wheeler warned over the commlink.

Skater heard the deep-throated *sproing* of the cable separating as it hummed past his ear.

"Jack."

He turned, recognizing Archangel's voice. The elven decker was still almost three meters out, and the grappling wire had snapped. Dropping his sword, taking the sweep and roll of the freighter into account, Skater grabbed the line, his hands partially protected by fingerless gloves. He gripped and yanked with everything he had. "Gotcha."

Archangel came over the side and joined him on the second deck, miraculously keeping her balance with his help. She was as tall as Skater, but slender and small-breasted, almost childlike. Her hair, platinum and normally worn long, was now tucked up under a tight black skull cap that showed the outline of her very pointed elven ears. Almond in shape, her bronze eyes held orbiting gold flecks that were strangely hypnotic. The gleam of the datajack on her right temple was masked by the same camou cosmetics that streaked her beautiful face. Her deck hung from a strap over her shoulder in a waterproof case, counter-balanced by an Ares Light Fire 70 in a crossdraw holster on her left hip.

She pushed herself out of his arms. Nothing personal, Skater knew, but the decker liked her space, didn't like being touched at all. Archangel wasn't her real name, but he'd never been given anything else to call her.

Skater took the lead. The storm was overtaking the freighter and rain was starting to fall, making the deck slippery. He raced to the stern, Archangel only steps behind him.

A trio of elven sailors met them at the companionway leading down into the private quarters of the *Sapphire Seahawk.*

Skater threw himself backward, flattening against the wall as bullets ripped long wooden splinters from the coaming. "Fraggit!" he swore. He sheathed the sword, drawing the Predator II and palming a flash grenade instead.

"Elvis," Skater called out over the commlink. "Fall back astern."

"You got it, chummer."

Skater peeled the pin from the flash grenade. Counting it down, he tossed it toward the companionway, then closed his eyes and told Archangel to do the same.

The instant the brunt of the explosion was over and the flare had died away, Skater ran toward the companionway. Looking over the side, he saw two elves beating embers from their clothing and coughing hard enough to hack up a lung. He leaped over the side and dropped on them. Swinging the Predator, he caught one man alongside the temple and put him down. Then he swung into a sleeper hold on the other elf, choking him into unconsciousness.

"Elvis," Skater cried out as he tried the door at the bottom of the companionway and found it locked. "The door."

"Step aside, stringbean." The troll came down the stairs, fitting tight with the armor and weapons on him.

Elvis drew back one enormous hobnailed boot, then drove it forward. The door was made of ceramic and steel and didn't give, but it was mounted in wooden framing that did, with a squealing shriek.

Skater dove through the door, the Predator gripped in his fist. The room was a private berth, filled with a bed, desk and chair, and a short sofa.

One of the four elves inside came at him, firing point-blank. The bullets smashed against Skater's armor like hammer blows, stealing his breath away. Skater grabbed one of the elves and drove him backward, firing as fast as he could over the man's shoulder.

He put three rounds into another guard's knees and cut his legs out from under him, tried to home in on a second man, but then the sailor he was holding brought his pistol up. Headbutting him in the face and braking his nose, Skater stripped the Ceska vz/120 from the elf's grip and threw it to the floor. He spun and caught the elf with a roundhouse kick that put him down.

An elven female dressed in street synthleather, looking as slender and unthreatening as Archangel, suddenly bared two sets of forearm snap-blades. Coolly and dispassionately, she rushed Elvis.

Setting himself with difficulty in the belowdecks room, the troll met her attack with a series of blocks and parries that were too quick for Skater to follow. Flesh slapped flesh, and three lines of blood appeared like magic over Elvis's left eye.

Another elf had been moving near the massive computer array against the wall, pulling the datajack out of hiding and toward his temple. Skater fired a round without warning, putting it through the elf's thigh while Elvis and his opponent fought. Keeping the elf covered, Skater glanced back and saw that the troll was bleeding from another cut on his cheek and two on his left arm. But a cruel smile raked his lips back. Without warning, Elvis popped out of a defensive posture and backhanded the woman with a paw the size of a two-liter bottle.

The razorgirl flew backward and struck the wall. She struggled briefly to get to her feet, then gave it up. Elvis moved in to secure her with pulse cuffs that would keep her cyberware inactive even if she woke before the team was done here.

"Down on the floor," Skater told the elf he'd shot. The sailor moved slowly, looking for an opening, but Skater didn't give it to him. By the time he and Elvis had cuffed the other elves, Archangel was jacked into her deck.

"Done," Elvis said, breathing hard. "Fraggin' dandelion-eater was slotting good." He touched his bloody forehead and gazed at the wet crimson.

Nodding, Skater moved over to join Archangel. "Any chance we simply rip out the drive and beat feet?"

She shook her head. "It's boosted for self-destruct if anyone tries to move it. I tripped to the sensors already, but whoever hid them really knew what they were doing."

"Get what you can." Then Skater told Elvis to search their prisoners while he tossed the drawers and traveling packs. In less than two minutes he knew they weren't going to find anything more.

"Skater."

Looking up, Skater saw Quint Duran standing at the top of the companionway. The ork's armor had fresh scratches.

"We could be overrun any minute," Duran said. "The elves are regrouping, getting ready to have another go. Trey's sleep spell didn't affect as many as we'd hoped."

"Stay with her," Skater instructed Elvis as he dropped a lockbar into place over the other door in the cabin. He went up the steps at a dead run and breathing hard. His ribs ached from the impacts of the bullets, promising bruises—if he lived long enough for them to show.

Shiva was nestled comfortably behind a Narcoject rifle, taking advantage of the cover provided at the side of the cabin. Trey was on the other side, his hands glowing, then flashing dimly.

"The sleep spell worked fine," Trey grumbled. "These guys came from belowdecks where I couldn't see them."

"Two minutes," Skater said. "Then we're outta here. Archangel's into their system."

"You don't have the two minutes," Wheeler said over the commlink. "We've got bogeys coming up from the east."

Skater spun, searching the wine-dark sky. Then he spotted them, a tight trio of helos aimed straight for the freighter. They were on the *Sapphire Seahawk* in seconds as heavy machine gun fire began smashing into the decks.

2

"Down there!" Skater ordered. "Move it!"

Nobody argued. There was nowhere else to go but back down the companionway stairs. Cullen Trey went first, gliding by in his cape, followed by Shiva.

"Go, kid," Quint Duran growled. He lifted the SPAS-22 as the first of the helo troops hit the freighter's deck, and took up a covering position.

A ruby laser sight blazed across Skater's face, sending him against the companionway for more cover. A bullet burned the air where he'd been a second before.

The helo teams moved with clockwork precision, breaking into groups that hurried to secure the command positions aboard the freighter. Duran's shotgun blasted twice, putting one gunner down and sparking fire from the rotorblades of the nearest helo. The pilot pulled back a few meters, then swiveled and rained hell across the companionway entrance with twin cannon.

"Yakuza," Duran said, following Skater as he rushed down the companionway stairs.

"You sure?" Skater demanded, looking around the room for any means of escape.

"You wanna go back and scan it yourself?"

Skater shot him a look as he leaned down to grab the door that had been ripped from its frame. "Elvis, lend me a hand."

The troll grabbed the door and helped Skater shove it roughly back into position. Skater pointed at the bed.

Quickly, the troll ripped the bed into pieces and brought the two long metal support struts over, wedging them between the floor and the door. "Not gonna hold much if they decide to play rough," Elvis said.

"You sure you don't know what's in that system?" Shiva asked, checking the loads on her Ares Crusader machine pistol.

Skater looked at her sharply. "I'm sure," he said coolly.

Shiva looked up just as sharply, but her expression was unreadable.

"I really don't think this is something we've got time for at the moment," Cullen Trey said dryly.

The first handful of bullets peppered the wedged door, causing it to vibrate. Shiva turned her attention there.

Skater accessed the Commlink IV. "Wheeler, talk to me."

"Yaks," the dwarf said. "Thick as ants at a fragging picnic."

"Can you home in on us?" Skater dropped to his knees and checked the flooring. It was wood, thick and gnarled, with scuff marks from years of use.

"Got you on the screen now, chummer."

"Stay with us, then," Skater said, "because we're getting the frag out of here."

"How?" Shiva demanded. "You figured out how to walk through walls and let bullets pass through you in the last couple minutes?"

"We go down." With a smooth motion, Skater drew the monofilament sword and used it to hack a large triangle in the center of the room's floor. It took two tries to kick the section of flooring away.

Just then a massive impact staggered the wedged door, forcing it back and leaving it listing open a few more centimeters than before. Smoke curled snarling tendrils around the door and reached into the room.

Thrusting the SPAS-22 through on his side of the door, Duran squeezed the trigger. The harsh *baloom* of the shotgun was near deafening in the confined space, but not loud enough to drown out Archangel's sudden screams of pain.

Skater whirled as she spilled from the chair onto the floor. As he rushed over, her eyes rolled back up in her head, her lids flickering like juiced Korean advertisements scaling buildings in downtown Seattle. She wasn't breathing.

"Dump shock," Trey said, joining Skater. "Whatever she ran into, the IC must have been rather nasty." The corps weren't shy about packing their systems with ever more vicious Intrusion Countermeasures, and no matter how good the decker, any Matrix run could be her last.

Skater silently agreed. Tilting Archangel's head back to make sure her breathing passages were clear, Skater clamped his lips to hers and started artificial respiration. Another few breaths and she was breathing on her own, though still unconscious.

"Stay with her," Skater told Trey.

"You got it," Trey said, stooping down to cradle the decker's head and shoulders gently.

Skater moved. Any time a decker rode a flaming board down, there was the chance of permanent neural damage. He'd met burned-out cowboy deckers who were worse than paraplegics.

Hunkering down beside the hole he'd cut into the floor, he palmed a flash from a pocket and pointed the hard yellow beam down into the bowels of the freighter. Support struts crisscrossed in a maze below him.

"Elvis," Skater said. "You take Archangel."

"Sure." Elvis slipped an arm almost tenderly under the unconscious elf. "Going to be some climbing, eh?"

"And that's the easy part," Skater admitted. It took another two slashes with the monofilament sword to make the hole big enough for the troll and the elf together. "Cullen, take the lead with your flash. Go all the way to the bottom and forward. Till you can't go anymore."

Trey dropped without a word, sinking through the maze of crisscrossed struts. Elvis followed, Archangel draped over one huge shoulder.

Taking out his Predator and checking that its magazine was full, Skater raced to the door blocking the companionway. Duran fired two rounds, then withdrew his shotgun long enough to thumb fresh shells into it.

"Go," Skater told Shiva.

"So we can take a chance on drowning?" she demanded. Blood seeped from scratches along her right cheek.

"Up to you if you want to live long enough to get out of here."

"You think you can pull this one off?" The harshness had gone out of her voice.

Skater had never quite gotten used to the mercurial changes in Shiva's temperament. "I've got a plan."

She recharged her weapon, then patted him on the cheek. "I fragging love it when you say that."

"Move."

Shiva dropped through the hole in a heartbeat.

Duran blasted another target, then ducked back. A renewed fusillade struck the door, making it quiver and jump. "You figure you can cowboy your way out of this one?" Duran asked.

"Won't know till we try," Skater said. He moved to the deck and quickly rigged a shaped explosive behind it that would create a blast of shrapnel when detonated. He accessed the Commlink IV. "Trey, use that tube of phosphorus and lay down a circle against the outer hull big enough that we can get through."

"The water pressure'll push it back in on us if we burn out a section," Trey said. "We won't be able to get out."

"Trust me on this one."

"Bad news," Duran said, pulling back from the door. "Looks like the yaks have got a shaman in one of the helos, and I don't think he's catching up on his t'ai chi."

Skater peered through the door and spotted the Japanese mage in the open cargo hold of a helo hovering out of range of either the shotgun or his pistol. The willowy movements of the man's arms and hands were careful and measured.

Suddenly the air in front of him rippled, disturbed by something even more fierce than the storm.

"Some kind of drekking spirit," Duran snarled.

The spirit whirled and twisted like a kite caught in the wind, then started for the companionway.

"Go!" Skater shouted, grabbing the ork and shoving him roughly toward the hole cut into the floor.

Duran scrambled between the struts, dropping toward the bottom of the ship.

Skater followed him, his boots slipping on the narrow steel beams. Before he could duck below the floor, a lightning bolt flared outside, visible through the uneven seams. Then the door jerked like it just got hit by a big Ford-Canada Bison running a full load. Reduced to smoking scraps of metal, it offered no barrier to the black thundercloud that flew into the room, internal lightnings flickering like pulsebeats. Then it disappeared as the first of the yakuza reached the opening it had made.

Skater dropped through the struts, Skater working his way

aft while Duran joined up with the others at the opposite end of the freighter. He played his flash over the bulkhead, trying to figure the stress points.

In the end, there was no time for finesse. He simply shoved the shaped plastic explosive charges onto the bulkhead toward the center, flicking the detonators to stagger them only a second or two apart, and fled back through the ankle-deep water sitting at the bottom of the hull. The others were almost thirty meters away, taking defensive positions.

"Trey," Skater transmitted. "Have you got that phosphorus circle ready?"

"Yes, but—"

"Detonate it when I tell you." Skater struggled through the maze of struts, catching his shin painfully against one that his flash didn't pick up in time. He tripped the first detonator switch via his commlink.

Sounding like basso drumbeats, the explosions ripped the stern right out of the *Sapphire Seahawk.* Roiling sea water spilled into the hull and raced the length of the ship, drinking it down. The stern dropped dramatically, throwing their yakuza pursuers off balance.

None of them had expected this run to turn out like this. "Wait, Trey," Skater said. The water around his boots got even deeper, then became a raging flood.

The torrent ripped the yakuza from the lattice-work of struts.

"Wheeler," Skater called. "What about those helos?"

"They're going in for emergency rescue, but they're playing hell with the elves now that most of them have recovered from the sleep spell."

"Works in our favor. We'll set off a smoke grenade once we're off the ship. We need you—fast."

"Won't be easy," the rigger said. "One of the deck guns just flamed a helo. The yaks have more problems than they thought, but we're a target, too."

Skater struggled through another tight spot. The water was swirling around his waist now, and he suddenly found himself pushing up a growing incline. He could see Trey up ahead, the water up to his knees. Skater also felt the air pressure thickening. The water slowed because of it, choked off by the huge air pocket that had formed.

"Okay, Trey," Skater transmitted. "Set the phosphorus

off." He was still eight meters away, sweating from his exertions in spite of the water.

He saw Trey perform an intricate series of gestures, then platinum fire jetted from his fingers. The phosphorus ignited at once, adding its sorcerous heat to the chemical's. The metal grew violently orange and red as a hole was sliced into it.

Elvis turned and held Archangel in both arms against his chest, shielding her. Duran and Shiva braced themselves to meet the falling oval of metal while Trey prepared another spell.

Instead, the cut piece was shoved outward. Skater grinned as he forced himself to a faster pace. The internal air pressure had increased enough to be a telling factor even though the hole he'd cut through the deck flooring in the stern had let some of the water and air pressures equalize.

The downside, however, was that the water pouring in through the holed stern had reached tidal wave proportions now, following the air bubble out. The water was up to Skater's chest and rising fast, knocking him off balance.

"Go!" he yelled.

Shiva hesitated only long enough to take the mini-scuba mask from Archangel's pocket and then seal it to the decker's lower face. Then she slipped her own mask into place and led the way through the hole in the side of the freighter. Elvis followed, stepping into one of the large bubbles spilling out of the ship.

Then the water level swelled up over Skater, turning everything black. He clapped his own mini-scuba to his face and sealed it to his skin. The mini-scubas were only good for about ten minutes of air at normal use. With the way his adrenaline was flowing, and the demands for oxygen his body was already making on his lungs, he knew he'd be lucky to get five minutes.

Then his hand found the semi-smooth edge of the cut hull. He pulled himself through, scraping a shoulder hard enough to rip his shirt and abrade the flesh beneath.

Despite the mini-scuba, Skater's lungs were aching for air by the time he reached the surface. Duran was only a short distance away, stubbornly treading water while holding onto the SPAS-22.

"You've got a smoke grenade," Skater said. "Set it off and let's fade."

"Done." Duran peeled the activation tab on the smoke grenade, then tossed it away. The grenade landed on the ocean surface and floated for a heartbeat. Then the contents ignited, spewing a dark lavender cloud across the water. Also visible were hot particles that obscured infrared detection the dwarf rigger could use to spot them.

Skater looked back at the *Sapphire Seahawk.* The freighter was definitely going down, dropping centimeters at a time while it shifted and rolled over on its port side. Fiery remnants of a yakuza helo lay scattered nearby.

"I see you," Wheeler radioed. "I'm on my way."

The amphibian heeled overhead like a gull spotting prey, and streaked for the ocean surface, pulling up sharply before dipping its pontoons into the water. Combined with the stiff traction of the sea, full flaps stopped the craft in short order.

A yellow floodlight suddenly raked the ocean surface ahead of Skater.

"We've been spotted," Shiva called out.

"Swim for it," Skater said. There was no other choice. He looked over his shoulder briefly, seeing the helo suddenly pull away from the floundering ship.

Trey reached the amphibian first, pulling himself up onto the pontoon and managing the door. He helped Elvis with Archangel, getting her up into the craft, then he pointed and shouted something.

Ten meters out from the amphibian, Skater couldn't hear or see what had set Trey off. But before he had time to think about it, a long, white tentacle with dark blue mottling snaked out of the water and lashed around Shiva as she clambered aboard the amphibian. It yanked once, pulling her beneath the surface before she had time to scream.

Skater swam, intending to call out to Duran, then coils of rubbery hard muscle closed around his chest and sucked him down.

3

His vision blurred by the depth, Skater saw the reflected lights of the yakuza helo slide by overhead on the ocean surface. His chest felt like it was being crushed, and black spots orbited before his eyes.

"Kraken!" he heard Duran shout over the headlink.

"Jack," Elvis called. "Trey says the fragging thing is shaman-controlled. He's working on it."

Skater tried to answer, but there wasn't enough air left in his lungs. He thought he could see the bulbous head of the kraken somewhere in the darkness further down and ahead of him, but he wasn't sure.

Sluggishly, his fingers found the haft of the sword and he pulled it free, then he somehow twisted and struggled enough to slice the monofilament edge straight through the tentacle. Blood clouded out of the stump, muddying the water, and the amputated coils of meat came bumping against his chest.

Skater came up out of the water, gasping harshly while his lungs burned. He shook the water out of his eyes and got his bearings.

Elvis was pulling Trey's body out of sight into the amphibian. Skater didn't know whether the mage had been hit or was seriously spent from his magical exertions.

The kraken was near the surface now, and all twelve of its appendages were visible as it flailed the water and stirred up undercurrents. Overhead, the yakuza helo circled the bobbing Fiat-Fokker while someone using a loudhailer demanded that everyone inside the plane debark.

Dodging one of the kraken's suckered tentacles, Skater swam for the amphibian. Laser sights lit up the water near him, the ruby ellipses giving him just enough warning to dive before the bullets chased him under.

He surfaced again, almost within reach. Duran was hauling Shiva from the water now. She was covered with blood. Clambering onto the pontoon, Skater managed to throw himself into the amphibian. Elvis was manning a Vindicator minigun, its multiple barrels chewing through a fifty-round belt in a handful of seconds.

Reluctantly, the helo backed off.

"Hang on," Wheeler called from the cockpit. "That fragging overgrown guppy-snatcher is coming for us again." The Fiat-Fokker shivered with increased power and began to skim along the water's surface.

Skater took his Predator II and fired through an entire clip, aiming at the monster's head.

Abruptly, the kraken broke off the attack and turned its attention to the yak helo. Three of its tentacles whipped around the chopper's landing skids and tightened, pulling the aircraft toward the ocean's surface.

Rotors whining, the helo struggled against the pull of the creature's tentacles. An instant after the first blade touched the water's surface and shattered to flying shrapnel, the helo exploded in an orange and black roil of fire and smoke. Hurt and surprised, the kraken released its prize and sank back into the black water.

Skater felt the amphibian's pontoons come free of the sea as the wings cut into the air and achieved lift. He took his flash from his pocket and played it over Shiva.

Her dead eyes gleamed wetly back at him. Bloody splotches left by the suckers of the kraken's tentacles marred her features.

Skater switched off the light, not wanting to see any more.

"Tough break," Duran commented.

Not for the first time, Skater wondered if that was the extent of a shadowrunner's lot. Seemed like not even your chummers missed you when you checked out. "What about Archangel and Trey?"

"Back among the living, chummer," the mage said as he sat up. "Nearly got my astral hoop kicked, though. That yakuza shaman was good." His cocky grin faded when he saw Shiva.

"I think Archangel's going to be okay," Elvis rumbled. He'd yanked a sleeping bag from the equipment stores and made her as comfortable as possible.

Skater glanced through the open cargo doors. The *Sapphire Seahawk* was still blazing merrily, embers chasing themselves up into the gray smoke stream.

"She'd better come through," Duran said, rolling the cargo door shut. "If she doesn't, then this whole run was a royal hose-up and we're all out a lot of capital investment. Not to mention Shiva dying for nothing."

Skater rested his forearms on his bent knees and concentrated first on breathing, then on dwindling inside himself to a place where nothing could touch him. It was the only place he'd ever felt safe, and the one he knew for sure was all an illusion.

* * *

Despite the active net Lone Star and the shore patrol put up, Wheeler managed an uninterrupted landing at the tourist puddle-jumper agency where the team had arranged docking for the amphibian. The rigger powered the amphib expertly into the U-shaped dock and cut the engine.

Throwing open the cargo door, Skater looked out across the smooth glimmer of Elliot Bay mirroring the kaleidoscopic scramble of neon advertising plastering the nearby buildings.

Long John Hurley stood in the shadows on the dock smoking a cigarro. He was gray, tall and lean, chromed over with obsolete cyberware.

"What the frag you people think you were doing?" Hurley groused. He paced along the dock nervously, sucking the cigarro like an automaton, his cyberleg whining with the effort.

Duran shoved his way out of the plane and onto the dock, ignoring Hurley.

"I mean, that drek with the *Sapphire Seahawk* was your handiwork tonight, right?" Hurley slunk back from Duran as the ork turned on him.

Without seeming to move quickly, Duran seized the tour owner by the shirt, ripping the material in one gnarled fist. A keen blade in his hand shattered the thin moonlight. "I'd say I got me a walkaway working here tonight," the ork told him. "I slit one more throat, ain't going to matter." He pulled Hurley closer. "Not to anyone else, and damn sure not to me. You scan?"

"Yeah." The iron drained right out of Hurley's spine. His eyes slid away. "I just don't want a blue crew knocking on my door in the morning."

"They find us," Skater said in a hard voice, "they find you. Simple math." Hurley had been as fair and as trustworthy as could be expected, but the team had never run a profile this high before.

The ork went into the small office, then returned moments later pushing a rolling cart. As they loaded the weapons they used aboard the Fiat-Fokker into the cart, Skater glanced around the marina. They'd chosen the place because it was berthed between two major domestic freight lines that ran "free trade" on the side and had enough grease to keep most groundhounds away.

With all the guns stashed, Elvis handed out Shiva's body, zipped up into one of the sleeping bags.

Skater took the weight with difficulty and forced himself not to think about what was inside. Death was a part of life; he'd learned that in the Council lands from his grandfather, but it had never become a casual thing for him in spite of everything the sprawl had taught him to the contrary. He laid the sleeping bag on top of the pile of weapons and pulled a dark sheet over everything.

Archangel climbed out of the amphibian on her own, her eyes smudged with dark circles. She wiped a small trickle of blood from her right nostril with a handkerchief.

"How you doing?" Skater asked.

"I'm alive," she said. "After a run like tonight's, I'd say that's pretty good."

Skater shook his head and looked over at the sleeping bag holding all that was left of Shiva. "Too bad Shiva can't say that."

Archangel's face was expressionless as ever, but her voice softened. "Don't get twisted with this, Jack. You told us things could get dicey. Shiva knew that as well as the rest of us."

Skater looked at her for a moment, but said nothing more. There was too much else to do. "You know the drill," he told them. "I'll stash our gear and weapons, then meet you back at base."

"I'm going with you." Callously, Duran plucked at the sleeping bag. "You got some extra baggage tonight. I want to make sure it's disposed of properly."

"Tell you the truth," Hyde Tallow said to Skater almost an hour later as he unzipped the sleeping bag and saw the bloody red hair spill from inside, "I've kind of been expecting this."

"Expecting what?" Skater asked. Duran stood behind him. Their voices were low and muffled by the stacks of crates and packages filling the small warehouse off Clay Street where Tallow did business. By day, the warehouse handled soy and artificial foods shipped in from the United Canadian and American States. By night, Tallow moonlighted as an organlegger for Nightingale's Body Parts when product was needed and wouldn't be too closely questioned as to the source. As long as it was good.

"You needing to dispose of a woman's body." Tallow slipped on a pair of transparent gloves with elastic snaps. "Shine that light over here."

Skater moved the flash beam over to Shiva's upper body.

"Wait." Tallow took a step closer and cupped Shiva's face in his hand. The street doc was years from practicing legally, but still ran parts and pieces through the shadows. He was short and broad, but had long white fingers on hands that looked like pale spiders crawling across Shiva's corpse. "This isn't the dancer from SybreSpace."

"No," Skater said. "It's not."

"I figured you two was quits when I started seeing her with other guys. Though I gotta tell you they seemed even less her style than you were."

Skater kept his face impassive, but he felt a twist of pain to think of Larisa with anyone else. It had been five months since he'd seen her, though only days since they'd talked.

Duran shifted uneasily beside Skater. "This guy know you?"

Skater shrugged. "Sometimes we hang at the same spots." That was how he'd first met Tallow, though he'd never used the man before, nor would he again.

Tallow turned to him and smiled. His gloves were already coated with Shiva's blood. "Don't have to worry about me," the street doc said. "Without guys like you, I'd be out combing the alleys looking for skells the Halloweeners or some other street gang might have iced and left for ratmeat." He patted Shiva's dead cheek. "At least this way, I get some healthy merch to deal. And well within the ischemic time of tissue survival for resale. Wouldn't do much good trying to sell dead organs. Bring her over here."

Skater and Duran grabbed the sides of the sleeping bag and followed the street doc into a barren office in the back. A nameplate announced that the office belonged to D. Madden. Congealed blood matted the material of the sleeping bag. They put the corpse on a desk Tallow cleared off. Talking to himself, the street doc opened a concealed vault hidden in the wall and removed a tray of medical instruments, all gleaming and sharp. The room had no windows, so when he switched on the high-intensity lamp over the desk after screwing in another bulb, the light died before leaving the room.

Tallow pushed Shiva's arms toward Skater. "Hold her.

I've got to cut her out of these clothes." A scalpel gleamed in his hand as it whisked through the clothing. In seconds, the corpse was naked.

Skater tried not to react. His grandfather had always insisted a new life awaited after the physical one was spent. He hoped it was so, and he hoped Shiva wasn't looking in on him as he helped cut up what remained of her.

Tallow switched on the laser saw and opened up the corpse's chest, then used a chest spreader that looked like a praying mantis to pull it apart. He talked to himself as he listed the organs that appeared to be in good shape. There wasn't much blood, and Skater was glad of it. By morning, what had once been Shiva would be scattered over the city as black-market organs and bone.

"So how'd Romeo happen to lose his fair Juliet?" Tallow lifted the undamaged heart from the chest cavity. He plopped it into a freon-chilled chamber that had come from the vault as well.

Face hard, tight with the effort to bottle up all the emotions of the moment as well as from memories of the past, Skater said, "She was afraid I'd end up on your table some night."

Duran leaned in, intimidating with his size and black synthleather. "More chopping," he said, "and less fragging yap."

"I don't know exactly what I snatched, but it was well-guarded," Archangel told them, seated in the rented room deep in the Ork Underground a couple of hours later. "I downloaded everything I could, but I still don't know what I got."

Skater stood behind Wheeler Iron-Nerve and beside Elvis, scanning the monitor as Archangel scrolled through the files. Figures and symbols raced across the screen, moving vertically and horizontally in random colors.

"It's coded," Skater said.

Archangel nodded. "If I had more time, maybe I'd be able to break it."

"The one thing we don't have is time," Duran muttered. He stood in one corner, dark and brooding, arms folded across his broad chest. "The yaks are combing the streets looking for the team that hit the *Sapphire Seahawk* tonight."

A cruel smile twisted Elvis's lips in the shadows of his

tusks. "You mean they're giving us all the credit?" The room was small, nearly filled to bursting by the 225-kilogram troll himself. Wooden casks of cheap wine and beer were stacked against the back wall. The Bloody Rosebud of Phelia, named after the ork warrior-woman who died defending her charges at a children's hospital during the Night of Rage, didn't have many customers at one a.m. of a Wednesday morning. A few cheap fuel-oil lanterns with the bar's logo printed on them filled a few handmade wooden shelves on the wall. Cullen Trey sat in a straight-backed chair, paging through a dusty book that had been painstakingly reassembled.

Duran nodded without mirth and ran a hand through his ork's thick mane. "That's exactly what I'm saying."

"What are we going to do with the load?" Archangel asked. "We don't have a buyer, and we're not even sure of what we've got to sell." As always, she looked like she was under zero-sweat.

"Can you copy it?" Skater asked.

"I copied it from the freighter's system, didn't I?"

"Then make four more copies," Skater said. "Give them to everyone else in the room. Not me."

"Why everyone else and not you?" Elvis demanded.

"Because," Wheeler said, "if he already had a buyer, he could cut us out of the loop in a heartbeat. Jack's trying to play square with us. This way he has nothing to sell without us."

"Maybe," Duran said, maintaining his icy expression. "And maybe copies of those files are a way to target the rest of the team."

Wheeler's face grew dark, but before he could respond, Skater told Archangel, "Give me a copy, too." He faced Duran. "You can trust me or not."

Archangel passed the duplicate chips out among them.

"What would you think?" the ork demanded. "You come to us out of the blue with this scam a few weeks ago. You're not sure exactly what we're after, but the buzz is it's worth a few million nuyen to the runners who can nick it and find a buyer. We've been doing well enough. We got plenty of Mr. Johnsons with biz for us. We didn't need this."

"No," Trey said agreeably. "But you didn't bat an eye when Jack laid it out, did you?"

"Stay out of this," Duran snarled.

"I would"—the combat mage smiled affably—"except that I'm already neck-deep in it, chummer. Same chopping block as you. Your own greed pushed you into this, not Jack."

Skater let the silence fill the room, stilling his impulse to say something in his own defense.

"So what's the plan?" Wheeler asked him.

"We separate and lay low till we find out how deep this goes. Then we try turn it around for ourselves. If we can."

"No matter what happens," Trey said, pushing himself up out of his chair and adjusting his cape, "no one can say these past three years haven't been a good run." He held out his hand to Skater. "If I don't see you again, chummer, it's been a slice." His smile seemed genuine.

In their own ways, Wheeler and Elvis echoed Trey's sentiments and offered their hands as well.

Archangel met Skater's glance full on, but didn't give him her hand. Skater knew it was her way. "This isn't over, Jack," she said softly. "Take care of yourself."

Skater didn't think it was over either, but he nodded.

"It was no coincidence the yakuza showed up almost at the same time we did," Duran said.

Skater knew it was true. With all the shipping in and out of Seattle, the *Sapphire Seahawk* would have been hard to identify without some kind of tracking device or foreknowledge of its route.

"That tells me that somebody crossed either us or the yakuza—or both." The ork's gaze hardened. "Any idea who that might be?"

"No," Skater said.

"Right." The sarcasm was as sharp as a monofilament edge. Without another word, Duran turned and walked through the door, and the others quickly trailed after him.

Skater grabbed one of the chairs and sat, waiting to be sure Duran and the rest were long gone before he took his own departure. He wouldn't let himself think about how he felt. The members of the team could never be called friends, but as runners they were all chummers, and there was no question they'd have laid down their lives for each other on a run. They'd already done it more than once over the past three years.

His grandfather had died when Skater was twelve, which was why he'd left the Council lands to live with his mother in Seattle. She'd been a fixer, surviving on the dirty edge of the shadows, and Skater had learned early not to trust the men she brought around. They were rough and uncaring, quick to swat when he didn't move fast enough.

For the past three years the team had been the closest Skater had ever come to feeling like he belonged somewhere. The closest to something he could call family, even though each one lived with his or her own secrets.

He couldn't remember the last time he'd considered the possibility of one of them betraying him or each other.

Now they were gone.

And his last words to them had been a lie, because Skater had a very good idea who'd set them up, even though he couldn't even begin to guess why. By rights he should have come clean and confessed his suspicions.

The only problem was, Skater was still in love with the woman.

4

"Cutting and running, eh?" the driver of the gypsy cab asked him maybe thirty minutes later.

For a moment Skater froze, halfway into the vehicle parked at the curbside. The trickers hustling the corner under a working street light only a few meters away took his indecision as possible interest. Dressed in a variety of street synthleathers and revealing lingerie, both sexes came at him, some entreating and some abrasive in their challenges.

"Get in, chummer," Kestrel said. "No big sweat that I know part of the score."

Skater dropped into the cab's vinyl-covered back seat only a step ahead of the most aggressive of the street hustlers.

A thin girl with spiky blond hair who'd found expression through synthleather and piercing pushed her palms and face against the window streaked with road grit. She leaned forward, spilling meaty breasts out of her white top, and dragged her tongue across the glass, leaving a twisting path of gleaming saliva that picked up the rainbow of colors from the neon advertising on the buildings. The earring piercing the tip of her tongue clicked hollowly against the glass.

"She's not shy, is she?" Kestrel said.

"No." Skater's hand circled the Predator's butt. "She's not." He kept watch on the pack of sleazers, ignoring the wet kisses the blond mouthed at him. Others wore neon body paint and looked like glimmering pools of perversion moving in the distance.

"Hang on," Kestrel warned. The big powerplant roared under the hood and he swerved the vehicle out into the street, cutting off a midnight blue Chrysler-Nissan Jackrabbit. A horn screeched loudly in their wake, and the blond tricker gave Skater the finger and a string of obscenities.

Skater tried to relax. It was no use. The cab's back seat was cramped and stank of urine. Smashed fast-food containers covered with days-old muddy footprints decorated the floorboard. A bulletproof and bombproof sheet of plastic separated him from Kestrel.

The cab knifed expertly through the traffic. "You didn't answer my question," Kestrel said through the speaker.

Skater grinned without humor. "I'm running."

"You got a funny way of showing it, chummer." Kestrel indicated the sprawl all around them. "You show up smack dab in the middle of Seattle with a lot of muscleboys looking to frag your hoop. For the nuyen you're paying me I'd have met you in Hell's Kitchen."

"You heard?"

"About the elf crate?" Kestrel nodded. "You didn't know the yaks had bought into the action?"

"No."

"Surprise."

"No drek." Skater shifted slightly in the seat, tensing. Kestrel was a street fixer, buried so deep in the web of crime and clout that most people didn't know about him—unless he wanted someone to.

Kestrel was dark and thin with hooded eyes. An angular scar, turned gray-white with age, lay like a private's chevron across the bridge of his hooked nose and leaked down onto both cheeks. His face was long, forgettable. He wore a baseball cap advertising the Seattle Timber Wolves combat bike team and a maroon tee shirt.

"So what's the plan?" Kestrel asked.

"Run," Skater said, "and don't look back."

"Then why you still here, chummer?"

Skater ignored the question. "What else have you heard about that elven freighter?"

Kestrel shrugged. "Scan's pretty tight on that. People are looking for you, *omae,* and spreading a lot of nuyen around while they're at it."

"Like who?"

"Word I get is they're working for Masaru Doyukai."

Skater ran the name through his mind. "Never heard of him."

"New boy in town," Kestrel replied. "Straight from the heart of Japan. Looking to make his way up quick. One of Shotozumi's godsons or some drek like that." The name of Hanzo Shotozumi was known to every runner on the street, and it was one feared by all. He was numero uno crime boss of Seattle, the man who'd forged the yakuza into the biggest, strongest, and deadliest crime organization in the sprawl.

"You don't know for sure?"

"No reason to. You want, I'll look him up. After tonight's action and the way he's leaning so heavy on everybody, I'll know him by morning anyway."

"I'll be long gone by then."

Kestrel nodded. "Good plan, kid. I always said you had a head on your shoulders. Nice to hear you're thinking of keeping it there."

"Why would Shotozumi be interested in an elven freighter?" Skater asked.

"No vendettas that I know of. Only thing I scan is that they were after some prize it carried." Kestrel glanced into the mirror. "What were you doing there?"

Skater met the man's gaze but said nothing.

Shaking his head, Kestrel reached for the pack on the dashboard and knocked a cigarette loose. He jammed it between his lips, gaze locked on the street ahead as he drove. "Kid, look . . . Much as I hate to admit it, I owe you. The day those Disassemblers hit your mom's place and killed her, they damn near killed me, too. If you hadn't gotten there, maybe they would have. You hear what I'm saying?"

"Yeah."

"Then, when you went after those trogs and evened the score, who helped you when you almost bought it?"

"You." The fixer had also worked out financial arrangements with the street docs who'd put Skater back together, this time with the addition of some wiz cybernetic enhancements. Revenge hadn't come easily, or without cost.

"Damn straight." Kestrel gave the accelerator a tap. "I'm not your nursemaid or even close to any kind of guardian angel, but I owe you. I'll nose around a little, do some digging, maybe find something out. You can call one of my message drops time to time and I'll let you know what kind of heat you're facing here."

"Sure," Skater said. "Problem is, I don't know for sure what we were after. Some kind of bioresearch supposed to be worth millions."

"A fragging pig in the poke?"

"I had an inside line."

"And the inside person? You trust him?"

Her, Skater silently corrected. "I did."

"Happens," Kestrel said. "You live life to figure out the people you can trust. If you're lucky, you survive the ones you're wrong about."

"You discover anything about this mess, you get a finder's fee."

Kestrel nodded.

"Where's my credstick?" Skater asked. The fixer also ran some of the best money-laundering schemes in the business.

"Under your new name down in the Cayman Islands. Some of it's still on the way, but it'll all be there by morning, long before you get there." Kestrel placed a small leather pouch into the vault pass-through mounted in the seat. With a wicked hiss, the vault shunted back toward Skater and opened with an electric pop.

Skater took out the ebony credstick and looked at it. Kestrel told him the SIN was in the name of Walter Dent.

Skater hit the doorlock and opened it as the light turned green, stepping out onto the curb. "Thanks, Kestrel." He kept moving, closing the door before the fixer could say anything else. He let the shadows take him, wishing they could drown the memories, too, because now those memories wouldn't turn loose, suddenly sharper and more insistent than ever. He couldn't quit the city without knowing why Larisa had betrayed him. It couldn't be love he felt for her, he knew. It was the attraction of the moth for the flame. And maybe a way of evening the score between them. She'd left him without reason, leaving him to feel like he just didn't make the grade. But he'd never sold someone out. He was better than that.

5

Skater got a once-over from one of the two bouncers working the main door to SybreSpace. He slotted his new credstick for the cover charge.

"You have a nice time while you're with us," the bouncer ordered in a gravelly voice as he popped the Wilkerson razors back into hiding. "And be nice to the working girls."

SybreSpace was still one of the trendiest bars in the sprawl, with a long history as a notorious hangout for deckers and wannabes. Others came for the music, which changed abruptly from style to style, depending on which dancer held the main stage.

Skater made his way to the bar, pushing through the packed bodies and haze of cigarette smoke that only partially blunted the scorching neon veins that made various Matrix-like designs pulse on the walls, ceiling, and floor.

Shielding his eyes, Skater spotted a bartender he knew and headed for the decorated bar lit up with glaring neon cubes and polyhedrons that whirled and spun, then exploded in myriad colors, only to be replaced by others. After a brief wait, he reached the head of the line, book-ended between two frazzled waitresses yelling drink orders.

"Can I get you something?" the bartender asked. He was slim and innocuous, but Skater knew for a fact that the guy's left arm held a Fichetti light pistol cybergun.

"A draw," Skater said. He didn't drink, a holdover from his upbringing on the Council lands, and from a personal belief that a shadowrunner had to stay sharp. Except for Shiva and Duran, who did indulge but never on the job, and Trey, who relished the occasional glass of vintage port when he could get it, no one else on the team drank either.

The bartender drew the soybeer into a thick glass, expertly moving the foaming head to the top in a smooth flood of amber.

Skater slotted his credstick, adding a twenty percent tip. This wasn't the Barrens, after all. "Something else."

The bartender went on filling orders for the waitresses, but he glanced back at Skater without missing a beat. His eyes narrowed only slightly, though the broad smile never faltered. "And that is?"

"Is Aggie working tonight?"

"Yes." The bartender sat a trio of drinks on one of the waitress's trays while she complained to the other one about the troll at a back table who was pinching her ass hard enough to leave bruises. "So are a half-dozen bouncers, *omae*."

"No problem." Skater took his drink and headed back to the shadows that extended just beyond the multicolored lights spilling from the main dance stage onto the floor. The crowd was already lathered up, shouting and hooting their encouragement to the stripper working her way out of her G-string with teasing abandon. She used the mirrors behind her and the gray fog from the stage filters to prolong visual frustration.

Memories came unbidden and started tumbling into Skater's mind. He'd first seen Larisa in the bar while discussing a possible run with a guy Archangel knew. From the very first Larisa Hartsinger had captivated him with her beauty and her dancing, then with her personality. He pushed the memories away with effort and some repressed pain, focusing on the task at hand.

Skater hugged the wall and stepped into the short hallway running to the back rooms. The overhead track lighting was intentionally dim so the dancers could come and go among the crowd without being seen.

He stopped at the second door on the left and let his knuckles find a rhythm on the reinforced wooden surface.

"Who is it?" a husky contralto demanded.

Skater hesitated only for a minute. "Aggie, it's Jack. I need to talk."

"Don't waste your time, chummer. She ain't here."

"I figured that. I need to know where she is."

There was a pause. "Why come to me?"

"Got no one else to ask, and I need to find her."

"Slot it, Jack, people are looking for you. The kind of people where you end up dead and turned to lawn mulch before you can blink your eyes." The old-fashioned peephole in the door darkened briefly.

"Larisa may be part of it. I need to know."

The door opened and Aggie ushered him in. She was tall and slender, with an overall bodymod that threw every luscious curve into the danger zone. A turquoise negligee overlaid a foundation of black lace undergarments that were shadows under the gauzy material. Her dark hair was hacked off at shoulder length but remained full, accentuating the Amerindian cheekbones and jawline.

Despite the pressing urgency, Skater found making small talk difficult. Before he'd taken up with Larisa, there'd been nights with Aggie. They'd had fun and the sex had been good, but never the magic that had fired him with Larisa.

The dressing room was small and spartan. Besides the vanity and the stool before it, there was only a loveseat and a coat rack.

Aggie smoothed her makeup on with practiced strokes, easily enhancing all her best features. "I don't have time for a lot of jaw." She made a moue of her lips and applied fiery red lipstick that held a neon glazed afterglow.

"Larisa," Skater prompted. The sounds coming from the main room had quieted.

"If she wanted contact with you, she'd have called."

"Aggie, this is serious."

She ignored him, quickly slashing on a pair of very arched brows. "Have you tried calling her?"

"I need to see her."

"Oh?" Aggie raised one of her new eyebrows. "You mean Larisa didn't give you her new number?" She closed her make-up case and dropped it into the slim purse sitting on the vanity. "What a surprise."

"You know they're looking for me," Skater said. "Maybe for Larisa, too."

Aggie's eyes trapped Skater's in the vanity mirror. "You mean somebody other than you?"

Skater let irritation sound in his voice. There'd been a little residual animosity between them after he'd started seeing Larisa, but no big drama. "I don't have time for games," he growled.

Spinning to face him, face darkened by anger, Aggie snapped, "Don't you? Everything's a game to you, Jack. You play hard, and you're one of the best, but it's all a game. Including Larisa. Get the hint, chummer: she doesn't want to see you. You didn't lose. Exactly. She's just not going to play anymore." Her voice softened. "Can't say I blame her. There's no use in hanging onto something that's not yours to have. She learned, just not soon enough."

"She set me up," Skater said in a low voice.

Aggie gave him a hard, doubtful look.

"Tonight," he went on, forcing her to hear. "A piece of action turned dirty and got one of my people killed." It was as much as he'd ever admitted to someone outside his own circle that he was involved in any kind of shadow biz. With one exception. "Larisa fed me the scan, cut herself in for a piece. I agreed because it sounded doable. Somewhere in there, the yakuza got double-crossed, either by Larisa or someone she knows. I want to know the score."

"And you think Larisa sold you out?"

Asked bare-faced and bluntly, Skater couldn't answer right away. "I don't know. I need to find out. If she didn't, she could be in danger."

Aggie's laugh was harsh and brittle. "You don't believe in anybody, do you?"

Skater didn't reply.

"Tell me," the dancer said, "when you get up in the morning and look in the mirror, do you ever believe the guy you see standing there?"

"Sometimes," Skater replied honestly.

"You don't even know yourself. How the hell can you expect to know anyone else?"

Skater was confused by the logic. "I need to see Larisa."

"Maybe she doesn't need to see you." Aggie turned and shook a long, gold-tipped black cigarette out of a pack and lit it. Smoke curled around her head. "She loved you, Jack. More than anything or anyone. I didn't think she'd ever leave you, no matter what kind of life you lead or the way you walled yourself off from her. Whatever you did to hurt her, it must have been bad."

"I didn't do anything to her," Skater said. He'd asked himself for months what it could have been, replayed every conversation he could remember. None of it seemed enough to drive her away. "What did she tell you?"

"Nothing. But we noticed you didn't come around anymore and Larisa didn't smile as much. A month later she couldn't hide it any longer, and we figured you'd left because of the baby."

Skater felt like he'd been juiced with a double string from a Super Shock taser. "Baby?"

"Yeah, a baby." Aggie held out her hands to measure dimensions angrily. "You know, about this big, pink and round. Cries a lot." She stared hard at him.

Skater flipped the possibility around inside his head, but it wouldn't stick to anything, like the inside of his skull was gel-coated.

"Spirits," Aggie said softly. "You *didn't* know."

"No." Skater felt battered and empty, all the anger he'd been holding onto to keep him moving suddenly blown out of him.

"We all figured you'd found out she was pregnant and decided to make tracks."

"I wouldn't have done that."

"You sure?"

Skater made himself answer honestly, more for himself than Aggie. He needed truth now. "No."

"Yeah. That's what I thought. Maybe that's what Larisa thought, too." She stubbed out her cigarette in an ashtray curled up inside a ceramic rock lizard. "You get to know them, guys are pretty much the same once you scratch that thin veneer. We tried to get her to see a street doc about eliminating the problem. But she refused. She had a nice nest egg set aside, and she was picking up more from new customers after you stopped coming around."

"Like who?"

"A connected guy named Synclair Tone." Aggie's voice and expression intimated scorn. "He's a Mafia guy who came up out of the Barrens. Still got the gutter written all over him, if you know where to look. He's cheap flash in a Vashon Island suit, but he's got mucho dinero backing any play he makes. And he liked Larisa a lot."

The knowledge soured inside Skater. From Aggie's expression, he knew she'd intended it to. He forced himself to get around it. "Who's Tone with?"

She shrugged. "You know how these guys are, Jack. Keep the mystery intact and they figure a girl will throw herself at his feet."

Had Larisa? He told himself he didn't want to know, but that was a lie. "Is it possible Tone's tied in with the yaks somehow?" Skater knew the Seattle Mafia and the yakuza were virtually at war, but he also knew the yaks were deep as drek in all this. No matter how unlikely, this Tone slag just might be stupid enough to try playing both ends against the middle.

"Not that I ever knew."

"Was Larisa?"

"No. The yakuza have a positively medieval outlook on women. She knew that. She stayed away."

Skater struggled to make sense of everything, but it wasn't happening. There was only one course of action he could pursue. "I need to see Larisa."

Someone knocked on the door. "Five minutes, Aggie."

"Coming," she yelled back.

"Don't be late or you'll get docked. Chloris got those suckers drooling and they ain't gonna wait long." Footsteps moved away from the door.

"I need to see Larisa," Skater repeated.

"Can't help you." Aggie gathered up her purse, something Skater knew she'd never take out on the stage.

"Maybe she's in trouble."

"And maybe she's not. Did you think about that?" Aggie challenged. "Maybe she sold your fragging ass down the river for a credstick so she could get you out of her system. Just so you'd be gone."

"I need to know how it was. For a lot of reasons. If I'd known about the baby, maybe things could have been different. But I didn't."

"Oh, hell, Jack, who knows if it was even your baby? There were other guys before you, maybe even during you. There can't help but be in this line of work. Frag it, they're in your face all the drekking time."

"It's not about the baby," Skater replied softly. "Not all of it. I didn't leave Larisa. She left me. No warning, and no reason why. She stayed in touch occasionally, even put me onto this piece of action tonight. I want to know why."

"What if she did?" Aggie demanded. The room's dim lights made her pinched features more severe. "Are you going to hurt her?"

"No." Skater knew it was the truth as soon as he spoke out loud. "When I know, one way or the other, I'll chill it and move on. Revenge is no piece of biz to buy into, unless it's not your own emotions burning you up. It's for my own piece of mind." He hesitated just a beat. "Like I told you, Larisa could be in danger, too."

For just a moment, indecision warred in Aggie's eyes. Then she shrugged, apparently making up her mind. "I'll call her. She can decide."

It wasn't what Skater wanted, and he searched for more words to offer.

Aggie read more into his reluctance to move. "Unless you're going to try to stop me." He fingers had drifted into her purse.

"No," Skater said, stepping aside. If Larisa ran from her doss, or didn't want to see him, that was an answer as well.

"Public telecoms are outside."

Skater opened the door and followed Aggie out. She walked down to the end of the hall where there were a couple of telecom cubes.

The music had changed to thunder out in the main lobby. It took Skater a few moments to recognize it as a popular biker thrash tune the Seattle Timber Wolves used as their theme song in combat matches.

Aggie tapped in a number on the keypad, then the two of them stood waiting for the face of Larisa Hartsinger to appear on the visual pickup. "That's strange." Aggie pushed the Disconnect key. "No answer. No message. Nothing."

But Skater's attention was already elsewhere, drawn by movement he caught out the corner of his eye. He'd sensed the two men stalking him even before he spotted them down at the other end of the hall. For a moment he wondered if they'd somehow recognized him.

Something told him the men were neither yakuza nor Lone Star or any other kind of blue crew. But his senses stuttered over the hard edge they broadcasted with their presence.

"Friends?" Aggie asked.

"No," Skater answered.

She crossed her arms over her breasts and kept her eyes on Skater, but he knew she was checking out the two figures down at the end of the hall. They were clearly visible as an elf and a troll. "Damn you, Jack Skater. This was a good place to work."

"Still could be." Skater didn't offer any misguided hope. He still didn't know how deep a hole he was in.

"I think I recognize one of those guys," Aggie said. "That

elf come up from the Barrens with Tone. If Larisa is with Tone in this thing, she's in way over her head. She'd never stand for someone flatlining you. Especially here."

Skater dropped his right hand into his duster pocket and gripped the Predator. His nerves were taut as piano strings and stretched thin as monowire, and he knew one wrong move would bust out the sturm and drang waiting between them. He used the reflection trapped in the dark Plexiglas over the bulletin board at the back of the hallway to keep watch over the two men. Neither of them appeared interested in closing in at the moment.

"Find her," Aggie said. "And get her out of this drek—if you can." She gave him the address.

He repeated it after her to be sure he got it right. The number was in the wealthy Bellevue District. If Larisa was living there these days, she'd certainly made her way up in the world.

Gently, Aggie touched his face. "And get yourself the hell out of there if you find out she's in too deep. I always hoped you were different than the other guys I've been with."

Before Skater could even say thanks, she was gone, turning into a swivel-hipped simsense wet dream on her way to the stage. Lust-filled applause and catcalls greeted her arrival.

He took advantage of the momentary confusion created by the music and the loud noises of the crowd to move quickly toward the club's rear exit. He didn't have to turn and look to know the two men were coming after him, closing in rapidly.

6

The instant he made the alley behind SybreSpace, Skater launched himself into a full run. High and narrow, the alley was a concrete chasm that twisted and ran without interruption to Cherry Street. A trio of Cutters jerked around at his approach, bringing weapons into view from under their leathers. The well-dressed woman with the gangers quickly ducked into the shadows. Moonlight danced off her earrings and amulets and sygils of protection.

"Personal problem," Skater yelled as he stayed to his side of the alley.

The three gangers huddled around the woman, protecting her.

He pounded past them, knees driving hard as his breath rasped in his lungs. A dumpster loomed before him, turned sideways. Gathering his strength and kicking in his boosted reflexes, he vaulted two meters up to the top of the metal containers, scanned the open ground before him, and leaped just as a blue-white laser beam cut through the air where he'd just been.

He hit the ground running, cutting back toward the building on his right. His shoulder slammed painfully into the brick wall, staggering him. Before he could make the corner, two more laser blasts sliced holes through the dumpster behind him.

One of the blasts faded out of existence just before it touched the plate glass window of a small restaurant across the street, at the end of its range. The other sheared through the rear tire of a green Volkswagen Elektro. Out of control, the little three-wheeler slammed into a light pole and sent a shower of yellow electrical sparks cascading down. A screamsheet vending machine sandwiched between the pole and the Elektro spilled out its load of chips while the sec-alarm emitted a high-pitched squeal in protest.

Skater figured the two guys tailing him were wetworkers, professional assassins whose one and only mission in life was to bring him back iced to whoever owned them. He turned the corner and ran west along Cherry Street, the canopies over the sidewalk deepening the shadows.

The three a.m. traffic slowed to a near halt around the crash site. He knew some of the drivers were probably calling in the accident right now, and the blue crews would soon descend over the area.

When the two shadows darted out of the alley, he pushed away from the side of the building and cut across the lines of traffic. Trying to get around the gawkers, a Gaz-Willys Nomad pickup started to pull around the Americar in front of it, but the driver was almost on top of Skater before he noticed him.

Skater put out an arm without breaking stride and caught

the Nomad's nose on his forearm. The driver applied the brakes and rubber shrilled. Rolling with the impact as much as he could, Skater slid across the vehicle's broad windshield and dropped to the street on the other side. He was close enough to feel the heat of the laser blast that hammered into the Nomad's cab.

The driver let out a string of curses above the din of frying metal and glass.

Wheeling and bringing up the Predator, Skater saw the driver leap from the wreckage of his vehicle as flames consumed it. His two pursuers knifed through the tangle of vehicles, dodging the ones that still moved as they sought their prey.

Switching to low-light vision, Skater scanned the two faces again, burning them into his memory and making sure that he'd never seen either one before. To Skater's right, the troll pulled himself up onto the cab of an Ares Roadmaster to take the high ground.

Focusing on the man's chest, Skater squeezed the Predator's trigger three times, ignoring the twisting gray smoke from the fiery Nomad that burned his nasal passages. The pistol jumped in his hands.

Caught full in the chest, the troll went backward off the truck. Realizing he was in the center of a bad situation, the Roadmaster's driver engaged the gears and pulled forward, ramming past a smaller car in front of him. In the cargo truck's wake, the troll got to his feet and unleashed another laser blast.

The blue-white beam slashed into the building behind Skater and set the festive canopy on fire.

Skater abandoned his position and ran for the alley behind him. Flaming bits of the canopy swirled around him and dropped to the pavement. Other drivers were bailing out of their cars now, many of them clutching weapons. Skater knew their anger would be directed at him as well as at the two men following him. If they felt frustrated enough at being trapped in their cars, the drivers would join the fight as well.

Perspiration coated him in a thin sheen, partly from the heat and partly from the exertion. He slapped burning debris from his duster, then took the corner and darted into the alley. He and Larisa had to walk a number of places that were only a short distance from the club. He knew the area, and he figured that gave him an edge over his pursuers.

Halfway down the alley, not more than three meters from ground level, a ring of advertising space jutted out from a closed simtheatre. Once, the meter-high advertising bands had pulsed clips from the latest releases. Now they were dark and dormant, burnt from years without maintenance and abuse by neon graffiti artists who'd left pornographic images charred into the reflective surface.

Measuring his pace, Skater shoved the Predator into the waistband of his pants and leaped upward behind the advert surface. He caught one of the support poles and pulled himself up into hiding, perched uncomfortably across three of the struts.

The alley continued on, butting into James Street. Across that was a wooded park area, mimicking Kobe Terrace Park on the other side of Yesler Way. With luck, Skater figured his pursuers would think he'd gone that way.

The pair came, running and working in tandem perfection. As each moved forward and took up a new position, the other kept a clear field of fire. Seeing the alley apparently deserted, the troll ran to the other end and peered out over James Street.

"No way," the elf called out. "He's not that fragging fast. The fragger's around here somewhere."

"We're pushing the clock, Dion," the troll grumbled, coming forward.

"You want to tell that to the big man later?" Dion asked.

Evidently his companion didn't because he decided to start searching. He was big and bulky even for a troll, no doubt chromed to the max. He carried the weighty laser pistol with no discernible effort.

"There's a door over here, Shayx." Dion drifted into place alongside it almost below Skater, his laser pistol lifted and ready. Like most elves, he was tall, with the exaggerated slenderness of that race. His dress was fashionable and expensive, a sharp contrast to his partner's street slouch.

Shayx put out a hand and tested the heavy wooden door. "Locked. But I can take it down."

Dion hesitated, scanning the alley. "You think he could have secured the damn door after him?"

"Maybe."

"I don't like it."

A snarl of mirth framed the troll's lips. "You want to call the big man and tell him that?"

"No." The reply was thoughtful, with no reaction to the taunt. "Take it down. He acted like he knew where he was headed. Maybe he had a key."

Shayx drew back a massive foot, then smashed it into the door, sundering it from its hinges with a series of snaps and metallic screeches.

"Go on," Dion said, pointing his pistol inside. "I've got you covered."

Shayx moved lithely into the room, following his weapon. "Nada, chummer. Room's full of dust. I spend any time in here, I'm gonna hack up a hairball the size of a Trailblazer truck."

The elf lowered his guard as he scanned the alley again. Eventually, his gaze wandered up in Skater's direction. His almond eyes widened in surprise and he tried to bring his weapon to bear.

Too late. Skater had already released his hold and dropped, hitting the elf as his weight knocked them both to the ground. Pushing himself up on one elbow, he extended the Predator before him, targeting the approaching Shayx bellowing a challenge. Skater snapped off six rounds and reduced the troll's head to a confused hunk of blood, bone, and ripped flesh. He didn't think anything less would have stopped the attack.

The augmentation kept the dead gillette on his feet for a few more staggered steps while Skater thrust the Predator's muzzle under the elf's chin. The elf froze at the touch of the heated metal. Reluctantly, Shayx's corpse dropped to its knees, then fell forward on what was left of his face.

Anger blazed in the elf's eyes, then his gaze flicked briefly toward the butt of the laser pistol only centimeters out of his reach.

"I really wouldn't advise that," Skater said. "I've had a long, hard night, and I won't hesitate a tick to shoot you. Roll over on your face. Slowly."

Dion did as he was ordered.

Skater kept watch over the alley exit to Cherry Street. He expected Lone Star to arrive any second now. But first he wanted to find out for sure if the elf and the samurai were working solo. He levered one of the elf's arms up behind his back, making it impossible for him to move well unless he was double-jointed. Skater didn't rule that out. The Predator lingered against the elf's skull.

"Who're you working for?" Skater demanded.

"Ask my friend," Dion suggested.

"Your friend's kind of dead right now."

"Well, he was always the talker."

Skater pressed the Predator a little harder against the base of Dion's skull. "Maybe it's time you start learning."

"Or else?"

"You and Shayx get a chance to pair up again in the next world."

The elf laughed delicately, not moving too much. "I appear to have an advantage over you. See, I know quite a lot about you. I know you're the kind of guy who'd rather cut a deal than use a gun."

"I'm not exactly adverse to using a gun," Skater pointed out. "You can check with your friend on that."

"True. But I'm just as dead if I talk. That, I can guarantee you, is a fact. And I really don't think you'll shoot a man who's so obviously at your mercy."

"What if you're wrong?" Skater nudged him again with the pistol barrel.

"Chummer," the elf said with a wry grin as he looked back at Skater, "will my face be red."

Still holding the Predator against the elf's skull, Skater searched his prisoner with his free hand.

"No credstick, I'm afraid. Never carry while I'm on assignment. You'll leave me knowing nothing about me."

"I know about Synclair Tone."

"Oh? Just what do you think you know?"

"Enough to start looking for him," Skater promised.

"If I should meet him, I'll be sure and tell him that."

Ignoring the jibe, Skater found the power-down button on the elf's Ares laser pistol harness and faded the present charge. It would take the soft-pack batteries a few minutes to power the unit back up. He planned on being gone by then. He did the same for the dead troll's.

"Do yourself a favor," Skater said, "and stay out of my way. I see you again, I'll figure a gun's the only way to set things straight between us."

The elf nodded. "I don't make the same mistake twice."

"Stay there." Skater pushed himself up and moved away, keeping the Predator trained on the elf. "Until you can't see me anymore." He kept backing away, noticing the hot white strobe lights of a Lone Star Northrop PRC-44B Yellowjacket helo descending on Cherry Street.

Holstering his weapon he moved at a fast walk and flagged down a cab. No one was following him.

Larisa's Bellevue address was a high-rise in Beaux Arts, just across a short expanse of Lake Washington from Council Island. The building was forty stories high, well landscaped and probably just as well protected by private security.

"This the place, bub?" the troll cabby asked, shifting a toothpick the size of a pencil around in his slash of a mouth. He wore a faded and stained plaid beret with a candy-striped pink button announcing I BRAKE FOR BLONDES.

"Yeah." Skater shoved his credstick into the pay slot and added a modest tip. The wind whipping in from the lake was cool and wet as he got out and stood for a moment looking up at the building. Skater took a deep breath and tried to shake off the fatigue he felt creeping up on him.

"You want to be careful in this neighborhood," the cabby advised. "Knight Errant does the general upkeep on security."

"Thanks. I will." Skater didn't bother to correct the cabby's assumption that he was here for some illicit reason.

The cabby touched his hat and pulled into the light traffic, within moments vanishing into the stream of ruby lights warring against moonlight and shadow.

Skater turned his duster collar up against the wind, then walked across the street and up to the door of what an elegant sign proclaimed as the Montgomery Building. The foyer was well-lit, glass on stainless steel, all buffed to perfection. The double doors were secured by cardkey locks, and were recessed enough that Skater figured a cage would form around anyone who tried to scam them.

Every nerve in him screamed to run as he ascended the seven short steps toward the front of the building. But it didn't matter. He couldn't leave Larisa in danger, no matter what had gone down between them.

He arrived at the door as an older couple also came up, and made a show out of retrieving his card from his wallet. They offered him the door and he took it, thanking them.

A public-service desk was to his right, prim and proper and polished, but totally deserted. A large framed watercolor print by Adam Alone depicting a forlorn troll gondolier in Venice covered the back wall between two electrical torch sconces. Potted pine trees stood formation around the outer perimeters. Grayish colors spewed from the security camera monitors running inside the small office behind the desk.

His senses clamoring a warning, Skater veered away from the old couple as they headed for the bank of elevators. As he approached the desk, he tasted the metallic stink of blood on the air even before he saw the first of it. Two bodies lay limbs akimbo behind the big counter, soaking crimson into the plush sand-colored carpet. The man wore professional dress and had Night Manager on his name tag. The woman was ten years older, well into her forties, and outfitted in the light-blue and gray uniform of Knight Errant Security. She'd been lasered through the abdomen, and part of the stylized KE belt buckle was missing.

Footsteps scraped carpet behind Skater.

He whirled, his moves riding the razor's edge of the boosted reflexes as adrenaline poured into his nervous system. The Predator came to a stop before him. He stared down the barrel at a thin guy in his fifties wearing a bathrobe.

"Don't shoot!" the man said. He elevated his arms quickly. "I just came down to complain about the noise coming from the apartment above me!"

Skater knew the man had seen the bodies on the other side of the desk. "What number are you?"

"Fourteen-eleven," the man answered.

Larisa was in fifteen-eleven. Skater dropped the gun away from the man. "You know the LTG number for Knight Errant Security?"

The man nodded, still not sure of himself.

"Call them," Skater said. "Tell them they've got someone down at this location." He pushed the man toward the deskcom, then sprinted for the elevator bank.

With a soft *ping* announcing its arrival, the doors to the elevator cage slid open. It was empty.

Skater stepped inside. After a brief hesitation, the elevator doors closed and the cage started up with a jerk. Seconds later, he stepped out onto the fifteenth floor.

Nothing moved in front of him. The corridor, soundproofed and deeply carpeted, the walls lined with expensive prints, was empty. Glass windows at both ends peered out over the other buildings in the neighborhood, filled with black space and diamond-hard stars. Red neon lights advertised the fire escape exits beside them.

He moved into the corridor and trotted toward Larisa's doss.

The doors were ornate bronze, filigreed with images from fables, which the Awakening had caused some to start speculating were possible history instead. The one on Larisa's door dealt with the Ashanti myth concerning the creation of rainbows.

Without warning, the frozen waves rolling out from a spilling waterfall in the frieze went from highlighted bronze to a gradually deepening scorched black that grew. Skater put his hand to the door. The heat soaked through the metal into his palm, already hot enough to burn. When he jerked his hand back, he saw that some of the black had come off on his skin. The soot flaked off easily.

The charred pattern spread even as he felt the heat radiate outward, quickly filling in the imprint of his palm. A fire extinguisher hung inside a cubicle in the wall down the corridor. He ran and got it, then hurried back.

Skater was sure someone had tampered with the building's security systems, or alarms would have been going off like fireworks by now. Shoving the Predator into his waistband, he kicked the door and broke the lock.

As the door opened, a sheet of flame dropped toward him. The Kevlar duster protected Skater for the most part, but he felt the fire licking at his exposed flesh. He triggered the fire extinguisher. A white cloud of fire retardent splashed against the fiery curtain confronting him. He stepped inside, carrying the extinguisher in one hand and the hose in the other.

Light from the flames illuminated the dark room. The furniture was ornate, expensive, nothing like the stuff Larisa usually went for. Fire ringed the room in a pattern that told him it was there by no accident. On the wall to his left, a fireplace blazed like a pit from hell, evidently the source of the initial flames.

"Larisa!" Skater's voice was tight, already made hoarse by the thick, coiling smoke. He laid down a pattern of flame retardent, trying to guess how the doss was laid out.

No one answered his call.

Skater avoided the flaming sofa and went around it. The floor changed from carpet to tile when he passed through a doorway, letting him know he'd stepped into the kitchen. Firelight gleamed and reflected from the metallic surfaces of the appliances. The effect was muted by the thick smoke.

He coughed and sat the extinguisher down long enough to take a bandanna from his pocket and knot it around his lower face. It helped, but only a little. He wouldn't be able to stay here long without succumbing to the smoke or lack of oxygen.

"Larisa!" Fear scattered inside him, rolling through him like a charge of DMSO invading his nervous system. He spotted a flight of stairs to his right when he evacuated the empty kitchen. So far the fire hadn't spread up the steps.

A pool of flames gathered at the foot of the stairs, further across than he could jump.

Thumbing the extinguisher's release, he laid down a solid sheet of spray before him. Stubbornly, the flames gave way, turning to smoldering embers in the craters they'd made in the carpet. He tossed the empty extinguisher away and started up the stairs.

Glass shattered to his left and he turned instinctively toward the sound. Mirror shards from the wall opposite the front door dropped into the meter-high flames. Dozens of little reflections were captured in the irregular pieces.

Skater recognized the leaping form of the hell hound at the same time he felt the blistering heat of the wrought-iron banister he was clutching. The soot-black animal reared out of the fire, apparently untouched by the flames, standing as tall as Skater on its hind legs. Its eyes were blazing red coals above a mouthful of huge fangs. Despite the heat, the ivory gleamed.

Pushing himself to the side and releasing the hot banister, Skater narrowly avoided the creature's initial lunge. Across the room, the curtains caught with a whoosh. The fire spread their length, paused at the ceiling for a heartbeat, and flowed across it like an in-rushing tide.

At the foot of the stairs, the hell hound dug in its feet and turned to face Skater just as the carpet below it caught fire again. It leaped at him from the flames, baying out a flaming breath that spread as it came at Skater.

7

Twisting to avoid the creature's attack, Skater reached for his Predator. As he drew the pistol, the hell hound's flaming breath slammed into his shoulder with more physical force than he expected. His first two rounds went over the beast's head as he stumbled back along the stairs.

Blue and yellow flames clung to the duster's shoulder from the beast's fiery breath. Heat soaked in through the Kevlar hot enough to burn. Before he could bring the pistol up again, the animal was on him. Its eyes burned red, and flaming slavers dripped from its blunt muzzle as it opened wide and reached for his face. Its front paws were heavy on Skater's chest.

Thrusting his free hand up between the creature's forelegs, Skater bent his arm at the side of the animal's neck and leveraged it away from his face. The glistening fangs took a bite out of the carpet covering the stairs instead of flesh.

Skater's muscles strained to hold the hound's muzzle from his face. It bayed again, spitting more fiery breath that singed the wall beside the stairs. Skater brought the Predator's barrel up behind the beast's ear and pulled the trigger. The detonations echoed through the room even above the snapping and crackling of the flames.

Blood and bone and fur covered Skater. With a spasmodic quiver, the huge black dog collapsed. Unable to take a deep breath because of the animal's weight, the smoke, and the heat, Skater struggled to push it off him. When he got to his feet, his vision was blurry. The Predator was starting to heat up in his hand, but he refused to release it. He'd heard rumors that some corps were using hellhounds as guard dogs, but he'd never run into one before. The hound's handler had to be somewhere close.

"Larisa!" Skater could hardly hear his own voice above the inferno swirling through the spacious apartment. He reached the landing and swept his gaze across the two closed doors in front of him. Perspiration dripped off him, soaking into his clothes as his body tried to compensate for the heat facing him. His chest burned with the effort of trying to breathe, and his lungs were wracked by fits of coughing.

He chose the door on his left. Using a fold of the duster to hold the knob that was already melting, he twisted and pulled it open. A mirror on the opposite wall picked up the incandescence given off by the flames and filled the bedroom with light.

No one was inside.

But for a moment Skater was hypnotized by the wallpaper covered with exotic animals wearing happy smiles. Just inside the door to his right was the crib. A small pillow sat at one end of a pile of bed clothes that were heaped enough to hide a small form beneath them.

Skater let the Predator drop at his side as he crossed to the crib. He shouted Larisa's name again, wondering how long a baby could have lasted in the noxious smoke.

A carousel mobile with a dozen multi-colored seahorses dangling from it was secured to the headboard. The pillowcase held more seahorses, and Skater recognized the stitch styling even through the smoke as something Larisa had done. The colors were bright and vivid.

Skater raked a hand through the bed clothes. Then he breathed a burning sigh of relief because no baby was in them, only a purple-furred teddy bear.

Even with his low-light vision kicked in, details in the room were hard to make out. However, judging from the furnishings and the stray bits of clothing in the hamper, the baby was a little girl.

Before he could stop to think about what he was doing, Skater picked up the teddy bear and shoved it into a pocket of his duster. Then he sprinted out of the room and hurried to the remaining door, knowing he was working on borrowed time.

When he tried the knob, again using the duster, he found he couldn't turn it. Stepping back, he raised a foot and kicked it. Wood splintered and tore. The door shivered open.

"Larisa!" he shouted as he stepped into the room.

A fat man wearing an expensive double-breasted pinstripe suit and a maroon cape turned to face Skater from a kneeling position. His jowls hung, framing a ruddy red nose that had surfaced in a sea of black and gray beard. With the gimlet eyes and his hands full of items from a wall safe, he looked like a larcenous Santa.

Skater lifted the Predator. He didn't think the man would see him clearly with the light from the fire filtering into the room from behind him—but he'd recognize the gun. "Where's Larisa Hartsinger?"

"I'm afraid you're far too late," the fat man said, then uttered some words Skater didn't understand.

Something told him this was magic, but before he could fire the Predator, a whirling mass of shimmering hot air came at Skater from one corner of the room.

The flaming creature knocked his arm aside, making the bullet go wide of its intended target. More than two meters high, the body roughly humanoid but definitely lizard-like, and the color and consistency of orange clay, the thing had to be a fire elemental. Fire clung to it like gossamer webs. Its eyes looked like they'd been poked into its head with a dull stick, and it had a crooked slash for a mouth.

Skater succeeded in partially deflecting the attack, but the sheer explosion of power knocked him backward. He slammed into the doorframe behind him, and bruising pain shot across his spine and his kidneys. Knowing the pistol wasn't any good against the elemental, he holstered it, continuing to give ground at the thing's approach. He tried to slam the door in its caricature of a face.

The elemental howled again as it pushed through the door. Fiery, four-fingered handprints lingered on the wooden surface, then sank into the door as they burned more deeply.

Skater yanked a pole from the second-floor hallway railing and swung it at the elemental. He'd been told that madmen had the best chance against elementals on the physical plane because they became obsessed.

The pole collided with the elemental's face hard enough to jar the thing's head. Flaming yellow blood trickled down its snout.

The fat man came to the door, maintaining visual contact with the elemental.

With a ragged howl of rage, the elemental filled one hand with a spinning ball of flaming plasma and threw it at Skater. The ball grew as it passed through the air.

By the time it reached Skater, the fireball was the size of a pumpkin. A fiery vine trailed after it. Skater grabbed the edge of his duster and raised it before him. The Kevlar took the brunt of the small, gaseous explosion, but the force was still enough to knock him back.

Then the fragging fire thing came at him again.

Abandoning any pretense at holding his position, Skater raced for the railing overlooking the lower floor. He vaulted over the edge as another fireball whizzed past him. There was a frozen moment of free-fall that twisted his stomach, then the expectation of being engulfed in the flames claiming the lower floor.

The fire licked at him as soon as he landed, drawn to him as a source of fuel. He was in motion at once, his knees protesting the continued abuse. A few islands of carpet still remained and he directed his steps toward the biggest one near the apartment door.

The elemental's roar filled the room.

Looking back over his shoulder, Skater saw the creature launch itself from the second-floor railing. Its arms were outspread as it kept its balance, and for a moment it looked like some kind of avenging angel wrapped in holy fire.

Then it landed with enough force to vibrate the floor. Its tail whipped around, scattering the flames. It roared again and started for Skater.

He sprinted for the door, cutting through the waist-high fire dug into the carpet. The trapped smoke was a rolling gray-black fog that was nearly impenetrable. Still, a metallic gleam above the door caught his attention. Eyes burning as he slammed against the doorframe and fumbled for the entry button, conscious of the fire elemental bearing down on him, he made out the gleam of the manual activation switch for the KIDDE fire-suppression system for the apartment.

The door was jammed.

Skater turned, one hand poised above the KIDDE switch. Even if the computer-driven automatic systems had been crashed, the manual switch should work. He hoped.

"Come on, you slotting freak bastard!" Skater yelled at the elemental.

The creature batted the remnants of the burning couch out of its way and came at him. The slash of a mouth was turned up in a rictus of a feral grin.

A fit of coughing consumed Skater. He had to force himself to remain erect enough to slam the KIDDE button. As soon as he did, jets of compressed foam and pressurized water sprayed from the ceiling nozzles.

The elemental was instantly drenched. Steam rose from its body, and its growls turned to howls of rage amid a cacophony of evil hisses. Wrapping its misshapen arms around itself and rolling up as tightly as possible, it vanished from the physical plane.

Spots whirled in Skater's vision. There was no oxygen left in his lungs. He pulled the Predator and fired the remainder of his clip into the door's locking mechanism, shattering it and ripping up the metal around it. He yanked again and the door opened.

The sudden supply of oxygen created a backdraft that rushed out into the corridor with Skater in a liquid whoosh. He sucked in the fresh air greedily as he leaned against the opposite wall.

Through the open door that held a fringe of stray flames seeking out the ceiling in the hallway, he saw that the smoldering apartment had been consumed by the fire. Nothing could have lived through that.

He thought about Larisa and felt hollow, wondering if he'd ever know the truth. The sudden clamor of alarms drove him to action.

Glancing up and down the hall, he saw that most of the dosses had their doors open. A small cluster of people was gathered at either fire escape while the pall of smoke from Larisa's apartment poured out into the corridor. Several of them had spotted Skater and were pointing him out to others.

Embers still clung to his clothing. He ran to the elevators and jammed his fingers between the doors to open them. He knew from the digital reader overhead that the cages were already near ground level.

"Get away from those fragging doors!"

Skater caught the Knight Errant sec-guard in his peripheral vision. The guard wore an armored uniform and was charging down the hall from the crowd around the fire escape route to his left.

Skater spread the elevator doors and looked inside. The cage was a dozen floors below and still moving. The tracked cables rolled with the cage.

"Last chance, brainwipe," the sec-guard yelled. He took a weaver stance with a Narcoject pistol pointed ahead of him. The blunt muzzle centered on Skater.

Without hesitation, Skater threw himself into the elevator shaft. Darts stabbed into the duster, needling their way through, then pinged into the corridor walls and the elevator doors. The darts were proof against most armor and would have nosed their way into his flesh if not for the layer of Kevlar next to his skin. Removing the duster later was going to be a cautious thing.

His leap carried him out into the elevator shaft. He wrapped his arms and boots around the tracked cable and moved with it.

The elevator doors banged shut overhead and filled the shaft with black so impenetrable that Skater's low-light vision couldn't make out any details. An instant later the doors reopened, spilling an elongated rectangle of harsh white light into the shaft. By then, Skater had dropped three floors and was gaining speed.

"He just left fifteen," the Knight Errant guard called out over the clamor from the hallway. "Elevator three-cee." He aimed the Narcoject pistol and fired a half-dozen rounds.

Skater dropped like a stone, nearly at terminal velocity. With the added speed and the narrow confines of the elevator shaft, the cage had the illusion of coming up at him.

"Not in the cage, damn it," the Knight Errant said. He stood in the open elevator doors nine or ten floors above Skater and reloaded the Narcoject. "On top of the slotting thing."

With less than two floors separating him from the descending cage, Skater tightened his grips again. Pain burned bone-deep into his arms, chest, feet, and knees. He held on as long as he was able, then abandoned the cable less than two meters above the top of the elevator cage. Going limp, he crashed to the hard, irregular metal surface waiting on him.

Before he could regain his breath, a pale ellipse of halogen-powered light fell over him, tearing away some of the protective shadows. He forced himself to his feet and stood swaying as the cage slowed. For the first time he noticed the meter-high numerals painted in red on the gray steel shaft walls next to the doors.

The three went by, and the cage was almost at a stop. Moving to the front of the it, he leaned out and caught the lip at the second-floor level. Even with the boosted reflexes kicking in extra adrenaline and adding speed to his nervous system, his endurance was flagging.

He kicked his feet against the wall and pulled himself up even with the second floor. Shoving his fingers into the space between the double doors, he pried them open and tried to ignore the double-imaging taking place in his vision. For a moment, he didn't think he was going to get the doors pushed back to the break-over point. Then they slid apart effortlessly.

Two Knight Errants stood in the doorway with drawn Narcoject pistols.

Skater held onto the lip because he had nowhere else to go. The cage below him blocked any escape to the first floor, and he didn't have the strength to climb back up the cables, much less dodge flying darts.

A steady ssshussh came from overhead. He glanced back over his shoulder to see the sec-man from fifteen sliding down the cable after him, at a sedate pace with his pistol pointed directly at Skater.

He was fragged no matter what he did.

"Looks like you're all crapped out," the grim-jawed Knight Errant ork with sergeant's chevrons said. He kept his pistol aimed at Skater's face.

8

Knight Errant worked the switch with Lone Star in a little over an hour. It wasn't a new record as far as Skater knew, but it was still pretty slotting quick. Knight Errant was merely the private security agency for the neighborhood, and had to bow to Lone Star's official position as police in and around Seattle.

By dawn, he was in an interrogation room in the Lone Star Security building on the corner of First Avenue and Union Street awaiting the arrival of two groundhounds. He'd been deloused in the biotech ward, retina-scanned and fingerprinted, DNA-scanned and cyber-scanned. The only conversation he'd gotten had been a steady stream of abuse. He'd already been tagged as a runner.

He sat in a flimsy metal chair in the interrogation room on the other side of a folding table that held a years-long collection of carved graffiti and cigarette burns. One of the tubes in the track lighting overhead flickered constantly, altering the shadows and driving the phalanx of flying insects that had made their way into the room crazy with frustration.

When they'd deloused him, they'd taken his clothing and given him an orange jumper with PROPERTY OF LONE STAR stenciled in black across his shoulders. Word on the street was that some Halloweeners liked to hack off the legs and sleeves and sport the jumpers proudly as gang colors if they'd been wearing them when they'd escaped from jail. There weren't many. Lone Star quietly offered a bounty to rival gangs for any returned jumpers—with or without return of the escaped prisoner, and the transactions were brokered by a third party.

Skater shifted and tried in vain to find a comfortable position. His hands were pulse-cuffed behind him to keep him from using his cyberware, secured to the chair, and ankle chains held his feet half a meter apart. He was bare-footed, and the stone floor was cold to the touch.

The pale green walls and ceiling offered no mental diversion, and the room's only window had been covered over in black paint years ago.

Instead of dwelling on what he didn't know and what might happen, Skater went inside himself the way his grandfather had taught him. Andrew Ghost-step had been a hard man, and not one easy to get close to. He'd been a leader in his community, and his daughter's excesses hadn't been easily put aside. Skater hadn't learned until later that when his mother abandoned him to her parents, many of his grandfather's political and personal friendships within the tribe had withered and not recovered.

Skater knew some of the Salish ways, though he didn't practice them, and some of the lore. But Ghost-step's teachings about self-discipline and control had helped him handle his problems then, and many since. There'd once been a hope that he might be a shaman because of some latent abilities, but that had died when no totem spirit had claimed him during his vision quest. He'd been twelve at the time, and the failure had distanced him further from his grandfather.

He let himself relax in his bonds, his muscles coiling naturally to spread out his weight.

The door creaked open, briefly letting in fragments of conversations, the steady slap of passing footsteps, and the stink of cigarette smoke and unwashed flesh.

Skater opened his eyes to slits, taking in the troll-sized

boots next to the human-sized ones in front of him. He didn't for a moment believe he was entirely safe inside Lone Star.

"You awake?" a whiskey-soured voice asked.

"Yeah," Skater replied, lifting his head.

"Good. For a minute there I thought you were dead and I'd wasted all this time thinking up questions to ask you." The speaker was the human, of average height and broad shoulders. He wore his beard short and his hair dark and long, pulled back in a ponytail. He had a large nose and thick eyebrows that looked like one woolly caterpillar crawling across both eyes. The blue and gold Lone Star jacket was held in one hand over his shoulder.

"There's not much I can tell you," Skater volunteered.

The man nodded and reached for one of the three remaining chairs at the table. "That's what I've heard." He dropped a portable microcam on the table. "We're going to go through it again, though. I'm Lance Paulson, you can think of me as an investigating officer." He jerked a thumb toward the troll. "And this is Nina, you can think of her as my partner."

The troll was only a few centimeters shorter than Elvis. Her horns were oiled and polished a jet-black, framing coarse hair that had been shaved into a six-centimeter tall mohawk done in chartreuse-tipped platinum. For a troll, she had curves. Skater figured Elvis would have been impressed, until he found out she was a cop.

"That much thinking," Skater said, "I'm liable to get confused."

"What I thought." Paulson nodded agreeably. He leaned over the portable microcam and switched it on. "That's why I brought datapics."

"Are you guys as high up as I go at Lone Star?" Skater asked.

"If you're referring to the way you've stone-walled everyone from the arresting Knight Errant team to the uniforms down in Booking," Nina said, "then, yes. We're it. From here you go to a lawyer and a trial, as soon as they can get it on the docket. With no help from you regarding your possible innocence, and your reluctance to say anything in your behalf, I doubt you'll make bail. And with the way the courts are jammed these days, you probably won't make your first appearance for three or four months. Gives you a long time to play with the other socially maladjusted drekheads in lock-up."

"A gloomy proposition," Paulson said. He relaxed in his chair with his hands folded behind his head. A smile curved his thin lips under the shadow of his hooked nose. "On the other hand, you can still talk to us."

"The cuffs?" Skater asked.

Paulson looked at Nina, who referred to a noteputer she took from inside her jacket.

"Boosted reflexes," she read. "Bone reinforcements in both arms and one leg. Eyes. Commlink IV. No implanted hardware that slices or dices."

"So that probably means no magic." Paulson said.

"Came back negative."

"Going in kind of naked for a shadowrunner, ain't you?" Paulson asked.

"I'm no gillette," Skater replied. "And I'm not a shadowrunner."

"Sure." Paulson got out of his chair and fished a key out of his pocket. "But let's get something straight before I unlock you: you do not want to try to slot me over when you're loose. I gave up original equipment a long time ago, but I wouldn't need chrome to get over on a guy like you in the first place. The ankle bracelets are staying on."

Once his wrists were free, Skater massaged them, trying to get circulation restored without all the pain.

"File came back with the name Otto Franks when it scanned your retina-prints and fingerprints," Nina said. "Is that your name?"

Skater nodded.

"This is being recorded, Mr. Franks. Could you answer verbally?"

"Sure."

"So your name is Otto Franks?"

"Yes." The name was a cover Archangel had implanted into the SIN database. If he got loose, Skater knew that she could erase all trace of him again and assign him another idee of his choice. Almost two years ago, she'd gotten into the system and erased every vestige of Jack Skater.

"And what's your occupation, Mr. Franks?" Paulson asked.

"I'm an investment counselor," Skater replied.

"With boosted reflexes? I guess the stocks change pretty fragging fast these days, don't they?"

"I was mugged a few years ago." Skater knew that record was on file, too, courtesy of Archangel. She was very efficient when she wove one of her webs. It also explained the reinforced limbs and the surgeries necessary to correct the damage the Disassemblers had done. "After I got out of the hospital, I had the boosted reflexes added. Figured it would give me an edge if I ever got into that situation again."

Paulson laughed out loud in disbelief. "Well, chummer, you certainly got yourself into some deep drek this morning, didn't you?"

"What am I charged with?" Skater asked.

"Arson, for starters," Nina said. "Besides the criminal action, there'll be a civil suit on behalf of the Montgomery Building owners."

"Which happens to be a joint venture of real-estate developers hardboosted into the megaplex's political and economic high-rollers scene," Paulson said. "They're pretty slotted off at the moment."

"And murder," the troll said.

Skater made himself ask, "Who was killed?"

Paulson pointed at him. "Maybe you want to tell us."

"The only thing I flatlined was a hell hound."

Nina looked at Paulson, who shrugged. "Crime Scene Unit reported a big dog. Forensics hasn't taken a whack at it yet. Could be."

"What about the desk clerk and the Knight Errant secguard working the lobby?" the troll asked.

"They were dead when I got there."

"When did you get there?"

"A little after four a.m."

"How much after?"

"Ten, fifteen minutes."

"Can anyone verify that?" Nina asked.

Skater thought of the cabby who'd taken him there, then dismissed the possibility. The driver was an ork. "An elderly couple let me in."

"That so?" Paulson stood and started pacing.

Skater knew the motion was purely to rattle him. His lies were all going to be simple, things he could easily remember. Nothing that would lead too far astray.

"How much money did you make last year, Mr. Franks?" Paulson asked.

"Check my tax return. I'm sure it's listed there." Archangel took care of those details, too.

"Oh, I have."

"Then why ask me?"

"To see if you knew. You don't. I find that interesting."

"My line of work," Skater said, "you do a lot of number-crunching."

"Give me a guess."

Skater remained quiet. His cover was holding, which was frustrating the detective team.

"I was playing the markets," Paulson went on, "could you recommend me a good buy at morning's open?"

"Maybe you could give us a client list," Nina said.

"Maybe I could get a lawyer in here," Skater said, "before we continue this discussion."

"What were you doing at the Montgomery?" Paulson asked.

"I went there to see someone."

"You normally do business at four in the morning?"

"A lot of my clients have strange schedules," Skater answered. "I don't mind working around their needs."

"Larisa Hartsinger was a client?" Nina asked.

"No."

"But you went there to see her?"

"Yes." By giving them part of the truth, Skater figured he could keep them off-balance, and bring the lies back on-line.

"Why?" Paulson queried.

"Personal reasons."

Paulson resumed his seat and put his hands behind his head again. "What kind of personal reasons?"

"She was a dancer at a club."

Paulson nodded. "SybreSpace. We've already talked to proprietress Amanda Silvereyes and some of Hartsinger's co-workers."

"Why were you interested in her?" the troll asked.

"I liked the way she danced."

"Hoping to get lucky?" Paulson asked.

Skater shrugged.

Nina punched up a new page in her noteputer. "According to Ms. Silvereyes, Larisa Hartsinger hadn't worked at the club in almost three months. Why pick now to try to see her?"

"I didn't want to put it off any longer," Skater said. It was also the truth.

"Let me tell you a story," Paulson said. "Stop me if you've heard this one before. But my partner and I thought it was great. This guy goes into SybreSpace tonight at about two-thirty. His name is Jack."

Skater knew then that they'd leaned on Aggie and she'd rolled over on him to save her own skin. He didn't blame her; she had no investment in the biz and everything to lose.

"We talked to one of the dancers, who says that two hard guys picked up on this Jack. She's not sure of their names, but she knows one's a troll." Paulson leaned forward and spoke with more animation. "Now don't lose it yet, because it gets funnier. See, there's a dust-up just outside the club, next street over, and one of the gillettes goes down. Turns out it's an electro-bodyware freak named Shayx who's known for low-level wetwork down in the Barrens. Nobody's talking about what he's doing up in Seattle, but word is he's a connected guy now. Oh, and did I mention that he was a troll?"

Skater remained silent, listening to the guy drive the nails into the box.

"We can't find Jack or the other hitman. After we dig a little more, we find out Larisa Hartsinger had an old boyfriend named Jack—we never got a last name—who may have been running the shadows for fun and profit. In the process, we turn up a snitch who's working for some yaks looking for three people, one of whom looks a lot like you."

Paulson tapped buttons on the microcam. The monitor rippled with color for just a moment, then produced a grainy black and white datapic of Skater. It had been shot somewhere on the street. In the holopic, Skater had his arm around Larisa.

He gazed at the image, remembering when it had been shot. It was no more than a month or two before Larisa had told him she didn't want to see him anymore. He studied the datapic, the pregnancy still on his mind. But he couldn't tell if she was or not. In the holopic, she wore her hair long, but the black and white didn't do justice to her coppery red hair and almond-shaped emerald green eyes. She was beautiful, her elven features looking chiseled and clean.

"Care to comment?" Nina asked.

"He could be anybody," Skater answered.

Paulson tapped the microcam again, opening another window. This one held a datapic of Skater in the lobby of Larisa's old doss, walking in through the door. It was black and white, too. The resemblance was undeniable. "You think so?"

"What I think doesn't seem to matter," Skater said.

"No, it fragging well doesn't, Jack, or maybe I should call you Walter Dent." Paulson tapped the control buttons again, and more datapics followed, this time ones that had been taken inside the building. "You always go around carrying an unregistered piece?" He held up a hand and spoke sarcastically. "Right. I forgot about you got mugged and all that slot."

"What happened to Larisa Hartsinger?" Skater asked.

"You tell me," Paulson challenged. "You went there to kill her."

"No."

"Sure you did. She dumped you."

"Yes."

There was a pause. "Yes what?" Paulson asked.

"Yes," Skater said. "She dumped me." It was another partial truth, and given just to keep them off-balance, unable to sort fact from fiction.

"Otto Franks or Jack somebody?"

"Where is she?"

"Give me a fragging name, Jack."

Skater fought the urge to jump up and make an attempt to reach the Lone Star man. But the way he felt, with the chains around his feet, he knew the effort was doomed to failure.

"What were you doing there?" Nina asked in a softer voice.

Skater knew it was pure good cop/bad cop, but he also knew he could use the ploy for his own purposes. He turned to face the troll. "I thought Larisa might be in danger."

Nina leaned in, giving the appearance of intense interest. For all Skater knew, it could have been real. "Why would you think that?"

He decided a small lie would work. "The troll in the alley told me."

"Shayx?"

"I didn't get his name."

"Why was he a threat to Larisa Hartsinger?"

"He didn't say. Just that he was going to kill her when he found her."

"Why did he attack you?"

"Because I went there asking questions about her."

Paulson slapped the desk, looking incredulous. "And you dusted him because he might at some point stumble across her address? I'm saying this because he apparently didn't have it or else he'd already gone there."

"He didn't give me much choice. It was self-defense."

"His head shot up like Swiss cheese," Paulson said, "there was no other way I could figure it."

Skater said nothing, returning the man's gaze full measure.

Paulson was still looking at Skater when he touched the base of his skull. Skater knew the guy was answering a commlink call. "Paulson." He listened intently for a moment, then turned to look at Nina. "That was the coroner. Thinks he identified that third body."

Nina looked the question.

"He says Larisa Hartsinger," Paulson said.

Skater kept his emotions from his face.

The Lone Star man turned to Skater. "So what do you think? Want to come take a look for yourself? A smart guy like you, maybe you'll see something we won't."

Skater kept his voice flat and neutral. "Sure." He had to see for himself.

9

The cold chill of death soaked into Jack Skater even as the elevator dropped through the Lone Star Security Services building to one of the basement levels. When the doors opened up, the stench of chemicals and blood surrounded him despite the efforts to cover it over with pine and lemon scents.

"Follow the purple line," Paulson ordered, giving him a shove to get him started.

Skater glanced at the floor and found a thin rainbow of colors traced across the linoleum. Locating the purple one near the center of the dozen or so colors, he started forward. The tile was cold underfoot, and the air was chill, crisp.

Men and women, human and meta, passed him in the hall, all dressed in white lab coats over their street clothes. Only a few gave him a second look. The orange jumpsuit made him stand out in the sterile environment. He flexed his cuffed hands behind his back in an effort to keep the circulation going.

He followed two lefts, then a right, ending up at a door as black as obsidian. The small lettering in the upper-right corner announced Richard Means, Ph.D., Forensics.

Nina swiped her passcard through the maglock and the door opened.

"Go," Paulson said, shoving again.

Skater went with it. He was deep inside himself, holding tight where no emotions could touch him. Maybe he'd already accepted Larisa's death; he wasn't sure. Maybe it was just that too much had happened. The numbness felt permanent, like nerve-death.

A small anteroom held a short black female who barely gave them a glance when they entered. She was studying diagrams on a deck. "Hello, Lance, Nina: Doc's inside waiting on you."

The smell filling the room was cloying and made the air thick in Skater's chest. He had to force himself to breathe it.

The only other door was to the left. A steady electronic whir came from it. Skater walked toward it, watching as more and more of the gleaming machinery covering the walls came into view.

A chromed ball hung from the ceiling, nearly two-dozen articulated arms jutting out from it. Each of them ended in another piece of medical hardware: scalpels, forceps, needles, bone saws, and a chest spreader.

"Doc," Nina said, staying back from the slanted table where a burned and blackened corpse lay stretched out in unclothed vulnerability. "We were told you had a confirmed idee."

Dr. Means sat in a chair at the corner of the room facing them. A helmet was fitted over his head, hardwired into the computers behind him. Rectangular glasses covered his eyes.

On the armrests, his hands played over a series of buttons, toggles, and joysticks. "I'm pretty sure of it."

In response to his movements the ball descended over the corpse and two of the articulated arms whirred smoothly into motion.

Skater felt Paulson's heavy hand drop onto his shoulder, pushing him closer. He stopped a few steps away and tried to breathe as shallowly as possible. Burned flesh seared his nostrils.

One look at the charred face let him know the corpse had once been Larisa Hartsinger. Somehow, the flames had caramelized her beauty, creating a hard, chitin-like exo-skeleton of her face. The shell was smooth, a deep burnished ebony with an undercurrent of dark red that gave off a glow around the edges. Her hair had been burnt off, leaving her skull with black stubble.

The long, slim body was ravaged and twisted by fire. Incisions had been made to allow different medical apparatus passage. Three of the arms on the surgical ball rummaged inside the corpse, one of them making sucking sounds.

"There's the face, of course," Means said. "The Crime Scene Unit made a tentative idee at the scene when they recovered the DB."

On the wall, one of the monitors flared to life. A picture of Larisa juiced the pixels.

"I got this from the Department of Licensing when I found out the DMV didn't have anything," Means said. "Because she worked as a dancer at SybreSpace, I knew Hartsinger would probably be registered. Some of them aren't, but Amanda Silvereyes runs a pretty tight ship."

Skater watched the monitor, keeping the memories at bay. The twisted thing on the lab table wasn't Larisa. Larisa was gone, hopefully to a better place, but he didn't know if he believed that.

The image of Larisa on the monitor shrank and moved over, making room for a view of her burned face. The eyes were open in the picture, looking like ice cubes that had gone gray with age, fixed in a thousand-meter stare.

"I ran tests on the DNA," Means said. "I was able to match the skin tone from pigmentation. I did the same for the hair and eyes."

The caramelized version of Larisa's face lightened up,

taking on a more human appearance. The gray eyes turned deep hunter's green.

"She'd had her eyes altered," the coroner said. "I was able to pick up enough of the traces of the cosmetic modifications to get a match on the color. I took a sample of her hair, also modified, from inside her scalp and made that match."

On the monitor, the burnt version of Larisa suddenly grew hair the coppery red color Skater remembered.

"This is what she looked like before she died," Means informed them. "I can show you what she looked like a few years ago. Before the cosmetic changes."

A third picture popped onto the other screen beside the other two. The girl in this one was not as pretty as Larisa. The bone structure was the same, but different. She was definitely slimmer, maybe anemic. Her eyes were a doe-brown, and her hair was mousy brunette, thin and plastered to her skull.

Skater had never seen that Larisa. It was like looking at a stranger. Except that he could see the other Larisa waiting to spring forth out of this one.

He was suddenly aware that there was so much he'd never known about her, that he'd never let her know about him. During the time they'd been together, he hadn't thought much about it. Life was to be lived now.

But standing there, looking at the three pictures of her on the coroner's wall, standing in front of her mortal remains and knowing she hadn't died an easy death, Skater felt the loss. It ached inside him, cold and hard and edged.

"You run a check on her?" Paulson asked.

"Yes. It's all in my report. The SIN was hers from birth. She has a mother still living in the sprawl. I assume you'll want to talk to her."

Skater didn't let the surprise show. Larisa had never mentioned a mother. But neither of them had been exactly forthcoming about their secrets.

"Yeah," Paulson said. "We'll talk to her. But I think we've already got the doer in custody."

Means slipped his head out of the helmet. Even sitting in the chair, Skater could see that he was tall. He had blond hair and blue eyes, and a lantern jaw. The guy could have been a new anchor on the trid. "Did you check him out for magic?"

"Came up negative," Nina said.

Means nodded. "Then you've possibly got one of the doers. This woman was shot first, then fried with some kind of fire blast."

"This guy's a shooter," Paulson said. "We didn't turn up a partner."

"Someone else was involved," Means said. "That woman was hit with a spell that left her like that. Whoever killed her wanted her identified, maybe as a warning. Was she connected?"

"Not anywhere that we could find," Nina said. "But working the dance floor at SybreSpace, she could have been. We're still looking."

Skater let the silence that followed draw out for a time, then, "What about the baby?"

"What baby?" Paulson demanded. "Nobody at the scene mentioned a baby."

"Ask him." Skater nodded at the corner.

"There was no baby found at the scene," Means replied. "But my tests show she'd given birth within the last three weeks."

A knot Skater hadn't known was inside him suddenly came loose. He breathed a little easier. Maybe some part of Larisa was still alive.

"Was there anything in the Montgomery files about a baby?" Paulson asked his partner.

The troll flipped through her notes. "No. The apartment was leased in Hartsinger's name only. The rent was paid to the Montgomery account by the first of the month ever since she moved in three months ago."

"She was making the payments?"

"Yes," Nina responded. "From an account with Garrison First."

"How old was the account?" Paulson asked.

"Three months."

"Amazing, huh?" Paulson asked sarcastically. "Can we trace the money that went into that account?"

"I'll make a note."

Without giving the appearance of listening, Skater memorized every word. He'd been set up. The team had been set up. Now, it was looking like Larisa had been set up, too. He still didn't know if she'd known his head was being put on the chopping block.

"What do you think about this?" Paulson asked, turning to face Skater. "You think your girlfriend could have made the kind of nuyen she needed to live in a place like the Montgomery from her salary and tips?"

"She was a good dancer," Skater answered. But he knew the high life wasn't something Larisa would have been comfortable with. She liked having people she could talk to.

"Damn sure doesn't look like it now."

With some difficulty, Skater managed to let the comment slide by. His grip on himself was tenuous, and he knew it could snap at any time if he wasn't careful.

"How did you know about the baby?" Nina asked.

"I saw the crib," Skater said.

"Nobody mentioned a crib," Paulson said, looking at Means.

The coroner shook his head. "After that fire, it's hard to say."

"That where you got the teddy bear you had on you?" Nina asked.

"Yeah."

"Any special reason for picking it up?"

"I figured if the baby got scared, the teddy bear might calm her."

"Her?"

Skater nodded. "The baby is a girl."

"You're sure about that?"

"I saw the room before it burned. It was made up for a little girl. The clothes were all for a girl."

"So where is she?"

"I don't know." Skater tried to answer in a neutral tone, like it didn't matter. He thought Nina might have seen through it.

"The baby could have already been gone," Means said as he poured soykaf from a thermos. "Larisa Hartsinger had been dead at least an hour before the fire got to her."

"You're sure?" Paulson asked.

The coroner nodded.

"You want to tell me about it now?" Paulson said, disgusted.

Skater just looked at him. "I'm tired of talking."

10

"You really think you're some kind of tough guy, don't you?" Paulson demanded. He swung the cell door hard. The lock clacked and clanked and seized up.

Seated on the cot bolted into the wall, two and a half meters away from the crossbars keeping the groundhound out, Skater sat back against the wall and didn't say anything. The cell was dark, spartan, and held a dank chill shoved deep into the bowels of the earth under the sprawl.

Without another word, Paulson stalked off. Nina stood there looking at Skater with her big troll eyes, softer than they had been. "If we hear about the missing baby, I'll make sure you know. And, here." She unfolded her big troll fingers to reveal the stuffed, purple bear.

"Thanks." Skater stuffed the toy into his jumpsuit and looked up at her gratefully. "I owe you one."

She nodded, but the look she gave him told him that the only time she expected him out of the cell was for relocation to Metroplex Prison a few streets down and over. She walked away without saying anything else.

The undercurrent of jail conversations broke out around him. Threats, wheedling, promises, crying, and the hopelessness of the lost surrounded him, mixed in the odors of blood, sweat, and sour flesh. Skater made himself comfortable on the cot and tried not to think about how many things might be living in the cell with him, six-legged as well as fungal.

Being locked up scared him. He'd always hated being confined. As a boy growing up on the Council lands, Skater often liked to slip away by himself for hours at a time. When he got older and the old man had begun teaching him what he knew about surviving on the land, the two would go out for days. Andrew Ghost-step was a loner who didn't talk much, leaving Skater to his own devices. It was a freedom the boy had savored.

He was exhausted and tried to sleep, but images of Larisa kept darting through his mind like blood kites riding rebellious thermals. He remembered her face when they'd been together, how hard it was when she told him she didn't want to see him anymore, and the way it was in the coroner's office.

He gave up and switched on the public trid built into the wall. A small retractable earpiece was mounted in the wall. He held it for a moment and considered the possibilities of someone jacking into the security system through the trid grid. Archangel would probably know how to do it, but he didn't. And even if he did, he had no deck.

Slipping the earplug in, he listened to most of a commercial put out by DeGear's Electronics. Then the news came on and the anchor switched to a reporter named Chelsea Sable. She was lanky and black, the irises in her eyes metallic gold with jet flakes. Her voice was calming and captured an audience easily with its huskiness.

"So far," Sable told the anchor and the trid audience, "it looks like the bio to open a Seattle branch of the Tir Tairngire corporation of NuGene is going to meet with none of the roadblocks originally threatened by local opponents of the move. If anything, support for NuGene CEO Tavis Silverstaff is gaining momentum."

The trid cut to footage of an elf getting out of a luxury sedan in front of the Charles Royer Building. He was tall and impressive, with blue-black hair styled long, and a beard and mustache that lent him an air of royalty. He wore a crimson suit that set him off from everyone around him, accessorized by a white cape with gold trim. The footage had been shot during the day, and the jewels set into his gold walking stick glinted in the sun. His bodyguards stayed near him at all times, a protective wall of flesh and bone.

Silverstaff reached back into the car and a female elf jointed him, clinging to his arm. She was a full head shorter than he was, delicate and slender, except for her obvious pregnancy. Her dress was conservative, in a crimson that went well with the man's.

"One of KTXX's sources today told this reporter that support for NuGene's expansion into Seattle is part of an effort to keep the elven nation of Tir Tairngire from redeveloping Portland as a major port city. As economists often point out, re-opening Portland to any degree would cut deeply into Seattle's position as prime port of entry for trade goods in the region. UCAS interests have also thrown in their support for

NuGene because a reinvigorated Portland would slash their tax-base in Seattle."

Silverstaff shook hands on his way into the building, a genuine smile on his face.

Skater closed his eyes and put his hands behind his head, willing himself to relax. The woman's voice was soothing, and he focused on it the way he used to do with his grandfather's words.

Harsh voices interrupted his unexpected drowsing. Opening his eyes, Skater glanced at the trid. For a moment, he thought he must have slept through the news into a movie. Then he realized the jerky quality of the footage wasn't from a cheap budget. It was because it was being filmed live from a hand-held unit.

Four Lone Star uniforms were inside a house wreathed in spider's webbing. Plywood sections covered the windows. The blue crew split into two groups, each armed with high-intensity flashlights and automatic weapons, which they fired freely into the dilapidated ceiling and walls. Trapped inside the house, the gunfire was a rolling onslaught of systematic thunder that challenged the trid's stereo capabilities.

Skater blinked, realizing he was scanning pictures of human beings that looked like they'd been torn apart and devoured by wild dogs. Two of them, their sex unknowable anymore, lay in the living room. The news team followed one group of uniforms into a dusty bedroom and turned the portacam on a young man who'd apparently been stabbed to death in his bed. Guts oozed out from huge rips in his torso. Another man, the supposed murderer, was stumbling around the room swinging what seemed to be one of his victim's organs, occasionally going back to the bed and hovering gleefully over the gruesome corpse. The man's clothes were soaked with blood and he was laughing, his head rolling around on his neck like a gyroscope. He seemed retarded, or demented. Skater watched, hypnotized.

The man's skin was yellowish, almost jaundiced-looking, and looked loose and flabby, as if he were hollow inside. His eyes were a mass of exploded blood vessels, rounded and red except for a small black dot for a pupil, the iris completely obliterated. He gazed stupidly at the high-intensity light and let out a peal of laughter.

The Lone Star uniforms ordered him to move away from the dead man, but the demented man suddenly lunged at them instead. In an instant a hail of bullets chewed him up and threw him to the floor like a rag doll.

The reporter's voice-over announced that this was the fourth reported case this week of what they'd started calling the laughing death disease, and that Lone Star had quarantined one of the maddened killers and turned her over to their labs for testing. The condition was apparently caused by a virus, but it was as yet unidentified. This was the first Skater had heard of it, but it seemed to fit right in with everything else that had happened since this night had begun.

"You got a service contract with DocWagon?" a man in the next cell asked.

Skater started at the question. Wheeler Iron-Nerve worked as a rigger for DocWagon as his straight job, and Duran, Shiva, and Elvis had all freelanced for the corp's paramedic teams from time to time. But calling for DocWagon while on a run wouldn't have been good biz.

"No," was all he said.

"Good thing. The skinny I get on this drek, these crazies popping up around town have all been clients of DocWagon."

"What does DocWagon say?"

"You kidding, chummer? At this point, nada. Ain't they just another corp? Cover-up's a specialty, if you know what I mean."

Skater listened to the man talk for a while, then exhaustion finally had its way and sucked him down into a maze of dark dreams that promised no rest at all.

Whispering voices woke Skater and he lay still in the cot, peering through slitted eyes and kicking in the low-light vision enhancement.

A handful of shadows drifted to a stop in front of his cell. He was still figuring the odds when the lock on the cell door snapped open. It was probably harder to break into Lone Star than any other place in the whole Seattle sprawl, yet these people were doing it. Since he was in general lock-up waiting for his appearance in court and not one of the high-sec levels, it would have been easier. But not much.

And they were after him.

"Breakout!" he shouted as he rose to his feet in a defensive crouch. Then he yelled again to attract attention and alert the security systems, and to push up his adrenaline levels as he swung a bunched fist at the lead elf rushing toward him.

Flesh gave way under Skater's fist, and an elf howled a curse in Sperethiel as he dropped backward. All the elves were dressed in loose black clothing and moved like a unit. Their reflexes were military, concise and telling.

Skater caught a long leg speeding toward his face. Grabbing the elf's ankle over his shoulder, he dropped into a crouch and hammered his other hand home into his attacker's groin. He straightened and used the leg as a fulcrum, propelling the man back into his mates.

More confused yelling, angry and frightened, filled the slammer as other prisoners came awake.

Skater fought from desperation, the confines of the cell not permitting much skill. He punched and kicked, and clawed and bit, focusing all his energies on reaching the cell door. He sent a wheel-kick rocketing, knocking an elf back into the arms of another behind him. For a moment, a path was clear to the door and he wasted no time making for it. He hurdled one elf who'd fallen and grabbed a bar to pull himself around the corner.

He didn't see the elf waiting for him until he was almost on top of him. This one was short and stocky, unusual for an elf, a few centimeters shorter than Skater and at least that much broader.

The elf came at Skater at a dead run, jamming a shoulder into his stomach, then crowding him up against the cell bars. Skater lost his breath as soon as the elf hit him, then heard the dull thunk of his head smashing up against one of the bars. A pyrotechnic display rattled the inside of his skull as his legs and arms turned rubbery.

"Secure him," the elf said, pushing back from Skater, barely breathing hard. "Let's get the frag out of here. The alert's gonna go off any minute now."

Skater felt cold steep clamp around his wrists and ankles, heard the ratcheting noises as they locked, then blacked out before he knew it.

11

Cold water splashed over Skater and brought him back to consciousness. This time he was handcuffed to a chair, his arms pinned painfully behind him and his ankles taped to the chair legs. A single bulb burned from a bell-shaped cover overhead, lighting up him, the chair, and the grease-stained concrete floor under them. People were in a ring around him. He saw their shoes just beyond the light's reach.

He didn't try to feign unconsciousness. He knew from the way the figures surrounding him shifted that they knew he was back on-line. A headache felt like a fusion processor reaching critical mass between his temples. His mouth was swollen, tasted of blood.

Fear filled him but he kept it under control. Whoever these elves were, they wanted something from him, and they wanted it bad enough to crack Lone Star to get him. Otherwise they'd have killed him long before now. As long as they wanted that something, he'd live. He hung on to that thought.

The smells of oils and fuels told him he was in a warehouse. And the smell of poverty—dust and dead meat—cutting through these industrial odors told him this was one that hadn't been used for any straight biz for quite awhile. Plenty of warehouses existed around the sprawl, some of them working and some empty. A lot of them changed hands regularly, few of them really traceable to an individual owner or a corporation through the straw companies that ostensibly owned them.

One of the elves moved forward, into the light. Judging from his build, Skater made him as the elf who'd put him down in the cell.

"Are you with us?" the elf demanded. "Or shall I have another bucket of water drawn?"

"I'm here," Skater said.

Besides being short and stocky, the elf appeared to be in his late middle years, with close-set charcoal eyes as polished as gunsights that marked him as a hunter. Scars crisscrossed his exposed flesh, including his face, war-maps of past battles he'd survived. His dark hair was cut short, not long enough to be grabbed, and was blistered with gray. One particular gray streak followed the jagged line of a knife scar along the side of his head to his right ear, which was missing at least three centimeters of its upper point.

He wore a gray pinstriped business suit, not too flashy, but not off-the-rack either. Navy suspenders held his pants up, as well as a shoulder holster containing a Seco pistol. His shirt sleeves were rolled to mid-forearm, but Skater didn't get the impression it was for appearance. The elf was a man who was used to work. He shook a cigarette from a pack in his shirt pocket and cracked a wooden match with his thumbnail to get it going.

Skater felt like he should know him. He was certain he'd seen the guy somewhere recently. But the cigarette pack was printed in Sperethiel, definitely an elven brand. Skater had never been to Tir Tairngire, and he sensed that was all this man had known.

"You took something from that freighter," the elf said. "I want it back, and I want the names of everyone who has copies of it."

"No matter what I say," Skater said, "you're not going to believe me. You're going to have to make sure."

A thin, mirthless smile scarred the man's mouth, looking out of place. "Of course."

"Then let's get to it," Skater said. "We're wasting time here."

"You've an admirable spirit, Mr. Skater," the elf said. "I would enjoy crossing swords with you at some other time, both verbal and steel, and I'm assured that you're no stranger to either. But I, too, am pressed by time. 'Work expands so as to fill the time available for its completion.' Parkinson's Law. You've probably never heard that before."

"Not to know who it came from," Skater agreed. He shifted slightly, like he was trying to work the circulation back into his legs. At the same time he was pulling on the handcuffs, testing the flex in the right one. "Did you kill Larisa Hartsinger?"

"No." The elf's face was stone, giving nothing away.

Except that he hadn't asked who Larisa Hartsinger was, Skater realized. "Who tipped you to me?"

"We had your picture from the ship. A few offers of financial reward here in Seattle, we had your name."

"The yakuza were out there, too. They hit the ship's system, not us."

"They're hunting you."

"Maybe they'd like you to think so."

The elf took the cigarette out of his mouth and blew on it till the coal was bright orange. "However it turns out, we're going to start with you and see where that takes us." He waved another man forward.

The new arrival was taller by a head than the first elf, and built like a rail. His dark red mohawk stood at least twenty centimeters high, and glittered from jeweled dust. He was young, maybe as little as nineteen or twenty, though Skater knew it was hard to tell with elves. In a synthleather vest over an open black shirt and dark denims and wearing gogang stomper boots, he looked like he knew his way around the sprawl. A series of hoops of increasing size ringed both pointy ears, alternating gold and silver. His black gloves had the fingers chopped out of them.

"Find out what he knows," the first elf said.

The elven mage smiled slightly, then touched the jeweled amulet at his throat as he gestured and spoke a string of words in Sperethiel.

Skater felt the spell take him, warned only a heartbeat before by the slight shimmering net of activity that jetted from the mage's fingers and jumped for him. It felt like a red-hot icicle had been jammed into his brain.

Memories of growing up on Council lands crashed through his synapses. He smelled his grandmother's cooking, felt the tug of the first fish he ever caught, and listened to the timbre of his grandfather voicing displeasure. There was a momentary flash of the wind in his face from the assault on the *Sapphire Seahawk,* the vibration of his sword clanging against one of the elven sailor's. He pulled the pain in deep until it consumed him and pushed everything else away.

In response, Skater felt the psychic knife filleting his mind shift angles. The number of memories became fewer, but their duration lasted longer.

Slick blood coated Skater's hand. Somewhere out there he could feel it. He hoped none of his captors noticed it was slowly coming free. Or maybe he was only imagining it. He forced his spasms to work with him, pulling on the arm till it felt like his shoulder was about to pop out of the socket.

"I've got the troll who was with him," the mage said confidently. "A few more minutes, I'll have the others, too."

"Lone Star confiscated his clothes and possessions," someone said.

"What about his doss?" the stocky elf asked.

"We didn't find anything," one of the other elves answered.

Skater focused on the lead elf, trying to fill his mind with how he looked. Shiva was in his mind again, and he knew the mage had her image as well.

"I've got two of them," the mage said. Perspiration gleamed in sliding diamonds on his pale face. "There were seven of them all together, but one may be dead."

The odor reached Skater first, rising up and separating itself out of all the rest. It was dense and suffocating, freshly turned, wet earth that had sat and mildewed for a long time.

Pain cut across the back of his right hand as he gained another centimeter or two on the cuff. He felt it resting across the first knuckle of his little finger. Blood pulsed against the steel. He knew he couldn't wait much longer. The damage was bruising his flesh and it was starting to swell. In another few seconds he wouldn't be able to get close to pulling his hand through.

Skater opened his eyes and focused on the mage. He was still shaking, like he had palsy. Fever spots burned on his cheeks and perspiration ran down his neck, soaking his clothes. Shadows lurked behind the elves. At first he thought it was just his imagination firing off the invasive mind filling his own. The shapes shambled toward the elves with a strange, almost drunken gait.

Then the shambling shadows closed on the elves. Skater recognized them for what they were, ghouls, and couldn't stop the insane laughter that cackled out of him. It was incredible. The smell was all around, but the elves weren't aware of it. Somehow the mage fragging around in his mind had magnified his olfactory nerves, maybe his vision and hearing too, because now he could spot the odd bit of gray-white scabrous hide and hear the scrape of near-dead flesh over the paved warehouse floor.

The psychic knife turned in Skater's mind again as he watched the things creep closer. The lamplight shone against their yellow fangs and long, gray nails. "They were able to download the files from the ship's system before the yuakuza got to them," the mage said.

"Where are the files?"

The mage hesitated, and Skater felt the mind probe penetrate further, questing with direction. "More than one copy exists."

Skater felt his trapped hand slide free. The handcuffs dangled from his other wrist, tapping against the back of the chair. He blinked perspiration out of his eyes, setting himself because he knew it was going down quick.

"I've got the decker's face," the mage said. "An elven female. She may be known to us."

"Only a little longer," the stocky elf said. "Then we'll dispose of him and get on about our business."

The ghouls closed the distance separating them from their prey. Skater couldn't believe they would attack seven armed men, even though they outnumbered the elves two to one. But who really knew what ghouls were like or how they behaved? One thing was obvious: the lure of human and metahuman flesh was irresistible to them. As ghouls, they existed on the edges of the sprawl, bringing down the weak, sick, or young, or dining on the freshly dead. Probably some sort of accident, no doubt involving dead bodies, had drawn them to this warehouse.

The leader of the pack wore a Mortimer of London longcoat over jeans and a lavender tanktop that emphasized the gray-white death pallor of the exposed flesh. He gestured, and two of the others peeled off and attacked the nearest elf, who was watching Skater with interest.

One of the scabrous creatures grabbed the elf by the shoulder and pulled him around. The elf started to say something, but a swipe of the long, hardened nails opened his throat, killing any noise he might have made. Still, the dying man's finger tightened on his Sandler. A line of bullets stuttered across the concrete floor and took out the second ghoul.

The stocky elf turned at once. Deadly quick, he dropped his hand, then had it up again pointing the Seco pistol as if by magic.

Skater felt the psychic knife leave his mind as soon as the mage's attention wavered. The ghouls moved forward, overwhelming the elves by sheer numbers.

The stocky elf killed one of them before it reached him. Another one was at pointblank range when he lifted the pistol and put a round through one of its eyes. The forward momentum didn't stop, and the dead ghoul came crashing across the stocky elf, knocking him to the floor.

The elven mage worked his hands, gathering the power needed to wield a spell. Before he could finish, a wall of force slammed into him. His broken body fell away, and from the slack way it landed, Skater was pretty sure the elf was history.

Skater stood, intending to get free of the chair. Guns blasted all around him, filling the warehouse with a blitzkrieg of flash and thunder. Screams and curses in Sperethiel punctuated the gunshots.

Before Skater could free one leg, a ghoul shoved its way through two elves who were trying to bring their weapons up and defend themselves at the same time. Skater straightened in time to catch the charging thing with a hand over its forehead. Skater's other hand knotted in the cloth remaining of the ghoul's stained, ripped shirt. Unable to get out of the way, the ghoul bowled him over with its sheer ferocity.

The wooden chair smashed when Skater and the ghoul landed on top of it. Skater's legs came free, carrying tatters of the tape and fragments of the chair. He was engulfed by the foul stench of the huge thing on top of him, and struggled not to throw up. It breathed on him, foul and heavy, wet against the bare skin of his neck.

He kept his hands locked in place, holding the thing at bay while its fangs gnashed for him. The ghoul swung a handful of claws in his face. Skater twisted, and the claws shattered against the pavement. It howled in frustrated anger.

An elf fell beside Skater, two of the ghouls on top of him. The elf shot one in the chest as it tried to smash his head between its hands. But even as the dead one fell away, the remaining one sank its fangs into his abdomen and slapped the gun away. The elf was screaming and trying to fight as the thing raised its head with crimson staining its mouth. With no wasted motion, the ghoul rammed a hand deep into the wound it had created in the elf's stomach, going all the way up to the elbow before it stopped. The elf shivered, went stiff, and died between heartbeats.

Releasing his hold on the ghoul's shirt, Skater bent its arm and with surprising ease, thrust its forearm and hand with the long, hardened nails into the side of its head. Blood spurted inside the creature's eye, threading a scarlet mosaic instantly through the ash-gray jelly.

Without mercy, Skater opened his hand and swung a short heel blow into the broken area of the ghoul's skull. The shattered plates of bone grated against each other, but sank inward to crush the brain. The sentient light in the creature's eyes went out and the muscles relaxed.

Skater rolled the dead body off him and forced himself to his feet. The teddy bear he'd picked up at Larisa's lay a few steps away, one of the ears nearly torn off. Reaching down, he plucked it from the floor and shoved it inside the loose jail jumper. Then he picked up a nearby chair leg.

A ghoul sprang at him, lips ricked back to expose the broken fangs. Strings of muscle tissue clotted with blood hung from them.

Side-stepping, Skater swung the short length of the chair leg. It wasn't heavy, so he knew he had to depend on speed and timing. The makeshift club landed with a satisfying thunk against the back of the ghoul's skull as it went stumbling by. The corpse sprawled and tumbled, fading back into the shadows.

"Freeze, rat-frag," an elf commanded. He moved out of the pile of bodies battling all around him. His pistol was centered on Skater's chest. Stray bullets impacted against the pavement from at least two other guns, spitting sparks.

Skater tensed, ready to throw himself behind a low wall of tarp-covered crates and machinery. The stink of the ghouls was overwhelming. Elves cursed and screamed as they fought and died.

A basso gunshot sounded from behind Skater, and for a moment he figured his luck had run out. Then his peripheral vision registered a long muzzle flash and the elf in front of him crumpled.

"C'mon, kid," a gruff voice said above the sound of a pump shotgun getting racked for another shot.

Skater whirled. Six meters away, Quint Duran stood in the cover afforded by the tarped crates. There was only a moment of indecision, then bullets cut wind around Skater and he was moving.

12

Duran stepped from cover and fired two double-ought blasts in the direction of the elves and ghouls, easily dropping some of both.

Skater stayed low, making his way toward the ork behind a row of crates. Rounds tore the canvas fabric and sent oblong pieces of material flying. Heavy return fire drove Duran back into hiding.

A flitting shadow warned Skater that he was about to be attacked. He turned to face the threat and caught an elf who was leaping over the covered crates. The elf's weight and momentum shoved Skater backward, but he locked a hand onto his attacker's gun-wrist.

He fell hard against the crates behind him and sent some of them spinning. Even in the darkness, he caught the gleam of edged metal in the elf's other hand. The knife came streaking for his face. Lifting his free arm, Skater parried the knife strike, then rammed his forehead into the elf's face. The crunch of breaking teeth echoed inside his skull, stepping up the pounding headache that was left over from the mind probe spell.

Before the elf could recover, Skater twisted the gun toward his attacker and jerked the trigger three times. All the rounds tore through the elf's chest. As the man lay dying, Skater stripped him of the Predator, then added two full clips to it from the belt at his attacker's waist.

Gray-white hands grabbed the tarp only centimeters from his face. The sharp talons sliced through the heavy material easily.

Skater lifted the Predator and squeezed off a round, wanting to make his ammunition last. The bullet shattered the ghoul's skull and sent it staggering back, bloody froth running down its misshapen muzzle.

He glanced up, searching for Duran. The ork was taking cover behind a crate.

"You need an invite at this point?" Duran asked as he thumbed more shells into the Remington Roomsweeper.

"Which way?" Skater asked. A glance showed him that the elves were starting to make headway against the ghouls. Several of the bodies lay strewn across the floor within reach of the ring of illumination coming from the overhead light. The elf mage's head had been removed by a blade, and the rest of the corpse lay stretched out near the broken chair.

Duran nodded across the empty space. "Door. Leads out into an alley. I got wheels waiting."

Skater pushed himself up, bringing the Predator around in both hands. "Go!" He was aware of Duran breaking cover as the elves who'd been firing at the ork's position came around to face him instead. The heavy pistol jumped in his hands as he squeezed the trigger rapidly. His first round extinguished the light, plunging the room into darkness.

He turned and dove as a fresh onslaught of bullets and fletchettes tore into the wall and door frame. Duran grabbed a fistful of the Lone Star jumper and yanked Skater to his feet in the short corridor, then gave him a shove toward the steel door with the panic bar still in place.

Skater dumped the empty clip and rammed the last full one in. He used his hip to slam against the panic bar. The door opened immediately, but the alarm *whoop-whoop-whooped* to life, the raucous noise echoing down the alley.

Afternoon had finally come to the sprawl, and so had the rain. Clouds obscured the sun, leaving the light washed out and fuzzy yellow. The drizzle coming down created a haze over the metroplex and left spattered pools of collected water across the uneven surface of the alley.

A yellow and black Harley Scorpion leaned on its kickstand next to the warehouse wall, partially hidden by the overgrowth springing out of the cracked asphalt. On the other side of the alley was the incline of a loading dock reaching to the warehouse bays.

"Run, kid," Duran said. He slid a long knife from his boot and rammed it through the door handle and the locking mechanism on the door frame. "This won't hold them long."

Skater sprinted for the motorcycle. The light hurt his eyes and he blinked rapidly to get rid of the pain. It didn't help. "Anyone else here?"

Duran slid into the Scorpion's saddle shoving the heavy pistol into a belt holster. "I'm solo." Pressing the electronic ignition, he brought the motorcycle roaring to life.

Skater dropped into place behind the ork.

"Drek, kid, you look like a fragging Halloween pumpkin sitting up there in all that orange." Duran shrugged out of his jacket and passed it back.

Skater took the jacket and pulled it on. Someone inside the warehouse was banging the hell out of the door.

"Hang on," Duran advised. The motorcycle engine revved up, then leveled out when the clutch was released. The rear tire spun for just a moment before finding traction.

Wrapping his free arm around the ork's midsection, Skater hung on. The Scorpion felt like it was moving along at the outside edge of control.

Tires shrieked at the mouth of the alley. A black Ford Americar backed into position, blocking access to the street. Skater pointed the Predator at the car and was about to start unloading, wondering where the drek they were going to find cover.

"Hold on." Duran tapped the rear brake and swooped the Scorpion up the slight incline leading to the loading dock fronting the boarded-over warehouse bays. "Tight." He accelerated and leaned forward.

Skater had both arms wrapped around the ork's waist when he saw the end of the loading dock suddenly come into view. Some years in the past, when it had still been active, steel safety bars had encircled the loading area. All that was left were a few centimeters above the concrete showing torch scarring where they'd been cut off. He didn't even have time to curse before they were suddenly airborne.

Duran pulled back on the handlebars, bringing the Scorpion's front wheel up. The motorcycle shot over the Americar's nose, landing meters away from the car on a broken and overgrown sidewalk with a harsh bounce. The ork handled the big motorcycle with muscle and weight, bending it to his will. Still moving, he geared down, then twisted the accelerator again. The motorcycle leaped the short curb and charged out onto the street just after a delivery van passed by.

The Americar wheeled around and came at them, tearing through a flower vendor's pushcart. A rainbow of blossoms and roses scattered as the wide red and white umbrella went spinning away. Barely escaping injury herself, the vendor came up on her knees firing, moving much younger and more adroitly than her baggy clothing suggested. One of the bullets hit the elf in the passenger seat in the back of the head, coating the windshield on the inside with blood.

Duran sent the Harley screaming around the corner, having to slow to keep the motorcycle on both wheels. The elves in the Americar had a broader base and four wheels. The driver overcontrolled as he tried to close the distance separating him from the Scorpion and momentarily lost his vehicle in the drift. Fishtailing, the Americar slammed against a Bulldog step-van. Metal screeched as the car pulled free and lunged forward again.

"The tires!" Duran shouted above the slipstream.

Skater didn't answer. He was already lifting the Predator and lining up the sights on the Americar's front tire. He got off two rounds before the driver figured what was happening and took evasive action. Three of the bullets smacked against the street, and two more holed the radiator, stringing out white steam across the Americar's hood.

"Hang on!" Duran shouted again as he popped them over the curb and cut across the sidewalk in front of a row of shops. Pedestrians reluctantly gave way before them, then moved in earnest when the sedan jumped up over the curb after them.

Skater couldn't fire again without fear of hitting a bystander. He glanced ahead of them and saw a Metro Transit bus parked at the corner. An advertising wraparound painted on the bus's skin showed scenes from the Seattle Aquarium, seals, dolphins, and killer whales slicing through the pale blue water alongside mermaids, merrow, torpedo sharks, and unicorn fish. "The bus," he said to Duran.

"I see it." The ork veered left.

On the other side of the street was a furniture outlet store, complete with a corner window that ran from floor to ceiling on the first floor of the building. "Go around it," Skater shouted, "and take a right. Then come around so we're broadside to the car as it comes after us."

"No," Duran said, "we're fragged." He thrust out his right leg and brought the Scorpion around in a tight circle, working the front brake. They narrowly missed an armored Fedex truck. The short muzzles sticking out of the gun ports had already started rotating in their direction.

Behind the truck, Duran cut the motorcycle to the left and brought it around in the middle of the street in the oncoming traffic lane. For the moment the lane was clear, but Skater could see the traffic light already shifting from yellow to red. He pushed himself off the back of the Scorpion and took the Predator in both hands.

The Americar slid around the corner. The elf in the passenger seat had shoved his head and chest out the window, his weapon laid along the top of the car. He fired as soon as Skater came into view.

"Kid," Duran said.

But Skater was already firing, holding the pistol in both hands and ignoring the swinging cuff hanging from one wrist. He squeezed the Predator's trigger methodically. The first two rounds hit only centimeters from their target, leaving pitted scars on the street as the bullets whined away. Skater felt at least one of the elf's rounds rip through the jacket Duran had given him, jerking the tail hard. He ignored the threat and lined up his next shot.

At least two of the heavy pistol's bullets sank into the vehicle's tire. The rubber shredded instantly when the air leaked out of the tire and there was no way to combat the centrifugal force of the sharp turn. The Americar flipped and skidded into the Fedex truck, bouncing from the heavy truck's armor and considerably greater weight. Thinking it was under attack, the Fedex truck's guns blazed for a split second, reducing the Americar to a flaming pyre for the men inside it an instant before it smashed through the plate glass windows of the furniture store.

"C'mon," Duran urged.

Skater hesitated only a second, feeling bad about the elf he saw stumble from the wreckage of the car completely wrapped in flames. He sprinted for the motorcycle and even before he got a leg all the way over, Duran was weaving through the traffic in a flat-out run.

By one p.m. they were down in the Ork Underground, Skater gratefully accepting the soykaf Duran brought him from the kiosk next to a tattoo parlor. The warmth soaked through the styrofoam cup and he held it in both palms, absorbing as much of the heat as he could.

"Hungry?" The low light gleamed off the ork's fangs springing up from his lower jaw.

"No." Truthfully, Skater was hungry, but he didn't think anything would stay down.

"Ready to walk?"

"Sure." Skater walked beside the ork. "Where are we going?"

"A bolthole I arranged with a guy." Duran's smile wasn't reassuring. "He works the downtown area from a small doss."

"I guess I owe you one for this."

Duran shrugged and took a narrow walkway leading off the main drag. It would take them back through a tunnel, and then on toward a door into a basement, which was one of the many secret entrances into and out of this underground city.

"How'd you find me?" Skater asked.

"Trailed you from Lone Star," Duran answered. "A guy I know scoped that you'd been arrested for murder over in Bellevue. I was hanging around Lone Star, hoping to scan the situation. I was still thinking maybe I'd get someone inside to talk to you when I saw the elves going into the building through the prisoner processing center."

"Who let them in?" Skater asked.

Duran paused in front of a small building painted in mismatched gray, some of the spots looking like they'd been coated over scorched surfaces. The door was scarred and nicked, showing the steel core underneath.

"I wasn't close enough to see," Duran said as he swiped a passcard through the maglock. "But you know the fix had to be set pretty high to bust into Lone Star and then get out with a prisoner. Lot of people got paid off."

Skater knew that, and it left a lot of questions.

"Null sweat following a bunch of elves and just luck some fragging ghouls showed up to distract them." The door opened and Duran stepped into the waiting darkness. Skater followed, feeling the tightness in his stomach.

The corpse of a dead dwarf lay sprawled in the center of the small living room. The look on his pasty white face was one of surprise. A black hole occupied the space at the top of his nose.

"I was in a hurry earlier," Duran explained. "Didn't have time to tidy up."

"Anybody I should know?" Skater asked calmly. He dropped his hand around the Predator in his pocket, carefully scanning the rest of the doss.

A trideo with illegal hookups leaking through the roof occupied one corner, offset by two speakers from a simrig. The sofa and easy chair were both covered in plaid, but neither from a set that belonged together. A ratty rug with an embroidered flock of colorful birds covered most of the open floor under a scarred soykaf table.

"A junkyen hustler named Archibald." Duran reached down to the gargoyle base of a lamp and switched on the light. Two moths leaped into flight and began circling the bulb. "Had a regular gig supplying some Aztechnology corpgeek for whatever experiments or other slot they're cooking up there. Human or meta, male or female, didn't matter as long as they were young. Tumbled across that little fact while doing some in-house work for Aztechnology a while back. Been meaning to speak to Archibald about it for some time, but I didn't know how well he was connected."

"I guess it was a short conversation."

Duran plopped down into the easy chair and looked at the dead dwarf. "I got in the final parting shot, you might say."

Skater briefly studied the bullet hole between the dwarf's eyes. "I'd say so."

"I also got the name of the corpgeek he's been supplying. Very high up on the ladder, but I'm learning some things about him. Time comes, there's going to be an opening for a new exec. Every now and then, the nitbrain gets out on his own without his bosses knowing about it. Likes to go without a sec-team knowing either. One night, he'll find me waiting instead."

Skater glanced back at the bushy-haired ork, waiting. His hand was still curled around the butt of the Predator. There'd always been tension between him and Duran, centering around the leadership of the team.

"In the meantime," Duran said, "old Archibald doesn't mind if we use his doss for a meeting place."

"So where does that leave us?" Skater asked. He remained standing, not moving toward the sofa.

"Talking," Duran replied. "Which is good."

"Okay."

"You don't trust me, do you?"

Skater returned the level gaze and answered honestly. "On a run, with profit waiting up ahead, yeah."

"But now?"

"No."

"Good. Keeps us even."

Skater raised his empty cup. "Old Archibald stock soykaf in his place?"

"Sure. Needed something to give color to his brandy." Duran pushed himself up from the easy chair and led the way to the small kitchenette, presenting his back to Skater.

Despite the offered vulnerability, Skater didn't let down his guard. All anyone ever got around Duran was one mistake. And he knew from experience that the ork never put himself into a position where he couldn't handle himself.

It turned out the dwarf kept his soykaf in the refrigerator next to liter bottles of cheap synthbrandy. The freezer unit yielded a half-dozen nuke meals, which stood the test of time better than the moldy cheese and blackened bag of wilted salad on the wire racks.

"Not exactly a cultured palate we're dealing with here," Duran said as he took the frozen dinners out and started chipping the ice from them.

Skater handled the soykaf, scooping it liberally into the electric kaf-maker so it would be strong. "Why were you looking for me?"

Duran slipped the first two dinners out of their wrap and popped them into the microwave. He set the parameters before answering. "We were set up on the *Sapphire Seahawk*. Doesn't take a gene-splicer to put that together." The microwave hummed along beneath the timbre of his voice, accompanied by the soykaf-maker juicing the mix. "Shiva got killed. Can't say I really liked her much, but she was a stand-up warrior. I figured if you were the one sold us out, I was going to offer her memory a revenge freebie."

Skater just stared at the ork, out of things to say.

Duran gave him a thin smile. "I'da done the same for you, chummer."

"Glad to hear it."

"Figured it would put your mind right to ease."

Skater opened the cabinets and found two chipped ceramic mugs. After a cursory glance inside them, he washed both in the sink, then filled each one with steaming kaf.

"The dancer set you up, didn't she?" Duran said as he accepted one of the cups. "The one the street doc was talking about when he was turning Shiva to chop?"

Wispy steam rose from the black liquid. Skater blew on it, getting his mind ready to taste and maybe sip. "I don't think she knew she was."

Duran pointed to the lopsided dining table with three chairs around it. The wall beside it held a poster of Slip-Shadow Sara singing at a local nightclub before becoming the megahit she was now. She was belting out the high notes, feeling the good pain. "Let's sit. Then you tell me about it."

"And then?"

The microwave pinged. Duran slipped on a mitt that had been burned in several places and retrieved the dinners. The smell of sirloin tips and applesauce temporarily won against the malaise of odors already in the doss and the new ones emanating from the ripening dwarf. "A lot of people out there seem to want us dead. We need to figure out who they are, who set us up, and what's so fraggin' important they'll spend a mountain of nuyen to put us down."

Skater took the fork the ork handed him. "And you think I know all this?"

"No way, chummer." Duran grinned without mirth as he took his seat across the table. "If you'da known, somebody woulda made sure you turned up geeked, not sitting nice and tidy in a Lone Star cell. My guess is that the elves used some heavy grease—some kinda clout—and got you quietly off the street. If my chummer wasn't tied in so tight to the network, I wouldn't have known about you, either. And I fragging sure wouldn't have been able to spring you from the cop shop."

"You could have checked that out without me," Skater replied.

"We tried."

Skater looked at him. "We?"

"We didn't exactly split up the way we said after leaving you." Duran forked a huge mouthful and chewed, juice oozing out between his fangs. "Chummer, when you got your head on straight, there ain't another runner in the biz whose action I'd back over yours. You're sharp and you're smart, and you scan people really well, especially the twisted ones."

Skater sipped the soykaf and considered the ork's words.

"The rest of us have noticed you seemed to have a lot on your mind lately. We figured, frag it, let you sort it out for yourself. But now it's boiled over on the team. Whatever this run was about, whoever's hunting us, if you're fragged, then we are too. The only way any of us is going to get our hoop outta this jam is together."

"It gets kind of complicated," Skater said, "and I don't know every angle myself. And I damn sure don't know where to start."

"Start with the woman."

"There's truths and there's lies. I haven't got it all sorted out myself yet."

"That's what you got me for, chummer. You're all caught up with it right now, but you tell me what you know and I see if I notice something you mighta missed."

Skater started talking. It was hard at first, because he was so used to being careful what he said to anyone. No one really knew everything there was to know about him. Larisa had come the closest. But now she was dead.

13

Skater peered through the peephole and found himself staring out at Elvis.

The troll was nonchalant, standing patiently at the door as if he had all day, not looking around to see if anyone was watching him. He carried a green and white-striped shopping bag in one huge-knuckled hand.

Skater dropped the Predator to his side and opened the door. He announced the troll to Duran, who sat watching the news round-up on the trideo, a pistol sitting on the armrest of his chair.

"Present for you," Elvis rumbled as he stepped into the room. He held the bag out for Skater. "I knew you'd probably still be drekking around in those Lone Star togs."

Skater opened the bag. Inside were several sets of clothing, denim jeans interwoven with Kevlar, a burgundy work shirt, a turquoise Seattle Mariners sweatshirt if he wanted to dress down even more, and ultra-thin black driving gloves. At the bottom of the bag was a brown bomber-style jacket. Last but not least were a pair of reinforced Doc Martins that laced up to the knee.

"Clothes make the man," Elvis said. "I thought maybe you'd feel more like yourself dressed right."

"Thanks," Skater said.

"This place always come with a geeked dwarf?" Elvis asked casually as he scanned the corpse in the center of the room.

"Duran threw him in for no extra charge," Skater said. He headed toward the small bedroom in the back.

"Well," the troll said, "I can throw him out for about the same." He fisted the corpse's shirt and lifted it from the floor. "You got a bathroom around here?"

Duran pointed.

"Probably a safe place to stash him. I don't figure anybody's gonna want to go in there after taking a look at this cheesebox anyway." The troll lumbered off with the dwarf in one hand.

In the bedroom, Skater stripped off the Lone Star one-piece and threw it on the floor. He wished he could shower, shave, sink into feeling a little more human. But there wasn't time.

He pulled on the jeans, then the Chambray work shirt, tucking the tails in. He was surprised at the fit. "Hey, Elvis, you did good with the sizes," Skater called through the door as he surveyed his reflection in the full-length mirror on the inside of the closet door. The troll was right; he felt better already.

"He had some help," a cool feminine voice said.

Skater turned and saw Archangel standing next to the door.

She was dressed in a caramel-colored skirt that hugged her thighs, a white blouse with a tiger's-eye studded collar chain, and a short-waisted blazer that matched the skirt. Bronze-lensed sunglasses covered her eyes, and her hair was pulled back in a French braid. "You look much more like yourself."

"How long have you been there?" Skater asked.

A wintry smile flickered at her lips. "Long enough to see the difference."

"And the others? When are they coming?"

"They're already here."

"Oh." Skater slipped the Predator into the waistband of his jeans, then walked back into the living room.

Duran was still in the easy chair. Elvis was sharing the

sofa with Cullen Trey, who was deftly using a pair of chopsticks to work his way through a carton of Chinese take-out from Lee Chee Garden. The mage nodded a hello, as elegantly dressed as ever. His cloak was spread out beneath him so his clothing wouldn't touch the sofa.

Wheeler Iron-Nerve was carrying two chairs in from the kitchen. He placed one for Archangel, then looked at Skater. "Chair?"

Skater shook his head. He liked to move around while he talked, and he had a lot to say. He started with Larisa, then let them have it all.

"She tipped you to the *Sapphire Seahawk,*" Elvis said, "and you thought you could trust her, but who gave *her* the scan?"

"She never really told me, just kept the whole thing kind of vague."

"Then why trust her?"

"I did some legwork of my own before taking the run to Archangel. It looked good." Skater let his eyes travel over all their faces. "We all agreed on that."

"She was a dancer," Trey said. "She could have gotten the scan from anywhere."

"That freighter was from Tir Tairngire," Duran said. "They're pretty fragging tight-lipped about anything they do. Hard to believe somebody connected with that ship would have been in SybreSpace bragging to some joygirl."

A spark of anger ignited in Skater, bringing him around to face the ork.

"Jack," Archangel interrupted softly. "Duran didn't mean anything. He's just saying how someone else might see it."

Taking in a tight, deep breath, Skater held it for just a moment, not meeting anyone's eyes, then releasing. "The information Larisa gave me was about as much as we ever get from any corporate Mr. Johnson. If you take out the bald-faced lies, the layers of bulldrek they shovel at us, and the info they think is on the level, we had about as much on the freighter as for any other run we've ever pulled. The manifests weren't on the level. Archangel found that out. Not much else, granted."

"But even the way those files were protected in the freighter's system told us it was a prize worth going after," Archangel said.

"Okay," Duran said, "we agreed we had a target. What about Larisa's info? Where did it come from?"

"She was looking for frag-you money," Skater said with a conviction he suddenly felt. "She got hold of some information she knew I could use—she knew what I did even if she didn't know who I did it with—and she thought she could cut herself in for a percentage."

"You gave it to her," Trey said.

Skater nodded. "Until this, I never had a reason not to trust her."

"She was holding out on you, though," Duran said.

Skater turned the possibility around in his mind. He didn't like it, but it felt right. Larisa had been scared at the end; he knew that as well as he knew his own heart was still beating. "She was frightened," he said softly. Then repeated the conjecture with more conviction.

"But she was obviously doing okay," Elvis said. "That Bellevue doss didn't come cheap."

Skater glanced at Archangel. "Have you checked out her numbers?" He was sure Duran would have asked Archangel to chip whatever she could about Larisa when he'd called the team in.

Archangel nodded. "Prelim's done. Some things I'm still chasing. Considering her income from four months ago, she was living well past her means."

"Can you trace the rent transfers?"

"I can try."

"Do it." Skater put his cup on the low table in front of the sofa and returned to the kitchen long enough to pick up packets of salt, pepper, ketchup, and sugar. Archibald had evidently frequented McHugh's, because they all bore the fast-food restaurant's logo. "Any luck with the files we boosted from the *Sapphire Seahawk*?"

"No. I've run some home-grown edit utilities with a decrypt cocktail to crash any scramble IC, and an evaluate program as an after-dinner mint. If I can crack any of the files, I may be able to find some bits that will give us more to work with. But I'm certain it's not all there."

Skater placed the salt packet on the low table. "Makes you wonder if it was all there to begin with."

Duran leaned forward. "What are you saying?"

Skater pointed to the red and white salt packet. "O.K., just to simplify things. Let's say we're the salt." He placed the black and gray pepper packet a few centimeters above the salt. "This represents the elves—Tir Tairngire—and their interest in recovering the files we stole."

"Damage control?" Elvis asked.

"On the surface, I think so. The people who broke out of Lone Star seemed to be more interested in getting those files back than anything else."

"Means they're worth something to someone," Trey said. "Which, incidentally, could work in our favor."

"If we live to collect," Wheeler put in.

"True, chummer, but let's look at this optimistically." Trey shifted, then leaned forward and tapped the pepper packet. "What if we tried selling the files back to the elves? Cut out the middle man?"

"If it comes to that," Skater said, "maybe we will. The downside is they'll find out fragging quick that we don't *have* all the files. In which case they're going think we're either trying to stiff them, or that we didn't have them to begin with, or that we're just trying to get them off our backs to make another deal."

"Either way," Elvis said, "we stand a good chance of getting our hoops flushed down the tubes so they can bury this."

"It also keeps us from tracking down whoever set us up to begin with." Skater looked around the table as he placed the ketchup packet below the salt. "Personally, I want a shot at whoever it was. They killed Larisa and, by proxy, they killed Shiva. Someone's got to pay."

"I agree," Duran stated. "The elf and troll who tried to scrag Skater outside SybreSpace, they're connected somewhere. Probably to whoever was pulling your girl's strings."

"Dion and Shayx," Skater said. "They might be working for a guy named Synclair Tone. He and Dion came up out of the Barrens together. A chummer's trying to find out more for me right now." If Kestrel would only return his call.

"I can make some discreet inquiries into Tone's affiliations," Trey said. "Some of my own contacts wouldn't mind trading info for some handy little trinkets I could whip up for them."

"Do that." Skater put the pink sugar envelope down, equidistant from the pepper and ketchup. "This here's the yakuza. I'm not sure where they fit in yet, but we can't ignore them."

"Not with them hunting us," Wheeler said.

"Even if we were able to cut a deal with the Tir Tairngire folks," Skater said, "the yaks just might think we kept a copy of the files as a bargaining chip for some later opportunity. There's a good possibility they'll keep coming at us unless we get certain closure on this."

"I'll look into the yak angle," Elvis said.

Skater nodded. "Outside of those three groups, we're also up against the best Lone Star has to offer, as well as every street hustler who figures on chiseling a piece of our butts." He stood and let his eyes travel over the faces of the others. "Could be our best bet is to do a quick fade and forget we ever heard of Seattle."

"Me," Duran said, "I never liked running from a fight, and I absolutely hate being set up."

"As for myself," Trey said, "I've become accustomed to a certain lifestyle in this town, and that lifestyle has been augmented by our various forays. To venture from here would mean losing that."

Wheeler and Elvis echoed the sentiments with reasons of their own.

"I'm in," Archangel stated simply.

Skater guessed that whatever past she was hiding might not be quite so easily lost if she had to pull up stakes and go elsewhere. "Archangel will do some fishing in the Matrix for any card we might play, while Trey checks out Synclair Tone and Elvis does the same for the yaks. We need an ops base, plus a bolthole in case things turn nasty."

"This place?" Wheeler obviously didn't like the idea.

"For the moment," Duran said, "this is as good as it gets."

"I'll see what I can do," Wheeler said. "You ask me, though, this is the end of the road even for losers."

"And transport," Skater said.

"What kind?"

"Ground and air. Keep it ready to jump." Skater turned away and walked to the kitchen. He took the stuffed bear from the table and brought it back to Trey. "I need to know about this."

The mage took the stuffed animal, absently wiping at the soot stains. "You serious?"

"Yeah." Even though his mind was racing, planning and counter-planning, shooting him onto an adrenaline edge, Skater felt the cold fear that came from touching the bear.

"Whose was it?" Trey asked.

"That's part of what I need to know." Skater told him about finding the stuffed animal in Larisa's apartment.

"You think it belonged to the child?" Trey asked.

"If there was one," Skater said. "If it was hers."

"Was it yours?"

The question hung out there, naked and blunt. "I don't know," Skater replied. "I don't think so. Larisa would have told me."

Trey stood up, shaking the wrinkles from his cloak. "I'll need some things. Paper. Something to mark with. I'll be back." He laid the stuffed bear on the table and walked into the kitchen.

Skater looked over at Archangel. "There may be hospital records on the birth."

"I'll check."

"And if the father is named—"

"I'll let you know." Her face never changed expression.

"What are you going to be doing all this time?" Wheeler asked.

"Looking through Larisa's life. Trying to figure out as many of the things she didn't tell me as I can." Skater looked at the ork. "You'll cover me because I can't grow eyes in the back of my head. If she was lying to me, her friends will try it too. I can't keep my eyes on them and watch to see I don't get my hoop fragged at the same time."

Duran nodded.

Returning from the other room, Trey pulled the bird-embroidered rug from the plascrete floor, then sat with his legs crossed. He ripped up a McHugh's paper bag till he had a flat surface to lay on the floor. After putting the stuffed bear in the center of it, he used a green pen advertising a bank service to mark sygils on the paper at six different positions around the stuffed animal.

"You've never seen this child?" Trey asked.

"No." Skater shook his head.

"A shame. That might have helped. Still, I'll see what I can do." The mage closed his eyes, his arms relaxed on his thighs. After a few minutes, he opened his eyes and looked over at Skater. "There was something. Maybe. It moved so quickly that I'm not sure. The spell would work better if I knew the child's name. Give me something of yours."

Skater thought a minute, then handed Trey the Predator.

Trey put it into the circle, then inscribed a new sygil over three pre-existing symbols. Then he closed his eyes again. Minutes passed. Perspiration dewed across Trey's broad forehead. This time his shirt was drenched and he slumped after coming out of his astral search.

"The child's alive," Trey said in a frayed voice. "But she's either very far away, or is being warded by someone. If I had a more secure connect, I'd be able to tell." He pushed himself to his feet. "As to whether she's your daughter, Jack, I can't honestly say. I was able to reach her, but I don't know if it's because she's yours, or because of your connection with her mother."

"Thanks for trying."

Trey bowed his head. "Of course."

Skater returned to the bedroom and gathered the synthleather bomber jacket. He slid into it on his way back out, adjusting the Predator so it couldn't be seen. "You ready?" he asked Duran.

"Yeah." The ork stood up, cracked the knuckles of his gnarled hands, and went to the door.

Skater pulled on the driving gloves Elvis had brought him, not totally surprised to find that the fingers and palm edges were lined with macroplast armor, turning them into a not-too-modest set of dusters. He went out the door, driven by a need for vengeance that would have shamed a fallen angel. Duran followed.

It wasn't about profit anymore. Not all of it.

14

"Kestrel," Skater said into the public telecom, "this is Skater. When you get this message, give me a call back." He read off the number with difficulty because it was sun-faded and weather-beaten. "I'll be here five minutes, then I'm smoke." He tapped the Disconnect, then walked down the street to join Duran leaning against the wall around the corner.

The ork looked completely at ease. Dressed in a modest suit and wearing wrap-around Whitelaw sunglasses, he could almost have passed for a corpgeek waiting for an after-work dinner date. Both of them were bone-tired from lack of sleep, and both were using stimulants on top of sheer will-power to keep going.

The telecom chirped two minutes later, and Skater was in motion at once. As he rounded the corner, he spotted two thrillers dressed in the Cutters' green and gold making for the cube. They were a salt and pepper team, a white female with spiky blonde hair and a shiny cyberarm, and a black male sporting a goatee and an open shirt revealing a pornographic chest tattoo of a troll abusing a sheep.

"Call's for me," Skater said.

The two gangers wheeled toward him. The black guy shoved his hand inside his shirt and grabbed something, but he made no move to pull it. Finger razors shot out of the girl's cyberarm, complete with a long elbow spur.

The telecom beeped a second time.

"I think you got that wrong, wackweed," the blonde said. "This is Cutter turf. That phone belongs to us. You'd best be on about your business."

Cars passed on the street. It was getting dark. Even in daylight the inner city was no place for someone to stop unless they had a fragging good reason, and went fully armed.

"Your choice," Skater said softly, still moving forward in a straight line. He opened the bomber jacket, letting them see the Ares Predator in its shoulder holster under the coat. "I'm prepared to die for that call. How about you?"

The male ganger released his weapon and stepped back. "Chill, Pebbles," he told the girl. "Let's pack it in. He's got a yabo over his shoulder. This drek don't mean nothing to us." He caught her flesh and blood arm and gently tugged her after him.

Her face set in angry lines, the girl whirled suddenly and dragged her razors across the window of the collectibles shop next to the telecom cube. The sharp points left scars in the glass.

Keeping one hand on the Predator, Skater tapped the Connect key. "Yeah," he said.

"I found out it was you who called," Kestrel said, sounding like he was talking from the bottom of a well, "you could have knocked me over with a fragging feather. I heard about you getting busted by Knight Errant and getting passed over to Lone Star. I also heard you escaped."

Skater had heard about the escape as well, sandwiched in between more trideo reports of the so-called laughing death disease. An ork woman working at a fast-food restaurant had gone berserk and attacked her own leg with a kitchen knife, then sat on the counter throwing her toes and chunks of flesh at the customers, all the while giggling like a little girl. There was also more footage on the fire at the Montgomery Building in Bellevue, and the terrorist bombing at Sea-Tac International Airport that morning. But not a peep about any dead elves being found in a warehouse.

"I need help," Skater said.

"If you're still in town after all the drek that went down," the fixer said, "you need your fragging head examined."

"What have you found out about the yak who's after me? Dokai something?"

"Masaru Doyukai," Kestrel said. "All I know is that he's still looking, and he's offering big nuyen to anyone who can finger you."

"What's his interest?"

"Still haven't scanned it, but the guy must be getting desperate. He put the squeeze on some stoolies in the area, killed two of them and put another in the hospital to make his point. Hasn't exactly endeared himself to the locals."

"Stick with it as best you can without getting caught in the middle," Skater said. "I'll pay for your time."

"Have you got a stash besides the one you had down in the Caribbean?" the fixer asked.

"Why?" Skater couldn't be sure the call wasn't being traced.

"The new idee I fixed you up with?" Kestrel said. "Lone Star got it. I tried to get into the accounts as soon as I heard they nabbed you. I wanted to shift them around so you'd have something if and when you got out. I got some of it, but not much."

"The rest of it?"

"Evaporated, chummer, absorbed back into Lone Star's legal acquisitions. Frozen till you can prove you're not guilty of any infractions of the law."

Skater felt a cold emptiness swell up inside him, threatening to envelop him. For eight years he'd been running the shadows—and that was a long time to survive in this biz—hustling and dodging bullets on every bit of action he could sign on for. There'd been a vague plan, an amorphous dream of getting out of the sprawl and the biz, but more than anything else, he'd been buying the security he'd never known.

Now it was gone, taken away.

"I've got some set aside," Skater said in a tight voice. "What I can't pay you immediately, I'll make good."

"Sure, sure," Kestrel said. "But I'd feel better if you were on your way out of Seattle right now."

"Can't," Skater said. "Somebody stuck it in me and broke it off. I can't be sure they're going to crawl off my back anywhere unless I can get them off. I'll be in touch." He hit the Disconnect.

Duran looked at him. "That look on your face, can't be anything but bad news."

"I moved my money around, getting ready to shake this town," Skater said. "But Lone Star seized my accounts. I've still got some put by in a few others places, but I'm going to be sucking air real soon."

"Tough break." Duran fell into step beside him, sweeping the street with his gaze. "But don't forget we're all in this together, kid. We pool our resources, we'll get by. Bet on it."

"We already are," Skater said.

15

"Hi, this is Brynna. I'm either not home now, or I'm engaged in a sexual fantasy come true that you can only dream about. If you're a chummer, leave a message and I'll get back to you when I recover. If you're selling something, frag off and don't be gentle about it. Bye."

A beep followed.

Skater chose not to leave a message. He stood at the cube of public telecoms near Renton Mall's southern entrance, in the wide hallway sandwiched between 2Fast Arcades and Shiloh's, a specialty costume shop.

"She home?" Duran asked as he walked up with two Sloppies and two big soft drinks.

"No." Skater took one of the drinks and a Sloppie. "But I got her recorded message."

"So she's probably still around." Duran pointed toward

the trideos stacked in the window further down the hallway at Matt & Matt's Trideo Concepts. "I was standing in line, I heard KTXX announce it was going live soon with some big news bulletin."

A locally produced syndicated talk show was on in a showcase window a few steps from where they stood. A handful of people were already gathered there, talking among themselves and watching the program.

On the screens, Perri Twyst, the host, was leaning intently toward her two guests. The trideo personality had widely spaced limpid blue pools for eyes, a strong chin, and a lime-green pageboy that emphasized her lean jawline and the earring in her left nostril chained to the ear on that same side. As usual, she wore faded jeans and a plaid Oxford button-down with the sleeves ripped out, emphasizing her street background.

"Knowing the resistance you would encounter trying to establish yourself in Seattle," Twyst was saying, "why would you be willing to undertake such a challenge?"

Her guests were the same elves Skater had seen on the trid in the Lone Star slam. He couldn't remember their names. Then, as the camera panned in for a close-up, block letters flashed onto the screen below the male: Tavis Silverstaff, CEO of NuGene, a biomed corp in Portland. He wore purples today, with a gold brocade that set everything off. His long fingers were wrapped around the head of a glittering cane, and his royal plum cape fell in cascades behind him across the plush chair. His smile was white and generous, totally confident.

"Because I believe we've got a good product," Silverstaff said.

"Fragging elf," one of the two young men to Skater's right said, "that's what he is. Ain't no man at all. Pointy-eared dandelion sniffer. Needs a little Order to bring him to the light, then he'd see."

The other young man laughed, clapping his friend on the back.

From the thinly disguised pun, Skater guessed that they were members of the Order, a white human-supremacy policlub. He glanced at Duran, but the ork was ignoring them.

"You've yet to unveil that product," Perri said. "But judging from NuGene's past work in pioneering tissue transplantation, organ transplantation, and reconstruction through biological agents instead of cyberware, I'd have to guess it must be something along those lines."

"Yes," Silverstaff said. "My father was a leader in introducing biomedial services in the Tir. Most elves don't like the idea of invasive surgeries except as life-threatening conditions warrant. But my father and his R&D teams came up with medical procedures, medicines, and tissue treatments that have saved and improved many lives. At NuGene, we've wanted to continue that."

"And you're going to try to develop that new market here in Seattle?"

"Ever since Portland shut down as a port city," Silverstaff said, "we knew we'd have to move on to become viable in the economic community again. Seattle is where the action is. People come here from all over the world. We want to be able to get our products and services to those who need them. Perhaps this will lead the way for other elven corporations. We elves of Tir Tairngire run the risk of becoming stagnant if we wall ourselves off from the world."

"Keep the pointy-eared little freaks at home if you want them to live," the other policlubber suggested. His friend high-fived him and they both laughed.

"And speaking of children," Twyst went on smoothly, "I'm told you're going to have an addition to your household."

The camera cut to Ariadne Silverstaff, her name conveniently filled in below her picture, too. She wore a conservatively pastel pink dress that echoed some of the purple from her husband's clothing. She touched her round stomach. "The doctor says any day now."

Twyst leaned back in her chair and faced the camera, making some glib comment about what a devoted couple these two were.

Silverstaff took up his wife's hand and kissed it. "Aye, but it is the touch of this fine lady's fingers that has captured the heart of a rogue."

"Frag," Duran whispered, "you can taste the NewSweet from here."

A caption suddenly appeared at the bottom of the trideo screens, announcing that a live transmission from downtown Seattle was about to be joined.

The policlubbers were more vocal in their denouncements

and started yelling for the managers of the trideo outlet to change the channel.

"So what do you want?" Perri Twyst asked. "A son or a daughter?"

"Whatever it is, boy or girl, we will love the child. Our physician didn't want Ariadne traveling at this time . . ."

". . . but I didn't want to be away from my husband's side," the woman added. "If the baby should be born here . . ."

". . . we'll take that as a good omen for our recent efforts in Seattle," Silverstaff said.

"That sounds great," Twyst said. "And you'll have to come back on the show and let us introduce him—or her—to the world. Please."

The canned applause was interrupted by the switch from televised show to a street scene. Chelsea Sable, KTXX Action Eye reporter, was dressed in a white low-cut blouse that left her shoulders exposed, and tight purple jeans that left little to the imagination.

The reporter was crossing the street against the traffic with her cameraman following closely behind. Cars had stopped and a few honked in mild irritation. In the background, the warehouse where the elves had brought Skater that morning had been roped off in yellow tape. Lone Star uniforms held the perimeters with automatic weapons.

Sable spoke in her normal tone, a sub-dermal microphone making her voice clear and resonant. "—you're joining us here live, at the site of what I've been told was a major gun battle today at noon." The reporter kept moving toward the police line. Three Lone Star uniforms broke from their posts and moved in an interception path. "However, investigating authorities declined to mention that in their reports earlier this afternoon."

The cameraman panned around the street, picking up the crowd that was starting to form. The KTXX mobile van was parked with two wheels up on the curb in front of Esoteric's Lore Store & More across the street. Going Out Of Business banners covered the tops of the two plate-glass windows.

"Come on," Skater said as he looked at the sea of faces the camera was picking up. He led the way into the trideo store.

The sales clerk behind the glass display counter was thin and angular. His hair had been cut to leave three stripes that ran from his forehead to the nape of his neck. All the stripes were done in black and white.

"Something I can do for you, chummer?" the clerk asked.

"Can you record that?" Skater asked, pointing to the trideo showing Sable's telecast.

"I can sell you a recorder, or I can sell you a trideo set," the clerk said.

"If you've got something set up and ready to roll," Skater said, "I'm sure I can make it worth your while." He showed a credstick he'd recovered from one of his small stashes. "What do you think?"

The clerk reached up to a shelf behind him and popped a chip into the recorder sitting there. "KTXX, huh?"

"Yeah." Skater watched the screen, barely registering the security camera that locked onto him from the upper corner of the ceiling. He knew Duran had noticed it, too, because the ork stood with his back to the camera.

Sable was having no luck at all in crossing the police barrier. She talked to a plainclothes detective in the end, though, right before she got the boot. The warehouse was the scene of an ongoing investigation, the groundhound yelled at her, and there was no way the media was going to be allowed access. Sable and her production team retreated to the other side of the street. During all of that, the camera had been busy moving, scanning the crowd that had gathered, partly out of interest and partly because the street was blocked.

In the middle of the reporter's explanation to the camera that she'd been tipped off about the shooting and that it was possibly related to the jailbreak from Lone Star Security Services that morning, Sable's transmission was cut short. The channel went to a popular game show, already in progress.

"That's it," Skater said. "I'll take the chip."

The clerk nodded, popping his gum in careless abandon, and retrieved the optical chip from the recorder. "Pleasure doing business with you."

Skater nodded and pocketed the chip as he headed for the door. Outside, he made straight for the telcoms again. He connected to the illegal line Wheeler had arranged at Archibald's apartment.

Wheeler answered on the first ring. "Yeah."

"I need to talk to Archangel."

"Done."

"You want to tell me what's going on?" the ork said in a low voice that wouldn't carry.

"Faces," Skater replied.

"Faces?" Duran echoed.

"That newscast went out live and got pulled," Skater said. "If the fix is really in, there won't be any copies of that transmission to be had."

"So?"

"I'm here," Archangel said, sounding distant, like she'd just jacked out of the Matrix.

"We're at the Renton Mall," Skater told her. "I just got a celebrity spot on a security camera in a shop called Matt & Matt's Trideo Concepts. I need to know if you can access it and bone the security system's memory."

"Shouldn't take more than a simple sleaze utility to get in and a chaotic crash and edit program to scramble their sec-cam files," Archangel said. "Does this have to be subtle?"

"No. Duran and I are clear. And if the security memory goes missing, there's nothing to tie us to the place."

"Jack." The decker seemed hesitant, then just pushed the words out. "I checked Larisa's med records. She had the baby three weeks ago at Harborview Hospital. It was still-born. I'm sorry."

Skater felt the cold chill of an unexplained loss drift through him. "Thanks," he made himself say. He punched the Disconnect.

"What's this about faces?" Duran asked.

"Let's make ourselves scarce." Skater headed for the southern exit. Bright bars of sunlight slashed through the glass doors and lay in straight lines against the tiled floor. "There's an outside chance that some of the elves we braced today might have been nosing around the warehouse area during the investigation. If we can identify them for Archangel, she might be able to find out who they were."

"We stand still long enough, they're going to make a run at us. We could idee them then."

"If we could be sure we'd live long enough to get it done," Skater said. "When the time comes to go up against these people, I want some aces in my pocket. I like moving."

Duran nodded. "Something to keep in mind, though: a moving target only has the illusion of being safe. Kind of fades away when you hear somebody yell, pull! And you figure out you're just another skeet."

* * *

Brynna Rose lived in the same three-story walk-up apartment overlooking Seattle University that she'd had when Skater had first met her over a year ago. The neighborhood was run-down in places, victimized by the students who haunted the area for cheap housing.

They left the car a block away and walked through a maze of dumpsters, broken and discarded furniture, and makeshift clothes lines that held sheets and other articles. From his two previous visits, Skater knew that, one way or another, the clothing would be gone by the time it was fully dark.

"Tell me who we're going to see," Duran said, walking around a vinyl-covered sofa with one end missing and a drunk passed out on it. A scrawny beagle perched on the drunk's chest watched them with baleful eyes.

"Her name's Brynna Rose." Skater paused at the bottom of the outside stairway and peered up. The landings were all small, peeling white paint over abused wood. "She was a friend of Larisa's."

"And yours?"

"We weren't exactly big on sharing friends. The only time I ever came here was a couple of times when Larisa had to pick up some things. They roomed together for a while too. There was a guy who came into the picture."

"Still around?"

"No." Skater stopped on the third floor landing. Angry voices barely penetrated the door. One was male, and the other sounded like Brynna's.

"She's not alone tonight," Duran observed, stepping into position on the other side of the door. He held his Roomsweeper in both hands.

Skater leaned against the wall. The doorknob was within easy reach on his side. He scanned the landing. Besides the few plants on the wire stands in two corners and a WELCOME mat knitted in a floral design, there was nothing else.

He tried the door and found it unlocked. Glancing at Duran, he nodded. The ork touched the pistol barrel to his forehead in a salute.

The sound of a slap, flesh on flesh, slipped through the door. A woman screamed in pain and fear.

Skater checked his impulse to enter. Though night was falling, the air was still humid enough to leave him drenched in perspiration. Drops ran down his face. Slowly, he moved to peer through the security-barred window to his right. Beneath the window, a flowerbox bursting with yellow blooms held a whirling mobile of cockatrice in full flight on a slender metal pole.

Two men were inside the room with Brynna Rose. The woman was small, with short-cropped brunette hair and dusky skin that advertised her Thai heritage. She wore red synthleather pants that fit her like a second skin and a black halter top with one of the shoulder straps ripped loose. She was lying half on the lemon-yellow couch, one hand held to the side of her face where her lipstick mixed with her bleeding mouth.

Two men were in the room with her. Both of them looked like street talent, yabos or bagmen, used to fast, direct action. They wore Armanté suits and expensive haircuts that would lend them anonymity in the corp scene, and respect while working the dives, maybe coming across like a blue crew.

One of them was dusky, similar to Brynna, but his features were clearly Amerind. The other guy was blond and thin, so pale as to be almost colorless. He held a silenced Manhunter in one hand like it was part of him, no expression on his face.

The dusky one reached for Brynna and yanked her around by the arm. Her face was mottled red in the shape of a palm print. Skater heard his name mentioned but couldn't make out the rest. Brynna screamed that she didn't know where he was. The guy drew his hand back to slap again.

Skater turned away, shutting down the anger till it was something he could use. He drew his Predator II and showed Duran two fingers as the slap sounded again. When the ork nodded, he closed the two fingers together, signaling that they were close.

"Do it," Duran urged.

Holding the Predator at shoulder height, Skater turned the knob and followed the door inside.

16

The pale gunman came around with smooth quickness, like he was moving on ball bearings, not flesh and blood. His eyes were cold, merciless gray above the black lenses of his sunglasses. The pistol in his fist moved with him.

Calmly, Skater shot the man in the left shoulder. The big bullet mushroomed, carrying enough weight and force to spin the gunman around and knock the sunglasses off.

The guy got off three rounds, the silencer reducing the noise to coughs, but all of them went into the ceiling as he fell back over the coffee table.

Skater surged forward, aware that Duran had the other man covered before he could draw a weapon. The pale man tried to bring his pistol back around and push himself up from the ground. Skater kicked out hard, the reinforced toe of his boot connecting with the thin man's gun-wrist, and splintered bone. The gun tumbled to the carpet.

"Your move," Skater grated as he pointed the Predator at the man's face. "But I guarantee an instant lobotomy a heartbeat after you make the wrong one."

"Frag off, mate," the man said. Instead of going for the gun, though, he laid back quietly on the carpet and held his broken wrist in his other hand.

Keeping his pistol in hand and leaving Duran a clear field of fire, Skater approached the downed gunner. He kicked the pistol under the love seat. "Brynna. Are these the only ones here?"

"Yes. Frag, Jack, what the hell do they want? I told them I didn't know where you were. I didn't even know your slotting name. Just Jack."

"I know. I'm sorry you got mixed up in this." Skater glanced at the pale man's shoulder. The bullet hadn't penetrated the Kevlar and cloth mesh, but he knew it had left one fragging big bruise. "Turn over, nitbrain, or I'll turn you over."

"Sure." Placing both hands on his head, the yabo rolled over facedown, totally professional.

Skater patted him down, turning up another gun and two credsticks. He threw the gun away and kept the credsticks, then moved on to the second guy, who was also lying on the floor now.

"Do you know who these slotters are, Brynna?" Skater asked as he lifted two credsticks from the second man's pockets.

"They said they were friends of yours." Wiping her face free of tears, Brynna struggled to her feet. Duran made no move to help her, giving the prisoners his full attention, a scowl making his fangs more prominent and threatening. "I told them that I hadn't seen you in months, and that Larisa had stopped seeing you some time ago. They thought I was lying."

Skater went to the closet and took out four empty wire hangers. Quickly, he bound the two men's hands behind their backs, then wired their feet together. He made sure they were turned tight. They'd get free eventually, but not anytime soon.

"You can't stay here," Skater said. He touched Brynna's face gently, inspecting the damage. She'd be bruised for a few days, but nothing looked permanent. Her left eye showed a spreading scarlet from broken blood vessels. "Go pack a few things. Quick. We don't want any more slotheads to come along and hassle you."

The woman nodded and moved off.

Skater went over and squatted next to the dusky-skinned man, opening the pouch he'd found. "You make much beating up on helpless women?"

The guy was resting on his chin, so when he smiled, it was crooked. "Not all of them are helpless."

"Kind of evens out over the long run, I guess." Skater poured the contents of the pouch onto the floor. "You want to tell me who you are, save me the trouble of looking?"

"I'd rather see you get slotted by a bull-dyke troll in full heat, manning a prosthesis the size of your fragging arm."

The pouch held a book of matches from a bar in the Sea-Tac airport terminal, breath mints, a folding knife, a pack of domestic cigarettes, and three condoms.

Skater shoved everything away but one of the condoms. He held up the package for Duran's inspection. "Australian. So's the price tag. Genuine sheepskin. We're dealing with a fragging barbarian here. Doesn't look new, either."

"Guess he's carried it around for awhile," the ork said.

"Something I've noticed about guys who travel a lot in their line of work," Skater said. "They smoke whatever cigarettes they can get. Same for throat lozenges and breath mints. But something they really worry about—say a social disease, for instance—they'd rather have a home-town brand. Something they trust. Just in case." He flipped the condom onto the bound man's back. "I'll know where to come looking for you if I need to."

"You talk tough," the guy said, anger flushing his face. "But I don't think I'll worry about it much. If my mate and I don't find you, the yaks or the elves will leave you in bloody tatters."

"Shut up," the pale man said.

Skater drew his pistol again and leaned in on the man. His interest was intense. "You're not a cop. You're not with the yakuza. And you're not with the elves. So who are you working for?"

"Bleeding Santa Claus, mate."

"Then I guess you're here to fill an early Christmas stalking." Skater touched the back of the man's head with the pistol. "I'm going to bet I can put a couple bullets through your head, and your friend will think maybe it's not so bad to talk to me about Larisa Hartsinger. What do you think? Because you drekking sure won't be around to check it out."

The guy swallowed hard and closed his eyes, then reopened them. "All I know about Larisa Hartsinger is that she's dead and you were her boyfriend. The woman in there, she was supposed to be one of her friends. Maybe she'd know where you were."

"See. Talking's not so hard. Who hired you?" Seeing the fear radiating out of the man, the liquid gleam in his eyes, and knowing he was putting it there, turned Skater's stomach. He was used to the heat of a run, danger nipping at his heels, giving him impetus to do whatever was necessary to survive. But then he thought of Larisa, the way she'd died, and he didn't let any of the weakness he felt show.

"A guy named Tone," the yabo said.

Skater nodded. "What for?"

"Find you. Sit on you. Give him a call when it was done."

"How were you supposed to get in touch with him?"

"He gave us a number." The yabo recited it without being asked.

Skater memorized it easily. He pulled the gun away from the man's head. "You did good. Now I'm going to give you a word of advice. Go catch the next suborbital and get as far away from Seattle as you can."

Neither of the gunmen said anything.

Brynna returned to the room, make-up intact again, a fresh layer of foundation partially covering the bruises.

"You look good," Skater said, knowing it wouldn't take away the pain or the fear, but that it might make her feel a little better. He took her arm and led her out of the doss into the early evening heat, trying to act like he had it all together. Duran covered them all the way to the car.

"Larisa didn't leave you, Jack," Brynna Rose said, lifting her brandy snifter and taking a healthy slug. "This guy made her do it."

Skater sat in his seat and felt his breath grow tight inside him. He, Duran, and Brynna were seated at a round table in the back of Murphy's Law, a bar the ork had suggested. Skater had never been in a seedier one, but the dark interior and the accumulated grime assured them of anonymity from the players working the streets.

"But she did leave me," Skater said. "Five months ago."

Brynna reached out and patted his hand. "He made her leave you, but I think she hoped you'd come after her."

"She said she didn't want me around," Skater said, listening to Larisa's words again in his mind.

"Of course she did. She had to be convincing or he'd have turned you over to Lone Star." Brynna nodded, like it was perfectly understandable.

Skater took a deep breath and let it out. It was frustrating being this close to some of the answers he needed and still not be able to make any sense of them. "Who is this 'he' you keep referring to?"

"A street sleaze named Ridge Maddock. He's a fixer, definitely small-time, but he had this jones for Larisa like you wouldn't believe."

"How was he able to force Larisa to leave me?"

"First he found out you were a runner, then he found out you were involved in something that happened to someone named Scharnhorn."

Skater flicked his eyes over to Duran's. The ork met his gaze but gave no outward sign that he recognized the name.

The Scharnhorn deal had gone down almost two years ago, and the closest the team had ever come to a full-fledged disaster.

"If she didn't do what Maddock wanted," Brynna said, "he threatened to squeal you to the people looking for you, and maybe Lone Star as well. If she told you, she'd save you, but she'd lose you that way, too. She didn't want that."

"So she made the deal," Duran said.

Brynna nodded. "And she got to keep you at least a little longer, at least until the pregnancy started to show. I guess she was hoping something would happen."

Skater turned away and stared hard through the cigarette smoke at the elongating shadows starting to drape themselves across the front of Murphy's Law, filling up the hollow spots in the sprawl. The low conversations at the other tables were punctuated by the click of balls coming from the pool table further in the back under long fluorescent lights. A half-dozen humans and metas were scattered down the length of the bar on his right.

"What was the deal?" Duran prompted.

"He wanted her to be a surrogate mother," Brynna said.

"That's whacked," Skater growled angrily, facing the woman. "Larisa didn't even use skillsofts to enhance her dancing. She'd never have gone for something like that."

"But she did, Jack. She did it for you."

Skater's mind reeled. He fell back in his chair, feeling numb and disoriented.

"She should be having the baby any time," Brynna said, laying her hand on Skater's. "Maybe it's not too late. Maybe if you see her—"

"It is too late," Duran said in a gruff voice. "Larisa's dead."

"She can't be," Brynna said in a small voice. "I just talked to her a couple days ago."

"She was killed yesterday," the ork said.

Brynna lifted her glass with a shaking hand and drained it. She wiped her mouth with the back of her hand, biting her lip as she worked through Duran's words. Fresh tears glinted in her eyes. Her voice was hoarse when she spoke. "Who killed her? Those guys back at my place?"

"We don't know," Duran said with uncharacteristic softness. "Maybe." He signaled for a round of drinks and the waitress brought them.

Skater watched the exchange, knowing the ork was taking his position as the soft-sell since he wasn't staying with the conversation. He seized on what Brynna had said. "You talked to Larisa a couple days ago?"

The woman nodded.

"She didn't mention the baby?"

"No."

"She had it three weeks ago," Skater said.

Brynna shook her head. "She would have told me. Toward the end, she started talking about the baby all the time. She could hardly wait. She said she thought being a mother would be the first thing she'd ever had a chance to do right."

Skater worked on keeping his distance from the subject matter. Images of Larisa lying asleep at his side, all baby-soft and cuddly in the early morning light, invaded his mind.

"She was living in Bellevue when she died," Duran said.

"I know. She wasn't as happy as I thought she would be. Drek, we used to talk about living in a place like that when we roomed together. Maddock paid for it."

"Because she was having the baby?"

"Right."

"What was going to happen to the child?" Duran asked.

"I didn't ask," Brynna replied. "See, Larisa got into this thing for all the wrong reasons, but she really got attached to the little guy. The way she could feel him inside her. She told me some days it was like he was turning somersaults and she didn't know how she was going to make it through."

"The little guy?" Skater repeated.

Brynna nodded. "Larisa didn't know for sure, but she hoped the baby was going to be a boy."

Skater remembered the way the second bedroom had been set up, the little girl's bedclothes in the crib. He couldn't help wondering where the baby was. And how many babies there actually were.

"Larisa was planning to keep it?" Duran asked.

Mentally kicking himself for not paying better attention to all the angles being laid out on the table, Skater took a sip of his juice and listened more closely.

"Yes. She had a piece of biz working," Brynna said. "If it came through, she figured she'd have enough to get away from Maddock and take the baby with her. I got the impression Jack was supposed to help her with it."

Skater looked at Duran, and the ork returned his gaze,

letting him know they shared the same opinion. "Did she mention any names?"

"No. Drek, Jack, she was going crazy there at the end, trying to figure out what she was going to do. Everything was mixed up for her. There's nothing else I can tell you, because I don't know any more." Tears ran down her face as she fought against it. She wiped a sleeve across her cheeks and sniffled.

"Did Larisa ever mention a guy named Tone?"

"I don't know . . . I don't think so, but I can't be sure. Why, is it important?"

"Maybe," Skater said. "Maybe not." Reaching into his jacket, Skater took out a certified credstick with a few thousand nuyen on it.

"I can't take this," Brynna protested.

Skater rolled it up in her fist. "Yes you can. You can't go back to your doss. And you can't access your own credstick for a few days. You're going to need something to live on. I wish I had more to give you, but I'm pretty tapped out myself at the moment."

Her eyes widened as she realized what he was saying. "I can't go off and leave everything I own."

"You will," Duran said gruffly, "if you want to go on breathing."

"Just give me a few days," Skater said. "Everything should be back to zero-sweat by then." He spoke with more confidence than he felt.

"How will I know?"

"Call this number and let me know where you're staying." Skater wrote the number of a message drop he used under another name on a cocktail napkin and gave it to her. The message drop, set up like the one he was using with Kestrel, went through an answering service. Once a call was made and another password entered, the message dropped through a trapdoor in the system, where it waited to be retrieved by another passcode. For all intents and purposes, he couldn't be made. Even the SIN he had on file with the answering service was false. Since he could call in and pick up whatever messages were recorded, it had a built-in layer of security. "If you don't hear from me, you might want to stay lost awhile longer."

Brynna nodded, looking more scared than ever.

"One other thing," Skater said. "Tell me where I can find Ridge Maddock."

17

"It's me," Skater said when Archangel answered the telecom at the safe house. "I've got a name I want to run by you. Ridge Maddock. Small-time fixer. He was connected with Larisa, and maybe to the accounts at the Montgomery doss."

"Maybe you should stop pushing for a little while," Archangel said. "Get some distance on things."

The comment confused Skater. He figured she was concerned he'd blow their cover and somehow lead the people who were hunting them back to the team. But for a moment, it sounded like she was concerned about him, too. "I'm okay. Duran's here to make sure I don't hose up too bad."

She didn't say anything.

"Have you found out anything about the diplomatic plates?" he asked. He didn't really expect anything, but asking was a way of ending the tense silence. Skater had noticed the official vehicles when viewing the newscast around the warehouse, and it seemed worth looking into.

"No." Her voice was cool, distant, like all this had nothing to do with her. "There's a lot of IC around those files, and cracking anything political runs the risk of getting my brain fried to a crisp."

"Be careful in there."

"Unlike you, I know when to stop, no matter how responsible I feel." The connection broke.

Puzzled and more than a little irritated over the conversation even though he didn't know why, Skater broke the connection and walked back to the Eurowind. "She's running Maddock."

Duran nodded, glanced quickly in the rearview mirrors, and screeched into traffic. "Something wrong?"

"Nothing I know of," Skater replied as he watched the street around them. A Lone Star cruiser passed them, going the other way fast enough that he knew the blue crew had a definite destination in mind. "We're not any deeper in drek than we were before, but Archangel sounded bent about something."

Duran handled the car easily, sweeping around the corner of Vine Street and heading north. "What'd she say?"

Skater told him.

"It's hard for her," Duran said when he finished.

"What?"

"Ties."

"Between us?"

"Between her and anybody," the ork answered. "I don't know much about Archangel, including her real name, even though I've known her longer than you. What I do know, though, is that I've never seen her with a friend, or ever mention having one."

It had been Archangel who'd brought Duran in after working with Skater off and off for three or four months. Elvis was already working with Skater, and he'd brought in Wheeler. Skater had recruited Cullen Trey from a number of possibilities when it became obvious they needed a mage with combat skills. Duran had suggested Shiva to round out the team with chromed muscle.

"Whatever happened to her along the way to getting here," Duran continued, "she doesn't let anyone next to her."

"I've noticed," Skater said.

"Right now," the ork said, "she's scared. She's let herself get closer to us than she planned." He paused. "I think maybe all of us have. Otherwise, we'd have split when we said we were going to. It was the best course of action at first glance."

"Then why didn't you?"

"I was checking you out," Duran said. "We discussed that. Elvis had already said he wasn't turning his back on you."

"I didn't know that."

"Wheeler stuck by you last night, too, when we were talking about divvying up the files. And Trey isn't the kind of guy to leave a chummer in the lurch if there's something he can do. And Archangel, well, she stuck for her own reasons."

Skater let the ork's words spin in his head, trying to get used to them. He remembered how alone he'd felt the previous night when the team had left him in the back room of the Bloody Rosebud of Phelia.

Duran stopped at a red light. "You put together a good team," he said, studying the rearview mirrors. "That's an achievement all by itself. If this had been some private action on your part and you'd gotten your hoop in the wringer all on your own, maybe none of us would have wanted to get mixed up in it. But it wasn't. You went into this thinking it was going to be a big score for all of us, and you got hosed for it."

"We all did," Skater pointed out.

"Yeah, but it's beginning to shape up like some of this was personal. Someone used you, and us along with you." The ork made a lane change, running a sedate ten kilometers over the posted speed limit. His fangs were edged ivory against his scarred cheeks. "A fragging lot of weight is hanging out there, waiting to come down on somebody. Even if we ran we'd probably get chased down and geeked one by one. Since we don't know, there's a safety in numbers. Could be whoever set this up figured the team would split up and be easier to get to. Most would have."

"I know."

"We run the shadows together," Duran said. "Doesn't make us bosom chummers, but we do have a responsibility to each other. A leader sets the standard on that, Jack, and you've set a high one these past three years."

Skater started to disagree, feeling uncomfortable, but Duran cut him off.

"It's no bulldrek. When Archangel got me into that first piece of biz with you, I saw a punk kid standing where a man ought to have been. I'd worked with Archangel and couldn't believe she'd have the time of day for someone like you, much less consider following your lead on a run. I never intended to stay on, but in the end your smarts and your nerve sold me."

"I was surprised you stayed," Skater said, remembering the tension that had existed then.

"So was I. But the run came off just like you thought it would. And four runs later, it was still the same. Then, when Trey got zapped by that drone during the raid on the simporn blackmailing scam and you went back for him, I knew you were a guy who'd stick even when things got tough."

"No way I could have left him there."

"Sure you could have." Duran made the corner, beating out the yellow light at the intersection. "A lot of people would have. I've seen some do it. I respect how you handled it, and so do the others."

"That hasn't been the only close call," Skater pointed out. "Everyone on this team has covered somebody else's hoop when the chips were down."

Duran nodded. "Ain't none of us all good or all bad, but not everyone can do the biz together without rubbing each other raw. You kept some of us from each other's throats at different times and made the team work. Me and Shiva, we didn't exactly see eye to eye, but you kept us operational."

That was putting it mildly, Skater knew, but he didn't offer a comment.

"I couldn't ever see us getting social together," the ork said. "But the working relationship was good. Better than most I've been involved with. We live in the shadows, and life is just a run through the shadows, too. That's easy to forget sometimes. And when you're running through those shadows, it's good to know you've got someone you can trust watching your back door."

"You didn't sound so trusting last night," Skater said, looking at Duran.

The ork smiled, and the effect looked positively serrated. "You get pushy, kid."

"Yeah."

"That's what I meant about being a good leader. Why'd you say that?"

"So I'd know," Skater answered.

"And in order for you to know how I think?"

"You're going to have to know how you think," Skater said.

"Right. Squares me up with myself first. Takes the focus off whether I should trust you and puts it back where it belongs—on whether I should trust myself."

"Something like that."

"So where did you learn to think like that?"

"Inside my own skin. Lot of drek I had to sort out for myself. Best way I figured to do that was know for sure what was on my mind, how I felt about a person or a situation."

Duran shook his head. "You'd have made a hell of a first sergeant, kid. In answer to your questions, though, last night

I was questioning your loyalty more than I was questioning whether I could trust you. Today, I decided."

Skater nodded. It was fair.

"Another thing."

"What?"

"That elf dancer you were involved with. How do you feel about her now?"

Skater was silent for a moment, trying to skull it through but coming up cross-slotted every time. "I don't know. Too much I found out that I didn't know, and too many questions left about things I thought I did know."

"How about I give you something to kick around in your head?"

Skater was hesitant. He'd always liked to do his own thinking, then he realized that Duran had probably been leading up to this the whole time. The ork was no slouch, either. "Yeah."

"You trusted this woman, maybe even loved her. On the surface, it looks like she fragged you over, looking for some kind of score to keep her own hoop from getting jammed."

Skater remained silent, distancing himself from the emotions that suddenly twisted up through him.

"I'm going to walk through it for you, and you can make of it what you want. I don't know much about your track record with the ladies, but I've seen you with Archangel, and you don't cross any lines. I see this woman, she loves you enough to try to save you when this Maddock comes along. She gets herself in deeper, becomes a surrogate mother because Maddock tells her that's what she's got to do. So she does, and loses everything: you, her job, her independence. That's why she was living in Bellevue. Right?"

Skater nodded. He remembered the doss in the Montgomery, painted by the flames. Not much had existed of the Larisa he'd known. Suddenly he realized it wasn't because she'd changed. It was because she hadn't lived there. A prisoner had.

"Maddock obviously had a lot invested in this piece of biz, whatever it was," Duran went on. "Larisa takes a good look around. Maddock has her by the short hairs, hosed any which way she goes. Maybe she gets mad at you during this time, but not enough to simply frag you over. Some slitches would. But you're good at reading people, right, so she didn't come across like that?"

"No," Skater said, and felt the certainty of that conviction sink into him. There'd been other women before Larisa, and their various betrayals hadn't surprised him.

"She's trapped, not knowing what to do. By this time she's been able to take a good look around. You haven't been breaking down the door trying to see her at the old doss, so she knows she can trust you to keep your word about staying away. Probably she knew that anyway. Only this time, it's working against her."

The image of Larisa's caramelized face filled Skater's mind and brought a pain that hurt deep and sharp.

"She takes a good look," the ork said. "She sees you, a shadowrunner. Can she save you? Can she get you to stay away from the action?"

Skater recalled the few arguments he'd had with Larisa. She'd wanted him to leave the shadows, even threatened to end it if he didn't. But she'd never been able to. Not until five months ago. "No," he said in a tight voice.

"No," Duran repeated with emphasis. "Because you're not moving from it. Hooked by the nuyen, the lifestyle, or the pump of the jazz running brings."

Thinking of all the Caribbean accounts that had been seized, Skater knew it wasn't any of those. He'd been hooked by the lure of security, of having enough to simply vanish one day. Larisa had always said that would never happen, because he'd never know when he had enough.

"Could be for awhile she ignored that," Duran said. "Then Maddock comes along with his blackmail scheme. She took the deal hoping to buy some time. Brynna told us that. Only time is all she's buying, and suddenly she realizes that's running out. But during this last five months, she gets to thinking maybe there is someone she can save."

"The baby."

Duran nodded. "That's what I think. So when she got her hands on the info about the *Sapphire Seahawk*, she calls you. If the biz goes down right, she has a way out for the baby, and possibly she's even thinking about herself now."

"Why not just call me?" Skater asked. "I could have gotten her away from there."

"And lose everything in doing it?" Duran shook his head. "There was no reason to believe you'd do it. She'd asked you before and you'd always said no. I think she probably had her own plans together, and was just waiting for financing. She could disappear. And if it came off right, you'd still be free to do whatever the hell you wanted to and she'd have earned her own way clear."

Examining the scenario, Skater tested it for any flaws. It fit with what he knew of Larisa. She'd been fiercely independent in her own right.

Duran was quiet for a time. "I think you had a hell of a woman on your hands for a time, and she loved you down deep where it counts. I think, too, that you knew it and it scared the drek out of you. So when you look at this thing, look past the surface."

"I have been. I just haven't been able to find anything else there."

"We'll talk to Maddock," the ork replied, "and see where that takes us. Once we get this *Sapphire Seahawk* biz squared away, you can find out who killed her and why." Duran glanced over at him. "Out of respect for the lady, I'd like to give you a hand with that." He stuck out a fist.

After only a moment's hesitation, Skater closed his fist and dropped it on the ork's, knowing that the offer wasn't meant lightly. He also knew neither the offer nor the acceptance came without a price. He was stepping way beyond the limits he'd imposed on his relationships with the team and it scared the hell out of him. "I'd appreciate it," he said, because the price was worth paying.

"Got him," Duran said.

Without moving too fast, Skater turned from the long bar and scanned the throbbing crowd that filled one of the huge glass dance floors of Dante's Inferno. The pulsating lights and crisscrossing lasers were fragging up his low-light vision, and the thump of the shag metal blasting out of dozens of speakers made sub-dermals out of the question. The band's theme was the afterlife, but only a gruesome afterlife achieved through arcane means. Dressed as rotting corpses and writhing maggots, they occupied the third level stage.

Skater and Duran had been scoping out the lowest three of the nine dance floors—not including Hell. They'd paid six waitresses, two on each floor, to let them know when Ridge Maddock put in his appearance. Sophie, one of the cocktail servers working the second floor, came over to them. She was tall and shapely, her left cheek covered with a tattoo of a flaming angel.

"Maddock's here," she said. "Come with me and I'll point him out."

Duran slotted her tipstick the balance of the finder's fee, then started following her. Skater fell into step behind them.

After exiting on the second floor, Skater and Duran separated but stayed within sight of each other as they wound their way through the knots of dancers and party-goers in the waitress's wake. Dante's Inferno was one of the more popular nightclubs in the sprawl, and—if you could get in—it was usually standing room only, even at nine p.m.

Ridge Maddock had rated a small table by himself in the corner of an L-shaped plant box boasting a twisting jungle of bioengineered plants and flowers. Neon-pseudo-jewels glittered among the growth.

He was tall, standing over two meters in height. His broad shoulders and the cut of his jacket hid most of his paunch. The ponytail he wore was severely pulled back, and a crimson and black dragon was etched into pale skin, climbing from under his left ear, curling around his cheek, with its head and front legs up over his eyebrow. Cut green gems glinted in the lobes of both ears.

"He's heeled," Skater said, noting the bulge under Maddock's right arm. "Left-handed."

"I see it," Duran answered. "You see anyone with him?"

Skater scanned the crowd. "Company's coming," he said, then quietly pointed out the woman approaching Maddock.

She was elven, but of an oriental caste. Her blushed skin was flawless, and a lot of it showed. The chartreuse gown she wore had long sleeves, but ended well above mid-thigh.

"Pleasure," Duran asked, "or biz?"

Without preamble, the woman sat down at Maddock's table. She crossed her legs, exposing a healthy expanse of thigh that was visible to the fixer where he sat. He didn't bother trying to feign disinterest in the move. She shook out a long thin brown cigarette and he lit it for her, making small talk till her drink arrived. Then she thanked Maddock and drank without bashfulness.

"Business," Skater replied. "Slime-sucking sleaze like Maddock aren't the kind a woman like that's going to go for."

Duran's grin was without humor. "Kid, you don't know what that slitch is like."

"I'm operating out of an impaired perception," Skater said. "I don't like this guy."

"Understandable, but not very professional." Duran halted near the bar, standing close enough to the mob of people waiting to order drinks that it looked like they were in line. "The question now is, do we step in or wait?"

Skater watched the fixer talking smoothly to the woman, as if he held every ace in the deck. He wondered if Larisa had met Maddock here like this a year ago and been forced to listen to the deal he was offering.

Duran had a small Ares Squirt pistol loaded with a DMSO gamma-scopolamine sedative gel that was extremely quick-acting and would put Maddock out between heartbeats. There was very little talk planned.

Skater took the lead, thinking if Maddock did know him it would distract his attention until Duran could make his move.

Instead, the woman got up from the table and waited for Maddock to take her arm.

Changing directions at once, Skater cut away from the bulk of the crowd. A glance showed him Duran was at his heels.

"Trouble," the ork growled.

Skater had already spotted the three Japanese men who'd altered their course and were closing on Maddock and the woman. They wore black Vashon Island suits and dark sunglasses despite the gloom that filled the Inferno. A smile was on the leader's face.

"Maddock," the leader of the trio called out in a good-natured voice. His right hand was concealed under his jacket.

The fixer came around, and the smile he'd been showing off to the woman melted quickly from his face. "What do you want?"

"My oyabun would like a few moments of your time." The lead Japanese stopped a few meters from Maddock with his hand still out of sight under his jacket. The other two men dropped into flanking positions.

The elven woman beside Maddock moved with the fluid grace of someone who either had extraordinary reflexes or was chipped to the teeth. She stepped behind the fixer and grabbed him by the collar as the doors to the maglev opened with a ping.

"Drek," Duran said softly but with genuine feeling.

Skater fisted the Predator and slipped it free, holding it out of sight by his leg.

"Get out of the slotting cage," the woman ordered the passengers inside the maglev. She motioned with the gun and they departed with alacrity. Maddock tried to jerk away, but the woman jammed the muzzle of her Tiffani Self-Defender against his temple. "Not so fast, nitbrain. You and I are out of here." She yanked him back into the maglev cage.

The crowd around the maglev suddenly dropped back and pushed their way out onto the dance floor. There were a few screams from nearby women who suddenly realized they were in the wrong place at the wrong time.

Taking a step forward, sensing the violence about to be unleashed, Skater watched the yak leader make his move.

In the blink of an eye, the yakuza pulled out a Scorpion machine pistol. He barked orders to his two companions as he raked a blistering line of fire across the wall only a few meters from the maglev doors.

Skater pointed his weapon at the leader's knee. Whether the knee was chromed or covered by Kevlar-lined pants, the bullet wound would deliver enough force to knock the man off his feet. He wanted Maddock alive even if the yaks didn't.

Evidently the elven woman did as well, because she emptied all four shots from the Self-Defender into the yak's face even as Skater's bullet caught the dead man in the knee and hammered him off-balance.

The remaining two yakuza turned to face Skater and Duran as the maglev doors closed and the Inferno's sec-teams started vectoring in on them.

18

"Put the fragging guns down now!" one of the Inferno guards bellowed. He made the alternative clear by thrusting his own weapon out.

Skater ignored the command. Getting caught at this point wasn't an option.

The surviving yaks must have felt the same way, because one of them directed his pistol at Skater and Duran while the other unleashed half a clip at the nightclub's sec-team.

Leaping, accessing both boosted reflexes and extra adrenaline, Skater put himself over and behind the low wall holding the plants. He hoped the wall would block the bullets. He dropped with his back against the wall in a squatting position and his pistol in a two-handed Weaver grip.

"Kid," Duran called. "You in one piece?"

Skater glanced around the corner of the wall and saw the ork in a defensive position behind an overturned table. "Yeah."

The gun battle was quickly heating up. The sec-teams had a momentary advantage, but more yakuza gunners drifted in from the dance floor and pushed them back, firing from whatever defensive positions they could find.

Every tick of the clock, Skater knew, put that much more distance between them and Maddock. "The stairs?" he shouted to Duran.

The ork nodded. "On your go, chummer."

"Do it!" Skater threw himself from cover, angling away from the thrust of the firefight. Bullets cut the air before and behind him. He didn't break stride. A round caught him high on the left shoulder but was stopped by the Kevlar-lined bomber jacket. The impact drove him off-balance, but he managed a stagger that got him to the door just after Duran burst through.

The twisting maze of stairs with flights leading down and up only held subdued lighting. A sec-guard in Inferno colors was coming up the flight of stairs leading to the second-floor landing. Before the man could raise his pistol in self-defense, Duran shoved the Squirt forward at point-blank range and pulled the trigger.

The DMSO gel ball smashed against the man's face, spreading visibly, and immediately taking effect.

Skater grabbed the handrail leading down to steady himself as he raced past the falling guard. Duran hit the wall ahead of them and pushed off, making the corner and gaining speed again. Seizing the handrail, Skater leaped and hauled himself over, knowing he was chancing a broken or sprained ankle, and landed with a jar halfway down the switch-back steps. He followed as Duran exploded through the first-floor door.

The corridor was empty, but heads were popping out about twenty meters down where the main entrance was. No one seemed too eager to challenge them.

Skater glanced up at the maglev's floor indicator. "Says the cage is here."

"Only one way to find out." Duran plucked a broad-bladed combat knife from his sleeve in an eye-blurring movement. The edged metal flashed as he buried it to the hilt between the maglev doors and twisted.

The doors parted a few centimeters, enough for Skater to shove his fingers in and pull the door back, opening the other with it.

Maddock hung by a small wire that fitted snugly under his jawline and cut into the flesh enough to leave thin threads of blood seeping down his neck to stain his shirt. His arms hung loosely, and his feet were fifty centimeters from the floor. Splashes of crimson spotted the stainless steel interior of the maglev cage.

Skater moved into the cage and used his free hand, his legs, and both elbows to leverage his head and shoulders through the escape hatch. The cage was a round, shiny egg-shape that floated up and down the shaft. Two floors above him, he spotted the elf woman floating through a set of double doors, levitated by her own power or someone else's. The shadowrunner kicked in his low-light vision and picked up three other figures waiting to help the woman make her exit. One of them was the elf who'd led the team that busted Skater out of Lone Star.

The elf spotted Skater and moved almost faster than Skater could counter, bringing up a shotgun and firing immediately.

Skater released his hold on the sides of the exit and dropped. The pellets caromed from the top of the cage like a sudden burst of hail, then rattled in smaller echoes against the sides of the maglev shaft.

"She had a backup team waiting in the wings," Skater said as he got up. "We'll never snag her now."

"We can't hold this twenty," Duran stated. "And I'm two rounds away from no-more-mister-nice-guy. The situation being what it is, I'm not about to surrender."

Holding the pistol in one hand, Skater used his other to search through Maddock's clothing. There was nothing to be found; the woman had evidently gotten whatever she was looking for.

A glance back into the hallway showed that the possibility of retreat in either direction had been cut off by Inferno sec-teams. Duran put another man down with the last gel pellet from the Squirt, then hauled out his Roomsweeper heavy pistol.

"Inside," Skater told the ork. He fired three rounds and holed the standpipe fire extinguishing system near the group of men to their right. A hard spray of water jetted out from the punctures in the standpipe and created a rainbow-colored mist in the hallway that was difficult to see through as well as becoming an approach hazard.

For a moment, the return fire blistered the walls around the maglev doors.

"Kid, I sure as frag hope you've got a plan." Duran took up a position on the other side of the cage from Skater and fired a pair of shots into the hallway. The detonations were deafening trapped inside the small space. "Our escape menu is getting about as limited as an incestuous cannibal's diet."

"Worse than that," Skater said. "At least an incestuous cannibal knows where his next meal is coming from."

Duran gave him a wry look.

"Cover me," Skater said.

"Another slotting crack like that," Duran warned, "and I geek you myself."

Skater lunged through the door long enough to fire three bullets into the maglev level display. A puff of smoke ejected from the crunched plates, followed by sparks and the start of a small fire. He withdrew back into the cage a heart-beat ahead of the gunfire that smashed into the doors. He tapped the down button for the second basement level.

Erratically, the doors closed with metallic grindings and protesting squeaks. More bullets spanged across the stainless steel and ricocheted over his and Duran's heads before they were shut out. The maglev dropped at once, starting Skater's stomach spinning with the near-feeling of weightlessness.

"Down?" Duran growled. "Down means we're going to be wearing a straitjacket of plascrete and have the building sitting on top of us."

The maglev arrived with a slight bump that belied the swirling sensation in Skater's stomach. He took the lead when the doors opened, following the Predator into the corridor. No one was in either direction. The closer to Hell a person got, the fewer people were around.

"This floor's connected to an underground garage," Skater said, orienting himself to what he'd learned about the building. Low-wattage security lights painted gray stripes of illumination across the floor. While the ork had worked the portaphone to arrange invitations into the nightclub, Skater had been using the Eurowind's small computer to download maps of the building provided by Archangel, which he'd used to plot routes for a hasty retreat. He counted doors, then went through.

"They'll have the garage sealed and watched," Duran said.

"We're not going through the garage doors," Skater said as they entered the parking area.

"Ops guy will have made us by now," Duran said, pointing to the lens of a vidcam in the wall. "They'll know where we're at."

"Give me a hand," Skater said, shoving his fingers into the recessed handle of a manhole cover in the corner. "This fragging thing is heavy."

Duran reached down and hooked the cover as well. Even with them working together, it moved only with difficulty. "Tell me this is only an access tube for the utilities."

Skater didn't reply as they bent to the task. The stench that curled up from the darkness inside the manhole after the cover was removed was the only necessary answer.

"Drek, kid," the ork grumbled, "we've hit a new low for getaways."

Skater swung onto the ladder mounted on the wall and started down into the stinking gloom. "Just hope we've hit this one at low tide."

Standing under the heated pummeling of the shower, Skater let the water sluice away the fatigue and the drek from their escape through the sewer running under the Inferno. Wheeler had disposed of Archibald's corpse by pouring acid and bacteria-reinforced lime over it in the bathtub, so the surfaces around him gleamed. The process had taken a few hours, but by the time the rigger was done, their host was only a memory and bits of DNA drifting through the lines to the water recycling plant. Skater didn't like thinking that the nightclub was on the same system as the doss, nor that it might be downstream. The thought that some of Archibald might have made it back to the apartment with him to go through the pipes again was too much.

The small bathroom in the doss acted like an acoustic ear, attracting all the sounds from without. Wheeler, Elvis, and Trey, despite the tension of the present situation, were still laughing at the kvetching Duran was doing about the escape through the sewer system.

"I mean it was this fragging *big,*" the ork growled. "If it'd had eyes, I'da thought I'd been attacked by a slotting deathrattle. Drek, I'd already flamed a few shots in that direction when the kid told me to relax."

"You thought it was a snake?" Wheeler said. "A deathrattle?" The dwarf succumbed to a new wave of barking laughter. "Slot me, I wish I'd been there."

"You keep rubbing me raw, halfer," Duran promised, "and it can still be arranged."

Skater shut off the water, dried off, and got dressed. A bag on the sink contained deodorant, shaving cream, and a razor. He used them, then went to join the others. He almost felt human again.

The windows were blacked out with cloth, and Wheeler had established new perimeter security measures. The master control held a number of cables plugged into it, as well as three vidlinks covering possible approaches to the apartment. The unit sat on the table with quick-disconnects, blinking green. All the cameras were hidden, had motion-detecting capabilities, and IR functions.

Duran was clad in fresh clothes and sat on the floor cleaning the weapons they'd used at the nightclub. He wore gloves and was working over a shirt Archibald no longer had a need for.

Elvis sat on the couch in contemplative silence, but the muscles in his thighs flexed and shifted, letting Skater know the troll was keeping limber and ready with isometrics. His silver horntip gleamed as he polished both his tusks with wax. Wheeler occupied himself with tweaking up the kluged systems he'd set up in the apartment. His tool belt held various instruments, and his vest was festooned as well. Spare wiring leaked out of one pocket from a spool.

"Soykaf?" Trey called from the kitchen.

"The hotter the better." The run through the sewer system

had left Skater chilled. He stopped a few steps from Archangel.

She was downloading files, her elven features a study in ice, frosted grayish-green from the deck monitor. Fluidly, her fingers played the keyboard. Images rolled and shifted too fast for Skater to see. Bits and bytes of info traveled in linear fashion, scaling quickly to the top of the screen and disappearing.

"You called your friend?" Archangel asked.

"Yes." Kestrel had left a message at Skater's drop. "He confirmed that Dion and Shayx worked for Synclair Tone."

"And you've never bumped into this guy?"

"No."

Voice cold and impersonal, Archangel said, "So the only common denominator you have is Larisa Hartsinger."

Skater said yes.

"I used his LTG number and some of the buzz Trey was able to collect to find out more about him." Archangel's fingers kept moving, and the clack of the keys being struck became a constant background noise. "He's got a record from his days in the Barrens. I picked it up from a pirate board I'm connected to. A lot of private investigators use the service."

The monitor cleared and formed a face. The man was young, an elf with the look of a thriller blocked into the ragged cut of his fair hair, the mismatched cybereye in the left socket puckered by a knife scar, and the trio of burn scars interrupting the stubble growth on the right side of his chin.

"How long has Tone been operating in Seattle?"

"Five months. About the time since you and Larisa called it quits."

That was one way to put being dumped, Skater thought. Then he recalled Brynna's assurances that Larisa had been blackmailed into leaving him. He pushed his personal feelings aside for the time. "That means he came onto the scene after Maddock, but Aggie said the Synclair Tone Larisa knew was a polished guy."

The picture on the monitor shifted in response to Archangel's commands. The face that replaced the Lone Star mug shot was clean and made-over. Even the mismatched cybereye had been replaced with an organic one and the three burns on his chin had been excised, leaving a smooth and shaven face. His hair was style-shop perfect. "He became that."

"Expensive," Trey commented. Skater knew the mage would know. He hadn't been born to wealth or to good manners, but he'd chosen how he presented himself and taught himself how to enjoy finer things. "The knife scars and the burns required a vat job to eradicate completely." The rest of the team had drifted over, listening and looking.

"Did he have the nuyen?" Wheeler asked.

"Not much ever showed on his arrest record from Puyallup," Archangel answered. "Every time he went down, it was for nickel and dime crimes. But he had a reputation for being a hard guy to handle, and one who would never cut a deal with the blues to save himself."

"Has he been noosed since he's been here?"

"No."

Skater shelved that line of inquiry for the moment. "How far did you get into those files we jacked from the freighter?"

"I cracked them a little more," she replied. "But they're not going to tell us anything. They've been corrupted, and whoever did it knew what they were doing. I don't think there's anything more I can recover."

"Intentionally corrupted?" Trey asked.

She nodded. "But I got far enough in to confirm that they're some kind of medical reports and research development. Perhaps if we took it to someone who knows more about bioresearch, we could find out what we're dealing with."

"Is there a possibility you accidentally corrupted the files while boosting them from the *Seahawk*'s system?" Trey asked.

Archangel turned her cold gaze on the mage. "Was there any way you could have made that sleep spell that you mojoed the crew with any more potent?"

Trey touched his forehead as if doffing an imaginary hat. "Forgive me for questioning your professionalism, my lady."

"The question was legitimate," Archangel acknowledged. "However, I'm sure I didn't harm the files when I extracted them. They were already corrupt."

"The freighter was carrying worthless files," Skater said. "Only one reason why that I can think of."

Duran nodded. "Trojan horses have been around for a

long time. It should have worked, if that's what they were doing. You and Archangel checked the freighter out and it looked like a nice prize to you."

"And to the yaks," Wheeler pointed out.

Skater looked at the scenario and put a further spin on it. "We got there before them, making it a double Trojan horse. We go for the files and get them, and the yaks think we made off with them, not knowing what we have isn't worth drek."

"No one told the ship's crew or the people guarding the computer either," Elvis said. "Those sailors stood their ground hard. We didn't kill anyone, but the yaks sure fragging did."

"You think the real files have already reached Seattle," Duran said.

"If they did," Skater asked, "then why are the elves chasing us so hard?"

"Keeping up the smoke screen," the ork replied.

"Possible. But why go after Maddock?"

The big mercenary shrugged. "Same reason, maybe."

Skater shook his head. "Now we're getting too many maybes. Finesse is best when used least. How did the elves know about Maddock?"

"Brynna could have given you up to the elves after you left her."

Skater considered the supposition briefly, then rejected it. "I think she was on the level. It's possible Tone and Maddock are connected, but what would Tone be doing with an elven corp?" He glanced at Archangel. "Where did you get with those diplomatic plates?"

"As yet, nowhere," she said. "I've got a browser program running, and maybe it'll turn up something. But from everything I've seen in the files I've accessed, I'd be willing to bet those plates belonged to cars used by Tir representatives. If I can't get in through plate identification, I've got some capture programs standing by to access the car-pool maintenance files. At least one of those vehicles was seriously damaged, if not destroyed. When a replacement or an order for repairs comes through maintenance, I'll know."

"Good job," Skater said. "Do you have that copy of the news report I recorded tonight?"

Archangel nodded.

"Would you run it?"

She tapped a few keys on the keyboard.

Skater called for Duran. They watched it five times. At the end of the last showing, Skater knew they weren't going to find any more elves from the raiding party than the two he'd already identified.

"Run them through immigration," Skater told Archangel, "visitor's visa files and Seattle Port Authority. Those jokers didn't just appear over here from the Tir."

Archangel cut and pasted the first face, moving it into its own file. "I can set up a cross-reference for the rest of the people in this footage at the same places. It'll take time."

Skater left her with it and walked back to the security setup Wheeler had installed. "Duran, you need some rack time. So do the rest of you. Elvis, you've got first watch. It's eleven now. That gives us seven hours before dawn. If nothing's jumping by then, maybe we can all catch a few. Elvis, set up the rotation for every hour and a half."

Wheeler volunteered for the next watch, claiming it wouldn't be so bad because he'd managed a few winks that evening after disposing of the body and setting up the security system.

As Skater watched them, he was amazed at how quickly everything came together. On a shadowrun, they worked as a unit for only a few hours, each one returning to his or her own life shortly after. He'd never imagined any of them spending much time together. They were too different, too adamant about liking their privacy.

But he had to reconsider that, thinking maybe he'd let his own preferences color his perceptions. He didn't like the thought of getting close to anyone. Larisa had been the only one. Leaning on others was weak; his mother had hammered that into his brain, and most of the people he'd known in the Council lands seemed to shun his company.

Thinking of Larisa made him think of the baby. She was alone out there somewhere—if she was still alive, he reminded himself—and that could be a cruel world waiting. For a heartbeat, he felt that if he could find the child and touch it, it would be like touching Larisa again.

"Jack."

He looked at Archangel and shelved the thoughts, making himself concentrate on survival. He needed sleep. The stimulants he'd been taking to keep going were taxing his reserves. "Yeah?"

"I may have something."

Skater joined her at the deck. "What?"

"The *Sapphire Seahawk* went down in international waters," Archangel said as she stroked the keyboard. "I guessed that she would be carrying insurance, so I sent some sleaze fingers to snoop out civil data about the freighter and learned that a carrier in Seattle covered the trip once the freighter crossed the Tir Tairngire border. The loss was filed with the carrier this morning so a credstick could be issued within the next ten days. It didn't take long to find the carrier, because not that many of them are willing to handle foreign accounts, especially for that much."

A form file appeared on the monitor. Skater leaned in, struggling to read the fine print.

"Cutting to the bone," Archangel said, "the agreement lists the responsibilities of both parties."

"The carrier," Skater prompted.

"Wilcoxin Controlled Risk, Inc. And the insured party . . ." Archangel paused and pointed at the screen. "An outfit calling itself NuGene Inc."

The name rang a bell in Skater's mind. "Tell me more."

"I just found them," Archangel said. "On the surface, they're a biomedical research and development corporation."

"Yeah," Skater said, remembering the tridcast he'd seen. "In the Tir."

"Portland." Archangel hit more keys and a gridded map appeared on the monitor screen. "The address shows that it's on Southwest Terwilliger Boulevard, somewhere near Tir Tairngire Medical Center. I'm working up other data, but from what I've seen so far, the decision by the Council of Princes to use Seattle as a port created some serious economic problems for the corporation."

"That happened to a lot of businesses in Portland then," Skater said. "Dig into it a little and see what you get."

Archangel nodded, and Skater walked over to the telecom Wheeler had rigged up with cut-outs that would make it very difficult to trace back to the apartment. Even with the security measures built in, he didn't plan on calling any numbers that were at risk.

He tapped in the number for the message drop he was using to contact Kestrel and checked in. He was informed there was a message for him. He keyed in the four-digit play sequence.

"I picked up some new biz hustling through the streets," Kestrel's voice said. "There's a guy wants to meet with you about the run. Says he has a deal. Name's Conrad McKenzie. You've probably heard of him. If not, call me and I'll give you the score. He left a number."

Skater memorized the number, then tapped the Disconnect key. He was familiar with the name, and it sent a cold, electric spike of premonition through his spine.

"What's wrong?" Archangel asked.

"My chummer passed along some buzz on the streets," Skater said. "Conrad McKenzie wants to talk with us about the biz on the freighter."

"Conrad McKenzie?" Wheeler stepped out of the kitchen with a fresh cup of soykaf in his hand. "Joker's one of the biggest Mafia bosses in the sprawl. What does he want?"

"He didn't say," Skater replied as he pushed himself out of the chair. "But he left a number."

19

"Give me your number and I'll have Mr. McKenzie get back to you when it's convenient," the woman said, her voice as prim as her pinched expression on the telecom screen.

"No," Skater replied. "I'll get back to you so you can give me a number where I can reach him. I wait more than ten minutes and you can tell him it's no longer convenient for me." He broke the connection and looked around the group. Archangel was at her deck, managing the relocate and deception programs that would mask the telecom's signature through the regional telecommunications grids. Wheeler was monitoring the feedback, ready to cut off the power if something nasty started whispering up the lines at them.

At the end of ten minutes, he called the LTG number McKenzie had left again.

"Do you have that number?" he asked without preamble.

"Yes." She read it off and didn't look or sound happy about doing it.

"Slotting high-headed bastard," she said. Abruptly the line clicked dead at the other end.

Skater listened intently to discern any other noises that might suggest someone or something else was on the line. There was nothing. A few seconds later white noise filled his ear. He glanced at Wheeler.

"We're green."

Skater punched in the number and waited to play it out. Conrad McKenzie was no lightweight on the Seattle crime scene. As brutal as he was cold-blooded, he'd carved a grim empire out for himself and his Family. Duran had added to their store of knowledge, recounting the time McKenzie had killed a yak opponent who'd been trying to muscle into a territory McKenzie had operated when younger. McKenzie had found out everything he could about the man, then tracked down his family and slaughtered them. Then he'd crippled the yak himself, destroying bone joints that took months to rebuild and burning the man with a blowtorch so he had to spend more months in tissue vats. At the end of that time, when the yak was almost recovered enough to walk by himself, McKenzie had him murdered outright. The message was clear. Animosity between the Mafia and yaks in Seattle ran deep and strong, but McKenzie apparently wanted to prove he wasn't a man to slot over.

Elvis had overheard some street buzz that McKenzie was semi-retired of late, having set himself up in a kind of judiciary position, settling disputes between lesser crime bosses. If McKenzie had dealt himself a hand in the freighter deal, the stakes were scraping the ozone.

"Skater?" The voice that answered was deep and whiskey-roughened, devoid of feeling.

"Run it down for me," Skater said. "The clock's ticking and I'm not going to stay on the line long enough for you to trace the call."

McKenzie laughed, a harsh sound. "I've been contacted by a certain party who would like to buy back the goods you liberated from them. I have no interest. I'm merely the go-between."

"Why would they come to you?" Skater asked.

"Because I have a reputation in this city as a man who can deliver what I promise. They are without many resources here in Seattle. I, however, am not."

"And you're doing this out of the goodness of your heart."

"Wrong." McKenzie seemed not to notice the sarcasm.

"I'm in this for a percentage, which I intend to collect from you and the elves."

"If you're doing the brokering," Skater pointed out, "you should take your cut from them."

"I am. But I'm nicking you for another ten percent they don't know about."

"No."

"No?" The harsh laugh sounded again. "Listen, nitbrain, you don't have a lot of choices at the moment."

"I don't have to sell the files to the elves."

"I guess not. You could hang on to them and keep running till they catch you. And they will, I promise you that, because we've already negotiated a finder's fee if I have to help them. You scan?"

"We've made it this far."

"You've been lucky so far, that's all. And the trouble with luck is that it runs out. You've got the elves after you, the yakuza, Lone Star, and from what I hear, some other small-time losers. Do you really want to add me to the list?"

"Maybe you're already there," Skater said.

"I was there," McKenzie promised, "I'd be pissing on your corpse right now."

"How much are the elves offering?"

"Three million nuyen."

"Bump them," Skater said. "Double it."

"Done." McKenzie sounded happy. "I don't mind taking twenty percent of six million nuyen instead of three. They may balk, but they don't really have a choice. My finder's fee would run them more than that. You might have jam enough to stay out of my people's hands for a few days more, but don't count on more than that."

Skater didn't argue.

"But for a percentage both ways," McKenzie said, "and zero sweat involved, I'm willing to be a go-between."

"Why should I believe that you could leverage the elves off me and my team once the deal goes down?"

"You shouldn't," McKenzie said. "Get your nuyen up front and start running like hell."

"Doesn't sound all that enticing."

"Do you have any options here? I was you, that's the way I'd handle it. Face it, you're in way over your heads. And the drek's just getting deeper. I'm offering you a way out."

Skater ignored the comment, trying to regain some momentum of his own in the conversation. Time was running out. "How'd you get my drop number?"

"Let that be a lesson to you," McKenzie said. "I know more about you than you think. So, do we have a deal?"

"I'll call you," Skater replied, "and let you know."

McKenzie gave a dry chuckle. "You've got cojones. I'll give you that. And you better call me soon, Skater, or don't bother." The connection broke, becoming a steady buzz of static.

"Doesn't sound like he gives a good slot one way or the other," Wheeler commented.

"No, he doesn't." The man left Skater with a chill and a tightness in his stomach that wasn't going to go away. He felt like he was being asked to stick his head into the mouth of a dragon.

"I don't know enough of the science involved to tell if it's a design for a virus," Archangel said. "I got into the files with a couple of homegrown decode utilities I got from a chummer. I've never tried anything like this before, but he said he uses them to reconstruct scrambled files from crashed disks. By cracking the IC with a high-octane deception program that makes me act like a System Access Node and challenges the files as they follow the sleazes, they identify themselves long enough for my browser to log on and reassemble the bits and pieces I get."

Skater was hunkered down beside her, staring hard at the confusion of chemical symbols and esoteric terms that had surfaced from the files they'd taken off the elven freighter. The rest of the team ringed them. With the turn of events, sleep was no longer an option.

"Whatever it really is," Archangel said, "it's a hybrid."

Another image surfaced on the monitor, showing a stylish though modest building deep in the heart of a metropolitan area that had seen better days.

"Portland," Elvis said. "I've done some biz there. Back when the place was a boom town."

"These are the corporate headquarters of NuGene," Archangel told them. "Their primary field of interest, as we've already seen, is in biomed research and development."

"What type of biotech?" Wheeler asked.

"Well," Archangel said over her shoulder, "they started out developing biomed facilities, but after 2052 turned strictly R&D. They haven't come out with any major commercial products yet, but basically they specialize in wetware—transplants, gene therapy, tissue tech, and regeneration. Repairing cellular damage. Mostly muscle tissue, tendons. Ultimately, they'd like to induce damaged tissue to renew itself organically." Archangel turned back to the screen. "But no one knows what they've accomplished. They've operated solely in the Tir, never gone beyond its borders."

"Until now." Skater shifted, stretching out the bruises and aches he'd collected over the last two days.

"NuGene teetered on the verge of financial collapse when the Council of Princes switched to Seattle as the Tir's primary port of call in '52," Archangel explained. "Like I said, they were the first to pioneer biomed facilities in Tir Tairngire. Up till the time Portland went bust, they were raking in the nuyen."

"I'll bet that slotted off a lot of shareholders," Trey said.

Archangel nodded. "According to newsfaxes I accessed from Portland's public databanks, the CEO decided to reinvest in his corporation rather than let it go down the tubes. As the stocks dropped in value, he spent a fortune buying them back up, hoping to prevent a takeover. For awhile, Saeder-Krupp seemed to be trying for a buyout, but gradually this guy accumulated ownership of fifty-seven percent of NuGene."

"Brave soul," Trey commented. "Fifty-seven percent of nothing, though, is the equivalent of one percent of nothing. And a drekking lot harder to afford."

"He didn't see it that way. I've read some watered-down versions of his corporate statement and mission plans. If he couldn't compete with Seattle, he'd regain what he'd lost by coming up with a product no one else could provide."

"Did he say what that was?" Wheeler asked.

"No. But he promised it for years."

"Then nobody knows if he was just blowing smoke."

"Torin Silverstaff didn't have that reputation," Archangel said.

The name rang a bell in Skater's mind. "Who?"

The elven decker repeated herself.

"Got a datapic?"

"Yes." Archangel typed in some new commands and the screen shifted to a white-haired elf at some elegant social function. "This was taken at a ball given in Lugh Surehand's honor three years ago, a year after NuGene almost went belly up. Torin Silverstaff was a reluctant guest according to the reports I've read, but he'd never given up hope of seeing Portland reinstated as the major port city for the Tir."

Torin Silverstaff looked familiar to Skater. The features were classic elven and proud. "Any relation to Tavis Silverstaff?" He suddenly remembered the name from the interview with Perri Twyst.

"Torin was his father."

"Was?" Skater asked.

"Torin was murdered in a mugging in Portland three years ago, shortly after this pic was taken. The killer was never found."

"So his son is the heir apparent."

"Yes. There was rumor of a stipulation in the inheritance. Tavis Silverstaff has three younger sisters, and his mother is still alive. To inherit the controlling interest in NuGene, Silverstaff has to provide for all of them, including their families."

"Was NuGene generating a profit at this point?" Trey asked.

Archangel shook her head. "It was still being bankrolled by Silverstaff's own nuyen. He never stopped believing that the Council of Princes would see the error of their ways and reinstate Portland."

"Long time to go without a payday," Duran rumbled.

"The corp almost went broke nineteen months ago. It had over-extended itself funding new research." Tapping the keys Archangel shifted to a picture of Tavis Silverstaff dressed in business clothes thumbprinting a document on trid footage. "Then Silverstaff picked up a number of new investors, including some support from the Council of Princes, when he announced he was going to take a stab at the Seattle market."

The monitor screen flared, then reconstructed itself into a new picture. Silverstaff was at center stage, looking a few years younger and trimmer. His hair was tied back in a flowing ponytail and he wore a tank top, shorts, and gloves in uniform colors. He carried a long stick curved at the end.

"Silverstaff was a member of the Portland Marchers," Archangel said. "Part of the National Hurling Association. He was nominated MVP two of the three years he played."

"What happened the third year?" Wheeler asked.

"He lost a knee to a deliberate maiming attempt by a Bend Journeymen player. Even after two vat jobs, it was never the same again. Silverstaff refused cyberware, maybe because he was such a natural athlete."

The monitor screen flickered and showed a new shot of Silverstaff with his father at a corporate meeting in '54, the year of the elder Silverstaff's death.

"He went to work for his father at NuGene," Archangel said. "Silverstaff is still a very popular figure in the Tir because of his career in sports. But he'd also been groomed by his father for business. He has a natural proclivity for PR. And, as you can see from recent trid footage of him, for wheeling and dealing."

"Part of the package Silverstaff is pitching to the UCC is his support for maintaining Seattle as Tir Tairngire's main port," Elvis put in. "Sounds like a conflict of interest."

"Tavis Silverstaff's a lot different from his father. Torin was strictly a first-generation elf, supporting the segregation of the races that Walter Bright Water argued for when trying to convince NAN to grant land to form the Tir nation. Tavis believes that the elves of Tir Tairngire need more interface with the human culture, as well as other nations. Especially in business. One thing he does have in common with his father is that he continues to promise that NuGene is developing a revolutionary, new product."

"With fifty-seven percent of the corp in his pocket," Wheeler said, "Silverstaff would be doing pretty slotting good if NuGene suddenly started turning a profit."

More footage spooled across the screen, detailing other shots and other business of NuGene, including some of the recent footage Skater'd already seen.

"With Silverstaff in Seattle, who's minding the store at NuGene?" Skater asked.

"Regis Blackoak." Archangel stopped the montage of pictures. A heavily jowled man easily twenty years older than Silverstaff flipped onto the monitor. "He worked for the elder Silverstaff in an advisory capacity. His politics have changed so much that Torin Silverstaff is probably rolling over in his grave." Archangel restarted the flow of images.

"Hold on," Skater suddenly gestured at the screen as Archangel froze the motion on a scene of Silverstaff dancing with his wife at some formal event. She was pregnant, but he had her in a low dip regardless. "Silverstaff isn't using a cane. Where is it? I've never seen him on the trid without his cane."

"Skater's right," Elvis said. "Ain't nothing bum about that elf's leg."

"Didn't you say NuGene's been working on repair of cellular damage?" Wheeler asked. "See how this scans—NuGene finds a way to do that, right? The CEO is living proof that it works. What do you do with this tech? Sell it to DocWagon? Set up a new DocWagon? Or set up a situation where you compete with DocWagon for biz? A crisis situation, say, where you know you'll come out on top."

"Like what type of crisis?" Archangel asked.

"Like infect people with a degenerative disease, some tissue-destroying virus, like something we got on this chip here, then sell the antidote—for a price."

"Good for a short-term infusion of nuyen," Elvis said. "Would Silverstaff have been that desperate?"

"No way," Archangel said. "With the backing the corp is getting from the Council of Princes and other wealthy investors, NuGene's solvent for at least another three years. Besides, it doesn't fit. If NuGene has a great new product, why go to all that trouble? Just put it on the market. There's no shortage of cell-damaged vat cases. Another DocWagon, though, I don't think the yaks or the Mafia would be thrilled about that." She looked at the screen. "Besides, pics can be deceiving."

Archangel wrinkled her brow as she hit another key. "I also downloaded some information from a black website on business affairs in Seattle. According to it, Silverstaff might be asked to join the United Corporation Council."

Skater looked at her. "That's impossible. No one not connected to Seattle has ever been invited to the UCC." The United Corporation Council was a formal association of the sprawl's major corporations. Behind the scenes, they manipulated more than stock prices and buy-outs. They also had considerable pull with the local politics as well as considerable sway in UCAS interests.

"The UCC must figure NuGene is going to be a success," Skater said.

"So what was on the freighter?" Duran asked.

The montage of trid shots started across the screen again.

"It might have been start-up data for the NuGene branch they're setting up here in Seattle," Archangel said.

"What are they going to try to sell?"

"R&D, just like in Portland. Other than that, I can't say."

An image flickered across the screen and registered in Skater's memory banks. "Hold it."

Archangel pressed a button and the montage stopped.

"Go back a few frames."

Slowly, the footage started backward.

"There," Skater said, when he saw the figure that had caught his attention. The face on the screen was unmistakably like that of the elf who'd broken him out of Lone Star. "Who's that?"

Archangel opened a window, then read from the file. "Ellard Dragonfletcher. He's NuGene's top security man."

"For how long?" Skater asked.

"Seven years. He rose to that post under Torin Silverstaff. There's not much else on him."

"Do some snooping," Skater said. Then he explained why. He glanced at the clock. "Almost midnight, chummers. I don't want to keep McKenzie simmering too long. Do we take the deal, or do we leave it?"

20

"There are a couple ways to work this piece of biz," Cullen Trey said.

Skater turned to him, listening closely. Trey was one of the most powerful mages he'd ever met. Where most would have run out of juice by now, exhausted by the drain on their powers, he was still able to reach in for a little more. His training was formal, but Skater didn't know where he'd gotten it. And Trey wasn't telling. But he was no slouch in the thinking department either. "Jink it out and let's scan it."

Trey turned up a palm and small lightnings flickered there. Smoke rose from his flesh and wove itself into a circling falcon about the size of his thumb, the wings long and sharp. More smoke rolled out, creating the shadowy impression of a forestscape. Amid the pseudo-trees and bushes, a rabbit hopped along at a sedate pace, unaware of the hunter.

"We could simply walk away from McKenzie and let NuGene think we have their biotech files," Trey said. In the smoky jazz coming up from his palm, the falcon ceased flying aimlessly and began tracking the rabbit and losing altitude. "In which case McKenzie might make good on his threat to work for the elves and come after us."

"He'll do it anyway," Duran said with conviction. "Even if there was no financial gain in the picture. Joker's got his rep on the come-line now."

"As I, too, believe," Trey agreed. "Conrad McKenzie isn't a man to be trifled with, and he's gone to great lengths to prove it. Another option would be to go directly to the elves and sell them back the copies of the incomplete files and tell them we weren't able to get everything."

Wheeler growled his displeasure. "Then why pay us for the incomplete files? At best we're getting the elves off our necks and flushing any chance of seeing any nuyen from this fiasco right down the drekker. Besides, since when are elves known for their forgiving natures? Admitting that we haven't got what they want would be giving up our last defense. Kind of like declaring open season—on ourselves."

"Not if they think we're trying to hide what we really have," Trey said. The falcon closed the distance between itself and the rabbit, matching trajectories and readying itself for the kill.

"NuGene may try to whack us to keep anyone else from getting the bioresearch," Duran pointed out.

"Not," Trey said, "if they believe we've got backup copies ready to be released to all comers in the event of our untimely demise." As the falcon closed on its prey, the rabbit turned and launched itself at the would-be predator, changing into a bobcat and revealing itself as a shapeshifter in disguise.

"It could work," Archangel said. "At this juncture, we're running out of options."

"Agreed." Skater stood and worked the kinks out of his knees as Trey's smoke illusion vanished. "Remaining in hiding might buy us a few more days, but I think we've learned as much as we can by keeping out of the eye of the storm. NuGene has shadow biz working and someone sold them out. If we lay down and play dead hoping they'll go away, they've got a better chance of hiding it again. By confronting NuGene through McKenzie, we can keep the pot stirred up. Hopefully, something useful will float to the top during the confusion. Without us getting geeked."

"Sounds like a plan to me," Duran said.

Skater shrugged. "It's an opening gambit. If it's true the *Sapphire Seahawk* was a Trojan horse as we suspect, the elves know we're not holding anything. If we try to sell it back, they may have to buy it just to keep their cover intact even though they know our files are corrupted beyond use."

"Which would spell profit for us." Wheeler rubbed his hands together and grinned. "That, I like."

"One of the real questions about the situation hasn't been answered," Skater said. "How does NuGene know we haven't already sold the files to a Mr. Johnson?"

"They whacked Maddock," Elvis said. "Could be they found out from him that Larisa gave you the buzz on the Seahawk and that we worked the run as independents."

"Who gave them Maddock?" Skater asked.

"Better yet, who gave Maddock the elves?" Trey added.

"If NuGene found the leak in their own ranks," Archangel said, "they could have learned about Larisa, and through her, learned of Maddock."

"Another possibility," Elvis said, "is that NuGene's topdogs didn't tell their sec-teams about the Trojan horse and that they'd intentionally leaked the information. If the sec-teams were sold out and figure it out, there's going to be lawsuits galore, and maybe the more personal kilo of flesh demanded as well."

Skater nodded. "It scans." But he still wanted to know for sure. If the elves were so ready to kill over hijacked files they knew were corrupt—or even if they didn't know—it meant that a lot of nuyen was at risk and NuGene was still vulnerable somewhere. "However else we read this, we were set up. I want to know by who and I want to know why. First up, though, is Conrad McKenzie, and here's how I plan on dealing with that."

Skater bribed his way into a table on the lower level of the Gray Line, one of Seattle's most elegant eateries as well as claiming the distinction of actually sitting right in Puget Sound rather than alongside it. At high tide the waters of the Sound rose up enough to touch the transparent walls of the lower dining area.

With a sharp snap of his fingers, the maître d' directed an impeccably dressed hostess to take Skater and Duran to a large table. She led the way down the red carpeted stairs and through a foyer lined with paintings depicting the history of Puget Sound during the past four hundred years. All of the art centered on sailing vessels, from Indian canoes to American trading clippers to twentieth-century fishing boats to the latest Harland & Wolff "Classique" motor yacht, and were rendered in a variety of mediums.

Skater and Duran were dressed to fit in with the posh crowd, both wearing custom-made Vashon Island suits just as carefully tailored to hide the weapons they carried. The Gray Line sec-teams had no objection to patrons being armed with guns, only against someone trying to use them inside the restaurant.

The hostess led them through the islands of tables. Floating candles in the shape of flowers burned a delicate incense that sharpened the palate, and the soft glows were reflected against the floor-to-ceiling wall of glass that fronted Puget Sound. Underwater lights and beacons attracted the native marine life. Seals and otters, their biological clocks formed more from the feeding times and the lights put out by the restaurant than anything nature had intended, frolicked within view of the diners. The lights changed the water to shimmering greens and lit up fluorescent-bearing fish in glowing obelisks.

"Would you like to see a menu?" the hostess asked. "I'm afraid this late at night we don't serve our full line, but the sandwiches are quite good."

"Thanks, but I think we'll just be having drinks." Skater passed the menus back, then ordered a shot and a beer for Duran and mineral water for himself.

Duran leaned back casually against the plush cushions of the three-quarter booth surrounding the table as the waitress left. "We're not alone."

"I count five," Skater said, staring at the wall of glass keeping the Sound out.

"You missed two," the ork said. "Did you pick up the women?"

A cocktail waitress arrived with the drinks and set them down on imprinted napkins. In the sea scene, a sea turtle pursued a purple squid that Skater guessed the restaurant management had ordered infoetically altered for enhanced viewing ease, planing through the water like an undersea fighter plane and gaining by centimeters.

"One of them," Skater answered when the waitress left. "Hot number in pink flirting with the suit at the corner bar."

"The other woman's holding hands with the slag guarding the entrance. He's gotta be a shaman."

Skater checked the reflection in the wall of glass and noted the two people the ork had picked out. "You're right. I missed them both."

On the other side of the glass wall, the sea turtle clamped its sharp jaws on two of the purple glowing squid's tentacles. Although the infoe-coded coloring was interesting to watch, Skater figured it pretty much sealed the squid's doom, leaving it no way to hide. He wondered how many of the creatures the restaurant's owners had to import each week to keep the sport up.

He accessed the Commlink IV. "Wheeler, where the slot are you?" he subvocalized.

"Two minutes, chummer," the dwarf responded. "I'll have everything in place." The rigger was supposed to be setting up in a boat anchored at the dock above.

"Good enough." Skater watched as the turtle tried to pull the squid in closer, only to have the remaining tentacles suddenly wrap around its shell. With the tangle of tentacles and the hidden strength in the squid, the turtle was in trouble as well. If the squid could hold out long enough, Skater knew it would drown the turtle.

"Gutsy little fragger," Duran said appreciatively, then glanced over at the entrance. "McKenzie just made the party."

Skater glanced at the approaching group, recognized McKenzie from files Archangel had accessed for him, then glanced deliberately back at the neon clock hanging above the bar. It was two-thirteen.

Conrad McKenzie was in the lead, a solid, blocky man several centimeters taller than Skater, and weighing at least twice that many kilos more. Even at this hour of the morning, his face gleamed like he'd shaven only moments ago. His salt and pepper hair was cut long and swept back from his high forehead. His suit was obviously real silk, and he carried a long raincoat over one arm.

Ellard Dragonfletcher was at McKenzie's left looking almost military in his own crisp, immaculate garb. At his side was a young female elf in wraparound nightshades and Zoe exec wear.

"She's razored," Duran warned.

"She goes," Skater said. He stood, not wanting anyone to mistake his seated position as a sign of weakness or overconfidence because either was deadly.

"Mr. Trump," the hostess said, "your party has arrived."

"Thank you," Skater said, slotting her a tip. He remained standing, squaring off against McKenzie and Dragonfletcher as they came within a few steps of him. "The woman goes." He didn't offer to shake hands or make any other gesture to relieve the tension of the meeting.

McKenzie locked eyes with him and Skater returned the stare.

"Mr. Dragonfletcher?" McKenzie said.

Skater never took his eyes off the Mafia man.

"Might I suggest to you," the elf said to Skater, "that you're in no position to be making demands at this point."

"Sure. Suggest away. But you're going to be doing it to my back."

McKenzie's half-smile was cold and calculating. "You don't leave until I say you do."

Skater reached inside himself and turned off the feelings, letting the adrenaline take over. He went to that place where fear didn't exist and anger wasn't even a memory. "I noticed the torpedoes and yabos you've got stationed around this place. I count seven. But you need to reconsider your own position. If I don't think I'm getting out of here, why should I let you?"

There was only a moment's hesitation before McKenzie spoke. "Ellard, do you still wish to deal?"

"I don't call it dealing if I'm listening to terms," the elf said gruffly.

"The razorgirl sits at another table," Duran stated. "I'm not going to have a knife at my throat while I'm sitting here."

"Yet your man stays," Dragonfletcher said.

"He's a full partner in this," Skater said. "His vote counts. And while you're thinking that over, here's something else you can consider: if we don't walk away from this tête-à-tête tonight, copies of those files get dumped straight onto the Shadowland network for anybody to download and sell wherever they can."

"You can't do that." Dragonfletcher's voice was hard.

"Your choice," Skater said. "But I'd decide soon. Standing here like this, we're losing whatever anonymity we started out with."

Dragonfletcher nodded curtly at the razorgirl and she walked away. He and McKenzie took seats across the table from Duran and Skater.

"It's ready, Jack." That was Wheeler's voice coming over Skater's headlink.

Skater lifted his glass to drink and subvocalized over the link before the water touched his lips. The glass masked his response. "Stand by."

The turtle's corpse drifted lazily through the green waters behind McKenzie. The squid was a pastel purple haze drifting away, wounded but alive.

"There are just the two of you?" McKenzie asked.

"Here," Skater replied, "yes. On the operation, no."

"I'd heard you'd lost at least one of your people, perhaps more."

"You hear pretty good for someone just walking into the deal," Skater said.

McKenzie smiled. "I like to look over any interesting proposition before deciding to get in."

"You have the credstick?" Skater asked Dragonfletcher.

"Yes. Provided you've got the files."

Carefully, knowing there were at least eight guns on him, Skater reached inside his jacket and took out the chip Archangel had prepared. He laid the chip-holder on the table in front of him, not offering it to either man.

Dragonfletcher reached inside his jacket, slowly pulling out the credstick, gradually unveiling its length. He held it between his forefingers, then handed it to McKenzie to pass over, as if touching Skater was beneath him.

Skater knew the elf didn't see McKenzie switch the credstick for another, taking his ten percent from the team's fee. The original credstick disappeared and McKenzie extended the second one.

"I think you'll find everything here," McKenzie said.

"Will I?" Skater asked.

"Yes."

Skater took the credstick, but before his fingers could close around it, Dragonfletcher placed a restraining hand on top of his.

"We need to address a few things first," he said.

"I'm listening," Skater said as he flicked his gaze to the elf. He raised his other hand to warn Duran off. The ork had bridled and bared his fangs.

"The other copies of the files," Dragonfletcher said, "I'll want them destroyed."

"They will be," Skater said. He didn't fight against the restraining grip.

"I want to be able to trust you."

Skater nodded, but it was McKenzie who spoke. "I told him we could deal with you," he said, flipping open a gold case and taking out a French cigarette. A built-in lighter ignited the tip and he put the case away. He narrowed his eyes against the smoke as he exhaled. "I had you checked out."

"When?" Skater asked.

"This afternoon."

Skater turned the information over in his mind. He didn't trust McKenzie at all.

"Like I said," McKenzie told Dragonfletcher, "for a shadowrunner, I think you'll find Mr. Skater has scruples."

Reluctantly, the elf withdrew his hand.

"Since we're clearing things up," Skater said, "I've got a few questions myself." He turned his hand over and let the point of the credstick touch the table surface. He focused on Dragonfletcher. "I know you had Maddock killed. I want to know why."

"He's part of the reason you and I are here now," Dragonfletcher answered.

"He leaked information about the NuGene files?" Skater asked.

Looking puzzled, Dragonfletcher glanced at McKenzie, who shrugged.

"The way I heard it," the Mafia boss said, "Skater was doing business through Maddock. But there could have been a cut-out along the way. I also heard he's the guy who tipped the yaks."

Dragonfletcher's gaze hardened as he stared at Skater. "Now that you've got that credstick in your hand, are you trying to squeeze a few more nuyen out of us by selling out your contacts? If so, I question my judgment in dealing with you."

"No. This chip represents all the dealing I'm going to do with NuGene." Skater tapped it, reminding them that he hadn't pushed it across. "I want the name of whoever's responsible for Larisa Hartsinger's death."

"I don't know," Dragonfletcher said.

Anger coiled inside Skater, as restless as a deathrattle. "I don't believe you."

"You wound me," the elf replied.

"I want the name of her killer," Skater said, leaning in and making his voice harsh. "And I want to know where her child is." He was conscious of movement around him, including Duran, who was shifting for a better field of fire.

"I don't know, I tell you." Dragonfletcher's voice was calm, pitched low.

Skater knew it was possible that the elf had merely assigned some wetwork specialists to the hit without knowing a name. "You can find out."

"Why should I?"

"Because without that name," Skater said, "you've only got half a deal." Deliberately, he let the credstick drop, then pushed it back at the elf with a forefinger. From the corner of his eye, he saw that McKenzie's reaction was subtle, but the crime boss definitely didn't like the way things were shaping up.

"What are you doing?" Dragonfletcher demanded.

"Leaving," Skater told him. He picked up the chip-holder and slipped it back into his inside jacket pocket.

"You do and you're a dead man," McKenzie warned. "Nobody fragging tries to make me look like a slotting nitbrain. We've got a deal."

"I'm a dead man," Skater said fiercely, "and those files hit the Matrix the heartbeat after."

For a moment, McKenzie held his gaze. Then, "I don't believe you."

"McKenzie," Dragonfletcher interrupted.

"Let me handle this," McKenzie said. "That's what you're paying me for." He shifted his attention to Skater. "You move another muscle, drekhead, and I'm going to take that chip off your corpse."

Skater faced McKenzie, but he spoke to Dragonfletcher. "Is that how you want it? You want the files on that chip spread all over the Matrix?"

"No. McKenzie, sit down." The elf glanced around, aware that they were attracting unwanted attention.

McKenzie's expression was cold and calculated. Anger

burned deep in his dark eyes. "You're making a mistake here. I just want you to know that."

"Depends," Duran said softly. "Could be you're the one making the mistake." His posture remained loose, but his tone left no doubt about his readiness for action.

Suddenly, McKenzie sat. "No sense in fragging up a perfectly good deal when all I've got to do is sit here. Right?" He shook out a fresh cigarette and lit up.

Skater sat down too, but held himself ready to move in an instant.

"What if I can't get the name of the girl's killer?" Dragonfletcher asked.

"I'll give you till ten o'clock tomorrow morning," Skater replied. "If you can prove to me that you spent time and effort on the search, we can deal then."

"Ten o'clock." Dragonfletcher stared at him.

"Another eight hours isn't going to make a major difference to whatever you're involved in," Skater said.

"Ten o'clock is acceptable," the elf said. "Anything after that, we hunt you down and you can try to make good on your threats."

"It's no threat," Skater said. He took a card out of his pocket. "Here's a number where you can leave a message for me. It'll be operational in the morning, from nine-fifty-five to ten-oh-five a.m. You can't trace it, you can't find it. The number and the exchange won't exist until then, and it'll disappear forever afterwards." Archangel was redirecting the com-call trail.

Dragonfletcher put the card in his jacket pocket. "Why the interest in this woman?"

"She was a friend," Skater said. "I don't have many of those."

The elf nodded.

"Take care of this," Skater said, pushing the credstick toward the elf again. "We'll be wanting it back." He could tell from the way McKenzie shifted that he wanted the credstick back himself to make the switch again, but there was no way to ask for it. He knew that Dragonfletcher would check the credstick over, especially since Skater had held it for a time. When the elf did, he'd find the ten percent missing. It wouldn't make sense for Skater to take it and leave the rest, so Dragonfletcher would jump logically to the conclusion that McKenzie had tried to cut himself in for a bigger piece of the biz. Skater wondered how the partnership would weather that revelation.

Dragonfletcher pocketed the credstick but didn't say anything.

Skater stood up and looked at McKenzie. "Maybe we'll be seeing each other again."

"Count on it," the Mafia boss said.

No matter what else happened, Skater knew he'd made a dangerous enemy by double-crossing McKenzie.

No sooner had the thought crossed his mind than a fusillade of gunshots suddenly exploded the quiet decorum of the restaurant. Skater ducked immediately and palmed the Predator II from the streamlined holster on his belt.

"C'mon!" Duran roared, grabbing the back of Skater's jacket and hustling him away from the entrance to the lower dining room. He had a Ceska Black Scorpion in his hand spitting flame and thunder.

At first, Skater thought that one of McKenzie's gunners had opened fire. Then he spotted the grim faces of what could only be yakuza marching into the room, systematically setting up fields of fire and burning down anyone who tried to stop them. The yaks were easy to spot, dressed in black suits and wearing enhanced sunglasses even at night.

The Mafia gunners held their ground, overturning tables to set up makeshift gunports. Bullets chewed into the furniture, but the noise level was low as the snarl of silencers wound through the restaurant.

"Wheeler," Duran called over the commlink, "get ready."

"Call it," the dwarf replied, "and I'm there."

Skater brought up his pistol and fired two rounds at a yakuza who was moving into the main dining area and sweeping the diners mercilessly. He aimed for the man's chest, not wanting to chance a headshot.

The bullets crashed and knocked the dark-suited man back. Skater wasn't sure if the bullets actually struck flesh or just flattened out against Kevlar. Duran released Skater's jacket, evidently satisfied that he was keeping up.

They reached the corner opposite the entrance at the same instant someone cut the power to the dining room. Darkness swallowed the recessed lighting in an eyeblink. Only the floodlights outside the glass wall and the uncertain scattering of muzzle flashes trapped inside the room provided any kind of illumination.

Skater switched over to low-light vision and scanned the impromptu battlefield. Evidently the yakuza had come prepared for the lights-out situation, because they were moving freely. Obviously many of them were wearing low-light glasses. However, a squadron of elves had also rushed onto the scene, outnumbering the yakuza in seconds. McKenzie and Dragonfletcher must have had an army standing by outside the restaurant. The bloody tide of the small war quickly turned.

"Skater fragging sold us out to the yakuza!" McKenzie roared. "It's a set-up!"

Tracking the voice, Skater scanned the dining area and spotted McKenzie kneeling behind a yakuza slumped across an overturned chair. The crime boss had both hands wrapped around a Manhunter that was sprouting a ruby beam.

Light blinded Skater for a second, then he was aware of the ruby dot that took shape just below his left eye. He was moving when he felt the force hit him, knocking his head back against the wall. He struggled with consciousness as his back scraped and bumped him down the wall and the blood ran warm down his face.

21

Throbbing pain filled Skater's head and he had to fight to get his arms and legs moving. His vision doubled, then blurred, and the low-light enhancers fragged up his depth perception altogether by overreacting to light and shadow.

"Kid!" Duran roared from somewhere nearby.

Skater tracked the ork's voice amid the gunfire and screams. Gunpowder stink filled the air. He turned his head and concentrated on the rectangle of light coming from the wall of glass. Evidently the floodlights out in the Sound operated independently of the ones inside the Gray Line. Shapes slipped across the glass surface and threw moving shadows into the room, but he couldn't distinguish what they were.

A yakuza came out of the darkness at him, chipped eyes

gleaming in the dark. He carried a taser, and the dart on the end sparked blue-white electricity.

Skater raised the Predator and fired till the man went down. Dumping the empty clip, he shoved another one home. He activated the commlink. "Trey."

"I'm here, chummer." Trey was positioned out of sight and using an external mike.

Skater threw himself behind an overturned table and had to shove the corpse of one of McKenzie's men out of the way. Bullets and fletchettes thudded into the table top. One of them skidded off the Kevlar weave of his jacket. The side of his face was covered with a warm, bloody mask. He couldn't tell how bad it was, but his vision was coming back on-line. "Time to go."

"I'm ready. On your mark."

At the back of the room, highlighted by the uneven illumination coming from the glass wall, McKenzie's shaman stood making intricate gestures while his razored girlfriend stood guard. She'd taken a clear bulletproof shield from a shopping bag at her feet and was holding it in front of their faces. Bullets drew lines of fire across the surface.

"Shaman's scanning a bead on us," Duran warned.

"I see him," Skater said. Another fusillade of bullets tore chunks from the table as two Mafia yabos came streaking toward his position. He got his feet under him, knowing it was all going to happen quickly. Blood blurred the vision in his left eye and tasted of salt on his lips.

A fireball flickered into view in the shaman's hand, then arced the length of the room with a fiery tail twisting out behind it. As Skater abandoned his position, the ball of fire struck the table and reduced it to flaming splinters that pinwheeled through the air.

The smoke given off by the blast cut deep into his lungs. Oxygen in the nearby area was reduced.

Counting on the distraction of the fireball exploding so close to the two men rushing him, Skater threw himself into the air and hit the second man with a flying kick. He landed, keeping his footing with difficulty as the after-effect of the fireball shot a glare of light across the room. Before the first man could turn, Skater shoved the Predator to the back of the man's skull and pulled the trigger.

The corpse dropped to the restaurant floor, most of its head missing.

McKenzie was in front of him, but partially blocked by yak gunners and the restaurant's panicked clientele. Gripped by a berserker rage, McKenzie shot into the screaming crowd. A mother and a small child went spinning away from the gunfire. They'd never had a chance to get clear.

The sight made Skater sick, but he couldn't fire at McKenzie without hitting innocents himself. "Wheeler!" he yelled over the subdermal radio. "Blow the glass!"

"Fire in the hole!" the dwarf responded from the boat waiting at the dock above.

Skater looked at the wall of glass in front of him. A frozen instant juiced by the adrenaline hitting his nervous system afforded him a crystal-clear clarity. He felt a bullet smash into the back of his leg against the Kevlar, buckling his knee with numbing force. He almost went down, but maintained his stance through an effort of will.

The glass wall had been pockmarked by earlier gunfire. Bullets were stuck in the glass in misshapen chunks of lead. Cracks bled away from them like crater veins. The damage distorted the view and affected magnification.

Without warning, but right on cue, the glass wall shattered into thousands of shards and the water rushed in. Emergency klaxons shrilled. Panels moved away from the baseboards of the walls, revealing drains. Pump engines fired to life, the sound venting through the drains.

It was all going as planned. Skater had known about the pumps because of a robbery a few years ago here at the Gray Line. The incident had escalated to a gun battle with Lone Star and to the shattering of the original glass panes in the restaurant's wall. Twelve people had drowned and jewelry worth a hundred thousand nuyen had been washed out into the Sound. Divers still occasionally combed the area looking for it, but it had never been found. Lawrence Bjelland, the owner of the Gray Line, had rebuilt the room and added in the emergency pumping stations against further accidents and incidents.

The water came over Skater in a rush, cold and briny, and filled with the flip-flop of the rainbow-colored fish that glowed in the dark. He remained standing with difficulty, the Predator tight in his hand. Salt burned in the wound along the side of his head. In a heartbeat, the water level had risen from his ankles to his thighs, swirling across chairs and tables, pushing everything before it.

He shoved an approaching chair out of the way and looked around for Duran. The ork was out of the torrent's way, holding his own in the corner beside the shattered glass wall, his hair matted to him like an animal's. He was firing measured shots in various directions, targeting both Mafia and yakuza gunners.

"Duran!" Skater yelled.

"Move!" the ork responded, dropping an empty clip from the Scorpion and feeding in another.

Angry voices were lost over the rush of the invading water, but Skater could hear McKenzie yelling orders to kill Duran and him. He tapped the subdermal radio, hoping Trey would still be able to hear him. "Trey."

"I'm still here, chummer."

Skater fought his way through the water as it flooded up to his waist. It would be only seconds before he could no longer challenge the incoming tide, and the strength of the water didn't appear to be flagging. He spared a glance toward the entrance and spotted Trey at the side of the open double doors, where he'd been waiting in reserve. Skater was relieved to see that the restaurant's patrons were beating a hasty retreat from the dining room through the double doors, guided by the Gray Line wait staff.

Trey gestured and a shimmering wave descended on the water around Skater. A small typhoon took shape in front of him, then whirled up to four meters over Skater's head. Bits and pieces of silverware, cocktail napkins, glasses, bottles, and furniture swirled within it.

Fully formed, the murky giant stood in the midst of the rushing water on legs as thick as telephone poles. Tracer rounds burned hot and bright as they ripped through its liquid flesh without doing any damage. The water elemental's features were barely formed, but conveyed intense anger. Trey had summoned it hours before, then held it ready to perform whatever service he required. Waves rolled in obedience to its outstretched hands, engulfing yakuza and Mafia gunners who dared stand before it.

"Go, Jack," Trey said. "I'll meet you topside." Without another word, the mage left his position and sprinted across the room, diving headfirst into the surging water.

"I've got your back," Duran said, "then I'll be along."

Skater dived into the water too, striking out for the collapsed wall. Instead of having to fight the in-rush of the

Sound, the current carried him along, flowing in the opposite direction of the liters of water pouring in. He knew it was Trey's doing, bending the water elemental's powers to his will.

He twisted and shot through the jagged fangs of the glass shards still hanging in the slots of the wall. The fish were swept away from him as well. Then the force moving him disappeared, leaving him weightless in the dark. A sense of buoyancy returned and he followed it up, the wet clothes slowing his ascent.

The water thinned above him. Moonlight pushed its way into the depths, except for a rough triangular shape to his left. He broke the surface and glanced back at the shadow, his breath burning in his lungs.

Wheeler Iron-Nerve, still clad in the scuba gear he'd used to plant the charges around the restaurant's glass wall, impatiently paced the deck of the Aztech Nightrunner he'd borrowed—for a price—from another rigger. Spotting Skater, the dwarf hurried over and offered a hand. "Get a fragging move on. We hang around here much longer, we're going to get our tickets punched."

Skater took the hand and fought down the nausea spinning from his wound. The dwarf was strong enough to lift him almost bodily from the water.

"Catch one?" Wheeler asked, running a rough hand across Skater's head. He peered closely.

"Almost." Skater brushed the hand away irritably. He turned and glanced back into the black depths. He accessed the subdermal. "Duran."

"On our way, kid," Duran answered. An instant later he broke the surface, shaking the water from his eyes, then getting his bearings. Trey came up less than a meter away. They swam for the boat.

Skater looked back toward the dock area, listening to the swelling voices drifting in from the Gray Line. The Nightrunner's low-slung design kept it lower than the docks jutting up as a bulwark against the storm season and blocking the restaurant itself from his view.

"They're coming," Wheeler said as he bolted for the enclosed cockpit.

Skater knew the rigger wasn't referring to Duran and Trey, who were scrambling over the side of the boat onto the deck. Even with the nausea swirling inside his brain, he could tell that some of the voices beyond the docks were getting closer. He lifted the Predator and readied himself.

The Nightrunner's cockpit only held two seats. Wheeler took one and jacked himself into the vehicle's control panel. The engine rumbled to life, quiet, even though the quiver that ran through the boat like the anticipatory wiggles of a BTL chiphead was something short of a low-Richter earthquake.

Trey stumbled as he tried to get to his feet on the Nightrunner's soaked deck. Even with the anti-skid matting overlaying the nonmetallic composites making up the hull, walking across the craft wasn't easy.

Skater reached out to help, but the mage drew his arm away.

"Easy, chummer," Trey cautioned in a drained tone. "I zigged when I should have zagged back there." He held up his arm. A gash ran the length of his forearm from wrist to elbow. Ivory bone gleamed through the blood that dripped onto the hull and stained his clothing. His face was blanched white. "Kevlar wasn't exactly designed to handled glass. I can fix this, though."

The mage's voice dropped off to a whisper, and Skater wasn't sure if the last comment was made to him or was intended as self-reassurance.

Skater pushed Trey toward the cockpit. "Get in and keep your head down."

Almost listlessly, the mage dropped into the other seat, cradling his wounded arm. His head lolled backward suddenly, and the sight drained out of his open eyes.

"Take care of him," Skater told Wheeler.

The dwarf nodded. "I've got him. You two hold on back there, because we're going to be fragging hell for leather."

Duran was already crouched down at the back of the cockpit with one hand on a grip, and the barrel of his gun propped on the edge of the boat. He ripped loose a sustained burst from the Scorpion across the front of the docks, driving back the shadows that had suddenly clustered there. Muzzle flashes streaked the night and highlighted the ancient wooden ramparts mixed in with the plascrete replacements.

Skater grabbed the other grip at the back of the cockpit. "Go!" he yelled to Wheeler.

Bullets pounded against the Nightrunner's hull and

bounced off the reinforced cockpit with a flurry of sparks. Chunks of the anti-skid matting ripped loose and went spinning away.

The inboard Marine turbine kicked in with a vengeance. The boat sank a few centimeters at first as the power shoved it forward, then gradually rose out of the water as speed and the curved prow lifted it clear.

Skater hung on, closing his fist and willing the flesh to meld into a single unit around the grip. The flickering muzzle flashes grew rapidly smaller along the dock and the sparks of bullets striking the Nightrunner ended.

"No pursuit," Duran yelled over the roar of the engine and the slap of the waves out on the flat surface of the Sound. "We'll make it."

Skater nodded. The only thing that could shut them down at this point was a quick-response helo team from Lone Star. He gazed at the cloud-filled sky. That, however, didn't appear in the offing.

Trey had slumped over even farther, but the blood coming from the wound seemed to be slowing down.

"How is he?" Skater asked Wheeler.

The dwarf remained concentrated on the controls. "He's hanging in there. Still breathing. That's always a good sign."

Skater nodded and hunkered down beside the cockpit.

"I guess we don't have to wonder about McKenzie anymore," Duran said. The ork's face was tight against the chill wind, but his eyes burned. "Son of a slitch had no problem turning on us back there. Probably would have given Dragonfletcher our heads on a pike if the price was right."

Skater nodded.

"He figured you were lying about dumping the files into the Matrix," the ork said.

"Maybe," Skater agreed. "And maybe he knew that the files were corrupt."

"You know that?" Duran asked. "Or you think that?"

"At the moment, I'm wondering," Skater answered honestly. "A lot." He cursed quietly, worrying about Trey, about the baby, and feeling the loss of Larisa even more as he realized he was running from the gunfight and didn't really have anything to run to. Somewhere in the mix of violent events of the last thirty hours, the pieces to the puzzle were there. He just couldn't find them.

22

"That's the second Lone Star heavy cruiser I've seen in the last five minutes," Wheeler said from the driver's seat of the Leyland-Rover as they cut through the streets of downtown Seattle.

Seated in the back so he could watch over the sleeping form of Cullen Trey, Skater stared through the bug-crusted windshield as the van rolled toward Archibald's apartment. He watched the ruby taillights of the Lone Star cruiser glide through the narrow streets away from them.

"They're running sections," Duran commented. He sat forward in the shotgun seat, the Scorpion still clutched in one hand. "Got foot patrols equipped with crawlers out, too." He pointed.

Skater followed the line of sight as the van passed through an intersection. Two blocks down, a trio of Lone Star uniforms in their distinctive colors were kicking open a door. An Aztechnology GCR-23C Crawler painted Lone Star blue and yellow waited in automated bliss at their feet, no larger than a bread box. It was a snooper drone, designed to penetrate buildings with vidscanners, keeping risk to flesh and blood at a minimum.

"I doubt they're out canvassing the neighborhood for opinions on how to improve their service," Skater said. He used the commlink to try the number they'd set up at the apartment.

A tinny female voice informed him that he'd reached a number that was no longer in service. He broke the connection, then tried Archibald's original number. It rang five times but went unanswered. Trey was still unconscious, but the ripped flesh along his arm was showing signs of reknitting.

"Pull over and stop," Skater told Wheeler three blocks from the apartment. "Give Duran and me five minutes to hit the apartment and scan the scene. If you get a call from me, at that time or before, come ahead. Anything after that, take off and save your own hoops."

Wheeler nodded and began pulling over, killing the van's lights as he glided in next to the curb.

Skater ditched his tie as the Leyland-Rover came to a stop. In suits, they were definitely overdressed for the neighborhood. Even if they didn't attract Lone Star attention, the night would already have unleashed plenty of street predators. He left the jacket unbuttoned and rolled up the sleeves. Flashing a grin at Duran, he said, "We dress down enough, maybe the local sleazers will think we've already been rolled tonight."

Duran tucked the Scorpion up into the shoulder sling under his jacket. "They don't want to make the mistake of jumping us. I ain't in the mood anymore."

Skater unlocked the back door and stepped out. After being out on Puget Sound, he found the city air muggy and doughy, making him sweat under the wet clothes even before they'd covered the first block. Duran was to his right and a half-step back. Glancing in the shop windows as he went, Skater used the ones not covered over by gray duct tape and plastiboard to scan for anyone who might be showing unwanted interest in their passage. The reflected images were dark and ghostly as they drifted along the street.

He thought about the times Larisa had argued with him, trying to persuade him to leave the biz, get out of shadowrunning. He remembered only too vividly how abandoned he'd felt when she'd left him, and how that had evoked all the baggage he'd carried with him from the Council lands into his mother's home and beyond. Thinking about all that had happened tonight while dodging and fleeing and fighting for his life, he realized how closed-in he'd kept his world. The people he was now depending on were ones he'd deliberately kept at arm's length. He suddenly realized how little he knew about them, how little he knew about anyone in his life. The insight trickled through his mind like cold mercury.

He glanced at Archibald's door a short way ahead. The security light over the door was still dark from when Elvis had removed the bulb. Three minutes and eleven seconds had passed.

"Duran," Skater said.

"Yeah, kid."

"You got a hobby?"

Three steps passed in silence. "A hobby?"

"Yeah." Skater stepped off the curb, looked up and down

the street, then started across. A breeze kicked up and blew papers, wrappers, and plastifoam cups bouncing along ahead of them. "Something you do in between jobs. You know."

"You sure you didn't get your wetware scrambled back there?" Duran asked in a casual tone.

"I'm sure." Less than a hundred paces separated them from the darkened door. Skater slid the Predator free and kept it hidden beside his leg.

"You want to tell me why you're interested in this now?"

"Because there might not be a later." Skater didn't want to try to put all the tangled emotions he was feeling into words. There was so much going on, so much to sort out, and his time might already be nearly up.

"Horses," Duran said. "I like to go to the races. Straight ones, though, where it's only heart and muscle that makes the difference. Not tech."

"Win much?" Skater looked at the big ork beside him, surprised at his own interest now that he'd breached forbidden ground.

Duran shook his head. "I never bet."

"Then why go?"

"To see 'em run," Duran said. "I just like to see 'em run."

Skater considered it, then decided that was probably as good a reason as any.

"And I like the Sloppies, too," Duran went on as they gained the other side of the street. "And watching the women. Females get crazy when money's changing hands and they never know if they've won until the horses hit the wire. And they dress nice. Synthleather pants that fit like a monofilament edge."

"Have you got somebody . . ." Skater hesitated over the word choice as they walked under a tattered steel-framed awning. ". . . somebody special?"

"A woman, you mean?"

"Yeah."

"Sometimes. Me and women, it's a nice thought, but kind of like mixing oil and vinegar. Got to keep it really shook up to make it run smooth. I don't have that kind of time to invest, and I've never found one who could keep my interest for that long. I've been told I'm hard to get to know."

Skater nodded, remembering conversations with Larisa. "And you're too controlling, too guarded, too paranoid."

"Bingo."

"But you try."

"Not as often as I used to."

Skater felt perspiration run down the side of his face. A crimson-tinted bead paused at the corner of his eye till he blinked it away. He took a fresh grip on the pistol as he walked to within knocking range of the apartment door. Four minutes thirty-seven seconds had elapsed. "I hope you get to see the horses run again once this is over."

"Me too, kid."

Before Skater could touch his knuckles to the door's surface, it opened. He hadn't walked right in just in case the apartment had already been invaded by Lone Star and no one was watching the door. Surprising a lax sentry could have led to a gun battle that he definitely didn't want.

At the side of the door, Duran was already in position with the Scorpion out in the open.

"We're leaving," Archangel said as she came to the door. "The lease is up on this place." She had her deck in its case and was dressed to go. "Anything we couldn't carry has been destroyed. Where's the car?"

Elvis stood behind her, a large suitcase in each hand. He eyed the street warily.

Skater called Wheeler over the link. "Let's go."

"On my way," the dwarf replied. Three blocks down, the van's headlights came on and carved tunnels in the shadows. The vehicle pulled smoothly out into the street.

Archangel obviously didn't feel comfortable standing in the doorway. She started toward the van at a sedate pace.

Skater fell into step beside her, feeling her tension and seeing it in the rigidity of her movements. "Problem?"

"You and Duran were made to this area by some street snitch," Archangel said. "They broke it on the trid not long ago. You're still wanted in connection with Larisa's murder. Lone Star only started the house-to-house searches about forty-five minutes ago. Some of the crews got pulled once the action began at the restaurant." The van pulled up alongside them, and she took a seat beside Trey, who was conscious once again.

The seam on the mage's arm looked shiny and pink and new, like a sunburned strip. Skater didn't think it would scar at all.

"I take it the meeting didn't go well," Archangel said.

"No," Skater told her as he took a seat further back.

"McKenzie's not exactly thrilled with us at the moment." He explained about the switched credsticks. "I was figuring on cutting him out of the loop so we'd have only the elves to deal with. I'm sure they don't have their own base of operations here in Seattle yet. I thought maybe it would give us some breathing room with McKenzie out of the way. But it seems like McKenzie fed the elves some lies."

Duran took the passenger seat up front again while Elvis dumped the baggage into the back and shut the door. He had a hard time getting his bulk comfortable as he took a seat beside Skater.

"The yakuza showed up too," Trey said. "Unannounced. Which means someone tipped them off. Again. All in all, the whole little party was absolutely fascinating. It's hard to keep up with who might be double-crossing who at any given moment."

"Doyukai's people?" Elvis asked.

"Probably," Duran answered. "What with all the hell breaking loose, we didn't have time to check their bonafides."

"So you're thinking someone in Dragonfletcher's group sold him out to the yaks?" Elvis asked.

Wheeler had the van rolling steadily now, headed out of downtown. "Where to?" he asked.

"It could have been somebody from NuGene," Skater said to Elvis, then turned to Wheeler. "I'm open to suggestions."

"I've got a warehouse with the Fiat-Fokker juiced up and ready to fly."

"We took damage on the freighter raid."

"Yeah." The dwarf rigger nodded. "She may not be pretty, but she's navigable."

"How secure is this place?"

"I left the amphibian there," Wheeler pointed out. "We've got considerable investment wrapped up in that bird."

"Easy in, easy out?" Skater asked.

"It's wiz. Place is totally chill. I've had access for awhile, just never used it. One of those hidey-holes you keep like an ace up your sleeve."

"Let's do it."

"It's also possible that one of McKenzie's men sold out the meeting," Archangel said.

Skater nodded. "With the meet arranged the way it was,

I'd say there are only three avenues for the information to get to the yakuza. McKenzie, NuGene, and us."

"Since *us* have nearly got our collective hoops shot off on different occasions during the last twenty-four hours," Trey said, "I vote we be left out of the running."

"No problem," Skater said. "The only other option is that Doyukai has someone planted in either McKenzie's or NuGene's camp."

"Doubtful," Duran said. "Those slags seem to play things pretty fraggin' close to the vest."

"Then how did we get tipped to the cargo aboard the *Sapphire Seahawk*?" Skater retorted.

"True," the ork growled. "Me, it's jamming my hoop where the word came from. I'd like to get the scan before we go much further."

"McKenzie's a pretty involved man at this point," Archangel said.

Skater raised an inquiring eyebrow.

"I don't have anything solid," she said, "but I was able to do some prowling around. From what I hear, McKenzie's trying hard to retire."

"You'd never know it," Trey said. "The slag I saw in action tonight was pure street savage."

"Where would he go?" Skater asked.

"He's got millions stashed in dozens of accounts," Archangel said. "I don't have any solid figures or bank names or the aliases he might be using for the accounts. But I got enough to know he won't be deprived of anything he enjoys right now. Maybe he's been skimming from the biz he handles for the Family."

"Think he's about to get caught with his hand in the cookie jar and wants to get out before they take his head too?" Skater asked.

"The Mafia expects a little graft," Elvis said. "It's figured in. A slag who's good at what he does can afford to get greedy because he's keeping the Family coffers full."

"And McKenzie's been that kind of guy."

"Without question," Archangel stated. "But lately he's been investing in more legitimate enterprises."

"Have they been good investments or has he been losing his shirt?" Skater asked. "From the way he acted about the money tonight, he must be strapped."

Archangel shook her head. "It sounds to me like he's built

up quite an impressive portfolio." She glanced at notes she'd scribbled. "He's not really making any profit, but he's leveraging money from different banks to buy interests in companies and businesses and stocks."

"Laundering his own money," Skater said.

Archangel nodded. "I think so, too, but it would be hard to prove."

"Then he's dealing with considerable shrinkage working through the money scammers," Wheeler said. The lights of the sprawl washed over the van's windshield, a neon jungle war waged in advertising. "Joker taking financial hits like that, this biz with NuGene could sound pretty good."

"He came up out of the gutter, kid," Duran said. "Tonight you kicked dirt in his face. No matter what social ladder he might be trying to climb, he's not just going to turn the other cheek."

Trey smiled wanly. "I get the feeling McKenzie works out of the other testament."

"How accessible is the info on McKenzie?" Skater asked Archangel.

"To who?" she asked.

"The yabos working for him."

She appeared to consider that, then nodded. "The ones that are well-connected could probably find out."

"Makes you wonder if any of them has designs on the hole McKenzie would leave behind," Skater said. "They said nature abhors a vacuum. One of them could have cut a deal with the yakuza and sold McKenzie out."

"I also traced the nuyen that paid Larisa Hartsinger's bills for the last few months," Archangel said. "It took quite a bit of doing."

Skater felt his stomach tighten. "And?"

"The payments were drawn on an account in Exchange First, a smaller bank that does a lot of out-of-sprawl biz. I had to run some real burners to figure out who was ultimately on the bottom line."

"Who?"

"NuGene."

"Dragonfletcher said he didn't know who Larisa was," Skater said.

"Maybe he doesn't."

"Did you get a name at NuGene?"

"Arial Baerenwald," Archangel said. "She's an accounts

clerk. Probably ran the payments through the bank without ever knowing what they were for."

"But someone knows," Skater said. He began ticking off points on his fingers. "Larisa sets us up with the raid on the freighter. We get the files, which are corrupt and aren't worth a twisted slot. One step ahead of the yakuza, who've evidently also been tipped about the cargo. Dragonfletcher, head of NuGene security, starts trying to move heaven and earth to catch the people responsible. Someone kills Larisa only a few hours before I can get to her, and takes her baby—which was arranged by Ridge Maddock. She'd been hanging around someone named Synclair Tone, who just happens to be very interested in getting rid of me. Now we discover her expenses have been paid by NuGene. And NuGene, a corp that's been near financial collapse, is suddenly given a new lease on life because Tavis Silverstaff is promoting a new product line. And along comes Conrad McKenzie, Mr. Mafia, taking his own percentage of the action." He raked the team with his gaze. "Am I missing anything here?"

"Quite a package," Duran commented.

"No drek," Skater retorted. He gazed out the window at the dark streets of the sprawl rushing by. "We need to know more about NuGene. What it's got on the books. Where the special interest groups came from. And what exactly's in those fragging files." He glanced at Archangel. "How tight is the ice around the Seattle operation?"

"I couldn't get inside without major effort and time—lots more time than we've got."

"Then that leaves the parent crop."

"NuGene in Tir Tairngire?" Trey said.

Skater nodded. "We've got two choices: Roll over and play dead, or try to figure out where all the heat is and leverage us some back." He met the gaze of every member of the team. "Either way you vote, I'm in for the long haul. There's too many questions I need answers to."

"Listen to you," Archangel said sharply. "You're talking about invading the elf lands like it was nothing."

"Can you get into NuGene from here?" Skater asked.

She hesitated. "No," she admitted. "I've already tried. The corp's R&D computers aren't tied in to the Matrix. They're keeping them isolated."

"We're not talking about raiding the elven strongholds,"

Skater pointed out. "Just Portland. Security's not as tight there."

"It's still a suicide run."

"One misstep," Skater said evenly, "and they all are."

"Portland security's no cakewalk," Archangel said.

"I wasn't thinking it was." Skater looked at her, sensing he had to win her over more than the others. Fear was in her eyes, something he'd never seen before. "The people who set us up, whether it's NuGene or the yakuza or someone else, they aren't going to take the hammer off of us until we're dead. Even if we try to vanish, I don't know if it can be done."

"I'm slotting good at disappearing," Archangel said in a cold voice. "I can do it again."

Skater leaned back, not knowing what else to say. "I've got to go."

There wasn't much hesitation from anyone else. Wheeler and Elvis agreed readily, followed somewhat reluctantly by Trey.

"I'm in, too," Duran growled. "When push comes to shove and the down and dirty gets ugly, I want to see if these stump-skankers can upload it as well as they download it."

Archangel shook her head. "I can't go. Not to Tir Tairngire." She looked away. "I'm sorry."

"Okay," Skater said softly. He knew from a glance there was no arguing with the cold, angry fear that suddenly shone in her eyes.

23

"Gonna be chancey as hell humping it into the Tir like this," Duran said.

"Not quite as bad as betting against loaded dice," Skater replied. He peered into the cargo hold of the Fiat-Fokker. Tightly packed cases filled almost the entire area. "And the odds are a lot fragging better than hanging around Seattle." Satisfied, he closed the cargo-hold door and locked it tight.

"And checking on that stuff is a waste of time," Duran pointed out. "We aren't going to use none of it."

"Who knows? Depending on who canvasses the scene first, maybe some of those weapons will end up in rebel hands. I've heard Kate Mustaffah never misses a trick when it comes to turning a profit." Mustaffah was an ex-arms runner turned businesswoman and crusader for the failing economic sector in Portland, but rumor had it she still kept her hand in.

Fatigue ate into Skater to the bone despite the few hours of sleep he'd managed in since they'd left Archibald's the night before. Not all of those hours of sleep had been consecutive, and none had been without dreams of the immediate past and nightmares of what the immediate future might hold.

He looked up at the ork. "We roll in twenty-six minutes, Duran. You get any bright ideas, let me know."

Quint Duran dropped a big hand on Skater's shoulder and gave a thin, ork grin that had never been stained by honest mirth. "Just grousing, kid. Drek, I think this is going to be one of the best slotting runs that's ever been put together. The only thing I'm dreading is the long walk back."

"Who knows? Maybe we can package a deal on that, too. Depending on what hole cards NuGene is hiding."

Ten meters down from them, Elvis pulled the Leyland-Rover to a stop inside the warehouse and yelled for Duran to come help him. Wheeler was finishing the final check on the plane, wearing oil-stained dark blue coveralls and a red and gold San Francisco Forty-Niners ballcap that had seen better days.

Skater ran a careful hand through his hair. The wound he'd taken the previous night had been tended but was still sore. He walked back to the office set against the wall to his 'eft.

The amphibian bobbed in a channel of water that cut through the heart of the warehouse while plascrete shoulders on both sides held parking areas and spaces for heavy equipment. According to Wheeler, the place had once been used for marine salvage and was now operated as a front for black-market goods moving through UCAS. The dwarf had earned the right to use the warehouse, but he didn't tell any stories about why.

The building smelled of diesel fuel and machine oil, with

only faint wafts from the sea-scent of the Sound. The windows were all whole, but had been painted black, giving the place a run-down appearance that belied the expansive security system it housed.

Cullen Trey sat inside the office watching the quartet of sec-cameras with overlapping fields of view. He was dressed casually, but Skater knew it was a casualness that wasn't casually afforded. The mage still looked out of place in front of the three-year-old calendar sporting holopics from a trid-action series about three scantily clad women fighting crime with big guns and deadly magic. The show had a cult audience and stayed in syndication despite repeated vicious slams by critics. August showed a bare-breasted Jolie wrestling a hellbender in a swampy bayou. Standing all around her in their boats were Gulf pirates holding automatic weapons and watching her struggle with lust-filled eyes.

A trid turned to twenty-four-hours news was showing footage from a grisly piece of biz that had happened in the Renton Mall. Evidently a mother who'd been stricken with the mysterious laughing death disease had gone mad and attacked her own children. The woman had been ill and displayed symptoms now associated with the disease: yellowing of the skin, reddening of the eyes, loss of motor coordination, and dementia. Somehow, she'd got herself out of bed and followed her two children to the Mall where she'd severely mauled them both before sec-guards put her down in a blaze of gunfire. Unconfirmed reports said she had recently been treated by DocWagon and, despite lack of definitive proof, reporters were starting to refer to the diseased people as "DocWackos." Lone Star had not released any report on their findings as to the cause of the disease, stating only that it was a virus.

Skater listened intently as the aroma of fresh soykaf filled the small room.

"Ready?" Trey asked. Before him, an arrangement of charms, bracelets, and rings lay on piece of silk embroidered with what Skater assumed to be some kind of arcane symbols. The mage touched them as he watched the screens, then began placing them on his person.

"Ready." Skater turned away from the trid and poured himself a cup from the kaf-maker tucked neatly into the corner under three shelves of mechanical reference manuals.

"She hasn't contacted you?" Trey asked.

Skater shook his head. There was only one *she* the mage could have been referring to.

Trey finished the last of his preparations. "I really thought she'd be here to see this thing through."

"She's got her reasons for not wanting to go."

"True. But we're operating under a death sentence here. Could it really be any worse?"

Skater remembered the fear he'd seen in Archangel's eyes. "Yeah, I think maybe it could." He checked the time. "It's almost eight. Let's button up here."

Less than ten minutes later, he and Trey had shut down the office, leaving up the bare-bones security systems. Wheeler was already in the cockpit warming the engine, and Elvis and Duran stood beside the door.

They loaded into the plane with no attempt at small talk. They'd all been tense since making the decision to hit NuGene, but the various tasks each one had assumed to prepare for the operation had kept them from taking it out on each other. A few hours of rest had helped, too.

Skater had heard snatches from Kestrel overnight and throughout the day that everyone looking for them—McKenzie, the elves, and the yakuza—was heated up to almost a fever pitch. The net was drawing tighter around Seattle.

Skater cast the mooring line loose and pulled himself up into the co-pilot's seat, adjusting to the rocking movement of the amphibian on the water. "Get us out of here," he told Wheeler.

The dwarf nodded. He sealed himself off in the plastic rigger's cocoon to totally immerse himself in the plane's operations. From now on, Skater knew, all communication with Wheeler would have to be through the aircraft's radio headsets. Sluggish at first, the plane gained speed, pushing toward the double doors. A press of a button on the control panel to bounce an IR signal off a servo mounted at the front of the warehouse made the doors slide sideways.

The waterway cut through fifty meters of plascrete and led directly into Puget Sound. Night lay like a cloak over the sprawl.

As the Fiat-Fokker passed the double doors, Skater spotted the figure standing there. "Hold it," he told Wheeler over the amphibian's com.

The dwarf cut the engine immediately, but the plane continued on across the water surface a few meters more.

Even without his low-light enhancement, Skater recognized Archangel in the dark.

She wore black synthdenim jeans and a black turtleneck under a gray trench coat. She held the straps of a heavy backpack tight in one white-knuckled fist. Tense anger darkened her features.

Skater popped the door and threw it back. He stood up so she could clearly see him.

"You're going through with this then?" she demanded.

"No choice," Skater said. Her hesitation probably lasted only an instant, but he felt the weight of it and knew she did too.

"Damn you, Jack, if we get caught." Her voice was hard and fierce, and he knew she meant every word of it. She stepped forward and offered her hand.

Skater took it and pulled her aboard. Even before she could get to her seat, Wheeler had pushed the throttle forward. In seconds, the Fiat-Fokker powered out onto the lake, then rose quickly into the black sky, cutting through the heavy cloud cover.

"How much time before we make the border?" Archangel asked.

Skater checked the time. They'd been in the air—in silence—for almost twenty minutes, getting up to altitude and speed. "Couple hours, give or take ten minutes. We're going in slow, looping back in from the Pacific. If everything works out, we'll meet up with an approaching storm front and should be able to use that for cover part of the way in."

"And after that?" she asked.

Skater looked at her. "After that, we're black-market arms dealers making a border run. We meet up with resistance, and we take the fall."

"Losing the plane?"

"We have to in order to make it look good. We'll go down near the Willamette River north of the city and just over the Wall, well beyond the river lock. Once in the river, we've got two undersea sleds and scuba gear. With all the action we'll stir up in the area, both land and sea, we should be clear before the first shock troops arrive. It's about five kilometers into Portland."

"They're going to be looking for bodies," Archangel said.

"Yepper," Duran said. He held up two thick fingers. "And they'll find them. Me and Elvis did a little recruiting while these guys were putting together the ordnance packages. We were gonna find us a street doc to sell us a coupla bodies, but then we tripped over a pair of Halloweeners all nice and geeked in some turf action." He twitched his lips back to show his fangs.

"Do they have believable histories if the Border Patrol does a check on them?" Archangel reached into her backpack and brought out her deck and a portable telecom. She handed the ork the datacord to jack the deck into the plane's computer.

Skater watched her as she worked. The tension was still with her, and her face was paler than usual. He felt guilty that she'd come almost in spite of herself and was having to face old fears she'd obviously left in the Tir. But the guilt wasn't professional and it wasn't going to do anyone a fragging bit of good, so he shelved it.

"They're going to explode," Duran said. "Probably won't be any pieces big enough to identify."

Archangel powered up her deck and started tapping at the keys. "But if there are, the Border Patrol's going to be suspicious about why two thrill-gangers suddenly went into the arms business. FitzWallace is no babe in the woods."

Skater knew the name from his scan on Portland. Colonel Jacob FitzWallace was the head of the Border Patrol. And Archangel was right; the guy was savvy.

"Did you get a SIN on either of them?" she asked.

"There wasn't exactly time."

Archangel dug through her backpack and pulled out a surface scanner/reader. She carried it for times the team needed to check fingerprints or steal them for future reference. She passed it back to Trey. "Get me their prints."

"They're dead." Trey didn't look at all happy about the assignment.

Archangel gave him a hard look. "Chummer, we're hours behind on the setup for this run. Part of it's my fault, but I can't play catch-up if you're dragging your hoop."

"Right." The mage made his way to the back, pulling a handkerchief from a shirt pocket.

"I can loop into the harbor patrol's crime files and set up records and SINs for both these guys. It's a lot easier than trying to crack Lone Star's systems. If FitzWallace asks Lone Star to do a background check on those bodies, the Star will do a search of all its precincts, triggering a general info dump from all the law-enforcement agencies in the area. The files I set up will feed right into Lone Star's resources and they'll accept them as good. All we have to do is make sure the Halloweener SINs turn up for the Border Patrol to find."

"But don't you need to get into the Matrix to do all that?" Skater asked.

"If we had a satellite uplink, there'd be no prob. But we don't, so I'll just create the files, compress them for a faster delivery, and tag a friend who's got access to a satlink through a black BBS. I can manage all that very nicely over this portaphone." Archangel looked up. "Buying time on the satlink's going to be expensive, but it's worth it." She hooked the telecom up to her deck as Skater watched.

"The amphibian's registration could be altered," Skater said.

"Who's it registered to now?" Archangel asked.

"A joker named Kennedy who's been dead for seventeen months," Wheeler replied. "Skater and I met him during a run that fell through. He was a hawker for a line of antiques and elf talismans coming out of some of the best little backdoor art factories you'd ever want to see. But none of them had ever seen the Old Country, whichever Old Country he was referring to at the time. He was a fragging artist. Had to be to support the gambling jones he had.

"The last time we went to see him, someone got to him before we did. Put a couple fletchettes through his wetware and left him at an outside table at the Renton Hole in the Wall. Nobody saw anything or even knew he was dead. We didn't know it either till we walked up on him. We'd already been noticed, so we had a drink each, then grabbed Kennedy and got the hell out of there. We arranged for the body to disappear, then when the time came to register the amphibian, we used his name."

Archangel nodded. "I can show that he sold our gangers the plane yesterday, log it in through licensing. Their SINs will pop up and should leave us clear. For awhile. When someone looks really close, those SINs are going to crumble and fall away."

Trey returned and handed the scanner over. Archangel jacked it into her deck and downloaded the images.

"How do you plan to get into NuGene?" she asked as she worked.

Skater shifted in his seat. "It's going to be tough. The place is maxxed out on security right now." Kestrel had turned up quite a bit of information on the current situation. "At least the perimeter stations are. Knight Errant is handling the account. But they're not being let inside. NuGene is taking care of its own internal security."

"Meaning Ellard Dragonfletcher."

"Yeah. The only option we've got is kidnapping one of NuGene's researchers and using him or her to get through the outer defenses."

"That's risky."

"Depends on how much the person we get wants to live," Duran said. "I'm pretty good at convincing someone their life is on the line."

"I've got another idea. When Torin Silverstaff was first building up the company, he constructed as cheaply as possible." Archangel tapped a key and transferred an image to the plane's large vidscreen so the team could see. A datapic of the NuGene building formed, all hard lines and angles. "He knocked down pre-existing buildings, scraped the rubble out of the way, and built on top of them. But he had to use the existing foundations and utility hookups."

The building image became translucent and remained sitting at the side of the street. Below it, a schematic of the foundation formed with grids in red lines and in yellow.

"The red lines are the current architecture," Archangel said, "and the yellow is where the previous buildings were."

Skater studied the schematic. "They've put up some false walls and floors."

Archangel tapped more keys. "The construction crews who rebuilt NuGene weren't able to completely incorporate the pre-existing foundations. They had to sink some new support columns."

"But there may be some pockets inside the foundation that aren't covered by Knight Errant or the internal secsystems." Skater peered at the gridded sections of the building's two foundations, excitement flaring to life inside him. Using one of the R&D people as a means of getting into the building hadn't been his preference, but it had seemed executable. "If we can get into those lower levels—"

"We might be able to tap the computer lines without them ever knowing we were there," Archangel said.

"Next best thing to a zipless frag," Duran said.

"They could have filled in the holes," Skater said, playing the devil's advocate.

Archangel shook her head. "I went over the blueprints I raided from the Portland City Commissioner's Office. Putting that much concrete in the ground near the river for a purely cosmetic reason would have cost serious nuyen in environmental taxes."

"The elves were already pushing for a back-to-nature movement then," Duran commented. "I guess they worry about other contaminants corps might want to hide in something built along the lines of a tomb."

"With good reason," Trey said. "Toxic waste is expensive to get rid of through legitimate means."

"There were letters from Silverstaff requesting that the Commissioner's office waive the tax," Archangel said, "but they turned him down. Silverstaff didn't invest the capital because the pouring was expensive as well."

"Is there a way to get to the foundation?" Skater asked.

"The city's been honeycombed with drainage systems to help prevent flooding." Archangel hit more keys and more lines took shape on the screen. "I found two likely prospects. Both of them come in from the river."

On the screen, the NuGene building reduced in size as the rest of the city came into view around it. An eyeblink later, two green tubes raced in from different positions along the curvature of the Willamette River, coming together at a juncture almost at NuGene's doorstep.

"From here," Archangel said, "we should be able to cut through the drainage tunnel into one of those pockets under the building. The other tunnel I found here"—a yellow tube formed on the screen almost touching the green joint and extended under NuGene—"has been abandoned."

"You don't know if it's clear?"

"No." Archangel looked at Skater. "We won't know that till we're there."

"How big are the tunnels?"

"The ones coming from the river, we can walk through. Even Elvis."

The troll stroked his silver-capped tusk. "That's good news."

"The downside is that they'll be patrolled by maintenance drones that could alert security. But I think I've got a utility that'll get us by them." Archangel touched the yellow line on the screen. "This tunnel, though, is less than a meter across."

"Crawlspace," Skater said.

Archangel leaned back in the bench seat. "At best."

"Then that's what we'll do. Can you print out a copy of those schematics? I want to overlay them with the maps I've got."

In seconds, she handed him the hardcopies. Briefly, their hands touched and she met his gaze. "Don't start feeling responsible for me being here," she said softly, in a voice the others couldn't hear. "I was bitchy when I caught up with you at the warehouse. That wasn't how I really feel. I'm just scared. Haven't had any sleep, and I've been running on kaf and sheer nerves. I came along for myself. Life may not be great in the sprawl, but at least it's mine and no one else's. It means a lot to me to be able to say that."

Before Skater could respond, she turned back to her deck and immediately became absorbed in working on it. He watched her for a moment, checking the throb along her neck, then faced forward again.

Abruptly, sheets of rain fell across the amphibian's nose and blotted out a discernible view of the sky. The roaring winds buffeted the small plane. Skater studied the maps and the hardcopy as the light in the Fiat-Fokker's cabin dimmed intermittently. Lightning blazed a ragged rip of color and heat only a few meters from the right wing, drawing a curse from Duran.

Wheeler juked the controls to bring the amphibian back on-line. "And to think," the dwarf cracked in the silence that had filled the plane, "this is the easy part."

Even watching the power of the storm envelop them, Skater knew it was the truth.

"Look alive, chummers," Wheeler said over the radio two hours later. He sounded like he was far away. Jacked into the amphibian's controls, he *was* the plane. "We've been tagged. Portland Border Patrol has given us a knock-knock, wants to know who we are and do we know we've violated Portland airspace."

Skater roused himself and glanced out the window, which showed him they were still enmeshed in roiling black clouds.

They'd ridden the edge of the storm into the area, sometimes bucking hard, alternately losing altitude, then climbing frantically to regain it. All of them had stayed buckled into their seats while the cargo shifted in the hold.

"How far out are we?" Skater asked over the headset.

"Seven kilometers," the rigger answered.

"How soon will we be there?"

"Three minutes, give or take. If this drekking storm isn't shoving us forward, it's sucking us back in thermals."

"The next time there's a good jolt of lightning," Skater said, "shed some altitude and make it look like we're having a harder time than we are." He leaned forward in his seat, captured by the harness.

"We catch another near one," Wheeler said with genuine feeling, "it might not be play-acting."

The signal from the Portland Border Patrol was garbled and broken up. A glance at the altimeter showed Skater they were at something over three thousand meters. He shifted his attention to the sweep of the arm across the radar screen. Two green blips appeared and the Fiat-Fokker's navigational computer began tracking them, showing their increasing altitude in rapidly changing red numerals.

"They've got two away," Skater said over the headset.

"I feel them out there. They won't hesitate."

"Fiat-Fokker," a harsh voice barked over the radio, "be advised that you are on the verge of entering Tir Tairngire airspace. Identify yourself and your business, or be shot down." The message was repeated in Sperethiel.

"Those are EuroFighter aircraft," Wheeler said. "They'll come fully loaded. And if they don't get us, there's always the SAM-sites."

Skater peered through the heavy rain as the warning was repeated, broken up by the electricity swirling around them. He couldn't see anything. The amphibian was hanging there like a kid's kite, waiting for a load of buckshot to take it down. His mouth was dry.

"Fiat-Fokker, this is your last—"

The lightning knifed a blinding arc through the storm-tossed clouds, cutting out the radio. Less than a heartbeat later, the peal of thunder cracked a sonic whip across the sky.

By then Wheeler was already moving. The amphibian heeled over sideways in response to his command. "No holding back now. We hesitate, we're soup meat."

"Go," Skater told him.

The amphibian's motor screamed. Under other circumstances the noise trapped in the cabin would have been deafening, but it was drowned out by the storm's fury. Another heated blast of cold white lightning slashed through the bowels of the dark clouds, momentarily creating a light funnel.

The altimeter dropped to twelve hundred meters. From what Skater had learned, the Border Patrol had standing orders to shoot anything that went below the thousand-meter mark. He glanced at the compass, a swirling ball suspended in a silicon mixture. The latitude and longitude, fed into the Fiat-Fokker's computer by a GPS satellite overhead, printed on the sides of the vibrating ball. The numbers shifted erratically as the amphibian tumbled.

Skater peered out the window but couldn't see anything. Lightning cracked again, but this time it was echoed by 20mm cannonfire that blew white-hot holes in the cloud cover less than thirty meters away. The concussions battered the amphibian. He brought up the IR panel, using the forward-looking infrared Wheeler had added to the plane's nose. Even with the IR and the memorization of the terrain maps he'd studied, he had a hard time spotting the Portland Wall until they were almost on top of it. The Wall surrounded the city and was controlled by heavily armed and well-guarded checkpoint stations. The Willamette River was a black ribbon that twisted through the green-hued landscape on either side of the Wall.

"Someone's got a target lock." Wheeler juked the amphibian left and down.

The Wall swept by below them, and a fresh swarm of cannonfire lit up the airspace in front of them. Wheeler powered through the twisting gray smoke that was being quickly ripped apart by the storm winds. Screaming in protest against the abuse and the howling gale of the storm, the Fiat-Fokker shivered.

"Find a spot," Skater told Wheeler. "Put it down." He

tapped on the radio com and put out a message that he guessed would be picked up by the Border Patrol. If it wasn't, it wouldn't affect the outcome. "Bushwhacker, this is Special Delivery. We're coming in hot and heavy. If you can assist, give me some kind of fragging response here." He repeated the message, then stopped in the middle of another ragged streak of lightning that nuked the cloudfront.

"Drek," Wheeler said. "Those jets have just kicked loose a pair of missiles."

24

Wheeler dropped altitude quickly, hitting five hundred meters and still plunging. The two heat-seeking missiles the EuroFighters had fired impacted against the heat flares the dwarf dumped out of the tail section. For the most part, the flares did the job of keeping the warheads away, but fragments holed the amphibian in a deadly drumbeat.

At two hundred meters and low enough now that Skater could see the landscape with his low-light enhancement, cannonfire ripped through the right wing, shearing off the last third of it.

"Frag me running," the dwarf groaned. "This is going to get ugly now." He tried to level the amphibian out, but it was no use. The tallest trees in the forest scratched against the Fiat-Fokker's underbelly while white phosphorus flames chewed the amputated wing. The plane flipped, twisted sideways as it sheared through a copse of trees. The amphib pancaked, rammed its good wing into the ground long enough to rip it free of its moorings, then skidded to a stop against a rocky hillside.

The silence after the crash was eerie.

Even with his low-light vision working, Skater had a hard time seeing. Worse than that, his safety harness was jammed. Using a knife he'd stuffed into his boot, he cut through the straps and managed to fall somewhat gracefully.

Wheeler shucked his harness and held onto it as he flipped over to land on his feet.

Archangel managed on her own, then immediately began

checking on her deck. Elvis's straps had jammed too, and he finally gave up and ripped them free. Cullen Trey was the first out the crumpled door after Duran kicked it open.

Skater moved to the cargo hold with Duran. He peered into the sky, but not much was visible through the canopy of trees overhead. He hoped it meant the EuroFighters couldn't spot them either. "Wheeler, how far to the river?"

"Half a kilometer," the dwarf answered. "We came down just about where we planned it."

Opening the cargo hold with effort, Skater yanked out the first undersea sled and passed it over to Elvis. "Grab your gear," he ordered. "We're going to get clear of this area as soon as possible."

Duran took up a position on the other side of him and began passing out scuba equipment. "Elvis, you've got point. Archangel, Wheeler, and Cullen are with you. Duran and I will bring up drag as soon as we finish here."

In addition to a scuba tank and flippers, each team member also carried their own gear and a canvas bag of equipment. The trek through the forest was going to be grueling.

"Let me have your airtank," Archangel said. They hadn't brought one for her, but each undersea sled had both an emergency tank and a regulator built in, and all had rebreathers to eradicate the telltale bubbles. "It'll lessen some of the weight while you bring the other sled."

Skater didn't argue.

A cocky grin was on Trey's face. "I guess we'll all gather at the river, then? How pagan." He took off, closing distance with the others quickly.

Skater reached into the hold and hefted out one of the bodies. Duran was busy beating the access panel off the engine area. Once he had it open, the ork knelt down with a broad-bladed knife in his fist. The smell of fuel quickly blotted out the odor of death that had been trapped in the hold.

The ground around the impact area was rocky and hard. The scars from the crash cut deeply into it, revealing shattered white rock.

Skater shoved the first corpse into the cockpit, then followed it with the second in short order. By then the leaking fuel was already making pools on the ground.

"Ready?" Duran asked.

Skater nodded and hoisted the undersea sled over his shoulder. It was constructed of composite materials, mainly polymers and ceramics, and weighed thirty-two-point-seven kilos. At a meter and a half long and two meters across and triangular in shape, it wasn't hard to lift and carry, but getting it through the forest was going to be slotting tricky. He started toward the river as Duran twisted the cap off a flare.

The fuse lit, and bright, hard scarlet fire burned the night away. He pitched the flare into one of the fuel puddles.

Yellow and blue alcohol flames jetted up from the pool nearly a meter away. They seemed to pause for an instant, then raced toward the broken amphibian.

Flames engulfed the Fiat-Fokker as more of the ordnance did increasing damage. Fiery comets spewed into the air in all directions, and flaming bits of the wreckage hung in the trees and against the hillside.

Despite the terrain and the weight, Skater and Duran made the river in less than five minutes. The first of the Border Patrol helos were closing in on the burning pyre of the amphibian further up the slope. The ground troops wouldn't be far behind.

The other members of the team were already in the cold water. Wheeler was jacked into the sled, the datacord for the machine's on-board computer plugged into his temple. The packs all had buoyancy bladders to keep them from floating or sinking, and Archangel was lashing the last one to the undersea sled. She'd already changed into the black thermal wetsuit Skater had packed for her against the chance that she might change her mind.

"Let's go," Skater said as he dropped his sled into the water. He keyed the ignition, and the electric motor started at once. After punching in the rest of the sequence and pushing the sled further out into the cold water, it sank and sat docilely in one place, using the dog-brain and negating the current automatically.

Wheeler tied onto the first sled, while Trey and Elvis tied on in succession after him, each with a longer piece of line. The dwarf walked them out into the river till the water closed over their heads.

After pulling the thermal lined hood over his head, Skater sealed it and grabbed the undersea sled's control bar. The goggles he wore had infrared and low-light capabilities, duplicating what his eyes could do and more, but providing protection from the water and corrections against the depths.

He slid them on and flicked the menu to IR. Archangel tied on after him, followed by Duran.

The roar of ground-based vehicles was in his ears as he walked out into the water. He shoved the regulator into his mouth and switched on his airtank, then handed the regulator for the emergency tank to Archangel.

She took it, but Skater thought she looked more distant and withdrawn than he'd ever seen. With the fear in her eyes and the uncertainty about what she was doing, she was too human.

Too easy to care about, Skater realized. The distance he'd always maintained to get him through a run was no longer there. They weren't pieces of a chess game anymore.

The knowledge hit him and stripped some of his confidence as he waded out into the water. The current of the river pushed at him as it closed over his head. Oozing silt sucked at his feet. He kicked out of his boots and slid his flippers on. After threading a line through his boot loops and tying them to his belt, he glanced back to make sure the others were ready.

"Do it," Duran said, and Archangel echoed him.

Skater accelerated the sled smoothly, gradually taking them all into motion. Peering back toward the bank, he could see the flames of the burning amphibian and the lights of the helos and the ground units through the meter of water that separated him from the surface.

Turning his attention back to the sled's controls, he increased the power again and took them deeper. The cold seeped in to claim him even through the thermal wetsuit. The thought that he might not be able to get the others out of this jam he'd gotten them into made him even colder.

Memory came to Skater as the water glided past him. It was something from one of the last camping trips he'd taken with his grandfather. The old man was sitting across the campfire from him, a rabbit roasting on a spit that he had Skater turning. The firelight illuminated the old man's craggy face and held back the blush of the stars.

"I want you to think about something." Daniel Ghost-step had said then. "There won't be an answer now or in the morning, or maybe for years." He'd reached down and pinched a bit of the rabbit's flesh off, tasting to see if it was done enough. "Keep turning and listen to this: A man is foolish and yet made strong of heart because he lives with one foot in the past and one foot in what is yet to be. If he does not do these things, he is only the wind and never rooted. When the time comes, and I hope that it will, you'll have to make the decision about being a man or just being the wind."

Skater hadn't understood then. Many Amerinds of the time were trying to figure out their history, piecing it together from half-remembered folk tales and books. In a way, they were as bad as the elves, forging a new past and calling it the Old Way.

But now Skater thought he understood at last. A man lived with his regrets and cherished his dreams, and made peace with life the rest of the time. The wind just blew wherever it went, never remembering, never caring, till it died away.

Inside the Tir, hanging onto the undersea sled like part of a human kite's tail, Skater knew he wasn't the wind anymore.

And he wasn't sure if he ever would be again.

Forty-seven minutes later, chilled to the bone, Skater released his hold on the sled and left it tethered in the water. He swam upward and joined Elvis and Trey at the mouth of a drainage tunnel spewing an impressive deluge of water into the river. The rain brought in by the storm had calmed, but hadn't completely gone away. Thunder still boomed occasionally.

"This it?" Elvis asked, standing in water up to his waist.

Skater swam to where he could stand up, then took the regulator out of his mouth and peered at the markings made on the collar holding the plascrete drainage pipe. "Yeah."

The drainage tunnel was almost two meters up the steep riverbank, and was three meters in height. It jutted out over the river at least another three meters.

The river twisted around them, turning more southerly. The opposite bank was filled with wooden and concrete docks as well as more modern plascrete ones. But the docks way outnumbered the boats. Lights tried to cut through the fog overlaying the river and the banks, but they were only half-hearted attempts.

Archangel surfaced behind Skater, pulling his pack as well as her own. Duran was next, followed by Wheeler.

Storm sounds and engine noises floated over the river. A

patrol boat came into view through the fog, lightning illuminating the Peace Force insignia on the prow. Searchlights burned across the banks in a tired fashion.

Skater and the others sank back into the water till the boat passed, evidently on routine patrol and not looking for them at all.

"Sleds are tied up below," Wheeler said. "But the batteries are about geeked. You can forget using them to get back."

"That way is out anyway," Skater replied. "The area's going to be crawling with Border Patrol for hours. We don't have that kind of time to spend waiting." He glanced at Elvis. "Can you give me a leg up?"

The troll laced his fingers together and bent over slightly.

Skater put one foot into Elvis's hands and pushed himself up toward the drainage pipe. The troll helped, almost shoving him into the pipe. Once he had his hands on the lip, Skater pulled himself into the tunnel. Sludge stained the front of his clothing brown and green.

Rats as long as his forearm sat in clusters above the waterline on both sides of the water cascading through the pipe. The thunder of the water rushing through the drainage system resonated, sounding near and far at the same time. Tracked grids ran along the sides of the pipe and he guessed they were for the maintenance drones Archangel had told him about.

In minutes they were all inside the pipe, scattering rats before them. The sludge and the rushing water made footing precarious. Skater led, a half-step in front of Archangel.

Elvis cursed and kicked. Flying rats banged into the metal sides of the tunnel. "Fragging things are trying to climb up on me."

"I would say something about kindred spirits," Trey volunteered.

The troll gave him a baleful look.

"But I won't," the mage promised.

Less than a hundred meters in, Skater stopped and looked at the wall to the right. "Should be about here." He took out his knife and banged the handle against the metal. The echo sounded hollow. "According to the schematics, the pipes touch. Spread out and let's see if we can find the other one."

In seconds the drainage pipe was filled with tapping, until Wheeler called out, "I think I've got it."

Skater tramped through the running water and nearly lost his footing in the sludge. He looked up at Elvis. "Cut it, and let's find out."

The troll nodded and unlimbered the laser torch he had in his equipment pack. He crossed to the wall and thumped it solidly.

"Duran," Skater called out, "see if you can get something over that grate so the laser won't show through."

Duran stripped off his jacket and blocked the grate, leaving enough room to allow the passage of water down the tunnel.

Strapping on a pair of protective goggles and thick gloves, Elvis switched on the laser and moved forward. Skater had the Predator in his fist and kept watch over the mouth of the pipe the way they'd come. There was a clang, then the laser light died away. When he turned, a hole big enough to crawl through was sliced through the pipe. The plascrete around the hole glowed hot orange a few centimeters deep. He holstered his weapon and removed his flash from his pocket, joining Archangel at the hole.

"The pipe's there," Archangel said, "but I can't tell what kind of shape it's in." She pointed her flash into the hole.

Skater added his to hers, but the distance was only illuminated a few meters. "It curves. Those specs didn't show a fragging curve." The light revealed the plascrete twisting out of sight nearly eight meters up.

"They're not that exact," Archangel replied. "They didn't have to be. Maybe it doesn't curve much."

Skater took a roll of ordnance tape from his pack and quickly strapped the flash to his gunwrist. He took off his street clothes and dragged them through the running water at his feet, then threw them across the heated edges of the lasered hole.

The cold water and soaked material hissed when they came in contact with the hot plascrete. The orange dimmed almost instantly, and steam rose up, drifting lazily with the flow of the water.

Skater crawled through the hole and pulled himself into the pipe. The fit was tight; there was barely enough room for his shoulders. Duran, Elvis, and Wheeler would never have made it.

On his stomach with the Predator and the flash aimed before him, he pulled himself forward. Panic whispered in his ear that he was going to get stuck at any moment, causing him to take bigger breaths than he actually needed. Once, because of a deep inhalation, his shoulders did get pinned and he found himself unable to move. Instinctively he took even more air in and found he couldn't. At the edge of losing it, he forced himself to be calm, to breathe out. He became unstuck, then worked to keep moving.

The curve was hard to navigate. He had to turn sideways and bend around it, not breathing till he was through.

His movements had stirred up clouds of dust that obscured the light from his flash. It took real effort to see the other end of the tunnel seven more meters along. A plascrete plug blocked it. He cursed silently for just a moment, then activated the Crypto Circuit link. "Duran, I'm going to need a drain opener. We've got a blockage up here." Skater played the flash over the rough plascrete surface, trying to estimate its depth.

"What are you looking at?'

"Plascrete cap. I don't know how thick."

"Probably only a few centimeters. Builders figured they needed some kind of safeguard to keep rodents and insects from using the pipe as a means of egress."

"According to the blueprints," Archangel said, "the wall on the other side of it is twenty centimeters thick. That'll have to be blown as well."

"Okay, kid," Duran said, "I'll get you a package fixed up. You coming back for it?"

Skater glanced back at the curve and thought about having to crawl through the pipe again. "No. Send it up with Archangel."

He twisted around so that he was lying on his back. His neck and shoulders were already burning from the exertion of keeping his head up. The thought of Archangel being in the pipe with him, blocking the way, was unsettling.

"Elvis sent this along," she said. "He thought it might help shield us from the blast."

Looking down, Skater saw that it was the troll's Kevlar-lined synthleather jacket. "It will. Go back to the bend in the pipe and hold onto it. I'll join you there."

As Archangel wriggled back, Skater moved forward with the explosive in his hand. His elbows were sore from crawling, and he felt the warmth of blood soaking into the wetsuit's sleeve from his left one.

Duran had shaped the charge and put a sticky surface on it. With care, Skater placed the explosive in the center of the plascrete plug. Going backward was every bit as difficult as he'd expected.

He stopped short of the curve in the pipe, knowing he didn't want to be trapped in it if anything went wrong. His nerves were jumping as Archangel passed up the heavy jacket. He wadded it deliberately, making as many layers as he could.

He tagged the commlink. "O.K., Duran. Blow it." He ducked his head into the jacket, smelling the strong troll smell.

Then the world inside the tunnel came apart as the detonation rocketed against his eardrums.

25

"Kid."

Duran's voice came to Skater as if from a long way off. The ringing in his ears didn't help. "We're here," he answered over the link. Then a fit of coughing wracked him as his lungs rebelled against the dusty debris floating through the air. When he shone his light along the length of the pipe, it looked like the fog hugging the river had invaded the crawlspace.

At the other end of the pipe, the plascrete plug was gone.

"How's it look?" the ork asked.

"Wide open. You did good." Skater tried to go forward, but the plascrete chips tortured his knees and chest. Coughing and wheezing and in pain, he decided his best course of action was to simply fist Elvis's jacket and shove it ahead of him. It also served to sweep most of the chips out of his way.

The opening into the building's foundation was irregular. Jagged remnants of plascrete and stone jutted around the rough circle. Cracks ran the width of the wall for nearly a meter in all directions. The dark was so complete Skater's low-light enhancement didn't work and he had to use his flash.

"Trey," Skater said as he crawled through the opening and dropped to the floor almost two meters below. He turned to help Archangel down.

"I'm here, chummer," the mage said.

"Check around and see if you can find the power-supply cables and whether or not we've been found out." Skater played his flash over the walls of the room. It was rectangular in shape, nine meters by three meters, and at least four meters from floor to ceiling. The stone surfaces were chipped and cracked, and fresh scars from the explosion showed through the layers of decades-old dust.

"Be right back," Trey said. His voice was already starting to fade as he went astral to do his assensing.

Plascrete chips ground under Skater's boots. It didn't take very long to see that none of the utility lines were in the room.

"According to the blueprints," Archangel said, "the power and supply umbilical should be on this side of the wall." She kept her light moving hopefully, but the frustrated frown on her high-boned elven features deepened. Gray dust coated her face.

After a few minutes more of fruitless searching, Cullen Trey climbed through the pipe and dropped into the room. He reached back into the opening for his pack. "The lines are on the other side of the wall. All the utilities, as well as the computer lines leading to the Portland Matrix, are there."

"What about security?" Skater asked.

The mage removed a drill from his pack and attached a large plascrete bit. "It's major, but I didn't sense any special alert. They're making the usual rounds, strictly routine. The blast was probably covered by the storm." He paced the wall, closed his eyes briefly as if trying to remember, then chose a spot on the wall. "It's here. Give me some room."

Skater and Archangel backed away. While Trey attacked the wall with the drill, Skater checked in with the other half of the team holding steady in the drainage pipe, letting them know what was going on.

The drill bit chewed into the thin wall and expelled a cloud of gray dust in the light cones given off by the flashes. Skater had his adjusted to its widest aperture and aimed at the ceiling so it partially lit up the room. Archangel kept hers directed at the spot where Trey was drilling.

Without warning, the keening of the drill changed pitches.

Trey, standing tightly muscled behind the tool, suddenly surged forward, then cut the power. He pushed his goggles up on his face and wiped away dust and plascrete chips. Stepping back, he pulled the bit out of the three-centimeter hole. "I'm through."

Archangel moved forward and peered through the hole. The flash beam was bigger than the drill bit had been, and the residual light bounced back over her face. "I see it."

When she moved back to the gear she'd brought, Skater shone his flash through the drilled hole. He could barely see the thick cable trunk to his right, only three or four centimeters away. From what he could make of the room on the other side of the wall, it was an electronics sublet. Banks of service computers filled two of the walls. A desk and a chair sat in front of the third wall, but no one was there.

Skater turned to Trey. "You didn't say there was an office."

"Those are just back-up and relay stations. There's no reason anyone would come down here much." Archangel held a probe device with a flexible end in her hand. A small monitor on the other end above a waldo flickered to life when she turned it on. "Arthoscope. I should be able to implant a tap into the circuitry." She flexed her hand, and the long probe wiggled in response.

Skater peered over her shoulder as she inserted the probe into the hole. The monitor was rendered in gray tones and showed the thick trunk of the cable. It swelled until it filled the whole screen.

Archangel worked the controls and a humming became an undercurrent running through the room. On the small screen, a tube restricted the camera eye's view and sank into the trunk. The end of the tube was jagged, cut at an angle and filled with sawteeth. There was a buzz, then a circular section of the outer shell of the trunk about the size of a shirt button tumbled inside.

Adjusting the focus of the camera, Archangel brought the wiring inside into view. She worked quickly and confidently. The tap looked like an ovoid insect with six stumpy legs. A heartbeat later, the legs wrapped around one of the wires.

"That should get me into their system." Archangel said. She fed a datajack with attached line through the scope and linked up. The other end slotted into her deck, then she jacked into the unit.

Skater moved toward the deck and activated the floppy-screened display Wheeler had set up so he could monitor Archangel's progression through the NuGene system. In case things went really bad for her, he could attempt to manually pull her out. Dealing with dump shock beat certain death from black or gray killer IC.

Archangel formed on the screen, a lambent green version of herself with feathered wings almost a meter longer than she was tall. The setup usually only showed the decker's point of view, but Archangel had modified it to also show the persona icon she used to maneuver in the Matrix by creating a double-image that shadowed her moves. The words I'M HERE typed across the bottom of the screen as she used the one-way communications link.

Then icon flapped its wings and the world of cyberspace came to life around her.

Archangel flew through multicolored flares of data pulsing through NuGene's system. The System Access Node was the first to challenge her. A gray gargoyle of a thing with amputated leathery wings and a face full of scars, it rose from the asteroid that blocked the path Archangel wanted to take. Broken silver chains hung from its thick wrists.

She paused and plucked a feather from her wings. She held it in her open palm and blew it at the fist-waving gargoyle. When the green feather touched the SAN, the feather popped, then the gargoyle calmed and sat back down on his prison of rock. A pucker opened in the rock and Archangel swooped toward it, her wings tightly closed around her.

FAKED PASSCODE WORKED, Archangel transmitted as the world went black around her.

Skater felt tense, counting the seconds that she'd disappeared. Then the Matrix appeared again, becoming a shimmering waterfall that represented NuGene's central switching office.

Archangel exploded through the rainbow-colored spray, her wings spread. It looked like a hundred different tunnels were stacked on the river's surface ahead of her. IF THIS BROWSE PROGRAM WORKS, ONE OF THE TUNNELS SHOULD—

One of the tunnels darkened. Archangel swooped toward it, almost out of control. I'M IN. NOW IF THE DECEPTION AND SLEAZE UTILITIES WORK, I SHOULD BE AT THE CPU IN SECONDS.

Skater knew Archangel had set up her icon to resemble a preventive maintenance program that was used primarily in elven computer systems. Whether it would get her into the heart of the security-encoded CPU was another matter.

Suddenly, the tunnel she was in widened and became a hexagon, then just as quickly shifted into a museum wall of niches filled with precious artifacts. NEED TO FIGURE OUT WHICH ONE WE WANT.

Archangel stood in the center of the room. A glow surrounded her, golden and full. Jagged scarlet threads unfurled from her fingers and snaked out toward the various artifacts.

In just a few seconds, a porcelain cup formed from a casting of a leaping dolphin pulsed with white-hot energy. She walked toward it. GOT IT!

Before she could touch it, a green cloud swirled into the room, and a gnarled elf formed only a few meters away. He was rail-thin and hunch-backed, with pince-nez sitting on his blade of a nose. He demanded that Archangel identify herself.

IT'S NOT BUYING THE PREV-MAINT DISGUISE, she transmitted. I'M BOOTING IN A RELOCATE UTILITY. MAYBE IT WON'T KNOW WE'RE INSIDE THE BUILDING.

Skater watched in tense silence. He'd never seen Archangel do her work before. He didn't like the helpless feeling it left him with.

I'M GOING TO TRY TO GET THE FILE AND DOWNLOAD IT. SINCE I'M NOT TAKING ANYTHING OR CRASHING ANYTHING, MAYBE THE DISGUISE WILL HOLD. The winged creature reached for the cup, her fingers barely touching the surface. The deck hummed against Skater's palm, downloading the information.

Then the wizened elf exploded, becoming a humanoid figure that looked like it was made of obsidian. Fires shifted beneath its glassy skin as it closed on Archangel.

Her wings unfurled, Archangel stepped away from the cup as she assumed a defensive posture. She plucked another feather from her wings and threw it like a dart at the obsidian elf. The feather struck and was absorbed. Immediately, the killer IC showed in its approach. I'VE GOT A SLOW UTILITY TAGGED TO IT, FOLLOWING UP WITH ATTACK UTILITIES.

The figure reeled under the attack. Then it threw a complex multi-colored cube at Archangel. Before it reached her, a mirrored barrier rose around her. The cube struck sparks from it, and the colors clung to the shiny surface, whirling madly within it. TAGGED ME. THOSE VIRUSES ARE EATING AWAY AT MY DEFENSES. I'M GOING FOR IT. She stepped from the protective barrier and grabbed the cup as the obsidian figure threw itself at her, its scarred face twisted in rage.

NO WAY TO BE QUIET ABOUT THIS NOW, Archangel transmitted. She shattered the cup against the stone floor and breathed in all the cinnamon-brown vapors that came up from it. The obsidian figure was almost on top of her when she wrapped her wings around herself and disappeared. JACKING OUT! The screen went blank.

Alarms shuddered to life within the building.

Skater activated the commlink. "Okay, we're blown. Grab the gear and get ready to beat feet."

Duran growled an affirmative.

"There!" a voice on the other side of the wall yelled. "They drilled through the wall. Look at that mess!"

With a groan, Archangel sat up, pulled the probe, and snatched the cord from her datajack. She was pale, and dark circles showed under her eyes.

A wavy shimmering left Cullen Trey's hand and shot through the hole. An instant later, he turned to face Skater with a smile. "Those guards won't bother us now, but there'll be more."

Archangel got to her feet and grabbed her gear with difficulty as Skater laced his hands together and let her step up into them. She slid her deck over her shoulder, then pushed up, almost tumbling over backward but managing to grasp the pipe's lip. "What'd you get?" he asked.

"More than I expected." Archangel pulled herself into the pipe, but kept on talking. Her voice echoed and resonated within the confines. "I'll have to decode it to figure out everything."

On the other side of the wall, security alarms cut loose with all the flair of a mauled barghest.

"NuGene has created some kind of new organic replacement tissue," she said, switching over to the commlink as she made her way down the tunnel.

Skater helped Trey up, watched the mage disappear into the pipe, then reached up and pulled himself along with considerable effort. He lost a couple layers of skin off his cheek as he wormed his way in.

Skater knew it was only his imagination, but the pipe felt tighter as he crawled back to the drainage spillway. He pushed the claustrophobic thoughts aside and tried to figure out how the hell they were going to get out of here. They couldn't go back the way they came, so it seemed the only choice was to go deeper into the city.

"Dragonfletcher was working security," Archangel said over the commlink. "The kicker is, he'd linked up with someone in Seattle who was supposed to help him handle things at that end."

"I'll bite," Wheeler said. "Who?"

"Conrad McKenzie."

"Not Lone Star?" Duran asked.

"No."

Skater considered that, feeling the suppositions turn suddenly nasty in his head. "How long has that been going on?"

"From the quick take I got while downloading files," Archangel said, "the earliest mention of McKenzie was maybe a couple months ago."

Skater started through the bend, working to stave off the increased panic that flooded through him as soon as he felt his shoulders wedge. Gently, he loosened them and went on. "Does Silverstaff know about McKenzie?"

"There's no way to be certain."

A blast echoed through the pipe from the other end. Skater felt the heat and force of it wash over him. Voices followed, sounding loud and excited. He pushed himself harder, trying to get around the bend. If the NuGene security guards fired up into the pipe, he'd be an easy target. The ragged plascrete burned across his back, shredding fabric.

The deep basso baying of dogs on the hunt sounded. A clatter of nails scratching frantically at metal rattled through the pipe. Then the howling resonated differently, letting Skater know the dogs were inside the pipe.

"Move," Duran yelled over the commlink. "Those fragging yabos have sicced beasties on you."

At the end of the pipe, Archangel pulled herself out and fell. Trey hesitated, watching her. Hearing the clatter of claws coming closer, Skater reached forward and grabbed the mage's foot. Bracing himself against the side of the pipe and wedging in tight, he shoved the foot as hard as he could.

With a cry of protest, Trey scooted out of the pipe and went down, flailing haphazardly. Water splashed and there were some painful grunts.

When he was within reach, Skater grabbed the lip of the pipe and hauled himself through just as the first pair of reddish eyes gleamed in the shadows behind him. He twisted as he fell, bringing the boosted reflexes on line as he reached for the Predator. His hand closed around the cold grip an instant before he slammed against the bottom of the drain pipe.

Elvis was facing the pipe's mouth with his forearm snap blades bared. The carbide tips gleamed darkly. "Get clear, chummer," he told Skater.

Duran was on one side of him, holding a pair of full-size Cougar Fine Blade knives in a martial arts stance, and Wheeler was on the other, wearing his jacket wrapped around his arm and waving a stun baton above his head.

Archangel had Trey by the arm and was hurrying him out of the way. Elvis's jacket was lying in the water where she'd dropped it.

The first animal to appear was a huge black Labrador with bullet-proof armor over its head and chest. The pink tongue lolled out over the ivory fangs for just an instant, then it launched itself at the troll. The reflexes as well as the distance of the dog's jump let Skater know it was razored. It streaked for Elvis's throat at once, almost too fast for the troll to counter. The snap blades crashed against the dog's skull plate with enough force to shoot sparks, and the dog sank its fangs into Elvis's shoulder instead of ripping out his throat.

Then Skater's attention was yanked back to his own situation. Another dog, this one big and heavy, but not as immediately identifiable, leaped from the pipe and landed on Skater's chest with enough weight to knock the wind from his lungs and put him flat on his back in the running water.

He didn't know how many other dogs came out of the pipe, but the sounds of animal growls and the team fighting for their lives blotted out all other noises. Struggling, the teeth only centimeters from his eyes, the stink of the dog's fetid breath over his face, he managed to leverage an arm under the animal's chin and keep it momentarily at bay.

The claws ripped at him, the slashing efforts blunted by the wetsuit. Hot saliva dripped on his face as the dog whined and growled in its frustration to get at him. Skater smashed the dog on the end of the snout with the Predator's barrel, drawing blood and a sudden yelp of pain.

The dog shook its head and backed away. Skater rolled to his knees, but before he could get to his feet, the animal launched itself at him, mouth gaping almost wide enough to clamp down on Skater's entire face.

Using the lightning-fast reflexes available to him, Skater rammed his right hand, pistol and all, into the dog's mouth. Before the fangs could close and break the skin of his arm, he fired three shots. The bullets cored through the back of the animal's head and sent it into spasmodic quivers. As the corpse shuddered to the ground, Skater stood and looked around.

A decapitated dog and a disemboweled dog lay at Elvis's feet. Bloody splash patterns covered his clothing. "Slot, I hate killing dogs," the big troll said. "I like dogs."

"These weren't dogs," Duran said as he extricated one of his knives from the skull of another animal. The shattered head dropped into the running water at the bottom of the drain. "They were just tasked killing machines. Being flesh and blood didn't change that."

Voices echoed through the pipe and let Skater know pursuit hadn't ended with the dogs. "Grab the gear," he said, fisting the straps of the pack nearest him.

"They'll have the river closed off," Wheeler said.

"We're not going to the river." Skater took the lead, using his flash for the benefit of Trey and Archangel, who weren't chipped for low-light vision. The elven decker's vision in the dark was better than a human's, but not enough to navigate by.

Duran asked Elvis to give him a hand as he shoved the corpse of the first dog into the access pipe leading to the building foundation.

"What's up?" the troll asked. But he complied with the request anyway, carrying a dead dog in each hand.

"Going to leave the sec-jokers a little surprise." The ork reached into an ordnance pouch, slipped the pins from two grenades, and wedged them under the pile of dead animals. He glanced at Skater. "Relax, kid, I know you figure these nitbrains were just doing their jobs, even if they sicced these razored hounds on us. This is just pepper gas. It'll make them uncomfortable for awhile, and definitely throw any other animals they bring up off the scent."

Settling the pack over his shoulder, Skater held the Predator in one hand and the flash other. He set out at a quick pace, but no one complained. Death was dogging their steps.

26

They'd been in the drainage tunnels for almost three hours, but Skater finally found the drainage system trunk line he was looking for. He'd discovered that some of the access drains were marked and some of them weren't. The one he wanted wasn't. He was bone-tired, feeling the effects of the last couple days. Adrenaline could be pushed only for so long before it gave out too.

The beam of his weakening flash was turning dirty gray as it splashed across the narrow breadth of the drain. This one was older, constructed of masonry rather than plascrete. Keeping the flash down, he used low-light vision to scan the ladder leading up to the manhole five meters up. There was no reason to think that Border Patrol guns were waiting at the top of the climb.

Still, he took a deep breath before shutting off his flash, grabbed the first rung and headed up. At the top, he gently shoved the manhole cover up and peered about. As he'd hoped, they'd come up in an alley beside an office building. Satisfied that he wasn't being watched, he pushed the cover to one side and climbed out.

The alley was narrow, framed by a tall hurricane fence and a three-story office building. One end was blocked by a plascrete wall that had been badly damaged in the past, and the other fronted a two-lane street. Cracks splintered the ground, allowing weeds to grow through. Some of them were almost knee-high.

Swan Island Industrial Park had become economically disenfranchised when the Council of Princes had moved the Tir's main port to Seattle. As Swan Island was one of the highest crime districts in the city, the police only came here when they had to—or so Kestrel had told Skater. He was sure they weren't very popular when they did, and that the locals would act as an alarm system if blue crews did start rolling the streets.

"Lights out," he told the others over the commlink, "and let's move. Elvis, you're up first. I need the lock on that building taken out pronto."

The troll surged up the ladder, full of vitality even after drekking around in the sewers for hours laying down false trails before finding their way here. "Which one, chummer?"

Skater pointed at the one back toward the ill-used Dumpster already filled to overflowing. Experience had taught him that all rear doors with Dumpster access were wired, but usually with dog-brain security systems instead of anything too exotic. Since employees used them frequently, they were generally set up user-friendly and not complicated.

Archangel followed the troll.

"I want a telecom line up and running as soon as you can get it," Skater told her. "I need to call a guy in Seattle."

"I'll take care of it. I've got a telecom swap utility that should do the trick."

"Good enough." Skater had hoped she would. A lot of deckers did. Usually such things were holdovers from their early days of prowling the Matrix and charging their time to other accounts.

When Wheeler, Duran, and Trey were topside, they closed the manhole. Elvis had the lock and the door to the office building open and they went inside.

The office belonged to The Chipped Pachyderm, a small company specializing in panic data-retrieval system software. It was divided up into twenty small cubicles, but only fourteen had computers. A quick inventory of those showed only five with personal effects hanging on the wall, suggesting that they were the only ones staffed.

"Wheeler," Skater said, pointing to the two security cameras hanging in opposite corners across the big room. The dog-brain alarm Elvis had taken out hadn't activated them. "They've got 'em inside, they've got to have 'em outside. Make them ours."

The dwarf gave him a brief salute and moved off.

Skater scanned the office. It would only be theirs free and clear for another few hours. By then they'd have to find another hiding place or some way out of the walled city. They had to make the most of it. "Trey. Start an inventory. Let me know what we have to work with."

"Done."

"Elvis, is that a trideo I see in that back office?"

The troll looked, then nodded.

"Scan headline news and see if we're anywhere near the top of the hit parade. Faces, names, or SINs."

"You got it." The troll lumbered off.

"Duran, security's yours until Wheeler brings the systems on-line."

"Right." The ork slipped back out into the alley and closed the door behind him without making a sound.

"Good news already," Trey reported from the other end of the office. "Place has fairly spacious washroom. No shower, but we can clean up a bit when there's time."

"We'll make time," Skater replied. Feeling clean meant feeling confident. He wasn't going to forego that easily accomplished weapon in his arsenal. "We'll go in shifts." He walked to the front windows and avoided skylining himself for anyone outside the building to see.

The street was mostly empty, and dark. None of the street lights worked, and there were none of the beautiful spires for which elven architecture had become famous. Along two of the thoroughfares he could see, there were huge cans of fire with transients gathered around them. It was the same kind of gutter scene you'd find in any of the darker corners of the sprawl. Skater figured that those pockets of humanity were the common denominator beyond all racial, political, or religious fervor. The problem was, that that common denominator stayed hungry, and compassion had generally been leeched out of them.

As he looked out over the unfamiliar city and recognized some of the familiar riffs, he had to admit he'd never been more afraid in his life. He'd led the team here, and he'd endangered them. And now he didn't have a clue how to get them back out again.

Archangel had most of the files she'd stolen from NuGene deciphered less than two hours later. She'd had to run a sample of them by a chummer in Seattle who specialized in biomed datasteals, and he'd given her a utility designed to get through the file encryption and archiving. It also had a special UnZip utility on it that she hadn't seen before. She'd handled that on her own.

When all that was done and the file open to them, the laborious reading gave Skater a headache.

"This could be worth millions," Archangel said, looking at the information. "Provided the research is on the money."

The files contained reports and documentation concerning new organic tissue implants that would end the need for immuno-suppressive drugs that caused almost as many problems for transplant patients as they solved. Skater didn't understand it all, but the gist was that NuGene had discovered a means of over-writing the DNA in the patient and in vat-grown donor tissue to create a hybrid that allowed the co-existence of both systems.

Usually, a transplant patient lived the rest of his or her life with some sort of immuno-suppressive drug, such as cyclosporine that prevented the granulocytes within the patient's body from attacking the new organs or tissues and in effect cannibalizing itself. However, that lowering of the body's defenses often resulted in reactions that could be just as life-threatening in the long run.

NuGene's new tissue was independently and singularly DNA-encoded to be absorbed by the host body. It wasn't a simple process, because the body's natural response to reject the new organic material as invasive wasn't easy to mute. The new organic material was recognized as antigens, and the granulocytes ingested it and killed it. But the research, including a bout of radiology to reorganize the tissue DNA, allowed the T-lymphocytes to rewrite the tissue as acceptable through phagocytization, altering the destruction of the new material to one of accepting.

"Okay," Skater said, looking at the material, "say a shadow team has this biotech in their hands. Why haven't they sold it to someone else?"

"No reason not to," Elvis said. "I'd have done it and gotten the hell out of there."

"Yeah, but this wasn't a simple run," Skater said. "We were set up to take the fall on this. It means there was a specific target in mind before the run. If NuGene can actually produce this new tissue, what's it going to mean for them in profits?"

"Through the fragging roof," Archangel said.

"Right. But what if these runners simply sold it to another corp?"

"Simple math," Duran said. "The profits get divided even if NuGene and the other corp don't try to cutthroat each other by lowering the prices."

Skater grinned to himself, feeling it now, knowing he was somewhere close to the target zone. "Right. If this was a simple shadowrun, the runners would have already fenced the files and pocketed whatever they could make on them. But the person behind this is in it for more than just the one-time score."

"How?" Duran asked.

Archangel paused at her deck and looked up at him, a puzzled look on her face.

"We agree that a corp's profits go down if it can't control the output of its product, right?"

Archangel and Duran agreed.

"Where are a corporation's profits shown? What are they put back into?"

"The company," Duran answered.

"The stocks," Archangel said.

Skater could tell by the look on her face that she'd followed him. "Dividends, yeah. Big money if this tissue-replacement tech is really wiz."

"But it wouldn't make sense for one of the shareholders to arrange something like this," Archangel said. "The profits were already theirs."

"What if news leaked out that NuGene just lost its little gold mine?" Skater asked. "How about this scenario: everyone who's been holding onto their shares for sentimental reasons or because they like backing a dark horse decides to dump them on the market. Whoever has arranged to steal the files, or even only give the impression that they've been stolen—which is a wiz little curve in the scheme of things all by itself—can then go and buy up the stock at cheap prices, then return the files to NuGene and watch the returns go through the roof."

"Frag, kid, do you know how risky that would be?" Duran asked.

"For the profit potential we're talking about, do you think anyone in a position to do this would think more than twice? We hit the *Sapphire Seahawk* hoping the tip would pan out. Whoever did this would have a lock."

"But we can always fade the heat," Duran said. "If they own the stock, their name is going to be written down somewhere in black and white."

"You have to know to look for them first. If you play for high stakes, you've got to be willing to stick your neck out. And remember, most of the time they've had *our* necks stuck out there."

A silence followed, and Skater knew they were thinking it over. Now that he'd said it out loud and fought for it, he felt more secure about it. The stolen files hadn't been about a simple datasteal; it had been a vicious and nasty play, thought out from the very first.

"At this point," Skater said, "everything NuGene's done so far indicates they thought we stole their tech. So now they think they're behind in the game and that someone sold them up the river. They might decide to rush their new discovery onto the market. To do that they're going to have to raise some capital."

"New stocks," Archangel said.

"Maybe." Skater stopped packing and looked at her. "We'll need to check that out."

She nodded. "Telecom's ready when you are."

He crossed the room and used it, accessing one of Kestrel's drops. Archangel was already working her deck with a vengeance. After Skater left a message for Kestrel to call him here at The Chipped Pachyderm, he walked into the office with Elvis. The troll had been waving to him.

The office showed an old pride. Documents and holopics lined the walls, as well as downloaded newsfaxes concerning deals the firm had made in the past. Most of them were more than five years old. The seat behind the desk was worn and comfortable, even though it was too small for the troll, who was perched on the edge of the desk.

"Starting the recap of the headline news," Elvis rumbled. "We made the cut."

The news bytes were announced by an elven male with capped teeth and broken veins in his nose from too many nights out late drinking that makeup couldn't quite cover. The crash landing of the arms dealers' plane, shot down by the ever-vigilant Border Guard, warranted some trid footage that showed the flaming wreckage and the shock troops beating the brush. So did news of the birth of a little girl to Ariadne and Tavis Silverstaff in Seattle. Stock footage rolled of the couple at public gatherings, as well as some stills from his sports career. And on an international note, a breaking story announced that the so-called laughing death disease had been traced to tainted DocWagon vats. The disease was caused by a new subvirus that converted healthy tissue into dangerous tissue, which then spread throughout the body, attacking muscle tissue and finally, the brain. The side effects of a body turned on itself were very disturbing. Seattle Governor Marilyn Schultz was attempting to suspend DocWagon's activities in the city.

Skater felt a sick cloud rise up inside him and spread through his guts, and he tried to force it out.

"Jack," Archangel called as the telecom beeped.

Skater shook himself and hustled over. "See if there's any more info on this laughing death disease. Something doesn't wash." He turned to the telecom. "Yeah."

"Where are you?" Kestrel asked, speaking only in audio mode.

"Would you believe, Portland?" Skater had no reason to hold back. NuGene already knew they were here. It couldn't cause more people to start looking for them. "I need something."

"Didn't have it figured any other way. What?"

"NuGene's Seattle operation. Has it become active since this morning?"

"You got a specific field, or do I just run this blind?"

"Stock," Skater said. "I think they may be out fishing for start-up capital."

"I thought they had that." In the background, keys clicked.

"They're thin for a really aggressive move. I'm guessing that whatever timetable they originally had has been drek-canned."

"I'll look around. Get back to you. This number still good for an hour or so?"

"Yeah. I'll be here."

"Wait," Archangel said, staring at her deck monitor. "Ask him about a stock called ReGEN." She spelled it.

Skater relayed the name as well as the spelling.

"It's a new player as of today. Not OTC stuff. It's selling at a fair piece of change, but the stock précis is pretty vague. New company, outstanding new product, blah-blah-blah, yahdee-yahdee-yahdee. I don't see anything exciting here."

"Tell him to track it back," Archangel said.

Skater did.

Kestrel sounded bored, and a little tense at having to stay on the line so long. It took him seven minutes to make the corporation behind the issued stock certificates even with Archangel guiding the way. Skater timed him. "Son of a slitch. NuGene. How'd you know?"

"Never mind. It's too long to go into. How's the stock trading?"

"For a new stock, it's done okay. Plus there's the fact that they issued a lot of it. Should I buy into this? I wouldn't mind a quick turn-around on something a little insider trading could guarantee."

"When I find out," Skater said, "I'll call you."

"Do that, kid, because you're going to owe me more for this than you can ever pay me. Is there anything else I can do?"

"I want to find a street guy, named Synclair Tone. Hardcase. He's in Seattle by way of Puyallup. I got a number off some of his yabos, that was my last line on him." Skater's stomach tightened when he thought of the man. But he was the last lead to Larisa that he hadn't checked out.

"I'll look around," Kestrel promised. "Let me know about ReGEN."

Skater said he would, then broke the connection. He looked at Archangel. "Where did you find the stock?"

"Here in Tir Tairngire. It went on-line this morning. Evidently issuing it had been in the works all along, just not so soon."

"They're in frenzy mode." Skater looked at the stock quotes culled from the Tir Tairngire exchange boards.

"I think so. The stock isn't selling so well over here."

"Less people wanting to take the risk."

"Or that can," Archangel agreed. "I also noticed something else." She punched the keyboard and brought up another screen of figures. "There's no tech info available on the laughing death subvirus, but it seems to be the evil twin of NuGene's. Also, DocWagon has been aggressively buying up NuGene stock here in Portland, spurring a resurgence of interest. Considering the pile of drek DocWagon's in, you wonder if they don't have an inside line. But it seems like a lot of NuGene's stockholders are seeing this as a chance to unload shares that haven't performed in years."

"Think DocWagon could be after a hostile take-over?"

"I don't see how. Tavis Silverstaff still owns over fifty percent of NuGene."

"But they could buy their way into being something more than a silent partner," Skater said.

"Yes."

"But they aren't taking any of the action on ReGEN."

"No. The information I turned up hasn't been released widely into the public." Archangel gestured at the deck. "Takes some concentrated digging by someone who's very good, and who is looking."

"How can the ReGEN stock be different from NuGene stock?"

"The way it's set up, NuGene represents the parent company. The Seattle office is going to be called something else, operate under different guidelines."

"Then Silverstaff doesn't own fifty percent of that company."

"It depends on how much stock they let out," Archangel said. "If they have to cover what the paper's worth and they're short, they're fragged."

Skater considered that. "So they're vulnerable now."

"Very. If anyone knew for sure they have something worthwhile. When they release the news that they've got this new tissue replacement, and it's as good as they say, that paper will turn to gold and they may be able to buy most of it back. Or at least issue and buy enough of it themselves to maintain controlling interest."

As he looked down the list of names, Skater saw one that caught his attention. "Saeder-Krupp was interested in acquiring NuGene at one time."

Archangel nodded.

"Want to find out if they still are?" Skater asked.

"What?" Her disbelief was evident.

Looking at the name of the German-based multinational corporation on the screen, Skater made himself believe it could happen. The art of the deal was in having something to sell to someone who wanted to believe you had something they wanted. "Saeder-Krupp is aggressive," he said, "and they own a few hundred other corps. If they were interested in NuGene before, they ought to really have a jones on once they find out about this new biotech."

Archangel stared at him in disbelief. "Have you gone totally glitched?"

Skater looked at her. "There's a wall between us and home, and a drekstorm waiting on us once we get there. I'm thinking that a partner at this time could be a good career move."

"Lofwyr?"

Skater nodded. "He carries a lot of weight. Fragging Charles Schwab of the Awakened age." Saeder-Krupp, the mightiest megacorp in the world, was Lofwyr's own personal plaything.

"He's a dragon." Archangel stared into his eyes. "He's a *dragon*, for frag's sake. No one ever knows for sure what they're going to do. The way they see the world, what they want out of it. You can't—."

"He believes in profit," Skater argued. "I'm prepared to give it to him. What more could he ask for?"

"Your stripped and bleached skull as a bedpan."

Skater looked at her, then lowered his voice. "It's a chance. Maybe the only one we've got. I'm not going to turn my back on it." He tried not to listen to the desperation in his own voice. Thankfully, Archangel didn't argue and just went to work.

Everyone knew that Lofwyr, a member of the Council of Princes who ruled Tir Tairngire, maintained an estate in the Royal Hill region of Portland. Skater couldn't be sure whether Lofwyr was actually there now, and he was even less sure whether it would be good luck or bad to find the dragon at home.

27

To his own surprise, Skater got through. Not to Lofwyr, of course, but to someone else fairly high up. She gave her name as Elschen. Despite the hair that apparently covered her from head to toe—judging from the view afforded by the telecom screen—Skater knew she was female. The blue-black body fur served as clothing and masked her breasts while hinting at the roundness only a touch would reveal. A silver amulet gleamed at her throat.

"Jack Skater," she said in a deep voice.

Skater had never talked to a sasquatch before. Especially one who worked for Lofwyr and knew his name before he gave it. "Yes," he confirmed.

"My people have been looking for you in Seattle." The sasquatch glanced at something out of the telecom's view. "However, it appears that you are not in Seattle."

Skater tensed. Archangel was jacked into her deck, overseeing the exchange and masking their real location at The Chipped Pachyderm. But if Elschen was already certain they weren't in Seattle, her capabilities made every second count. "Why were you looking for me?"

"For the NuGene files you stole," Elschen said. She folded her hands under her jawline. "Of course." Her eyes gleamed like a cat's.

"I was thinking more along the lines of making a deal," Skater replied.

"You would ask for more than your life—knowing whom you're dealing with?" She seemed amused.

"You're looking for me," Skater replied.

"And you're looking for Lofwyr. Touché, Mr. Skater." Elschen leaned back in her chair. The office behind her was baroque, filled with antiquities and stained glass. "For a time, it appears that we may need each other."

"Lofwyr knows about the replacement tissue NuGene has in development?"

"He has for months. The profits from that bit of biz will be astronomical, of course. That, however, is not our main interest. NuGene and Tavis Silverstaff have become an important cog in a much larger wheel. You are merely one of the teeth." She bared her own fangs for his inspection.

Skater struggled to remain at ease on the outside. Inside, his stomach was tight and rebellious. "Maybe the cog won't turn so well without that tooth," he pointed out.

"Maybe," Elschen said. "What you must realize is that your well-being isn't something that particularly concerns us. But I was instructed that you might be useful should you turn up. Lofwyr has mentioned that controlling your presence in these matters may facilitate the success of his own designs. If that were not the case, you'd never have gotten this far." She gave a soft laugh. "How many people do you think can just call me up on the telecom?"

Skater didn't like the way the conversation was going. But he didn't have a choice. He'd hoped to be bargaining from a position of power, offering the dragon a suitable prize in exchange for their own survival. Now he was like a pauper begging for table crumbs. But when crumbs came from the dragon's table, those crumbs could represent lives and small fortunes.

"But I have."

"Yes." Elschen came closer to the screen. Her eyes were as focused as gunsights. "You're in a position to beg for a favor, and Lofwyr has his own reasons for granting it. If—you do not ask for too much. I'll send a car to bring you to Royal Hill."

As easy as that, the sasquatch had let Skater know she knew he was in Portland. A cold feeling trailed down his spine.

"Yes. You see, we already knew about your raid on NuGene. It couldn't have been anyone else." She glared at him. "If you try to run, we'll simply hunt you down."

"I'll be at the Ivanhoe," Skater said. It was a seedy motel not far from their Swan Island location. "In thirty minutes."

The sasquatch cut the connection without another word.

The rest of the team tried to talk Skater out of making the meet. But they were only half-hearted attempts. In the end, there was really no choice at all.

Lofwyr maintained a small estate on Royal Hill. Small, at least, by the standards set by its neighbors. The black Rolls Royce Phaeton limousine delivered Skater to the tall, arched front doors just slightly more than an hour and a half later. It was almost dawn.

He got out and stretched, taking time to scan his surroundings. There was no way he could escape. With all the electronic and magical security around the castle, he'd have had better luck trying to cross a moat of alligators.

Lofwyr hadn't limited himself to mere electronic security measures and the low walls encircling the estate. Things roamed the grounds, some on great leathery wings and some on taloned feet. Elschen met him at the door, dressed in nothing more than the amulet. Her body hair somehow masked her nakedness and made her all the more alluring.

"You have a weapon." She held out her hand.

Reluctantly, Skater passed the Predator across. She took it casually and held it in her hand as she ushered him in.

The first things Skater noticed about the house were the huge doorways and immense, sweeping corridors. He felt incredibly small. Elschen walking at his side, being head and shoulders taller, didn't help.

She didn't speak to him, and exuded an air that she didn't want him speaking to her.

Skater took in the house as they walked. The floor was rough and dark cement, and the lighting was dim. Though Saeder-Krupp invested heavily in cutting-edge technology, it didn't show in the surroundings. The doors were unmarked, and security cameras were nestled in clear bubbles that hung from the ceiling.

"Go ahead," Elschen said, opening one of a final pair of doors. "He's expecting you."

Skater moved into the antechamber beyond the doors. His heels clicked on the concrete surface, ringing hollowly in the vast space the room contained. He was alone, and not another sound was in the house.

The walls held paintings that were both priceless and emotionally powerful. Sculptures of equal potency sat on stands and in niches in the walls beneath the paintings.

"Skater."

The dry, raspy voice formed in his mind, feeling like sandpaper next to his brain. He turned and stared down the long room.

A man suddenly stood at the other end next to a banquet table that must have stretched at least twenty meters. Candlesticks and flowers decorated the length of the polished wood. The man was almost two and a half meters tall, but the dark pinstriped silk suit fit him perfectly. Though troll-sized, he was perfectly proportioned. His bronze-colored hair was gathered behind him in a ponytail that went down his back. His features looked chiseled, but smooth and robust. He wore black wraparound sunglasses.

"I am Lofwyr," he said in that awesome silent voice of his.

Skater noticed that his lips never moved.

"I do not have much time. There are other matters that require my attention. I've freed this hour for you. Do not waste it."

The words were pure, naked threat. Skater had to steel his knees as he approached the dragon. He'd heard they could assume human as well as other forms; he'd just never expected to see it for himself. Quickly, aware of the tightness in his voice that he couldn't quite shake, he recounted the events of the last couple days.

"It appears that you've been someone's pawn in this game so far," Lofwyr said when he finished. *"Now you wish to be mine."*

Skater almost disagreed. He was there to become his own force in the scheme of things, leveraging himself in to get a shot at a profit and revenge. But looking at the dragon's cool, human facade, he knew that while he might have come to Lofwyr with that in mind, becoming a pawn in whatever game the dragon was playing was the best he could hope for. He answered in a small voice. "Yes."

"Elschen," Lofwyr said, *"bring up the stock quotes."*

Skater knew the dragon had intentionally allowed him to hear the conversation. A section of the inlaid wooden wall to his left separated and revealed a computer screen. In seconds, stock quotes were pulsing across it.

"Interesting. I hadn't thought Silverstaff would become vulnerable so quickly."

"I don't think he's aware of how exposed he's about to become," Skater said. He had to force himself to speak. The dragon's presence and the sheer power that surrounded him were almost overwhelming.

"Nor do I." Lofwyr eyed him speculatively from behind the dark glasses. *"What is it you wish to accomplish here, human?"*

"I want to get my team and myself out of Portland alive," Skater said, and as he said it, it sounded like more than the dragon would ever agree to. "And I want some payback against the people who set us up and killed Larisa Hartsinger."

The dragon's lips twitched in amusement. *"Why,"* he asked in that impossibly dry voice, *"should I care?"*

"Maybe you shouldn't," Skater replied. "But I may be in a position to give you NuGene."

"How?"

The feeling he was covering ground the dragon had already crossed plagued Skater as he tried to talk. He was tense and frightened confronting Lofwyr. Dragons didn't look at life the same as men. "We can represent your interests in Seattle on this. If it's played right, you stand to make a lot of profit over the next few days."

"Money doesn't interest me," Lofwyr stated. *"It's only a marker system designed to keep track of the games I play with others."*

"If that's true," Skater said, "then I've wasted your time and mine by coming here."

The dragon eyed him in cold regard. *"You border on insolence."*

Skater couldn't deny it, partly because it was true, and partly because his mouth had gone dry.

"Still, you and your team add a layer of deniability to my efforts, as well as concealment while I launch my own strikes." Lofwyr smiled. *"You have promise in these matters, I'll admit that. And in my own game, your presence here could eliminate some steps I would need to take."*

Skater waited, his breath tight in his chest. If the dragon hadn't wanted to use him, he'd never have been brought here in the first place.

"Besides passage from Portland," the dragon asked, *"what else would you want from me?"*

"A letter of credit at one of your Seattle banks. We're going to set up some straw accounts to get as much of the issued stock from ReGEN as we can. With the activity that can generate, the price should go up in hours. At the same time, we're going to release news to the trid channels that ReGEN's research has been stolen. Once that news hits, the prices will plummet again, and people will dump the shares they've bought, trying not to get stuck with them. We'll be able to buy even more of them then."

"To what end? It sounds like you're only wasting money. MY money."

"Because ReGEN stands to make a fortune on this tech," Skater said. "Someone has set them up, made it look like their research was stolen by us. But the stuff we got our hands on was no good. NuGene and Silverstaff don't know that. Right now they're living in terror that they're about to lose everything they've worked for. In order to save as much as they can, they're going into production immediately. That's why they're selling the stocks: to get the money necessary to open the Seattle office now."

"How do you know the tech hasn't been stolen by someone else and another company isn't already working on it?"

"If that was the case, NuGene would know about it. Something this big wouldn't stay a secret. Instead, they're totally concentrated on us."

"Maybe the buyer has his own reasons for keeping silent about this."

"NuGene hasn't patented this procedure yet," Skater said. "Even if they did patent it now, anyone who has the original process can change it up enough to get the same results and claim they discovered it through independent research. Someone who could pay for the tech probably also has the means to go into production immediately. If NuGene did contest the ownership, the court battle would take years to settle and be a continual drain on dividends and profits. No one would want to invest in them, meaning even less nuyen to fight back with. Their only hope is to find the people who swiped the tech, or manage to buy it back from them if at all possible."

The dragon was silent for a moment. *"I agree."*

"There's another facet to this," Skater said. "It could turn out that whoever really stole the tech, or at least made it look like my team did, is intending to return it to NuGene soon. In the meantime, they're going to be buying up stock as well. I have a feeling that whoever set me up, set up my friend Larisa too, and I'm going to nail him."

"For a human," the dragon said, *"you're capable of delightfully nefarious thought. Your exit from Portland and the letter of credit shall be accomplished and established. Is there anything that remains?"*

Skater shook his head, not daring to speak.

"You're lucky, human," Lofwyr said. *"You managed to put your foot into something that I'd already had designs on. I briefly considered having you killed and returning the tech to NuGene through a third party. I need Tavis Silverstaff to appear strong to the people I'm really after, then I'll humble them. For now, though, I find you quite useful. But have a care in your machinations."*

The dragon approached slowly. Skater stood his ground with difficulty. His knees wanted to tremble.

"I won't stand for being betrayed." The dragon's human face was implacable. He reached out a hand, leaving the fingers open and splayed, and stopped it only centimeters from

Skater's face. *"You and your kind have a saying—Never deal with a dragon. There is a history between your race and mine that you could not possibly be aware of. I would amend that wisdom: never break a deal with a dragon. The consequences can be most dire."*

The hand shifted suddenly, morphing almost within an eyeblink. It became a clawed talon three times its size and covered in scales the color of golden crystal, large enough to easily engulf Skater's head. The heavy nails clacked together as they sheared through air only a skin layer or two from Skater's face.

Skater thought he was going to throw up. There was no doubt that the talons could have neatly sliced the face from his skull too fast to let the blood run had the dragon wanted.

"Welcome to my game, Jack Skater, and to your small, almost insignificant part within it. Play it well and you'll find that I can be most generous. Do not, and hope that your enemies kill you. They'll be more merciful than I. That's a promise."

The taloned claw turned back into a hand.

Skater didn't feel any safer for it.

Lofwyr turned his back and walked away, a giant man striding through his kingdom. *"Go now. Your needs will have been attended. Deliver what you've promised."* Then he walked through a heavy wooden door and was gone.

"Oh drek, Jack," Skater said, struggling to keep from falling. The meeting had been worse than anything he'd imagined. He breathed in through his nose and out through his mouth, scrambling for self-control. Going back to face everything in Seattle seemed impossible enough.

But he knew he'd just stared death in the eye.

28

Skater was almost asleep in the padded luxury of the Lear-Cessna Platinum I jet when the portacom rang. Shifting the set forward, he powered it up and said hello.

"I've got the skinny on Synclair Tone," Kestrel said, returning Skater's call.

Archangel was the only one of the team still awake. She sat hunched over her deck, tied in through the luxury jet's onboard computers and the satlink. Not only had Saeder-Krupp supplied the jet, they'd even installed an Elvis-sized seat. The troll lay on his back, arms thrown out to his sides, snoring fitfully. Lofwyr had also sent a med-team to meet them when they'd boarded the jet, and the troll's shoulder had been bandaged where the dog bit him.

"Let me hear it."

"Joker's connected to the Mafia just as you suspected. He's working out of a stable of hitters managed by Tomasino Carbone."

"I'm not familiar with the name."

"No reason you should be. Carbone handles wetwork, matching the right job with the right guy. He stays in the background, no PR, no profile whatsoever. Lone Star's been trying to nail him for years."

"Tone is working for Carbone?" Skater asked.

"On the surface. See, there's a wrinkle."

"What?"

"Carbone has a rep for handling only top-notch hitters. Star-quality. Experts in mage work, physical adepts, street razors hardwired to hell. The people he services, sometimes they want their targets to simply disappear, or commit suicide, with no repercussions for them. Tone doesn't fit the profile. He's a fragging street animal. Finesse for him would be making sure the whole clip hit his target, not just making sure only one bullet was needed."

"Then what's Carbone doing with Tone?"

"I asked that very question," Kestrel said. "No definite word came back. But I was told that it was a favor."

"To Tone?" Skater asked.

"No way. To someone else higher up in the food chain."

"Can you find out who?"

"Kid, you've lived on the backstreets where I've gotta go to get this buzz. These wiseguys don't talk."

"What about a contact to Carbone? I'll ask him myself."

"Are you glitched?"

Larisa's ruined face slipped into Skater's mind, bringing with it a memory of the empty crib. "No."

"There's a bounty on your head, kid, or don't you remember?"

"I need this slag, Kestrel. No matter how I have to do it." Tone was all that remained of the ties back to Larisa.

The fixer sighed. "Okay, I'll check into it. In the meantime, I've heard that Tone has gotten himself a piece of an after-hours casino on the west side, down in the dock area. He's leaning on them for protection money."

"Carbone's doing?"

"Slot, no. Carbone wouldn't touch this place. It's called Stinky-Fingered Al's. Joker who owns it used to be a proctologist before he got busted from the doc biz for improprieties unbecoming a member of the profession. Makes you wonder about the improprieties that *are* becoming. The trade is strictly low-level gamblers and hustlers, mostly longshoremen and blue collar. There's about eight killings a year there, and maybe two attempted robberies."

"Tone has cut himself in on the gate?"

"Yepper. And Stinky-Fingered Al is none too happy about it, but he can't do a fragging thing about it. No matter what else is going on, Stinky-Finger isn't going to try to slot Tone over as long as Carbone is backing him."

"Has Tone done any wetwork for Carbone yet?"

"No way to tell that, chummer."

"Could be interesting to ask."

"Could be interesting to see if you're still standing when the question clears your lips."

"Do what you can," Skater said. "I'll be in touch." He punched the telecom off, then pushed himself out of the seat, wondering who might have leaned on Carbone for Tone. There wasn't a lot in the guy's resume to make someone go to bat for him. Meaning he'd done something, or was going to do something, for someone who could.

The sprawl turned on the cut of the deal, and there was always another one in the works.

"Stinky-Fingered Al's?" Duran said.

"You listened in."

"Kind of hard not to. No offense."

"None taken."

The ork shifted. "I know the place. Want company when you go? It's not really a joint where you want to go stag."

Skater looked at him. "I'd like that."

Duran nodded, then closed his eyes and relaxed again. "Just say when."

* * *

In addition to the trip out of the Tir and various kinds of financial support, Lofwyr had also provided a suite of apartments near the Aztechnology complex that had its own private elevator so they could come and go pretty much as they pleased. Four vehicles were also at their disposal in the underground parking area. Skater had no doubt that whatever the dragon's real scheme, the stakes were high. He wondered if he'd ever know what was going on, then hoped he wouldn't. Too much knowledge could be deadly.

The team arrived back in Seattle in the early afternoon. For the first day and a half, Skater had them all keep a low profile. They ordered take-out and charged it to the corporate account, and slept in shifts. Archangel set her own schedule, exhausting herself in the work of surreptitiously buying up the stocks through straw accounts as well as trying to find out who the other major players were. By the evening of the first day, she'd cut the list from six to four. On the morning of the second day after a round of heavy trading, she cut that list to three. But she still wasn't able to put names to the buyers.

Skater woke after each sleep, whether it was for his whole shift or a nap he'd managed, dripping wet from a cold sweat and in the throes of another nightmare about Larisa, and sometimes about the baby. After growing up on the Council lands, he'd never much liked being cooped up inside. Knowing the nightmares were just waiting for him to close his eyes didn't make it any easier.

When he stood trembling with the aftershocks of some nightmare and gazed out the bullet- and bomb-proof windows during the day or night, he could almost hear the streets calling out to him. It was where he needed to be, the battleground he was most familiar with.

That afternoon, while Archangel was searching down names of players, Skater arranged an untraceable telecom call to four of the major trid media groups and talked with their investigative reporters regarding NuGene's inability to make good on the stocks they were issuing.

The story broke across the networks that afternoon and again that night. NuGene spokesmen, including Tavis Silverstaff, were unavailable for comment.

At the end of the eleven o'clock news round-up, however, the society reporter for KOMA showed footage of Ariadne Silverstaff's new daughter.

Mother and infant were going home the following day, after staying in the hospital for routine observation. The delivery was easy, Ariadne Silverstaff was quoted as saying. The footage was short and to the point, taken in the private room where the two had stayed since birth. There were also a few seconds with Dr. Liam Reed, who said the pair were in the pink of health.

The segment ended with a close-up of mother and child.

"Is something wrong?" Archangel asked as she happened to come into the room.

Skater had stopped dead in the middle of the living room, galvanized by the sight of the round-faced baby ogling the people around her. "No," he said. But he was lying, because something was suddenly very wrong. What he'd seen in the face of that newborn infant was Larisa.

During the trading the next morning, ReGEN stock rained down like confetti on the trading floors. The going price dropped by thirty-five percent at open, then continued falling another twenty-two percent before the close of the day. None of the new stock issued had moved at all. But Archangel and the three other buyers kept adding to their hoards, buying up from the people who were afraid of losing all their investment.

At four o'clock, Skater found a message in one of his drops from a woman who claimed to be Larisa Hartsinger's mother. She wanted to meet, to give him something Larisa had left for him.

The apartment was in the Tukwila neighborhood in the south downtown section of Seattle. It was a third-floor walkup at the back where plastitwine ran stitches back and forth between the adjacent buildings, and clothing was hung on them. Human and meta kids played together in the grass and weeds that sprang up through the cracked plascrete that had once been a courtyard. Graffiti, both the old spray-paint kind and the new neon tubing that was the latest in use, scarred the pitted walls, violence and degradation and pride all wrapped up in bright colors.

Skater walked easily, dressed in street clothes and boots, the Predator tucked under his Kevlar jacket at the back. His heart was pounding in his chest when he reached the door of 305, but it wasn't from the exertion of the climb. The doorbell had been broken, and only two wires stuck out. He rapped his knuckles on the scratched surface of the door.

Archangel had checked the address out for him, finding that it was listed to Kalika Chilson, who was cross-referenced on both Larisa's birth and death certificates. Skater didn't think the message was a trap, but Elvis and Duran had ridden along as rearguard, maintaining a position in a van only a few blocks away.

The door opened hesitantly. "Yeah?" a harsh female's voice demanded.

"I'm Skater."

"You alone?"

"Yes."

The woman opened the door and stuck her face out suspiciously. She was short, thin, and frail, looking like a bleached mop that had been up-ended, given arms and legs, and shoved into a worn set of black synthleathers. She had on a white tee shirt that had gone sickly gray under the jacket, and the sagging breasts advertised that she wasn't wearing underclothes. Her ears and features were elven.

She didn't invite Skater in, taking time to fire up a cigarette butt that sent her into a fit of coughing. She squinted up at him when it passed. "Larisa said there'd probably be some money in it for me."

"Depends on what you have," Skater said.

"A telecom message chip she said you'd want."

"Did she say what it was about?"

"No." A black circle ringed under her left eye, a bruise already past its prime.

"Then why should I be so ready to pay you?" Skater asked.

"You come, didn't you?"

Skater didn't have a reply for that. "How much?"

She shrugged, trying to play it off and let him make the offer. She obviously didn't know what the message chip was worth. "Got my eye blacked over it," she said. "Two guys come to my squat yesterday. Wanted to know if I'd been in touch with Larisa before she died. I lied. Told them no. They hit me, wanting to make sure I was telling the truth. But I've been hit before. I can take a pretty good beating if I have to. Anyway, them showing up here like that made me start thinking Larisa wasn't lying when she said there'd be some profit in me calling you. At first, I was afraid it would only bring trouble. Since that had already got here, I figured I'd give you a call this morning."

Looking at the woman and listening to her, Skater wondered how Larisa could have even been in the same gene pool, much less the woman's daughter.

Evidently she thought he was still looking at her eye. "Larisa's father could throw a good punch when he wanted to." Kalika Chilson lit another cigarette from the stub of the first, then hacked her way through another coughing fit. This time it ended with a gob of phlegm sailing over the side of the railing and splatting near a trio of troll boys who immediately started yelling profanities at the woman.

"Who were the men who came here?" Skater asked.

"Gutterkin," she answered. "One of them had on a fancy suit and a new face, but the mark of the street was still there. Fragging pieces of drek is what they were."

"The name Synclair Tone mean anything to you?"

"One was called Tone. The other one was Bobby. It was Tone who done the hitting. He liked it; you could see it in his eyes."

"What's on the chip?" Skater asked.

The thin shoulders rose and fell. "Don't know. It's password protected." She smiled at him, showing gapped teeth. "I'll admit, I ain't no saint." She licked her lips. "Think you want to spend five thousand nuyen to find out what's on it?"

Skater dug his hand into his pocket and took out one of the credsticks he had there. A brief glance showed him it was one with five thousand nuyen keyed on it. Lofwyr's coffers ran deep. "It's open-coded. Put your passcode and SIN in and you're wiz."

She took the credstick hesitantly. "I don't suppose I could ask for more?"

"No."

Her gaze was belligerent. "And if I did?"

"I'd book," Skater replied. "Maybe you could find the two guys who showed up here before. Maybe I'd even call them and tell them you lied. It doesn't sound like you'd get more than I'm offering."

Without another word, Kalika Chilson reached into an inner pocket of her jacket and retrieved the message chip. "Don't suppose you'd want to see the things she left here."

"She hasn't been here recently?"

"No."

Skater shook his head. "I don't think so." He inserted the chip into the portacom he'd brought and powered up. Larisa formed on the display immediately.

"Jack," the message said, "if you get this, I guess it means—"

Skater shut it off. Whatever Larisa had left for him was private. He meant for it to stay that way. "I thought you said it was password protected."

"It is," the woman insisted. "You let it play a little longer, she'll tell you that."

Skater nodded and said thanks. He held the portacom as he went down the steps, wondering if the message held all the secrets. Some, he felt certain, he'd already guessed.

29

"Jack, if you get this, I guess it means I'm not around to talk to anymore." On the portacom screen, Larisa looked drawn and tired. She was wearing some kind of black outfit that looked good on her, and behind her was the living room of the Bellevue doss. Her figure hadn't quite bounced back from the pregnancy, but Jack thought she looked better than anytime he'd known her. And she'd changed her hair, wearing it shorter and more daring than before. The corpse Skater had viewed in the Lone Star morgue hadn't revealed that.

The time/date stamp in the lower-right corner showed that the message had been recorded only three days before she'd died. "First off, I want to tell you I'm sorry about what happened with us. There were a lot of things I never got to say to you that I wanted to. We fought, and I wish I'd had the chance to set that straight, too."

Seated in the back of the van as Elvis drove it back to their hideout, Skater felt a stab of pain at seeing her face and hearing her voice. Duran sat in the passenger seat with the Scorpion canted across his knees.

"I love you, Jack," Larisa said. "I just wish there was more time to explain. Everything got so twisted up so fragging fast." Tears glimmered in her eyes.

Skater's throat felt thick and tight, and he was uncomfortable knowing that Kalika Chilson had heard even this much of the recording. He rubbed his fingers lightly over the flat screen.

"It's hard to talk," she went on. "I promised myself I wasn't going to get emotional. I'm going to passcode the rest of this. One word. If you don't know about it, then you don't need to. Just remember that I love you."

The picture on the display faded out, leaving a password prompt blinking. Without hesitation, Skater hit the keypad control and converted the entry into letters instead of numerals. He punched in five letters. C—H—I—L—D.

The prompt showed a reject flag.

He tried again, this time thinking that Larisa would have ragged on him for being so impersonal. Four letters, this time. B—A—B—Y. A word with more promise, more joy.

The prompt flashed an accept.

The screen cleared again. When it did, Larisa was visible once more, this time with another room of her apartment in the background. "Her name is Emma, Jack. It means 'one who heals.' I hope you like it." Then she held up a baby in her arms.

The round face and wispy dark hair and pointed ears reminded Skater of Larisa. It was like he'd seen the baby before, like he knew exactly what she would look like. Part of it, he knew, was because of the resemblance between mother and daughter. Then, his heart seemed to thud to a stop inside his chest. The tiny face he'd seen on the trid the night before flashed in his mind. Ariadne Silverstaff's new baby. He peered closely at Emma and knew with cold certainty that the pictures had been of the same baby.

"She's your daughter," Larisa said, and there were tears that went along with the smile on her face. She kissed the baby, then gently laid her in the crib. "And if you're watching this, it means they've killed me and taken her." The flat screen grayed out.

"Oh frag," Skater said, feeling like a hole had suddenly materialized in the center of his chest.

"This all started about a year ago," Larisa went on, taking up the narrative after a brief pause. She no longer had the baby in her arms.

Skater paced the floor of the suite of apartments while the

others watched. He'd already seen it all in the van, but he wanted them to see it too.

"A man named Ridge Maddock came to me," Larisa said. "He said he had information about some shadow work you'd done. He told me if I didn't cooperate, he'd give you up to the people still looking for you and that they'd kill you the minute they laid eyes on you." Her voice broke. "I didn't want that to happen, Jack."

Skater worked hard to keep his face devoid of emotion. A lot of anger was moving in him, as well as confusion. He had a daughter. That was something that was going to take a lot of getting used to. Until now he'd always been alone, responsible for no one other than himself. That had been one of his laws. No extensions of self to render him more vulnerable. Larisa was as close as he'd ever come.

"He wanted me to have a child," Larisa said. "They were going to artificially inseminate me. You know how I feel about that. Machines poking inside my body. I'm a dancer, and a good one without being chipped. I couldn't handle that. So I went to a street mage I know, and he gave me a mojo that would prevent the embryo from taking. Sometimes they don't take anyway, and the procedure has to be done again. Maybe more than once."

Unable to face the hurt in her eyes anymore, Skater turned away from the screen and looked out the window. Night was coming to the sprawl, and the lurkers were starting to come to life.

"I used the mojo, but they agreed to wait another month and see if I'd gotten pregnant," Larisa said. "I was going out of my mind trying to figure out what to do—I still had to come up with a baby. Maddock is connected to someone named Synclair Tone. The whole deal came from him. If he'd found out what I'd done, he'd have killed me for sure."

Slowly, Skater sipped his soykaf, hoping it would wash the bitter taste from his mouth. It wouldn't cut the guilt. Larisa had been trapped and alone, and he hadn't even noticed.

"I could think of only one thing I could do," she said. "They were practically mainlining fertility drugs into me by then, and so I just let nature take its course when you and I were together. When I went back a month later, I was pregnant and they were satisfied. They never questioned whether it was the embryo they'd tried to plant in me. I thought maybe it would give us some time to work things out. Only you were never there to work things out with." She paused. "Part of it is my fault, because I didn't tell you. Spirits, with everything that had happened, I wouldn't have known where to begin."

Skater's fist clenched. Somewhere out there in the sprawl, Synclair Tone was enjoying himself, maybe making himself happy at someone else's expense. Skater was a shadowrunner; he stole, sometimes he even killed, and he lived between the cracks of society, but he didn't intentionally harm innocents. Most times he worked for one corp against another, and he hadn't met an innocent corporation yet.

And one thing he was sure of, Larisa had been one of those innocents. She wouldn't have ended up dead if it hadn't been for her association with him. He blamed himself as much as anyone.

"For the first few months it was no problem seeing you," Larisa said. "You were a ghost during that time, so it was easy for the other girls to cover for me when Maddock asked about it. He got pushy sometimes, and demanding, but it was easy to lie to him because I didn't like him. And to tell the truth, I don't think he cared what I did as long as I stayed pregnant."

As Skater listened, he dwindled down to the cold core of himself where he'd learned to live while with his grandfather.

"But then, five months ago, everything changed. I was starting to show. He told me I had to stop seeing you and two months later, he moved me to a new apartment. He said I didn't have a choice if I wanted to protect you. And even if I didn't, then I was protecting myself now, too, because he had an investment in me."

Glancing at the display, Skater saw Larisa sitting on the big couch in the living room. He suddenly remembered he'd never seen it all in one piece. She had her hands fisted together and squeezed between her knees. It was a habit she had whenever she felt stressed or overwhelmed.

"I realized that I was protecting more than that, then too. During the time I was pregnant, I started to feel the baby more and more." She paused, as if trying to find the words. "I can't explain, but it was like she was kicking and twisting and turning just to let me know she was there. It was the only way she had of getting my attention, of communicating with me. I knew she was ours. Mine. But I didn't know how I was going to keep her. That became my whole purpose in life. And now that I'm gone, Jack, know for chiptruth that I didn't give Emma to those drekkers. No matter what they say."

On the screen, Larisa stood up. Evidently she'd been too tense to sit any longer.

"I really wanted to tell you about her five months ago. I'd already started to lean on you more, and you know it. That's why you were pulling back. Looking back on it, I realize I'm partly to blame because I was pressuring you and you didn't have a clue why."

The suite's regular telecom suddenly beeped and Archangel started to get up to answer it, but Skater waved her back down again. He tapped a key even as Larisa's voice continued, and found a message waiting for him at one of his drops. It was from Kestrel.

"Then I thought maybe even if I did tell you," Larisa went on, "we wouldn't be able to run. Not without a lot of money. I didn't know how much you had put aside, but I had nada. And these people, Tone and Maddock, they weren't nitbrains. Maddock is slime, and Tone likes to hurt people; that's why they got him."

Skater keyed up the message from Kestrel. There was no vid, only the fixer's distinctive voice. "Carbone will talk to you." An LTG number followed.

"I overheard Maddock and Tone talking a few weeks ago," Larisa said. "Tone was bragging. He likes to do that anyway, but he was boasting even more than usual. He told Maddock about a Tir freighter called the *Sapphire Seahawk,* and said it was carrying some files worth millions of nuyen. Just like my baby."

Skater punched in Carbone's LTG number and listened to it ring. He wasn't worried about the call being traced; Archangel had seen to setting up cut-outs along the way.

"So I got hold of you," Larisa went on. "I knew if the paydata aboard the elf ship was worth anything, you'd see to it I got my share. I was hoping it would be enough to get Emma and me clear of Maddock and Tone."

A gruff voice answered the telecom.

Skater asked to speak to Carbone and added his name. He was told to wait a moment.

"Since you're getting this message," Larisa said, "I guess

something went wrong. Maddock has been acting edgy the last few days, so I suppose they're going to try to take Emma soon. I don't know everything that's behind the scam, but I do know that an elf couple somewhere is wanting to buy an elf baby, and that they've got millions to spend doing it. The doctors checked me to make sure Emma was an elf embryo. Maybe if she hadn't been, they'd have let us go. I don't know."

The gruff voice came back on-line and barked out another number, a private line to Mr. Carbone's office.

Skater said thanks, but the connection had already been cut.

"I don't think Tone is the brains behind it all, but he's definitely over Maddock," Larisa said. "Find him, Jack, because you're Emma's only hope. No one else will care. If you've got this, it means you've met my mother. You know it's true." Her voice broke, but she forced herself to go on. "You and I, we almost made it. But the secrets we kept got in the way. It's hard giving up those secrets when you've learned to close off so much of your life from other people. I know you didn't want ties or responsibilities. I didn't want them either. But Emma . . . she's got no one. And these people who took her, I don't want our daughter to be some kind of prize. Find her, Jack, and take care of her when you do."

The screen on Skater's telecom flatlined into a gray surface. No one said a word, but the group gradually broke up. Archangel returned to her deck and jacked in while the others went to see about assembling some kind of a meal. Even with Lofwyr's help, all were aware that they couldn't stay hidden forever. And there was the deal they'd made with the dragon. Time was running out on all fronts.

Skater had a call to make and he punched in the numbers, one by one.

"Carbone," came a cultured voice after a few moments. A brief instant later, the vid image flickered to life. The man had thin blond hair that lay plastered against his scalp. His eyebrows were almost colorless, thin edges against pink skin, but his dark blue eyes fit the Vashon Island suit he wore. He was inspecting a compound bow, plucking at the drawstring with his fingers. When he did, a laser aiming light fired a ruby shaft out of the telecom's view along the bow's sighting line.

Skater pushed all the swirling emotions out of his mind

and concentrated on dealing with Carbone. "I'm Jack Skater."

Carbone nodded. "I got your name when your call was transferred back." He plucked the bowstring again. "I know who you are. What I want to know is why I should give you the time of day."

"Because," Skater said, "I can take Synclair Tone off your hands. From what I gather, that's something akin to losing a cranial tumor."

"Interesting." Carbone laid the bow on an ornate desk that looked like it had been assembled by elven carpenters. Then he seated himself behind it. "Except that Tone happens to be protected property."

"And you're doing the protecting," Skater agreed. "Somewhat less than enthusiastically."

"But with no lack of professionalism." Carbone leaned back in his chair.

"Agreed. That's why I'm calling you. If I could do this without disrupting what you're doing, I would."

"And in the event that you somehow succeeded, I'd have you tracked down and geeked." Carbone steepled his hands in front of him. "Just so we both know where we stand in this thing."

Skater nodded. In his mind, Larisa was telling him again that the baby's name was Emma, that she was his daughter. He put a lid on the thought with real effort.

"Getting Tone flatlined while in my employ could be somewhat embarrassing," Carbone said.

"Keeping him around could prove to be even more embarrassing," Skate replied.

There was only a slight hesitation on Carbone's behalf. "Yes."

"And there could be rumors circulating that you paid for someone to whack Tone yourself. Of course, these would remain unfounded. You are not, however, in the protection business, so it shouldn't affect your real marketability."

"Indeed, I am not." Carbone laughed, and the sound of it was cold and brittle. "It would be poetic in a way, I suppose, people saying that even I wasn't safe from myself after the contract had been accepted. But—how do I know you can deliver?"

"Even if I wasn't able to remove Tone, you'd still be in a position of deniability."

"True."

"I'd consider that a win-win situation for you however it goes."

"What is it that you want from me?"

Skater didn't let a smile touch his face as he slid into position to deal. He knew he couldn't ask who Tone belonged to, but he knew the man's boss *had* to connect somehow to Silverstaff. "I know about the casino Tone has cut himself a part of. All I want from you is a bit of laxity."

"Later, it will be questioned how someone was able to take Tone from my watch."

"Are you Tone's keeper," Skater asked, "or are you being used as a cover?"

"Suggesting that my responsibility to Tone ends somewhere?"

"You didn't authorize him to cut into the casino."

"No," Carbone answered. "Though it's well-known that I keep a close eye on my staff."

"It's also known that Tone isn't exactly one of your staff."

Carbone took a long, slim cigarillo from an ornate box of worked metals. "Yes." He tapped one end and then lit it with a sculptured lighter. "What is your interest in Tone?"

"Personal."

Exhaling twin streams of smoke through his nose, Carbone said, "So you'd risk much to get him."

"I think I already have," Skater said. "Approaching you about getting rid of him isn't the wisest thing I could do. Especially when you could sell me out to any of a handful of interested parties. I'm betting that being rid of Tone is worth more than that. You'll let me know if I'm right."

Carbone blinked once, but otherwise his face might have been stone. "How soon could you make your move?"

"Five minutes after this transmission."

Carbone nodded. "Give me an hour. I'm sure arrangements can be made. But keep in mind one thing."

Skater listened.

"If there are repercussions, if I am asked to look into the matter and take care of it, I will. Never doubt that."

"I don't," Skater replied. "I'm gambling that whoever ultimately owns Tone doesn't really prize him. Tone is just a piece in a very deadly chess game. He has no real worth, except as a planned sacrifice. I'm just going to take him out of the game prematurely and change the relationship of cause and effect."

"We'll see if you're correct." Carbone leaned forward and broke the connection.

Skater let out a tense breath and hit his own Disconnect. It was time to find out if he was right.

30

Stinky-Fingered Al's occupied the bottom two floors of what had once been a four-story hotel. The new security bars over the windows and the reinforced security door creating an isosceles triangle with the two cross streets contradicted the peeling paint and graffiti.

Skater double-parked the Ford Americar he and Duran had boosted behind a delivery truck servicing a small troll restaurant across the street. A hand-lettered sign running down the length of the cafe door said RIBS. The scent of simmering barbecue sauce filled the air.

"I hear Stinky-Finger bought the hotel from a real estate company that was never able to get it out of the red," Duran said from the passenger seat. He ran a hand through his unruly coarse hair, then slipped the Scorpion's sling over his shoulder where it would be hidden by his combat-cut jacket. "Guess the gambling action here is wiz, though."

Skater had to agree. Sandwich boards on sawhorses advertised available parking in three different areas. A local go-gang called the Leather Devils had evidently set themselves up as the parking franchise for the casino.

Adrenaline surged inside Skater as he crossed the street. His focus was there, but not quite in reach. Thoughts of the baby—Larisa's daughter—kept cycling around in his head, moving but going nowhere. It was hard to keep from operating out of emotion, and the strongest one he felt was confusion.

"You chill?" Duran asked as they stepped up on the curb in front of the casino.

"Getting there." Skater shifted inside his duster, adjusting to the feel of the Predator in the break-out shoulder rig under his left arm.

"Don't worry about getting around everything right now. It's been coming at you too fast. Take care of the biz you can, and let the rest of it come when the time's right." The ork pushed one of the doors open and waited for Skater. "Tonight, it's time for Synclair Tone."

Skater nodded. He had to work on that too. The closer he got to Tone, the more tightly the anger inside him coiled. He knew that Duran was aware of it.

"What'll it be, gentlemen?" The woman lounged behind the bulletproof windows of the ticket booth. She was young and black, wearing a diaphanous top and tight shorts.

Two yabos in black pants and black tee shirts with SECURITY across their chests in red letters stood on either side of the entrance. Both held automatic rifles, and pistols were leathered at their hips.

One of them took up a wand plugged into a wall power outlet. "We need to check you over before you go in. Policy." His eyes were cybered, steely death.

"Mr. Carbone thought it would be no problem if we went on in," Skater said.

The gillette stared back hard, but didn't say anything.

"Anybody else going to come in here and tell you that?"

The yabo put the wand away. "They're expecting you," he said, sounding like he took it as a personal offense. "Go on in."

Duran followed Skater through the door.

On the other side of the entrance, the smell of the casino hit Skater like a physical force. Cigarette smoke, alcohol, beer, cheap perfume and sweat, interfaced with the sour smell of desperation, all combined to make an olfactory haze that thickened the canned air put out by the AC.

The tables were filled with the after-hours crowd. Several of the patrons still wore their uniforms and talked loudly as the booze worked in them. The carpet was worn, as tight against the floor as ligaments on a man dead two days, and suspiciously stained in wild patterns. The decor was lacking, but the lighting was low enough that most of the crowd wouldn't have missed it if they'd cared enough to look.

But the action at the tables was hot. Cards and dice and chips whisked out across the new green felt. Croupiers and dealers kept the players properly antagonized and sympathized with as the need arose. At least three tables were devoted to virtual-reality maze chases where the watchers bid against the house on the outcome. Floppy display monitors overhead charted the progress of the challenger and the house champion. Other games included simboxing and simdog-fights with aircraft ranging from Kitty Hawk to the latest Aztlan releases.

A long-legged brunette elf carrying a tray of bottles and drinks stopped in front of Skater and Duran on her way back to the bar. "What'll you have, chummers?"

"I'm looking for Synclair Tone," Skater said.

The smile didn't leave her face, but it tightened and all the warmth drained away. "He's in the back at his usual table. You can't miss him."

Skater nodded and walked around a blackjack table where a troll female was dealing, leaning forward from time to time to engage the players' interest with the incredible expanse of cleavage available. He stayed away from the pools of light as much as possible, and didn't make contact with anyone along the way.

Duran was an intangible shadow at his heels, covering his back.

Synclair Tone was seated at a rear table set on a dais raised almost two meters above the gaming floor. Two other tables sat around him, but they were unoccupied. Three women clustered around Tone, scantily dressed and hanging on him. One of them was a black elf, and the other two were human. The human woman on Tone's right moved like she was chromed, making all the curves dangerous. Skater mentally filed her away as he made for Tone.

"Any particular way you want to handle this, kid?" Duran asked.

Skater didn't reply, focusing on Tone and kicking his boosted reflexes on-line. Adrenaline rushed through his system, slick as quicksilver and throbbing like a jazzed salsa beat. Grabbing the handrail of the short flight of stairs leading up the tables, he had to force himself to breathe correctly.

"Just keep your head low when the drek hits the turbo," Duran said tersely. "Guy went to all that trouble to get himself handsome, he's probably tricked out in Arnie-Awesome hardware too. And he ain't gonna like it none, you trying to mess up what the docs have done."

The Predator was in Skater's fist as he hit the last step and wheeled toward Tone.

Tone picked up on him at once, but didn't move from behind the table. He kept both hands in view; and if he hadn't, Skater knew he'd have already opened fire. He stopped four meters from the table and groped for the twisting center of himself. Emotions and thoughts were all knotted up inside him. He forced out a long breath through his open mouth.

The lights from the gaming floor spilled over his shoulder and fell across. Tone and his table. Two of the women, the elf and the unchromed human, moved away, out of Tone's reach.

Tone grinned at Skater. "You got a problem, chummer?"

"No," Skater said in a level voice, "you do."

Scratching his smooth-shaven skin as if unconcerned, Tone said, "You come in here carrying heavy metal. Your friend too. Makes me wonder how you got past security."

"You don't exactly make friends where you go," Skater said.

"I think I'm doing okay these days." Tone glanced around, looking for the security teams working the floor.

Skater looked with him, never taking his eyes off Tone or the razorgirl. Evidently the yabos working the front door had passed the message, because the hard guys were leaving the floor.

"Some of those guys belong to me," Tone said. "Stinky-Fingered Al didn't buy you and send you in here."

"No. I've got a personal interest in you," Skater said slowly. "Remember a woman named Larisa Hartsinger?" The name hung in Skater's mind, bringing with it memories from the past. Memories of how Larisa looked in the morning light, the sound of her laughter, the silk of her skin under his fingertips, the scent of her favorite perfume, and the taste of her mouth when passion ran hot between them. An image of her, tearful yet smiling while she held her baby, froze in his mind. And the focus clicked in, turning him into a monofilament whip waiting to be unloosed.

"History," Tone said. "Days dead, and didn't even put up much of a fight." Skater felt the black rage drop on him, but it wasn't so much that he didn't see the small finger signal Tone gave the razorgirl. Without warning, she launched herself at him like a heat-seeking missile. Snap-blades jutted from her forearms, and spurs flicked out from her heels as she flipped through the air. Light glinted from the whirling mix of keen-edged steel as she knifed toward Skater.

The shadowrunner stood his ground, locking eyes with Tone, who was reaching under the table. Duran was back there, Skater knew, and backup didn't come any fiercer than the ork.

The fusillade of bullets from Duran's Scorpion whipped by Skater, a few of them actually cutting through the loose folds of the duster where there was no Kevlar lining. He didn't move.

But the rounds caught the razorgirl as she came out of her flip, her blades extended and reaching for Skater's throat and face. Centimeters from making contact with her prey, the bullets hammered into her and knocked her back, a shattered puppet with its strings cut.

The haze of blue gunsmoke drifted across the table as Tone pushed himself away and leaped up, a pistol in his fist.

Skater took two quick steps, his muscles and synapses firing with the boosted reflexes. Behind him, he could hear the screams and curses of the casino's patrons as they scrambled for safety. He threw himself at Tone.

The contact was hard, fierce, letting him know that the other man was definitely chromed up. His weight drove them to the floor, breaking chairs and scattering them in all directions.

Skater chopped out with the Predator and smashed the barrel alongside Tone's gun-hand hard enough to tear the flesh. The reinforced bone didn't break, but the pistol bounced away into the shadows.

They landed hard. Off-balance from his swing to disarm his opponent, Skater couldn't move away from the forearm shiver Tone threw with his other arm. Hard muscle and bone and cyberware crashed into his face and knocked his head backward.

He hung onto the Predator as he rolled away. Using his free hand, he caught himself and came up on his feet. He lifted the pistol, looking for Tone.

And caught a kick in the head that split the flesh over his eyebrow. Blood trickled into his vision, blinding him on the left. He let the force of the kick move him back a couple meters, listening for Tone's movements as well as trying to see them.

Material whipped and snapped.

Skater ducked, and the follow-up kick sailed over his head. He smashed the Predator's barrel into Tone's support leg, hard enough to shatter a normal kneecap.

Tone's scream let him know the pain was there, but his fluid movements showed that nothing had been broken.

Standing, Skater set himself and pointed the pistol at Tone's head. "Game's over," he growled. The anger was a chained thing striving to break its limits inside him. He saw two images of the Mafia man; one in normal view, and the other limned in crimson from his own blood.

Still in a defensive posture, Tone glanced around the nearly empty casino. He smiled derisively. "That how you want it, hoopfragger? You waving that gun in my face and making me back down?"

"I'll take it that way," Skater answered. He made no move to wipe away the blood streaming down the side of his face. The Predator didn't waver. "Of course, you don't have to leave it at that. You can try to jump me, and I'll test that dermal sheath you call skin. Let me know if I find any weak spots. But I'm betting I can shoot your eyes out before you reach me."

"And me," Duran called in a low voice, "I'll cover as much of that action as you want to handle."

Tone spat at Skater's feet but missed.

Skater didn't move.

"You're Skater, right?" Tone said. "You're here because of that elf slitch."

Skater didn't say anything.

Tone grinned maliciously. "Had it real bad for her, didn't you? That's what Maddock said."

Inside him, Skater felt the anger move, growing larger, consuming him.

Tone visibly relaxed. "You know who killed her, bozo? Anybody give you the lowdown on that?"

"Don't let him sucker you, kid," Duran advised in a rumbling voice.

"Frag you, tusker," Tone said. "This is between pretty boy and me." He smiled again. "Let me take that micro-mystery away from you, Skater. I killed your slitch. Put a bullet through her wetware. And by the time I was through with her, she was begging for it."

The anger devoured Skater completely. Without hesitation, he put the Predator's safety on, then flipped the weapon back to Duran.

"Kid," the ork said, snatching the weapon out of the air. "Don't try to be no fragging trid hero."

"No." Skater stepped forward. He was no hero. If he was, he'd have saved Larisa. But he was going to remove that cocky smile from Tone's made-over face.

"That's right, kid," Tone coaxed, turning the name into an insult, "come kick my hoop. You know you want to so bad you can taste it." He dropped into a defensive posture.

Skater kept moving.

31

As soon as he got within striking distance of Tone, Skater uncoiled, feinting with his left hand toward the main's midsection, then following up with a wheel-kick with his right foot.

Tone ignored the feint and went for Skater's foot, trapping it in both his hands. The bigger man wrenched viciously. In response, pain shot up Skater's leg from ankle to hip. He wavered off-balance.

Before Skater could recover, Tone brought a hammer-blow down against the side of his knee. A heartbeat before the blow landed, Skater was able to turn slightly and deflect it.

"Hold still, nitbrain," Tone grunted, "and I promise I'll make this as painless as possible." He yanked Skater off-balance again and readied himself for another punch.

Gathering his strength, Skater leaped up and plowed his free foot into Tone's face. He felt the man's nose break and the grip on his ankle released an instant later.

Tone yelled in pain, roared curses. Then as Skater pushed himself to his feet, favoring his wrenched ankle, Tone rushed him.

Crashing into him, he yanked Skater from the ground and propelled him back against the wall. One long-fingered hand gripped Skater under the chin and forced his head back.

"Fragging drekface." Tone's broken nose dripped bloody

strands of mucus down the front of his face. For the moment, the handsome look he'd purchased was erased. "I'm going to kill you, then I'm going to take out the tusker."

Over Tone's shoulder, Skater saw Duran closing in. "No," he croaked.

Reluctantly, the ork stopped advancing, but he continued to hold the Scorpion at the ready.

"Too proud to ask for help, boy?" Tone taunted. His breath pushed into Skater's face in nauseating waves. He gave a short jab that rocked Skater's head, snapping it back against the wall.

Sparks shimmered through Skater's vision from the double impact. He brought himself back into focus, letting the pain be his guide.

"You're just begging to get yourself geeked," Tone promised. He brought a knee up into Skater's side and knocked the wind out of him.

Gasping for his next breath, Skater straightened and slipped another jab. Tone's knuckles crashed into the wall.

"You think you're gonna avenge that elven slitch?" Tone asked. "You think that's gonna bring her back?" He punched again, connecting with Skater's temple. "You're dumb as a bag of hammers if you believe that."

The force turned Skater's head and he felt another stream of blood running down the side of his face, curling through his hair. He partially blocked the next blow, but it skidded off the back of his head.

Tone's breath was fetid and sour with alcohol. It gusted hotly into Skater's face as Tone struggled to hit him again. "I come from the streets, dweezle. I'm harder than you, tougher than you, faster than you. Fragging shadowrunner. You never learned how to stand up and fight, did you?"

Skater blocked the next few blows, running on the adrenaline of the boosted reflexes. Tone was going to beat him. He could feel it.

"One thing I got to say," Tone stated, "Your slitch put up a better fight than you did."

The anger swirled within Skater and he went with it, letting it give him some extra kick. "No!" he shouted, and pushed the bigger man back by sheer strength. He blocked Tone's next blow, but the force of it partially numbed his arm. Images of Larisa's corpse intermingled with his other memories. He remembered her telling him that he was

Emma's only chance. He remembered his grandfather's words about being the wind. Whether he'd wanted it or not, Larisa had given him roots. Shadowrunning had given him the chance to be the wind, and its call was seductive. No ties, no responsibilities.

But that wasn't true anymore.

Whatever possibilities Larisa had represented had been ripped away by Tone—and by whoever gave him his orders. But the baby still existed. She was still out there, almost within reach. He was determined to span the distance.

Tone came at him again, a whirlwind of augmented punches and kicks that whipped through the air.

Skater blocked them with increasing ease, finding the groove now. Tone was a force, battering and steady, but not inventive. Skater worked with that, countering, blocking, evading, finding the weak spots, letting the other man wear himself out. He listened, hearing his own breath coming hard in his ears, but Tone's was coming even harder, a bellows over a hot forge.

Whirling, Tone kicked out.

Skater ducked under the leg, letting it slide along his blocking arm to partially off-balance the other man, then standing and moving in. His attack arm bent into a vee, then the inside of his elbow smashed against Tone's exposed neck.

A strangled cry died in Tone's throat. He staggered and tried to set himself, but his lungs couldn't draw in oxygen.

If he'd hit much harder, Skater knew he'd have killed the man. He reeled in the anger, making it work for him. Stepping forward, he threw two overhand blows into Tone's face, snapping the man's head back both times. Skater concentrated on his breathing, pulling the air in and keeping himself loose.

"You're wrong," Skater said as he set himself for a front snap-kick, "I've been fighting all my life." The kick smashed against Tone's broken nose.

The man screamed out in pain and went over backward.

Skater brushed the blood out of his eye, clearing his vision some. As Tone pushed himself to his feet, he closed in. Skater kicked him in the face again, then waited until Tone got all the way up this time. "Who hired you?"

"Go frag yourself," Tone said. He wiped at his face and his hand came away covered with blood.

"Talk to me," Skater said, closing again. "It's the only way you're walking out of here alive."

"You talk big, drekface." Tone threw himself at Skater.

The big man was slower, but his cyber enhancements still made him deadly.

Skater spun, wasn't there when the other man arrived, and delivered a spinning backfist to Tone's face a heartbeat later.

Stunned, Tone dropped to his knees, then worked at getting back up.

Pain filled Skater's body, and his hands and feet ached from the repeated impacts. They were already swelling. "I know about you giving the bag to Silverstaff and his wife."

Tone threw a punch.

Skater moved under it easily, and delivered a short jab that cracked Tone's ribs. "I know you hired Ridge Maddock, and I know you leaked the information to him about the *Sapphire Seahawk*."

Tone's face went white with pain and he made an obvious effort to focus.

"I also know you're not smart enough to do any of that on your own. I want the guy behind you." Skater spun, delivering another side kick to Tone's mid-section. He worked on chopping the big man down, using his hands and feet to beat a vicious tattoo against every vulnerable part he could find. He didn't let the violence touch him, kept the anger in check, using just enough of it to be relentless.

In seconds, Tone collapsed to the floor and lay there facedown.

Skater stepped in and knotted his hand in the man's hair. Using his strength and weight, he pulled Tone to his knees.

Tone was groggy, batting out with his hands ineffectively.

Behind the big man now, Skater looped an arm under Tone's chin, putting a palm over the guy's ear on the other side of his head. He slid his other hand down, locking in the hair just above his other ear.

Tone reached up and tried to pry Skater's hands and arm away.

Skater maintained the hold, letting Tone feel the strength. He leaned down, breathing harsh in Tone's ear. "How about it? Think I can twist your head off?"

Tone pulled at the arm shutting off his wind, but couldn't budge it. His eyes were glazed with fear.

"Maybe I'll only break your neck," Skater whispered.

"Bad enough that no body doc can hotwire the damage. Maybe turn you into a quad. We can see." He tightened his grip.

"McKenzie," Tone croaked, struggling to take another shuddering breath.

"Tell me again," Skater said.

"Conrad McKenzie," Tone replied. "He promised me he'd move me up in his Family after everything was over and the time came. I can't breathe."

"McKenzie's working with the elves." Skater relaxed his grip slightly.

"He's working for himself." Tone sucked in a breath.

"He knew about the freighter?"

"Yeah. And he set up the deal with Silverstaff for the baby."

"Why did Silverstaff want her?"

"I don't know. I swear."

Skater believed him. He stepped away, having to concentrate to keep from stumbling. Looking out across the floor, he saw the casino's yabos standing around. None of them were close enough to have heard Tone's admission.

"Time to go, kid," Duran said. "Chances are the clientele of this place would be somewhat reluctant to notify Lone Star about what happened here tonight, but stranger things have happened." He came forward and slapped the containment manacles they'd brought on Tone, blocking off the man's access to his cyberware, and a headjammer to nullify any radio or phone link he might have. Then he jerked Tone to his feet.

Skater took his Predator back and followed Duran and their prisoner out of the casino. He considered McKenzie's involvement, looking for the angles that would allow him to access the man. McKenzie's world turned on money, and with the stocks in ReGEN and the dragon as his silent partner, Skater figured he had the hammer he needed to bring McKenzie down.

"Ready to hear about Ariadne Silverstaff?" Archangel asked.

Skater had stepped out of the shower in the suite and was wrapping a towel around his waist. He'd stood under the hot needle spray until most of the aches and all of the blood had disappeared, then followed it up with a cold deluge until he couldn't take it anymore. He felt more awake, but he knew the sensation was false. He was running on adrenaline, and there was little of that left.

"Tell me," he said.

Archangel seemed pleased with herself in spite of the fatigue revealed by the dark circles under her eyes. "I searched all through the Tir for mention of her, but Ariadne Silverstaff née Stonewater doesn't seem to have come into being until just a few years ago. There's a reason for that."

Skater nodded in understanding. "Because she didn't exist until a few years ago."

"Right. You guessed?"

"Yeah. Put it together on the way over. Tavis Silverstaff has been in the public eye in the Tir since he was a kid. Just like his father before him. If there were any skeletons in the closet, they'd have come out before now."

"Which left the woman," Archangel said. "But you were figuring something like this before you went to meet Tone."

"Yeah." Skater ushered Archangel out of the room and shut the door while he dressed, leaving just a crack for them to talk through. Steam covered the mirror.

Synclair Tone was being held in another room. Wheeler had seen to the damage with a medkit and Elvis had taken care of the incarceration. The Mafia soldier was going nowhere, and was going to live while he did it.

"It scans as a blackmail squeeze of some sort, otherwise the Silverstaffs would have found a less nefarious adoption agency," Skater said as he pulled on synthdenim pants and a soft gray pullover. He winced as the material grazed some of the injuries he'd taken over the last few days. "What's the bottom line?"

"Ariadne's not an elf," Archangel said.

Skater opened the door, picked up his boots and socks, and padded into the living room. He flashed on the face he'd seen on the trid. "She looks like an elf."

"Cosmetic surgery," Archangel said. "I haven't found out who did it, but I know that's what it's got to be. I also know who she was before she became Ariadne Stonewater."

The rest of the team was in the living room. Elvis and Trey occupied the long sofa, Duran and Wheeler the chairs. Trays of fruits and sandwiches lay spread across the long, low coffee table, as well as containers of soykaf and tea.

Skater sat on the couch when Elvis made room. He

dropped his boots in front of a steaming plate of noodles. Tasting it and finding it delicious, he realized he was hungrier than he'd thought. He glanced in Trey's direction.

The mage inclined his head. "My culinary skills improve with the materials that I have to work with."

"Yes," Skater said. "Thanks."

Archangel sat in front of her deck and tapped as she spoke. "After ruling out Tavis Silverstaff myself, I wondered about the woman, what she might be hiding."

A datapic of Ariadne Silverstaff popped onto the vidscreen.

"The lack of a family, of a past, bothered me some," the decker said, "but not too much. There are still some elves who develop through Unexplained Genetic Expression, and record-keeping wasn't all that good in the Tir when it was first formed after the start of UGE. However, it was all I had to work with."

Skater sipped his kaf, listening to Archangel talk, looking for the arsenal in her words that he hoped to find. Already a plan was forming in his mind.

"Women do a lot with how they look," Archangel said. "I started there, using some of the appearance utilities I have for making false documentation requiring a datapic base. I altered her appearance and kept the images cycling through a program I set up that cross-referenced them with various Seattle databases."

A multitude of Ariadne Silverstaffs flipped across the vidscreen. They looked older, younger, fatter, thinner, blonde, gray, and tens of other combinations. Then they froze, coming to rest on a sallow-faced young girl who definitely wasn't of elven blood.

"I asked myself what might be the most damaging secret for the wife of someone so prominent in the Tir," Archangel said. "So I took away the elven features. This is what I ended up with."

Skater studied the face, trying to fathom what story it told.

"A lot of people in the Tir might not consider Tavis Silverstaff such a fair-haired darling if they knew he was married to a human," Duran said.

"As prejudiced as most of those slotters are in the Tir," Wheeler said, "there's no way in hell."

"Why hasn't someone else figured this out?" Trey asked.

He steepled his forefingers under his chin and studied the image on the display.

"Why would they try?" Archangel asked. "Tavis Silverstaff, and perhaps his family, would be the only ones who might have wanted to check her out. Cosmetic surgery of this type wouldn't be visible through magical means. If she told her husband, and I'm thinking she probably did, he'd have helped make sure her elven identity was locked because he loved her. And with NuGene in such financial straits, why would anyone bother targeting Silverstaff for blackmail?"

"Who was she?" Skater asked, feeling drawn toward the girl's hollow eyes.

"Her name used to be Arlen Crenshaw," Archangel said, pulling up official-looking documents. "She was arrested a few times in the red-light district near the docks."

"Sex-for-sell?" Elvis asked.

Archangel nodded. "Two of the charges stuck and she served some time. Not quite a year in all."

"But enough to be kept on file," Skater said.

"Right. And somewhere in there, she got the nuyen together, had the cosmetic alterations done, moved to the Tir during one of the resettlement times under the Ariadne name, then met and married Tavis Silverstaff, star athlete and potential economic powerhouse."

"Then McKenzie's blackmailing Silverstaff because of his wife's past?" Wheeler asked.

"McKenzie may not even know about that part," Skater said. "He has Larisa's baby hanging over their heads." He still couldn't bring himself to say, his daughter. "McKenzie wouldn't need anything else."

"So that's how McKenzie got an easy in where we're concerned," Elvis said, rubbing his capped tusk thoughtfully. He shifted. In response, the troll's immense weight caused everything to shift.

"As we discovered, McKenzie was already working to make sure the NuGene branch opened in Seattle," Trey stated. "Business and crime often go hand in hand in this sprawl."

"It doesn't really matter," Skater said. "One led to the other, however it happened."

"She's an angle we can use," Duran stated.

"I know," Skater said. "But if we expose her, Silverstaff

goes down the drekker. Part of the deal we made with Lofwyr was to hand Silverstaff over—intact." He turned the various scenarios over in his mind. "Attacking McKenzie outright isn't an option. And we don't know how, or even, if NuGene is dirty."

"There's another problem with taking NuGene down," Archangel said. "If we do, and manage to smear their name around, the dragon's stock won't be worth slot."

"He's not going to be a happy camper if that happens," Elvis said. "Personally, I don't want to leave Lofwyr holding the bag—or even any part of it."

Skater nodded, looking at the face on the display. "Agreed. What I do want to do is keep Ariadne Silverstaff out of the line of fire. And the baby as well."

"In the elven embassy, she's going to be guarded pretty fragging tight," Duran growled.

"But she's not going to be there all day," Archangel said. "Tomorrow morning, she's due at KTXX at ten o'clock in the morning for an interview with Perri Twyst."

Skater glanced at the time. It was four a.m. "That doesn't give us much time to get ready," he said. "Archangel, see if you can access some building plans. Duran, let's ride. I want to eyeball this place in person before we put this thing together." He was up and moving, feeling the soreness that was clinging to him, but knowing it would wear away as he stayed in motion. There was no way he wanted Larisa's child caught in the crossfire that he knew for certain was coming.

32

The catnap he'd managed before the morning raid helped Skater make it through the waiting. Otherwise, he'd probably have been a basket case, worse than a BTL junkie coming down hard.

"Okay," Elvis called out over the commlink, "she's in the building."

"I read you," Skater said. He reached for the van's ignition, glancing at Duran as he keyed the engine.

The ork gave him a thumbs-up and shifted the Scorpion in his lap. Then he slid the Kevlar-lined mask over his features. With his wild hair and rough build, there was no mistaking that Duran was an ork, but hopefully their targets wouldn't know which ork he was until after the dust had settled.

Skater backed out into the underground parking garage. Security for the trideo station wasn't lax, but it wasn't anything like you'd find at a corp office building or arcology. Trid news dealt in secrets just like every other business in the sprawl, only the focus of the trideo companies was in giving those secrets away for public consumption, not using them for blackmail or to gain a favorable trade balance.

Rows of parked cars were on either side of them, interspersed with thick stone pillars that helped support the building above it. KTXX leased spaces out of an apartment and department store building, five floors up.

"If this doesn't go down right," Wheeler warned, "this could turn out to be a real cluster-frag. I've got her limo in sight."

"Stay on them," Skater said, pulling the wheel hard right and heading down into the lower stories of the parking garage. He was running with parking lights only, and they barely touched the gloom inside the garage. It was nine-thirty-one a.m. KTXX had arranged to meet Ariadne and her party on the third floor down at nine-forty-five.

The lady was arriving early.

Archangel had decked and sleazed her way into the building-security systems and retrieved the layout information before six that morning. Those systems had been easier to get into than the trideo corp's because the businesses they supported weren't corp-driven or financial institutions, and the info had been essentially the same.

"There're two Renault-Fiat Eurovans following the limo," Elvis said. "Figure a possibility of twelve guns added to the four aboard the limo."

Skater nodded to himself. It was all a matter of timing. "Everybody stay chill," he said. "This one's got to come off by the numbers."

Duran reached down and checked the seat belt harness, then flipped the safety off the Scorpion. All their weapons were loaded with gel rounds designed to incapacitate rather than harm. Skater wanted zero bloodshed. They hadn't sorted out who was zooming who on the stock score yet.

Running a hand across the back of his neck, Skater was surprised to feel the sheen of perspiration there. His palm came away wet. He got himself in position, seeing the dark Mitsubishi Nightsky limousine sail sedately down the tunnel leading to the lower levels. The escort vans were barely more than a car length behind.

"Trey," Skater said, accessing his commlink, aiming the van at the gap in the parking wall that allowed cars on this level to get to the exits more quickly.

"I'm ready," the mage said over his external link.

Skater glanced at Duran and got a nod of confirmation. The limousine moved past him. "Now!" he yelled, and floored the van's accelerator. The van shivered as the engine responded. The front-wheel drive screamed against the plascrete floor as they scrambled for purchase.

Then the van was shooting forward, skidding off one of the immense pylons framing the exit ramp, narrowly missing the limo's tail.

Skater only had to pull the wheel a fraction to neatly cut off the lead van trailing the limousine. Rending metal screeched into mega-velocity, filling the underground garage with unrelenting carnage. The elven van locked its bumper into the side of Skater's vehicle and started pushing it along. Skater didn't take his foot off the accelerator until the van slammed into the unmoving wall across the tunnel.

As they'd planned, the impact released the collision airbags, which ballooned to cushion them and keep them from bouncing off the dashboard. His face swaddled in the inflated bag, Skater was blinded for a few seconds till he fought his way free. A blade flicked out, only centimeters from his eyes, then sank into the airbag. It deflated with a pronounced hiss.

"Move," Duran growled, putting away his Cougar knife and kicking open the door on his side of the van.

Skater spared only a short glance at the elves boiling out of the two wrecked vans on the other side of his door like angry wasps. A pair of bullets shattered the window on his side, then punched fist-sized holes through the cracked windshield.

The van had temporarily blocked the tunnel, cutting the sec-teams off from Ariadne Silverstaff. But it wouldn't keep them from climbing over.

Skater threw himself through the door Duran had just

clambered out of. More bullets slammed into the van where he'd been sitting. He fisted the Predator and started running, less than two paces behind Duran's lead. Up ahead, he could see the brake lights of the limo flare into ruby glares nearly fifty meters away.

The limo driver veered sharply when Trey levitated into view from behind one of the support pylons, looking eerily impressive with the edge of his Kevlar cloak clutched in one hand at his side. In the dim light bouncing crazily through the underground garage, the mage's eyes seemed to glow from some inner source. As he gestured toward the limo with his free hand, the sleek, shining vehicle suddenly screeched to a stop, followed by an explosion that ripped the hood from the limo in a cloud of angry orange and black flames. The mage remained hovering, a target for the gunners onboard.

Skater pushed himself hard, trying to reach the battle zone before Trey could be overcome. The call would have by now gone out to Lone Star as well as the Tir embassy. Help would already be en route.

The first elf to leap from the Mitsubishi rattled off a series of shots at Trey, the bullets chopping at the mage's cloak as he gestured again. Abruptly, the gunman stopped firing as an invisible wall of force slammed into him and left him spread-eagled and stunned on the plascrete.

Elvis leaped from the shadows while the door on the limo's other side was opening. Catching the door in one massive hand, the troll ripped it from its hinges with a mighty screeching yank. As the elf turned to face him, Elvis slapped him with the door, knocking the man unconscious.

Bullets sparked off the troll's Kevlar jacket from the driver's side of the limo, but Duran was already reaching through the open window and yanking the man out. The driver was frantically working to bring his weapon around, then slumped an instant later as the butt of Duran's Scorpion hit his skull.

Skater was right behind Duran, glancing inside the limo.

Ariadne Silverstaff was in the back seat looking around fearfully. In front of her, belted securely in a portable seat, was the baby. She was red-faced, struggling, screaming her lungs out.

Emma. Skater thought her name as he reached for her, his usually quick fingers clumsy with the safety harness. Trey's ram spell had been exact. No one inside the limo had been hurt by the forced stop.

The baby continued to scream lustily.

Finally, the straps gave way. Skater plucked the baby out of the seat and glanced at Ariadne Silverstaff.

"Please don't hurt me or my baby," she pleaded. Bright tears shone in her eyes.

Skater backed away, tucking the baby under the folds of his duster. He had to restrain himself from checking her over. If she'd been injured, though, there would have been blood. There was none.

"Get out," he told Ariadne.

She looked like she was going to refuse.

Skater showed her the business end of the Predator. "Your choice," he said in a cold voice. "I'm running on a tight schedule."

Ariadne crawled out of the limousine, gazing at her sec-guards spread out in heaps around the target area. "What are you going to do?"

"This is no Q and A session going on here," Duran growled as he clamped containment cuffs on her slender wrists. Unceremoniously, he stooped long enough to gather the woman and throw her over his shoulder. "Those jokers are starting to catch up."

A glance over his shoulder showed Skater that more elven bodyguards had crossed over the tangled wreckage of the vans and were headed in their direction. He beat feet around the front of the stalled and burning limo as Trey came drifting to land standing.

"That went nicely," the mage said, wiping his hands together. He looked pale and fatigued, his dark eyes feverish from the strain of spellcasting. "At least, I thought so."

"You did good," Skater said. Then he accessed the commlink. "Wheeler, we're not planning on hiking out of here."

There was no answer, just the sudden scream of abused rubber from ahead of them. The dwarf brought another transport vehicle to a rocking halt only a few meters in front of them where it would be afforded partial cover by the limo blocking the tunnel.

Archangel threw open the side door and they climbed in as the first bullets slammed into the sides of the vehicle. "I'll take the baby," she said.

Skater handed Emma over more reluctantly than he would have thought, given the circumstances. She was all that was left of Larisa and their shattered dreams. He moved forward, sparing a look at Duran, who was seating Ariadne Silverstaff in the back of the vehicle, and took the passenger seat.

"Get us out of here," he told Wheeler.

Wheeler manually shot the car forward. Lights flashed over the windshield, white and hot from the elves' hand-torches, and neon from the various information prompts showing advertising as well as directions.

Elvis slammed the sliding door shut, closing out some of the noise. The baby was still screaming, but Archangel was tucking her in close.

"Lone Star's on the way," Wheeler said as he scanned the garage. "I monitored part of the transmission over their regular channels, but when Silverstaff's name was mentioned, they went black."

"Did you get an ETA?" Skater asked.

"Minute, minute and a half," Wheeler replied. "Don't usually get trouble this close to Lake Union so late in the morning."

Skater buckled himself in, watching as the transport vehicle launched itself up an incline leading to a heavy metal door that was sliding shut. "Elvis."

"Don't worry," the troll rumbled. "I already took care of the door. It's on Wheeler's frequency."

"I've got it," the dwarf responded. "Everybody hang tough, 'cause I'm blowing it—now!"

Halfway up the thirty-meter incline, with men and women in gray sec uniforms closing in on them from all directions inside the garage, a series of explosions rattled the massive door and ripped it from its moorings. Elvis's demolition work had been on the money. The clouds of dust and the noise were horrendous, amplified by being trapped in the garage.

Cut free and blown in a designed fall, the door toppled outward into the street only a heartbeat before Wheeler steered the vehicle over it. The ride was bumpy and rough, but over almost as soon as it began.

Out on Mercer Street, Wheeler cut illegally through the intersection of Mercer and Westlake Avenue North, shouldering a delivery wagon aside and zipping between the drivers waiting to proceed with the green light. A flurry of angry honking followed them, but the motorists didn't waste any time.

Skater watched the intersection fill up as they roared through, knowing whatever pursuit might have made it out of the garage would be effectively cut off for a few seconds more. He let out a tense breath. "Okay, let's lose this rolling bull's-eye and shift to some other transportation."

33

Skater looked up from Archangel's display as Duran led Ariadne Silverstaff into the living room of the suite serving as their safe house. Before returning here, Archangel had checked her over and found two tracking devices. One that the woman must have activated at the time of the attack, and the other set for an eight-hour delay if she didn't use a frequency modulator attached to her portacom. Both had been removed.

Standing, Skater waved to a chair in the circle that had formed around Archangel's work area. "Please. Have a seat."

Ariadne kept herself distant. Her arms were folded tightly over her breasts. She appeared hesitant, not wanting to give in so easily. More than two hours had passed since they'd gotten her, and the trideo stations were full of the news. "My husband," she said in a strong voice that carried a sense of brittleness with it, "I'm sure he will be glad to pay any reasonable ransom."

"You're not being held for ransom," Skater said. "Actually, we may be able to help you. It seems you and your husband have been blackmailed enough lately."

Color drained from her face slightly, but she didn't turn away. "I don't know what you're talking about."

"I'm talking about that baby in the other room." Skater returned her gaze full measure.

"My daughter? I don't understand."

"She's not your daughter," Skater said firmly. "That's the whole point." He let that sink in, watching as the woman drew into herself. Anger coiled restlessly inside him when he wondered how much Ariadne Silverstaff knew about Larisa's death.

He'd held the baby briefly while Archangel had been getting her squared away, purchasing diapers, milk, and other things. Surprisingly, it was Elvis, so huge next to Emma that she could almost lie in one big hand, who seemed to calm and soothe her most.

"I know the whole story . . . about McKenzie setting it all up . . . everything," Skater said. "But I wonder how much you know, like where the baby came from?"

"McKenzie told us he'd found a suitable surrogate mother. It was a business arrangement. No blackmail was involved." Ariadne's words came faster now, and with relief evident in them. "This whole thing, there was so much pressure on us, it was so hard to know what to do, who to trust, where to begin even."

"There was no surrogate mother," Skater said. "McKenzie coerced a young woman into having that baby for you and your husband. Once the baby was born, the mother became a liability so he had her killed, presumably to keep her from telling anyone about it."

She looked at him with knowing eyes. "You knew her."

Skater nodded.

"What are you going to do?"

"I don't know," he said honestly. "I was hoping talking to you might give me some ideas."

"My husband didn't know about the mother getting killed either," Ariadne said. "He could never have kept something like that from me."

Skater leaned forward, putting his elbows on his knees, making everything more conspiratorial now. Ariadne Silverstaff was going to be looking for a way out, and if his plan was going to work, she had to buy into the one he was going to offer. "I believe you, but I want Conrad McKenzie to pay for what he's done," he stated.

"He's a very powerful man," she said, "that's why Tavis went to him in the first place. We needed help getting NuGene into Seattle, and it looked like nothing could be done in this city without some kind of help from people like McKenzie. We knew that for a price McKenzie's influence could help protect NuGene's interests once we were established here. My husband linked up with him about a year ago."

Skater gave a short, bitter laugh. "The corps and the criminals may keep their books differently, but seems like they often have the same interests. And always with an eye on the same bottom line."

A look of desperation entered Ariadne's eyes. "NuGene has been in serious trouble ever since Seattle replaced Portland as the main port for goods going in and out of the Tir. Tavis's father had worked so hard to build NuGene into something, but then the Council of Princes took it all away from him. He'd sunk a lot of money into a new product, and suddenly got the market pulled out from under him. And he wasn't the only one. Hundreds went bankrupt. Portland was a boom town in those days, but that changed almost overnight. NuGene was among those who got hit hardest. It's taken years, but it looked like we'd finally found a way out."

Skater listened to the emotion behind the words, sensing that he was getting the truth.

"By the time Torin died, some very promising research had already begun on a promising new organic replacement tissue. The research continued after his death, though the financial strain was tremendous. Last year we were finally ready to go into production, but access to the market was virtually blocked. Tavis's only chance to save NuGene and his family was to get as many Portland backers as he could, promising to set up a branch of NuGene in Seattle. Tavis himself underwent a transplant treatment on his injured knee, using our new tissue. It worked wonderfully, but he was waiting until his position in Seattle was established before announcing it. Things seemed to be going fine until the raid on the *Sapphire Seahawk.* Tavis had no choice but to go public with the stock in hopes of making enough profit that he could buy it all back at a later date, or at least maintain a controlling interest. We had to go into production immediately before someone else beat us to it. But the cost overruns on moving so fast have been incredible."

"The company is vulnerable," Archangel said.

With the amount of stock that had surfaced in the various exchanges, Skater figured it would be two or three years before NuGene made it back into the black. Assuming the company survived.

"Yes," Ariadne admitted. "When the media picked up the rumor that someone had stolen the secret of NuGene's important new discovery, the stocks plummeted. We had to stop releasing it because we couldn't afford to cover the paper once people started to panic and sell. We'd never be able to buy it all back."

"Your husband told you copies of the files were stolen?" Duran asked.

"Yes. He tells me everything. That's why I'm so sure he didn't know anything about the baby's mother being murdered."

Skater stood up, pacing, working it through. Synclair Tone was in another room, kept drugged and cuffed. Now that they also had Ariadne, there were two people who could tie Larisa's murder to McKenzie.

"McKenzie knows you're a human passing as an elf?" Skater asked.

Ariadne stiffened, and then started to tremble. "Yes," she said in a faltering voice, the tears welling up. "We told him I was sterile and that was why we were looking for a surrogate mother. We never intended for him to know, but he's a clever man, cleverer than we thought. He found out somehow."

"Did he threaten you with what he'd found out?"

"No." Tears streamed down Ariadne's face. "But with me being human, we couldn't take the chance of conceiving a child of our own. The chances are fifty-fifty that it would have been born human, and then everyone would know Tavis had married outside the elves."

"And that would destroy him in the Tir," Archangel said.

Ariadne nodded. "Elves aren't the most tolerant of races." She wiped at her eyes. "After I had the cosmetic surgeries, I emigrated into the elflands hoping to find a better life. I found it wasn't that much different really. There were castles and princes, but none of them were mine. But I did find Tavis, and we love each other so. When he asked me to marry him, I told him the truth, but it didn't make any difference to him."

"But it does now," Duran said.

"Not to Tavis," Ariadne answered. "But we married when he thought his father was going to see NuGene through the hard times. With his death, all that responsibility fell to Tavis. I don't know how much longer either of us can handle the pressure."

"You had no problem taking the baby." Skater looked at her, wanting a full read on her answer.

"We were told the mother needed the money and had no interest in keeping the child. We knew we could give the baby a lot of love and a good home."

Skater crossed the room to Archangel and her deck. "McKenzie might not be blackmailing your husband outright, but he sure as drek is running him up the river. We stole the files from the freighter, but they were already trashed."

"Then how did they show up in Seattle?" Ariadne's brow furrowed. "Those are the same files we downloaded into our mainframes at ReGEN."

"My guess is that McKenzie had someone working for him aboard the freighter," Skater said. "He had them load the corrupted files into the ship's system, while the actual files came across on another ship. One that McKenzie controlled. The switch was made sometime before the download could be processed."

"You're talking about a conspiracy within NuGene."

"At the very least," Skater agreed. "What you don't know is that the tip I got on the freighter came from the baby's mother before she was killed. She heard a man named Synclair Tone talking about it—a man also on McKenzie's payroll—but it was all a setup. They intended for her to hear. They also tipped the yakuza that night, probably through a third party, so that everything that happened on the *Sapphire Seahawk* would be even more confusing. Covering up McKenzie all nice and pretty."

"But why would he do that?" Ariadne asked.

Skater pointed to the display as Archangel booted up the files she had waiting. "These are the figures for the ReGEN stock as they went on sale." He tapped the columns. "On the surface, it looks as though a lot of buyers are picking up the stock."

Ariadne glanced at the spinning digital numbers, her rapt attention showing she knew enough of the inner workings of NuGene's finances to understand what she was seeing. "The stocks were selling much more quickly than we'd imagined. Until the media coverage broke."

"Now we begin to break it down," Skater said. "We set up a controlled buy on the stocks, knowing that once NuGene brought the new tech to the market, it would probably go through the roof."

On the screen, a portion of the stocks slid in one direction, then renamed themselves Wayfarer, the gathering place for all stocks purchased through Lofwyr's Ocean Tiller Exports in Seattle. The corporation specialized in exotic trans-Pacific shipping and overseas investments in textile and food futures.

"Ultimately, these stocks became ours, under different holding names and fronts," Skater said.

Ariadne shook her head slowly as she watched the screen. "But how?"

"We brought in a backer," Skater said. "Someone with really deep pockets and an interest already developed in NuGene."

"Who?" Ariadne's tone became defensive and demanding.

"I'm not at liberty to say." Skater pointed to the display. "As you can see, we're currently holding about nineteen percent of ReGEN, even after the stock shut-down. Our representatives are still buying outstanding shares. But we've definitely got competition."

The screen shimmered again. The name McKenzie formed, then shares started flocking toward it like lemmings going over a cliff.

"McKenzie has been buying ReGEN stock since day one," Skater said as the screen continued to show stock certificates flowing into McKenzie's name. "As of the last hour, he controls thirty-nine percent of ReGEN. And he's gotten it cheap."

"I recognize some of those buyers' names," Ariadne said. "But I don't understand."

Skater turned to face her. "NuGene had to put this deal together. The company's survival depended on it. McKenzie cut himself in for a piece by agreeing to help set it up, but he got greedy. He staged the raid on the biotech files so your husband would have to rush into production to protect the research."

"He could have sold it to someone else if he had it," Ariadne said.

"Again," Skater replied, "McKenzie got greedy. He's been making noises about retiring. But in order to do that now, he'd have to forego a considerable amount of his cash flow. NuGene provided him an opportunity to get around that—as long as he could buy up enough of the stock and use it to help him launder other little nest eggs he's socked away. If he sold the files to someone else, all he'd get would be a one-time fee, and having two corps out marketing the same product would lessen the price cap. Competition kills the profit margin."

"So he leaked the story to the trid?" Ariadne asked.

"We did," Skater said. "To get a jump on the competition."

Ariadne slumped back in her chair. "Tavis doesn't know any of this."

"He's suckling a serpent to his breast," Trey said. He handed her a glass of water.

"What are you going to do?" she asked Skater, looking up at him.

"We're going to defang the serpent," Skater said, "then cut off its head."

34

"Do you realize the kind of risk you're asking Lofwyr to take?"

Skater looked at Elschen's dark image on the telecom screen. The sasquatch leaned forward, her fangs visible at the corners of her mouth. He suddenly remembered the dragon's taloned claw snapping shut in front of his face. "Yes, but there's no other way to handle this." He was in the living room of the suite, pacing, working off the nervous energy.

"If it were up to me," the sasquatch said, "you'd be dead just for daring to ask him to do this."

Skater didn't say anything, not wanting to antagonize her further.

"He'll do it, though, because he concedes there's some worth in the venture. But if you're wrong, human, I'll take care of you myself. And death won't be merciful." Elschen's image dissolved with a quick disconnect.

"Well," Trey said from the other side of the room, "that apparently went well."

Skater let out a tense breath. He couldn't wait to return to some semblance of his life before the raid on the *Sapphire Seahawk*. He clicked on the trid, which was set to NewsNet's financial reporting channel.

"Did he go for it?" Wheeler asked, looking up from a steering dog-brain he was working on.

"Yeah." Skater studied the stock quotes running across the bottom of the screen.

"I can freeze it on ReGEN's stock prices," Archangel offered.

Skater nodded.

She worked with the remote control and locked in the information about ReGEN.

The price was holding steady at 113 nuyen a share, with trading primarily sporadic. McKenzie's buyers, the ones Ariadne had identified, were quietly snatching up every stock they could. There'd been a report that even with the deflated interest in the stock, more certificates might be placed on sale before the close of day. Skater intended to make it happen.

Five minutes passed in silence as they waited to see what would happen. Then ten. At twelve minutes, the stock prices and the number of units moving started to go up. Four minutes more and units were moving across the board like they were jet-propelled, the going price jumping to 729 nuyen.

The financial channel broke for a special report, going on location to Wall Street. An excited female elf in a conservative black business suit talked over a dull roar of noise. Behind her, a cluster of people were standing and yelling in front of a huge video tote board that showed current stock prices as well as rotating advertisements from a battalion of corporations. "ReGEN, a little-known stock offered by NuGene out of their branch operation in Seattle, bottomed out yesterday after a small showing over the last few days. But now renewed activity has breathed life back into it. Saeder-Krupp announced only minutes ago that they're interested in purchasing the stock at above-market prices. Needless to say, fierce trading has begun." She went on about Lofwyr's economic prowess and a bit of the corporation's history, and mentioned that the dragon's activities rarely became public knowledge until long after he'd accomplished his aims. No one knew where the present tip on Lofwyr's interest had come from, but it had been confirmed.

When Skater turned off the trid, ReGEN had climbed to 1,024 nuyen a share. It wouldn't last for long, but it would be enough to make any future purchases by McKenzie extremely costly.

He glanced at Ariadne, who was sitting in a chair apart from the group. "It's showtime," he told her.

She nodded.

"Remember, let me do the talking. No signals, no words. You do anything to tip your husband off, and I figure out a new way to get McKenzie, and the two of you can go hang."

"I understand," the woman said.

"Ready?" Skater asked Archangel.

She sat next to her deck, ready to jack in. "Make your call. I'll be along."

Skater punched in the LTG number for Tavis Silverstaff's private line, then moved over to the window and peered out. The anxiety he'd been feeling for the last few hours as they'd put everything into play was thrumming inside him. Seattle lay spread out before him, alluring in the daylight, gleaming and shiny for the most part. Only the shadows betrayed the rot and decay that infected it.

The screen flickered to life and Silverstaff himself answered the call. He looked tired and drawn.

Skater had deliberately left the return vid portion of the call off. "I have your wife," he said, not wanting to waste words.

"I want to speak with her."

Skater glanced at Archangel sitting slumped at her deck; she was obviously hard at work. Duran stood beside Ariadne with his arms crossed, a big pistol showing on his belt. The ork nodded.

Crossing the room, Skater punched on the vid display so that Ariadne Silverstaff was visible to her husband. "One question," the elf said, "and that's all. Or I terminate the transmission."

Silverstaff's voice was hoarse with worry, but he wasn't about to walk into a trap. "On what day did you accept my proposal of marriage?"

Ariadne didn't hesitate, but fresh tears filled her eyes. Her own voice cracked when she replied. "June. June tenth."

Skater switched off the vid. "Convinced?"

"Yes. What do you want?"

"For starters, I want you to sell another seven thousand shares of ReGEN stock to Saeder-Krupp," Skater said. "You'll find the offer registered in your office by the time I end this call. It's a fair price. You're being offered the market price before the bottom dropped out yesterday."

Silverstaff answered almost at once, even though he had to know that selling that much more stock was going to seriously cripple his chances of maintaining control of the company. "Done. You're working for the dragon, then?"

"Indirectly," Skater said. "I've cut a deal with him. Mainly I'm working for myself."

"You said this is the first thing," Silverstaff reminded.

"I'm not going to ask you to turn over that stock transfer contract until I can put your wife back in your hands."

"When?" Silverstaff asked.

"Tonight," Skater answered. "Midnight." He stared across the intervening chasm of buildings and saw the monorail gliding by in a silvery streak four stories above the streets.

"Where?"

"I'll be in touch and let you know." Skater punched off the power, then looked over at Archangel.

She stayed slumped for a few seconds more before coming back to the physical world. Reaching up, she plucked the jack from its slot in her temple. "He was being monitored," she said.

"McKenzie?" Skater asked.

"I couldn't be certain," she answered. "I had to work to trace the bug. I figured if McKenzie did have a way of keeping tabs on everything that's going on at ReGEN, he'd have a dump file. Some stepped-up smoke and mirrors utilities got me into the ReGEN system so I could locate the file, but I had to do some heavy-duty sleazing to track the source down. The number picking up the bug is an import business called the Hidalgo Republic Trading Company."

Skater nodded. "Did they trace us?"

She shook her head. "No way. With all the relocate programs I had layered against your call, a decker would have taken hours to get through."

"McKenzie or someone else may recognize my voice if audio was made of the call," Skater said. "That would work in our favor, actually. But they still won't know where we are." He went over to the telecom again, punching in the number for one of Kestrel's message dumps.

The fixer was back in touch in less than two minutes.

"Hidalgo Republic Trading Company," Skater said. "I need to know who owns it."

"I'll get back to you," Kestrel promised, breaking the connection with a click.

Quickly and efficiently, the team started making their preparations. Everyone knew the waiting was over and the countdown had begun.

Three hours later, Skater stood in the doorway of the room where Emma lay sleeping, quietly watching the child. Her features were so much like Larisa's it hurt. Her hair was black, like his, and so fine he could see through it, but her doe-shaped eyes were Larisa's. She slept on her back, one pink-fingered hand knuckled up to her mouth. Her pointed ears looked longer than most elves' and were plastered against her head, running toward the crown. Elvis had fed and changed her only minutes ago, then dressed her in the yellow sleeper she wore now.

She looked so small, so frail and vulnerable on the big bed.

And Jack Skater was more afraid of her than anything he'd ever faced.

"Is she sleeping?"

He glanced over his shoulder at Archangel. "Yeah."

Archangel joined him in the doorway. "She's a pretty child, Jack."

"I thought I was just prejudiced."

Archangel smiled. "No."

"What are you going to do with her?"

"Tonight?" Skater asked. "Elvis has arranged for some troll chummers to take care of her. They'll stay here. No one has a fix on this doss yet. If we make it through the meet with Silverstaff and McKenzie, we should be okay."

"I knew about that," Archangel said. "I meant what are you going to do with her once this is all over?"

"You must be feeling awfully optimistic."

"You didn't answer the question."

Skater looked at the sleeping baby. "Larisa asked me to take care of her. No one's ever asked me to take care of anyone. And I've never asked anyone to take care of me."

Archangel looked at him quietly, and he could feel her eyes on him. But he didn't know what she was thinking.

"I don't know if I can do it."

"Do you want to?"

"I don't know that either."

"Guilt's not a reason to take something on," Archangel said. "Feeling responsible is a somewhat stronger reason, but it's still not one that's going to help you through the hard times. And there will be hard times."

He nodded. "It's going to take some time to sort all this out. I wasn't expecting any of it."

"Whatever it is," she said. "You'll make the right decision."

"If everything comes off the way we've planned tonight," Skater said, "Ariadne and Silverstaff should get out of this in one piece. I could leave her with them. They've got more to offer her than I do."

"Do they?" Archangel reached out and laid cool fingers on his cheek, turning his head to face her. "Do they really?"

"He's the head of a corporation. They're a couple. They wanted a baby. They don't live in the shadows with each heartbeat dependent on how quick your next move is or whether or not you can smell a setup. Are you forgetting I'm the frag-up who got us into this jam in the first place?"

"No, I'm not forgetting. But you had no way of knowing how it would turn out."

Skater gave a shrug of hopelessness. "I'm just trying to survive."

"That's the first and biggest adjustment anybody has to make. You've got that edge, Jack. Something inside you wants to live so fiercely that you've got the strength to do it. That's only one of the things I admire about you. Not all of us have that edge."

Skater didn't know what to say when he saw the unshed tears glimmer in her eyes.

"You're a builder," she said. "Your survival instinct is only part of that. Whatever you need, whatever Emma needs, you'll find a way to get it. You haven't lived outside your own skin because you haven't had to. But that child in there, she has the power to make you live from the best of yourself."

"Yeah. Maybe you're right."

"I am right." Archangel turned away and crossed her arms over her breasts, bringing the icy cool back to herself. The tears went away, still unshed. "As for the Silverstaffs, NuGene is no longer his. They're a couple, for now, but the secrets they're going to have to carry around, even if we're successful tonight, may be more than they can handle, no matter how much they love each other. And even though they say they wanted a baby, they never had the guts to do it on their own. A child would have been another secret they'd have had to protect; not a baby. And the shadows? The shadows can reach out and take anyone down at any time. You know that."

Skater turned her words over in his mind, his gaze fixed on Emma. There was a lot to think about. When he turned to Archangel once more, she was already gone.

Ariadne had been asked to return to her room and stay there while they finished gearing up for the run. Not once had she asked to see the baby. Skater thought about that and it hurt. He remembered the little boy who'd been left in the Council lands, waving goodbye to his own mother, abandoned to strangers. The memory brought a tightness to his chest that was overwhelming, but he knew he couldn't leave this baby. He felt the ties that bound them. What he didn't know was if giving in to those feelings was going to be good for her.

He crossed the room and sat down on the side of the bed, careful not to wake her. He ran a finger along her arm, watching how her soft skin pinked up at his touch. He stopped at her hand, marveling at how small it was up against his finger.

"How about you?" he whispered. "Do you think I can pull this off, too?"

Her hand came open for an instant, then curled tightly around his finger when he froze, trying to stay still and not wake her. She hung on to him tight.

And he let her.

Kestrel's call came in an hour later, just before eight. It was brief and to the point. "Hidalgo Republic Trading Company is a front for the Seattle Mafia to move contraband around. But Conrad McKenzie pulls the strings."

Skater thanked the fixer and hung up. Elvis, Wheeler, and Duran were already hours gone, taking care of the setups they needed at the meeting site. After he told Archangel and Trey what he'd just learned, he called the others over the commlink, letting them know the op was green.

By ten, Archangel had finished with her part of the mission and presented Skater with an ebony credstick.

"It activates with a cellular scan that registers your DNA," she said.

"Silverstaff has it too?"

"Along with your passcode."

Skater took the slender rod and slipped it into his shirt pocket in a protective case.

"It's loaded with everything I could think of," Archangel promised. "I've got attack utilities programmed into that credstick that'll bring most portable decks to their knees, backed by mirror utilities and a shield program that should buy me the time I need. I also layered in browse and decrypt utilities that will get me to the files and break them into information I can use almost immediately. The deception and sleaze utilities are some of the best stuff I've ever written. Seconds after that credstick slots into a reader, the programming will unleash a virus that will create a node slaved to my deck that temporarily establishes itself as their system's CPU, giving me control of their deck for a minute or two until the IC reacts and dumps me back out. It should be enough to get what we need."

"We're going to find out soon," Skater said.

At eleven-thirty-two, Wheeler called and let Skater know everything was set. The troll chummers of Elvis arrived a few minutes after that. While Trey gave them their orders concerning Emma and Synclair Tone, Skater called Tavis Silverstaff. Once again he left the vid function off.

Archangel jacked into her deck.

"Have you got it?" Skater asked.

"Yes," Silverstaff said.

"You're familiar with the monorail circling the inner city?"

"Yes."

"Board it at the King Street Station at twelve-oh-seven. Car eight. If you leave now, you can make it."

"How will I know you?" Silverstaff asked.

"I'll know you," Skater promised. "And you'll know your wife." He broke the connection and glanced over at Archangel as she surfaced from her deck.

"Hidalgo Republic Trading Company again," she reported. "They were there from the beginning."

Skater nodded as Trey brought Ariadne into the room. She looked tense and nervous. All of them were dressed in the stolen orange repair suits worn by monorail maintenance crews that they'd gotten from a fixer Trey knew.

"Let's do it," Skater said, and led the way to the private elevator.

35

Skater and his team caught the monorail at the Belmont Avenue station. Midnight was still eleven minutes away when they boarded.

The original Seattle monorail had been destroyed in 2036 during the Night of Rage, and since been rebuilt. Where it had once risen only eight meters off the ground and traveled along a linear track, the new monorail operated on a maglev propulsion system that circled the inner city four stories above the streets. Two trains worked twenty-four hours a day, passing each other in opposite directions. At the front of the trains were the bullet-nosed control stations that regulated the magnetic fields generated that pulled the train along the superconductive metal rail housed in the center of the track. The original monorail had been built for the 1962 World's Fair, and had sailed along an electrified track. With the new maglev system, the trains could never be sabotaged by someone simply shutting down the electricity.

The station was raucous even at this late hour. Few innocents were abroad because the thriller gangs ruled the night and the streets of the inner city. Dressed in their colors, they pushed and shoved at each other, laughing when someone got mad and took a real swing. A knife flashed as Trey reached back to help Ariadne Silverstaff into the monorail car, and one of the thrillers went down with a blade buried in his gut. His companions boarded the next car up from the shadowrunners and yelled obscenities as the downed ganger dragged himself away, leaving a bloody trail.

A double row of seats ran down either side of the car, with synthleather loops hanging from the ceiling for passengers who had to stand. In the mornings and afternoons, the monorails were crowded with commuter traffic. Now, the weak lights barely illuminated the interior of the car.

Trey led Ariadne to a seat, then sat beside her, keeping up a calm and cool front to reassure her. The woman's face had blanched white as they waited for the train and she still looked pale.

Archangel moved immediately to a corner in the back of the car and removed an access plate, quickly dropping a tap into the car's emergency com and booting up her deck, hidden inside a scarred orange toolbox.

"Please secure all items and keep hands and feet inside the cars," the pleasant male voice recording announced over the intercom systems.

With a lurch and a hiss, the monorail took off.

Skater jerked with the sudden acceleration. Adrenaline was pounding inside him, setting him on the razor's edge of awareness. The boosted reflexes were only a heartbeat away.

The monorail car was twenty meters long, three meters high so most trolls only had to duck slightly, and seven meters across. On the outside, it looked like a flat-gray sausage and bore the blue pattern of Line Two. Line One cars were painted with red patterns. The colors were always layered over with graffiti, and the city had given up trying to keep the trains unmarked. Emergency access doors were at either end, and were never supposed to be opened without authorization. Usually, at night, that rule was violated.

There were four other passengers in the car, all of them looking like late-shift workers just trying to survive the trip home. None of them looked like McKenzie's people. But then, Skater supposed, none of them would.

"Something wrong with this car?" a slender girl asked. She wore ripped clothing, had her face pierced above both eyebrows and through one side of her mouth, and sported a brilliant chartreuse bowl cut. Her eyes were dead behind the rectangular sunglasses.

"No," Skater replied. "Regular monthly maintenance."

"And it takes four of you?"

Skater looked at her. "It's not exactly safe."

"Yeah." The girl showed him a bloodthirsty grin. "No drek." She leaned her head back and closed her eyes.

Looking out the smeared and streaked windows, Skater watched the sprawl pass by four stories below. He seldom rode the monorail. Larisa had liked it, but it always left him feeling exposed and vulnerable. The train wound between some of the buildings, and soared over others, moving along the support track.

During the day, it took almost forty-five minutes to circle

the city, even with the automated stops and locked doors keeping the lines moving. But at night the time was nearly halved.

Skater accessed his headlink to make sure they hadn't been jammed as they approached the King Street Station.

"We're ready," Duran reported.

The ork, Wheeler, and Elvis were further back in the train, waiting to back up the play.

Skater glanced at Archangel, and she gave him a nod. Her spot offered some protection and would keep her out of sight for awhile.

The monorail eased to a stop. The automated voice announced the station and opened the doors.

Three of the passengers off-loaded, leaving the young girl behind.

Skater unfurled a TEMPORARILY CLOSED FOR MAINTENANCE banner with suction cups at the four corners and affixed it to the windows. He walked to the door and turned away a half-dozen passengers and pointed to the sign. They grumbled but moved on. Still blocking the door, he turned to the girl and said, "I'm afraid you're going to have to find another car for the rest of your trip."

"I like it here just fine."

Skater gave her a hard look. "You'll like it more somewhere else, or you'll have to catch the next circuit."

"Fragging ditbrained sprawl service-drone," the girl muttered as she gathered her bag and pushed herself up. She ignored the door and used the forward emergency exit to get into the next car.

"There he is," Ariadne said. She was looking through the window.

Peering through the gloom of the King Street Station, Skater saw Tavis Silverstaff walking hurriedly toward the monorail car.

The elf was dressed in casual wear that had already drawn a pack of Cutter thrillers, their gold and green colors marking them even in the shadows. Silverstaff merely ignored them, stepping quickly into the car.

"Hold it right there," Skater said, unzipping his jumpsuit to get at his Predator in its shoulder leather. He wore Kevlar under the jumpsuit as well, and he was already sweating with the heat of it.

Silverstaff froze in the center of the car, his eyes locked on his wife.

Trey moved slightly, revealing the pistol he was holding.

The thrillers tried to follow Silverstaff into the car, but Skater stepped in front of them, blocking the way. "Car's closed," he said, indicating the banner in the window.

The lead Cutter was a gap-toothed male with sandy hair that looked like it had been styled by a blind man wielding a lawn edger. "Think you can keep all of us out?" he taunted.

Skater lifted the Predator and shoved it between the thriller's eyes. "You won't be around to know."

Angry noises started in the back, egging the leader on. But he didn't move, even after the canned message about the doors started up. As the train pulled away from the station, Skater put the pistol away and turned to Silverstaff.

"You've got the credstick?" he asked.

"Yes." Silverstaff reached inside his jacket and pulled out the ebony rod. "I received the payment earlier. The credstick holds the stock. Your DNA is locked into the access codes."

Skater plucked the credstick from the man's fingers. He'd already sensed the shadows gathering on the other side of the emergency exit when he heard Elvis's warning over his headware.

"It's happening," the troll samurai said. "They've got guys coming at you from both ends."

Wheeler had replaced the monorail's dog-brain remote control with the one he'd rebuilt at the suite. As a result of the new dog-brain interface—equipped with masking utilities courtesy of Archangel so the replacement wouldn't be detected by the main transport CPU downtown—the dwarf rigger not only had access to the monorail's controls, but the security cameras as well. The other members of the team could see everything that was going on in all the cars.

"We're on our way," Duran promised.

Over Silverstaff's shoulder, Skater saw the front emergency door yanked outward. He drew the Predator again and pointed it at Silverstaff. He also took advantage of the confusion long enough to switch the credstick for the one Archangel had prepared.

"I told you to come alone," Skater told Silverstaff.

Ten yabos filled that side of the car, pulling weapons. They were obviously McKenzie's muscle.

"Skater," Trey called, playing out his part of the scenario. He stood up facing the rear door to the car, holding his gun out and using Ariadne as a shield.

"I see them."

"We're almost there, chummer," Elvis said over the Crypto Circuit. The sound of the wind whipped in over his transmission, blotting out some of the words.

Skater knew Elvis, Wheeler, and Duran were by now making their way across the top of the train. He couldn't stop them, because the train would be pulling into another station soon and the passengers getting on or off would give them away. They were only two cars away; things would have to happen quick.

Grabbing Silverstaff, Skater jammed the pistol to the elf's head. "Stay back," he warned, "or I'm going to start a direct oxygen feed to his wetware."

A scarred man with big hands just smiled and said, "Don't mean nothing to us, drekhead. You're the joker we want."

"Don't hurt my wife," Silverstaff said to Skater. "Please. I didn't know anything about this."

Skater glanced around the car, seeing that they'd garnered interest from people in the cars ahead and behind them. Some of those passengers had begun to file out, moving in the other direction from the yabos filling the cars. The monorail kept clattering along. Archangel had jacked into her deck and lay slumped out of sight between the seats. Trey had turned and, like Skater, had dropped back to the center of the car, menacing the yabos at his end with a pistol.

"He didn't know anything about this," someone said.

Then the yabos in front of Skater parted ranks, letting Conrad McKenzie pass through. As before, his outward appearance was elegant, but carried an undercurrent of potential threat, like a well-oiled pistol on display.

Skater lifted the Predator and aimed it at McKenzie. In response, every hostile gun in the car was directed at him.

"If you're smart," the Mafia man said, "you'll put away your popgun before you get hurt unnecessarily."

"You walked in here," Skater pointed out. "Maybe we can just be dumb together this once and sort it out in hell."

McKenzie removed his fedora. "Look, punk, you can't

hurt me, and I don't need to hurt you." He shrugged. "Of course, I don't need to not hurt you either."

Skater didn't put the gun away, but he did keep Silverstaff in front of him, playing the role to the hilt. He knew McKenzie wouldn't want to hurt the elf if he didn't have to.

"Silverstaff didn't know I was coming," McKenzie said. "I invited myself." He took a seat near the front exit, making himself comfortable even with the gun pointed at his face.

"What are you doing here?" Silverstaff demanded.

"He had your line tapped," Skater said. "If you didn't invite him, how else would he be here?"

"You're smart, Skater," McKenzie said evenly. "I like that. I guess I have you to thank for tipping the media that ReGEN wasn't as solid as everyone wanted to believe. Of course you kind of balanced the scales with that other biz today."

Skater didn't answer.

"We're here, kid," Duran whispered in his head.

Skater shifted behind Silverstaff. "Wait," he subvocalized.

"I managed to acquire a lot more stock that way," McKenzie continued. "And with the way the prices skyrocketed today, I was able to do a lot of laundry by selling the stock to other fronts of mine. By the time my accounts quit looping all the profit involved, I'll be sitting pretty."

"What's all this?" Silverstaff asked.

"He's been buying up ReGEN stock," Skater said.

McKenzie applauded silently, like a teacher rewarding a struggling student. "I'd wondered how much you'd put together once the stock prices dropped. When they rose again today, and you told Silverstaff you'd cut a deal with Lofwyr, I figured you had most of it."

"My team and I raided the *Seahawk* because of information McKenzie leaked through a sleaze named Tone," Slater told Silverstaff. "But the files we boosted from the freighter were trashed, nothing of use on them."

"That's not possible," Silverstaff said. "We downloaded those files onto the mainframe at ReGEN."

"Not the same files," Skater said. "He set us up, even sicced the yakuza on us by giving them the same information."

"A little later, of course," McKenzie said. "I knew the yaks'd crack the files soon enough and realize they'd been had. You, on the other hand, I thought were without resources. Even after you'd discovered the files were just so much drek, I never thought you'd be able to use that information. Not even to save yourselves. Apparently I was wrong."

"Not from lack of trying," Skater said.

"You made me think those files had been compromised," Silverstaff said to McKenzie. "Why?"

"Because he knew you were vulnerable," Skater said. "If you didn't get the tissue replacement into production pronto, you'd lose everything. And in order to finance a crash program, you'd have to sell stock. If you got desperate enough and sold enough, he could make a fortune."

McKenzie grinned at Silverstaff. "Afraid so. Me and you, we're going to be partners for a long time. The seven thousand shares of stock on that credstick will put me over the top with fifty-three percent ownership of ReGEN." He shifted his harsh gaze over to Skater. "Hand it over."

Skater didn't answer for a moment. "I do and there's nothing to keep you from killing me."

"There's nothing to keep me from killing you now," McKenzie said. "All I've got to do is take that credstick off your corpse."

Releasing his hold on Silverstaff, Skater held up the credstick in his free hand. The anger was moving in him now, but he kept it in a controlled flow. "Not if I destroy it. I don't think you'll find Silverstaff so quick to cut another one of these."

"Sure he would. I've got his wife. I've got you. He does what I tell him to, he gets to live." McKenzie paused. "Just like you. Getting the credstick tonight will be convenient, nothing more."

"That's why you're here," Skater said, "because it's convenient?"

"I'm here because it's about time both of you learned who the frag you're dealing with." McKenzie softened his voice, then laughed. "We've been pretty good partners until now, Skater. I don't want to have to kill you."

Skater knew it was a lie. He and the rest of the team represented loose ends. He wrapped his free arm around Silverstaff's neck, then screwed the muzzle into the man's temple again. "I give you the credstick, but I keep Silverstaff. Until we're safely off the train. If Silverstaff turns up dead, things at ReGEN are going to be up for grabs for a long time, no matter how much stock you think you own."

Mckenzie nodded. "Deal."

Skater flipped him the credstick and it turned through the air until one of McKenzie's big hands snatched it.

36

Skater watched McKenzie intently, knowing things would happen fast now.

McKenzie held the credstick up in his fingers. "Gaberyl."

A slim young man came forward, a deck in a protective case under his arm. He was all in black and wore sunglasses despite the hour. His hair was cut short enough to show the S&M tattooing on his head. Long, silvery earrings hung nearly to his shoulders. He took the credstick from McKenzie and plugged his deck into the emergency com. Then he slotted the credstick. Seconds later, he was jacked in.

"Broad Street station's coming up fragging fast," Duran cautioned over the commlink.

"Null sweat," Wheeler said. "One of McKenzie's people just slapped an override program into the monorail's dog-brain. We're going to bypass the station. It happens sometimes anyway. But it don't matter, because when I jump into that dog-brain, it knows who's boss."

McKenzie's decker blinked his eyes open and looked at his boss. "It's there, but I'm going to need a DNA scan to get in."

Skater knew the decker had read the false programs Archangel had loaded onto the credstick to lure him in. They were surface view only. She and her other nasty surprises lay in wait in cyberspace.

The windows outside the monorail car grew dark as the train shot through the station, pushing back the wave of passengers waiting to board. Skater knew those already on board were surely starting to get nervous, and some might complicate things by becoming violent themselves. He slipped a claspknife from his pocket, opened it, and ran the blade along his arm, picking up skin cells. He handed the knife to the decker. Trey was at his back, tense and ready.

Gaberyl passed the skin sample under the deck's built-in cellular scanner. "Here goes," he said, jacking back into the deck.

Things started to go wrong for the decker at once. First he began to shudder loosely like a man overcome with palsy, then he dropped to his knees, his deck crashing to the floor but still connected to his datajack. Blood poured from his ears.

McKenzie turned his hot gaze on Skater. "Kill those fraggers!" he roared to his men. "Kill them now!"

"Get down!" Skater shouted, pushing Silverstaff down with his free arm as he opened fire with the other hand. Two of his bullets caught McKenzie in the chest, but were stopped by the Kevlar woven into the suit. After that, he was covered by a wall of his yabos and Skater couldn't get a clear shot.

Trey had shoved Ariadne Silverstaff down as well, and was shielding her with his Kevlar cloak.

"Skater!" Elvis called.

"Do it!" Skater said. He fired the Predator dry, even as he felt bullets thud against the Kevlar under his jumpsuit, hitting hard from some ten meters away. Silverstaff crawled to his wife and pulled her behind one of the seats, bleeding from a neck wound.

For a few seconds, McKenzie's men were slow to react, crammed into too little space and trying to move too fast, getting in each other's way. That would change in heartbeats, though, as the quick separated from the dead.

Skater knew he'd put at least three of the yabos down with mortal wounds. Seven of them were still moving. Two of them opened the emergency door and shoved McKenzie through, going with him. Skater wanted to pursue, but he knew that would be suicide.

"Stay down, kid," Duran said calmly over the commlink. "The calvary's here."

Skater rolled behind a seat opposite Silverstaff and Ariadne. They had their arms around each other, one trying to protect the other. Bullets from Mafia guns ripped into the padding and sent the thin foam into the air in streamers.

Then the windows on both sides of the monorail car came apart and a blaze of gunfire followed. Elvis and Duran hung from webbing on either side of the car with the muzzles of their shotguns pointed at the pack of men standing in front of the exit through which McKenzie had just passed. They fired as quickly as the semiautos would reload, emptying the magazine tubes. The muzzle flashes lit up the interior of the car as pellets left scars on the walls. The din rendered everyone deaf while it lasted.

Dumping the empty clip from his pistol and reloading, Skater turned his attention to Trey's end of the car. Nothing human was going to survive the hellish onslaught Duran and Elvis had unleashed at the front end.

A Mafia yabo broke cover and tried to open the emergency exit.

Taking deliberate aim, his ears still ringing from the shotgun noise, Skater shot the man through the head and watched the corpse drop.

Trey gestured toward another. A second later, the man was swept off his feet by an invisible force and smashed against the wall. When he fell, he didn't move again.

Trey turned, his hands empty and ready to deal more magic. "We're alive," he said with a crooked grin. "I didn't really expect that."

"Neither did they," Skater said, nodding at the dead and unconscious men the mage's spells had left in their wake. He glanced back at Silverstaff and his wife. "Time to get you clear of this."

Silverstaff didn't look any too happy that his welfare depended on the runners, but he got his wife up and moving.

Skater watched through the broken windows of the car as Elvis and Duran tried to climb back to the top. The monorail was clattering along the single track below, the line of cars picking up the wind now and shaking from side to side. The ork and the troll were both having trouble getting back to the top. They hung at the side of the car like fat fruit waiting to be picked off.

In the car behind them, Skater saw more Mafia guns swarming at the door. He opened his arms wide and slammed into the Silverstaffs, driving them back against the wall as a hail of gunfire ripped through the car's interior.

"Wheeler," Skater called over the commlink. "Can we lose the car behind us?"

"I'm working on it."

The door to the car in front of them opened suddenly and

a man dived through, a machine pistol in his fist. He rolled, bringing the weapon up in a semicircle that swept a new line of holes across the ceiling of the car.

Skater fired from almost point-blank range, putting two bullets into the man's face as he tried to correct his aim. He looked through the broken window facing the car behind them, then fired another trio of shots that took out another gunner walking the connections between the cars.

The Mafia soldier shouted something when he got hit, then toppled from the connection and screamed louder as he started the long, four-story-fall to the streets.

"It's not the fall that kills you," Trey yelled across the car on the other side of the door. "It's that sudden stop at the end."

Skater kept watch, wondering how long before someone realized a grenade lobbed into the car would make all the difference in the world. He accessed the commlink. "Wheeler."

"I'm done," the dwarf replied. "Stand by. I've had to override the emergency relays. It's not going to be pretty, but it should work."

"Bloody frag," Trey said. "Somebody brought a rocket launcher as a party favor."

"Son of a slitch," Duran said with real feeling over the commlink.

Skater peered around the edge of the window frame and saw it was true. The Mafia gunners had pulled back from the front of the next car, giving the one with the collapsible M79B1 LAW rocket launcher over his shoulder room to fire the weapon.

The LAW was a telescoping length of sudden death, its wide maw gaping at them. It wasn't designed to be used at such close quarters, but the warhead didn't know that.

Skater shoved the Predator's snout through the window and aimed the whole rest of the clip at the coupling linking the two cars. Ejected brass caught the moonlight and the wind, then disappeared instantly.

The sound of screeching metal screamed just before the whoosh of the rocket launcher, and Skater hoped the blown coupling had thrown the LAW-operator off balance even as he fired the thing.

He got his wish. Instead of smashing into the rear of the monorail car or plowing through the door into the interior, the warhead exploded against the car's undercarriage. Smoke and fire belched out from under the car, and the shock waves of the detonation shivered the length of the compartment.

Skater forced himself up from the floor where he'd fallen. He stared at the huge rip that had opened up only centimeters from where he'd been, followed the line of it for meters till it ended nearly halfway down the car.

Through the half-meter-wide tear given birth by the explosive, he could see the rail the car was running along. The ringing in his ears didn't die down and the smoke only got worse. When he saw the phosphorous-based flames clinging to the undercarriage, he understood why. The heat gathered intensity, becoming a live thing that whipped through the car's interior.

On either side of the monorail track, Skater saw the glow of neon adverts lighting up the sprawl below. The monorail lurched, and the split in the flooring grew even wider. Bullets continued to pound the rear of the car.

"Drek, Wheeler," Skater said as he tried to crouch down and press the magazine release on the Predator. He got it on the second attempt and the rectangle of metal clunked to the floor, slid toward his feet, then abruptly changed course and skittered through the widening hole at the side of the car. "I thought you were getting rid of the car."

"I cut it loose," the dwarf said. "Fragging explosion must have jammed the coupling releases."

Skater risked a glance out the window, and a rifle bullet nearly took his head off. Still, the momentary glance he got showed him that the coupling was barely hanging together. He brought his hand over the edge of the window and sighted from the point, banging out shot after shot to offer the mage cover. He accessed the headlink. "Elvis, Duran, you still with us?"

"We're on top of the car," came the ork's voice, "but those fraggers have us pinned down. We've also got some company coming from the troops in the car ahead of us."

Skater knew he was more than halfway through the clip even though he couldn't remember exactly how many shots he'd fired. So far none seemed to have done much harm.

Tavis Silverstaff left his wife's side long enough to retrieve the machine pistol from a dead man, kept in place by a blood-stained sling.

"I hope you've got a clear idea of who the enemy is here," Skater said. "Because if I have to, I'll drop you." He turned the Predator on the elf.

"You and McKenzie can fight all you want," the elf said. "I'm getting my wife out of here."

Skater nodded. A shimmering wave of force left Trey's hand just as the Predator's slide blew back empty and locked. His breath burned his lungs as it carried in the smoke and the searing heat.

With a loud *bamf,* flames jumped up through the hole in the car and started to spread. At the same time, the shimmering force slammed into the car behind them and finished shearing the couplings. The car immediately dropped behind.

But the redistribution of the weight caused the rear of the car Skater and the team were in to come free of the monorail. It swayed sickeningly, bouncing up and down and from side to side as the monorail engine kept pulling it along.

Skater glanced through the view afforded by the hole. The flames alternately reached for the ceiling of the car and were sucked back outside. He saw the street four stories down, then they were over a short building, then an alley where a wrecker with flashing red and blue lights was picking up a derelict car that had been turned into someone's graffiti *pièce de resistance.*

"We can't stay here," Trey said.

The monorail car swung wildly back the other way, snapping like an amusement park ride.

Skater glanced at Archangel. She lay slumped between the seats, still jacked into the deck. He could detect the rise and fall of her breasts.

"She's still jacked in," Skater said. "And we need her there. I'll stay with her while the rest of you get out of here."

Trey seemed on the verge of making some objection, but then simply nodded.

The monorail seemed to gain speed now that the last four cars were no longer with it. They turned a corner, and the warped car listed hard to Skater's right and stayed there, canted at a thirty-degree angle or more and turned diagonal across the track. He saw sparks through the hole in the floor and knew that the car was rubbing up against the monorail itself.

"Duran," Skater called.

"Still here, kid, but barely."

Looking toward the front of the car, Skater realized that the only good thing about the sudden shift was that it broke the field of fire for the Mafia gunners in the car ahead of them. "We're passing Ariadne along, then her husband."

"Which way?"

Skater looked at the window that was now pointed skyward. "Port side."

"Okay."

Skater turned his attention to Silverstaff. "We can get you out of here."

Silverstaff appeared hesitant. Then the monorail hit another section of track and the car slewed sideways even more. The gunfire at the front of the car died away. "It appears that's the wisest course of action." He held Ariadne, taking most of her weight, and muscled her up to the other side of the car against gravity and the incline.

"Fraggit, Jack," Wheeler called out, "this drekking car is going to pull the others off the track."

Skater peered through the shattered window behind and below him. The streets around him twisted dizzyingly. "Can you blow the coupling through the dog-brain?"

"I doubt it, chummer. That coupling is probably so jammed nothing short of an explosion is going to knock it loose."

"You've got plastic explosives in your kit?"

"Yeah, but I don't think those nitbrains up there are going to hold off on their shooting gallery practice while I rig something up."

"Then we're going to have to buy you some time." Skater used the Predator's butt to knock out the remaining glass shards in the window. Then he stripped a Kevlar jacket from one of the Mafia soldiers Trey had mojoed and laid it over the edge of the window. Ariadne would go through easily enough, but it would be a tight fit for the men.

"Gonna need something to tie on with," Duran advised.

Skater glanced around, then took out his claspknife and grabbed one of the hanging loops from overhead. "Cut them down," he told Trey. "We can tie them together."

Trey drew a knife from his boot and set to work. Silverstaff found another on one of the dead men and joined them. In seconds they had a number of them.

Skater worked quickly, tying three of the loop lengths together to use as a safety harness. Then he looped it around Ariadne's shoulders, telling Silverstaff to boost her up through the window.

Silverstaff embraced her quickly, then pushed his wife along as she climbed through the window. Duran caught one of her hands in his and pulled her quickly up.

"Okay," the ork called back. "Next."

Silverstaff fashioned his own harness and climbed through, the borrowed machine pistol slung around his neck.

"McKenzie or his people are trying to stop the monorail at the Fairview stop," Wheeler said over the commlink. "I'm not letting them. If we lose the momentum we've built up, gravity's going to take over and pull this car down. The rest of them will probably come right along with it."

"Keep him out of it," Skater said.

"I am," the dwarf replied. "For now. It's not going to take them long to find the power switches, though. They do that, we're toast."

The car hit another rough patch of track and jerked unexpectedly. Skater went down, sliding down the incline and thudding against the seats on the other side. Blood filled his mouth from a cut inside his lip. He spat it out and struggled to his feet. The flames in the center of the car were staying about the same, but he knew the phosphorus had burned away by now. The fire had found something else to feed on. He turned back to Trey.

"I can manage this," the mage said, levitating himself to hang less than a meter above the uneven footing.

Trey looked strange to Skater, hanging in the air with his balance correct instead of struggling against the incline. "Go on," Skater said. "Archangel and I will follow as soon as we can."

A pained look came over Trey's features.

"Dammit, Trey," Skater said. "You can be of more use up there. Our people can't stay up there. If the car goes, they go with it."

"You could do more good up there too, chummer."

Skater shook his head. "Duran and Elvis are better at the close-in work than I am. I can't work magic. And I can't leave Archangel here."

"I know. Take care of her." Trey rose like a wraith, gliding easily through the window, his cloak pulled close to the compact lines of his body.

Skater turned his attention back to Archangel. She'd been thrown around by the sliding monorail car and was lying under one of the seats. He made his way to her and pulled her out, careful of the datajack. She twitched in his arms, her muscles fighting against whatever she was up against inside the Matrix. A thin line of blood trickled from her right nostril. He wiped it away and cradled her in his arms, holding her tight so the whipping motions of the car wouldn't harm her and shielding her from the heat of the twisting flames behind him.

Abruptly, she opened her eyes and looked up at him. "Jack."

"I'm here."

Then an explosion ripped the front emergency exit open and sent a shiver coursing down the length of the monorail car. It shifted, moving into a forty-five-degree angle now, and the rear of the car bounced even more vigorously.

A pair of gunners came through the door, landing awkwardly, but their weapons were steady in their hands.

37

Skater brought the Predator up in one smooth motion and fired, putting two bullets through the lead man's face. The corpse stumbled back over his partner.

Pushing the dead man out of the way, the second gunner raced for the side of the car where the Mafia decker had gone down.

"Stop him," Archangel said in a weak voice. "If they get that deck, McKenzie could change the passcodes before I can get back in for the rest of the files we need. I couldn't retrieve everything. And they've got that piece of you, Jack. A mage could have a lot fun with that."

Skater shoved himself to his feet and raced alongside the crack as well as he could. The flames reached for him, attracted by the displaced air of his passage.

The Mafia gunman came up firing. A pair of bullets

slammed into Skater's armor over his heart, stopped dead by the Kevlar weave.

Pain wracked Skater's chest even though the bullets didn't penetrate. With the heat trapped in the car and the smoke boiling up, it was hard to breathe, and getting harder to see. Only ten meters away now, the gunman was a silhouette, dimly outlined by the illumination given off by the flames.

The man turned back toward the door, going with gravity this time. He held the dead man's deck in one hand, the datajack dangling loosely.

Skater tried to take aim, but ten or fifteen rounds from gunners still in the forward car ripped through the windows and door and drove him to cover. He caught a brief glimpse of the Mafia soldier making his way through the door.

The monorail hit another rough patch and the incline turned even more.

Returning to Archangel's side, Skater said, "We're going to lose the car. We've got to get out of here."

She was putting her equipment away. Soot streaked her pale features, and another thin ribbon of blood had snaked past her lip and leaked all the way down her chin. "Did you get the deck?" A coughing spasm racked her, almost doubling her over.

"No," Skater replied.

"Dammit, Jack," she snarled. "I almost got it all. McKenzie's files, access to where he's got the stocks, his accounts, the tech from NuGene. McKenzie got paid to dump that subvirus into DocWagon's vats. He's responsible for the laughing death disease, Jack. It was developed at NuGene, too." Archangel faced Skater. "Are you listening to me? It was supposed to be a new way to treat the mentally ill, but it totally backfired. One of the developers cut the deal with McKenzie—and he didn't even care—he probably thought it would help turn more profits once the new tissue came on the market. The antidote is there, but I didn't have time to snatch it." She started to walk toward the emergency exit, but Skater stopped her.

"Let's go." Skater put an arm around her waist and guided her away from the door and to the window. "Duran," he said over the link. "Archangel's coming up."

"I'm waiting." The ork sounded tense.

"Did you hear me?" Archangel demanded as she flailed at

the window almost above her now. "McKenzie's a fragging monster. He tainted the DocWagon vats. He's responsible for the deaths of dozens of innocent people."

"I heard." Skater lifted her. Archangel's reflexes were coming back, but the coughing was throwing her off. "But if we don't get out of here alive, us getting the antidote won't help anybody a fragging slot."

Duran pulled her through the window easily.

Another tremor ran through the car.

Skater holstered the Predator and grabbed the lip of the window. He hauled himself up with effort. The cool night air felt better at once, and triggered a coughing fit from him, too. He hung onto the quivering surface of the monorail car, blinking through tearing eyes as the inner hub of the sprawl went spinning by him in a swirl of neon lights and shadows.

"You can lollygag later," Duran told him in a hard voice. The ork fisted Skater's uniform and pulled him roughly to his feet. "We're still earning a credstick here."

Skater nodded and sucked in another deep breath. He stood with both hands on the ladder railing intended for use by the maintenance crews. Across the uneven top of the car canted at a steep angle, his team hung on, using the loops they'd cut from the passenger section. Silverstaff held his wife protectively.

A gust of wind slapped into the car, rocking it viciously. There was no doubt in Skater's mind that it was completely unhooked underneath, held only by the coupling to the car in front of it.

"We can't stay here," he yelled over the wind.

"Didn't plan on it," Duran said, unlimbering the Scorpion. "We were just waiting on you."

"Some good has come out of our present situation," Trey remarked. He was near the front of the car, prone and peering down. "Everyone seems to have abandoned this section."

Cautiously, sliding his hand along the railing, Skater made his way forward. By now reports should be pouring into Lone Star about the runaway monorail and the violence aboard it. The ops time had about run its course, like the car beneath them.

At the front of the car, Skater studied the forward car. Nothing moved inside it. "Wheeler."

"Yepper."

"You're on."

"I'm there." The dwarf slithered over the edge of the car and dropped onto the platform near the coupling. He dug around in his backpack and set to work at once.

"Trey, Elvis, Wheeler's going to need someone to watch his back." Skater eyed the distance between him and the next car. The leverage provided by the wrecked car had lifted the rear section of the forward car from the track, but it was still lower than his present position. The only problem was the three meters of distance and the fact that they'd be jumping into the wind.

"Take one of them with you," Archangel said. "I can hold a gun. We've got to get that deck."

Skater looked at her. Archangel's color looked better, and there was no denying that fierceness in her eyes. He nodded. "Elvis, you're with Duran and me."

"I'm ready," the troll said.

With the start of a prayer on his lips that quickly changed to an obscenity, Skater threw himself forward. He landed harder than he expected, the impact against the top of the car unforgiving. Numbness spread up his legs and he fell, unable to keep his balance. For a moment he thought he might go over the edge, then he gripped the maintenance ladder and brought himself to his feet again.

Duran and Elvis made the leap more easily. Behind them, Archangel was climbing down to the coupling link while Trey handed Ariadne down to Silverstaff.

Skater moved forward, going as fast as he dared. The wind cut and slashed at him, making him narrow his eyes to slits and almost robbing him of his breath. There were three cars remaining between them and the engine. The footing was treacherous, vibrating and slippery in spite of the friction pads running on either side of the maintenance ladder.

"Grab something," Wheeler advised. "The coupling's going in three, two, one—contact!"

Skater, Elvis, and Duran flattened against the top of the next car after making the jump. Even with a car separating them from the concussion, the impact and subsequent release of the car being dragged was terrific.

The wrecked car was turned loose at once, twisting and turning in the air as it fell, flames surging over it like tidal waves. Wheeler had evidently chosen his time, because the car landed on one of the above ground parking garages in the Seattle Center and exploded into a pile of flaming debris. There'd be property damage, but hopefully no lives lost.

The monorail kept going around the tight turn through the Seattle Center station. Somebody must have issued warnings over the PA system, because the turnstiles were empty, and only Lone Star uniforms were in place. None of them had the opportunity to board.

Up and moving again, Skater made for the engine. He still didn't know where McKenzie was. He called Wheeler over the commlink. "You still tied into those security cameras in the cars?"

"Yepper."

"Find McKenzie for me."

"It's done, chummer. He's in the engine."

Skater leaped to the second car back from the engine. His balance was coming more surely to him now. The drag created by the wrecked car had thrown everything off. He was aware of the passengers in the car below him. Screams sounded over the whipping wind and twice he was shot at by someone other than McKenzie's soldiers.

"Jack," Archangel said, "he's just entering the last car before the engine."

"And a lot of his soldiers trailing along with him," Trey put in.

"You've got to retrieve that deck," Archangel said. "Once McKenzie gets it, he can use the credstick to change all my passcodes and make all those accounts and files inaccessible to me. I'm trying to download what I have at this end now, but I'm going to have to borrow some hard-drive space somewhere. I'll need a few minutes to arrange that."

Skater made himself run harder. All of their futures hung in the balance. The deals they'd made with the dragon. ReGEN and NuGene. Ariadne and Tavis Silverstaff. With care, and a little time, most of it could be salvaged. He was certain of that. He made the leap onto the last passenger car, kicking in the boosted reflexes and feeling the adrenaline surge through him. He got his second wind, felt his senses become more acute and his body resume its coordination despite the fatigue eating at him.

Larisa had given her life for the information Archangel had tapped, and had staked her daughter's future on it. He'd gambled and lost everything himself. If Emma was going to have a chance, he couldn't fail.

He got to the edge of the car just as the Mafia soldier with the deck crashed through the door into the engine. Placing his free hand on the edge of the car, Skater vaulted onto the platform in front of the engine. His hip slammed painfully up against the railing and he grabbed it. When he tried the door, it was locked.

Stepping back, he rammed a foot into the door. The lock shattered and came open, the light inside spilling outward. He went forward with the Predator in his hand, his free hand cupping the butt of it as he tucked it in close to his face.

The interior of the monorail engine was built in a T-shape, with a short corridor between the electromagnets that led into the control cross-section. Voices came to Skater over the throb of the transformers. He recognized McKenzie's at once.

Gunfire broke out behind him, made alternately louder and muffled by the swinging door. Whoever was in the engine with McKenzie must have thought the sound of the breaking lock was part of the general racket echoing through the monorail.

"Kid," Duran called over the commlink, "we're pinned down. You're solo."

"I read you," Skater replied. He kept moving forward as gunfire crashed behind him.

"Look out," Wheeler called. "There's a maintenance rig coming at us up ahead."

Skater peered around the corner and saw McKenzie in the control booth with three other men. He was holding the deck in both hands, looking rumpled but not hurt. On the other side of the windshield, the lean lines of the skeletal maintenance rig designed for working on a monotrain that had stalled between stations swelled into view.

"It's matching our speed," Wheeler said. "Closing the gap between us. We're coming. Just hang on."

Skater knew McKenzie wasn't going to wait, though.

Even now, he'd managed to get another team aboard the monotrain. That maint-rig had to be his doing.

The control room was generally unoccupied except during safety inspections, Skater knew. There were no innocents in the area. He used the commlink. "Wheeler."

"Go."

"You've still got access to the engine's dog-brain?"

"Yepper."

"On my mark, put on the brakes. Does everyone copy?"

The rest of the team quickly checked in with an affirmative.

The maint-rig closed on them, only meters away now and moving fluidly enough to change speeds with them.

Sensing the presence at his back, Skater wheeled.

Duran stood there, breathing hard, blood covering his upper body. "I got your back, kid."

"Where's Elvis?"

"He got shot up pretty bad, but those slotting trogs are hard to kill. He's holding the rest of McKenzie's people off us till the others arrive."

In the control booth, Skater saw McKenzie toss the deck aside and take the steps down to the side door. The maint-rig was getting closer, filling the windshield now as it came at them.

"Wheeler," Skater called, "do it!" He hung onto the side, clutching at a pipe as tightly as he could.

A heartbeat later, the engine's brakes shrilled as they seized up. The engine and the cars had an antilocking system on the brakes to prevent derailment and compensate for load shifts, but anyone not belted down still got a hefty reminder about the physical laws of momentum and inertia. Screams and curses from the passengers cowering for their lives ripped through the noise.

Skater felt like his arm had been torn from its socket, but he held on grimly. Through the windshield, he saw the maint-rig shoot away quickly, then its brakes joined the shrill screaming of metal on metal.

The three Mafia soldiers were scattered across the control booth. But standing in the doorway as he was, McKenzie kept his feet, which told Skater that the man had cyberenhancements. There was no other way he could have stood against the braking action.

Even before the engine had come to a complete stop,

McKenzie was in motion. The side door let out over the four-story drop, but that didn't keep him from finding handholds along the bullet-shaped nose and scrambling toward the maint-rig.

The three Mafia soldiers were getting to their feet, looking back at Skater and Duran.

"Go, kid!" Duran growled. "I'll handle things here."

Skater broke cover at once, locked on McKenzie's fleeing form sliding across the engine's nose. A bullet hit him in the side, slipping around the Kevlar plates, and ripped into flesh. He was knocked off-balance but didn't know how bad he'd been wounded. Staggering, he made it into the doorway with difficulty and leathered the Predator.

Warm blood continued to run down his side as he swung out over the four-story drop and reached for the first handhold. He missed, and swung wildly back. Both feet came off the last rung in the doorway. For an instant he hung over the city, about to be dropped into it like a treat to a hell hound. The sprawl wouldn't even remember him once he was gone.

Then his feet found purchase and he pushed himself onward. He located the handholds and footholds he needed, crawled across the hot metal of the engine. Bullets cracked and whined around him as gunners in the maint-rig tried to shoot him.

Skater was aware of the bloody trail following him as he slid off the engine and dropped onto the monorail's track. The single metal rib was only slightly less than two meters wide, hammered smooth by the wear and tear of years of service.

McKenzie was moving rapidly, but not running, across it. The distance separating him from the maint-rig was less than sixty meters and closing.

Both monorail vehicles only had running lights, nothing that would project enough illumination to cut through the darkness around the track.

Skater was aware of the gunfire lighting up the inside of the engine he'd just quit, as well as the numbing chill that had spread up his side. He ran after McKenzie, keeping to the shadows and not pulling the Predator because it would give the Mafia guns a flash to fix on. The footing beneath his boots was uncertain, and his boosted reflexes were strained to keep him on the track.

Bullets whipped by his face, but as he closed on

McKenzie, he knew he was offering an increasingly smaller target for the hostile shooters to hit. McKenzie, whether he wanted to or not, was protecting him.

"Shoot the fragger!" McKenzie screamed, trying to pick up the pace.

Skater concentrated on his target, letting his reflexes do their job. He drew within ten meters of McKenzie. The maint-rig was shutting down, its brakes showering sparks that fell like plummeting comets and winked out long before they hit the ground. Beyond it were the advertising lights of the Warwick Hotel. Skater remembered staying there one weekend with Larisa. They'd been celebrating something, and it made him sad to realize he couldn't remember what it was.

And now he could never ask her.

The distance between him and McKenzie dropped to five meters. The maint-rig was almost at a standstill forty meters distant. None of the bullets were coming close. McKenzie was too big and too blocky to shoot around.

At three meters, Skater launched himself into the air. He crashed into McKenzie's back and sent the big man sprawling.

Even with his low-light vision, Skater got confused in the dark. He tried to control his slide across the slick surface of the rail, but couldn't. As he was about to go over the side, he hooked an arm back across the rail and brought himself to a stop. Grease and machine muck covered the front of the maintenance uniform as he pushed himself up.

McKenzie, larger and heavier, raised up in front of him. "You stupid son of a slitch," he said. "I've already left too many jokers like you lying in gutters on my way up. You came out here on this rail to die."

Skater stood and assumed a defensive position. The maint-rig was coasting to a full stop twenty meters behind McKenzie. Men were already climbing out onto the nose with weapons in their hands. "If I go, you're coming with me." He drew the Predator, but McKenzie knocked it away before he could take aim. The force of the blow numbed his arm.

A few rounds from the men on the engine danced around them. One slammed into the Kevlar plate over Skater's right thigh and knocked him off-balance. He recovered quickly, then slammed an overhand right into McKenzie's face as the big man closed in.

McKenzie shook his head and backed away. He snorted, blowing out bloody mucus across his lower face. He came in again, using his greater size and strength to push Skater back.

Skater scored with another overhand right, but McKenzie was able to slip some of the blow and returned a backhanded slap that almost lifted Skater out of his boots.

"You out here for the dragon?" McKenzie grunted, closing in again. His hands were up, guarding his face. "You really think that big worm gives a frag about you?" He popped out a hand, splitting Skater's cheek open.

Skater shook his head, trying to clear it. McKenzie could box, and for the kind of footing they had to work with, it was a better style than the martial arts Skater knew. He raised his hands and tried to cover himself.

McKenzie chopped at him, moving easily now, the natural skills melding with and taking advantage of the cyber enhancements. "Golden gloves for four years, punk. Nobody manhandles me. And you, you get the privilege of seeing why close up."

Skater tried to avoid the vicious jabs, but they were everywhere: his face, his body, and twice McKenzie tried to punch him in the crotch. He could feel his face swelling, his lips puffing. Everything he was able to connect with, the big man just seemed to shrug off.

Abruptly, gunfire sounded from the engine behind Skater.

"We're here, kid," Duran said over the link. "Get clear."

Over McKenzie's shoulder, Skater saw the Mafia gunners suddenly realizing their predicament. They scattered like pigeons, and three of them fell from the maint-rig, hit by bullets from Duran and the others.

Skater held his ground, feeling his legs go to rubber beneath him. McKenzie looked away for a moment, perhaps startled by the sound of gunfire. Drawing up his reserves, Skater went for him.

McKenzie glanced back and saw him coming. He turned, his hands bunching into fists. "Why didn't you quit when you had a chance, ditbrain?" He launched a right cross. "Now you're gonna die."

Skater blocked the blow and retaliated with a right hook to McKenzie's stomach that drew a cry of pain from the big man. Before McKenzie could draw back, Skater stepped on his foot, pinning him there, and shook him with two more vicious, stinging hooks.

McKenzie tried a roundhouse, but Skater blocked it too. The dark anger was working in him now, combining with the boosted reflexes and extra adrenaline to switch off the pain.

"Do you remember her name?" Skater demanded, hitting the man in the face with a left.

McKenzie was slowing down, out of gas. His guard was there, but loose, no longer invincible. He looked like he didn't know what Skater was talking about.

"Did you even know her name?" Skater asked. "The woman you had Synclair Tone murder?"

"Frag you," McKenzie snarled. "She was just another loser. Just like you."

"No," Skater said, balling up his right hand again. "She's the reason you're going down." His fist exploded on the big man's jaw. "I wanted you to know that. For me, this wasn't about money." Before Skater could swing again, something slammed into the right side of his face. Hot, bright pain went nova in his right eye, and the sticky warmth of blood cascaded down his cheek, already soaking into the material over his shoulder. Nausea reared up inside him, twisting like a beheaded snake. He struggled to remain on his feet.

McKenzie laughed. "Now we'll see who's going down tonight."

Half-blind, the pain pushing him so far out of his mind he was operating almost entirely on instinct, Skater grabbed one of the big hands that shoved at him. He felt himself go over the side of the monorail track, felt the drop yawn below him, and yanked on McKenzie.

Then gravity kicked in and started him down. McKenzie was yelling somewhere beside him. Twisting in the air, blood splashing over his face, Skater grabbed the lip of the track as he dropped, barely able to spot it. His left hand gripped it, but he couldn't close his right hand properly. It felt broken inside.

McKenzie's scream fell away from him, lasting a long time, then ending abruptly.

Skater looked down, seeing the four-story fall waiting on him. He tried to pull himself up, but he didn't have the strength to save himself. Already his fingers were beginning to slide; a moment more and they'd slip completely free.

He wasn't surprised when it happened. Suddenly there was nothing more under his palm, under his straining fingertips. He remembered thinking that he was sorry he wouldn't be able to take care of Emma the way Larisa had asked him to, because it was the first time she'd ever asked him to do something for her.

Gravity drew him in.

Then an iron grip slapped around his wrist and halted his fall.

Almost unconscious now, Skater looked up and saw Duran grinning at him, lying prone on the track, one scarred hand knuckled into a death grip. "What's the matter, kid? Get tired of hanging around?"

Skater tried to answer—something—but the waiting shadows took him in, giving him shelter from the pain and confusion.

About the Author

Mel Odom is the author of over forty books in the SF, action-adventure, horror, and gaming fields—many of them critically acclaimed by such publications as *Starlog* and *Science Fiction Chronicle.* His most recent novel, *F.R.E.E. Lancers,* was published by TSR Books. He has also had published numerous short stories and comic books.

In addition to writing in already-invented universes, Odom writes his own original fiction. Two SF thrillers involving serial killers: *Lethal Interface,* a Stephen Tall Award finalist, and *Stalker Analog* were published in 1992 and 1993 respectively by ROC/Penguin. These well-received novels have also been translated and published in both Russia and Germany. A third original SF thriller is upcoming.

Odom lives in Moore, Oklahoma, with his wife and four children.

Don't miss the next exciting
Shadowrun® novel,

DEAD AIR

by Jak Koke, coming in October

High up the blue, steel and glass side of the Venice Beach Hilton, Grids Desmond stared out the window of his room, watching the huge orange sun setting in an ocean of aquamarine green. A brilliant red streak reflected off the water, shimmering; glowing like a broad trail of fire between him and the sun. The Los Angeles smog had few redeeming qualities, but it helped turn the sunsets from merely beautiful into spectacular.

Grids was thin for a human, with little muscle on his bones and less fat. He subsisted mostly on a diet of cheese crackers and soykaf. His pale skin was untainted by any hue of melanin since he almost never ventured into the sun without his customary black jeans and Mickey Mouse t-shirt. Despite this, he was handsome in an old-fashioned film star way. Black, tousled hair, white skin. Thin face with delicate, almost feminine features. All but the eyes; his hawk-sharp, dark eyes hinted at what was behind them—a genius intelligence and a quick, if detached, wit.

Grids watched and waited. Waited for the sting to begin.

Nearer, the daytime spectacles of Venice Beach were winding down, and the evening shows were about to begin. Grids brought his Ares CCD binoculars up to his eyes and scanned the beach. At one spot a team of hugely muscled joyboys were performing acrobatics for a crowd of onlookers. The men looked like clones, surgically altered to look identical—all natural flesh, tanned to a deep brown, wavy blond hair.

Grids scanned across the rest of the area. There were magic illusions, dance routines, basketball, volleyball, and sparring matches. People were hawking 'ware of every shape, size, and prescription. Venice Beach was safe territory, bounded by a huge desalination plant on the south side and the walled-off corporate beaches of Santa Monica to the north. Venice Beach was protected by the Mafia and thus considered neutral turf by the local gangs who prowled the toxic beachfront district south of the desalination plant.

Grids brought his headclock into focus on his retina as he lowered the binox. 07:18:24 p.m. Almost time.

He'd been waiting for Tamara since just after one o'clock that afternoon, arriving at the Venice Hilton early to avert any suspicion, checking into room 2305 seemingly at random even though he'd chosen it from a list of rooms within range of Tamara's simlink transmitter stored in his internal headware memory. That had given him ample time to set up his Truman Realink simrecorder and double check the modifications he'd made so that the signals to and from Tamara's simrig would look, at a glance, like portable telecom carrier waves.

Tamara's simrig had been far easier to tweak than others Grids had worked with because it was military grade, from her years as a test pilot for UCAS—the United Canadian and American States. The virtual interface was clunky, but once he figured out what it could do, he marveled at its versatility. Commercial simlinks on actors and techs sometimes had wiz options and programs, but Tamara's signal could be encrypted in any number of ways. It had been harder to modify the Truman.

But now, the time for action was near at hand. Even though, technically, he wouldn't participate in the flesh. Simming Tamara's wet feed from five floors away was as close as he wanted to get. He never took action directly if he could help it.

Better living through vicarious reality.

Grids turned from the window and sat on the bed next to the Truman simrecorder. The Truman was a small semi-portable unit with a black plastic casing about the size of a briefcase. Grids set the small gray CCD binocs next to the Truman, took the last gulp of the cold soykaf from his cup, and double checked that the chip in the slot was still the ten gigapulse stack he'd popped in earlier. Wet record simsense gobbled memory like a ghoul in a graveyard—one megapulse per second at baseline. That meant he had just under three hours' worth.

Unless Andreas Michaelson was some sort of sexual marathoner, three hours would be plenty for what Tamara had planned.

Grids jacked in and made another pass at all the systems for lack of anything better to do. A few minutes later, as he was running a diagnostic on the on-the-fly decryption algorithm, the unit picked up Tamara's simlink signal and started recording.

A thrill of excitement shivered down his back as he sat back, placed his hand on the round bulge of his stomach and faded himself into her feed. The signal was strong and clear, the decryption working perfectly.

Ahh, it's so nice when things work.

Suddenly he was in a helicopter, feeling the resonating rhythm of the rotor blades as the machine descended toward the roof of the hotel. His body was tall and elven, lean and well muscled. And female, very female.

He drank in the ecstasy of her scent—the primal sex of this new body, Tamara's body. Drekking tailored pheromones. The signal coming from her was full-X, the entire spectrum of sensory and emotive tracks, but Grids had programmed the Truman only to record the baseline—the sensory tracks—to save on memory. Besides, Tamara had specifically requested that her emotions not be recorded, saying that they weren't important or relevant to what they were doing.

She was the boss on this one. He was just technical support. It felt like old times, really, back when he a runner, decking for Grayson Alexander. Burn ice. Those were really old times. Before his stint with Brilliant Genesis, before Amalgamated Studios.

At least he wasn't dueling IC on this one. He hated decking, and had never really gotten good enough at battling intrusion countermeasures to suit his sense of self-worth. Even though the Matrix was virtual, it was too real for him. In the consensual hallucination of cyberspace, the virtual became the real. Data turned physical. The drek in there could kill you.

It was harder to die in sim. Not impossible, but harder. The technology was the same in cyberdecks and sensedecks, but most commercial sensedecks had built-in peak controllers. Cyberdecks did not.

In the sim, Tamara's svelte elven form sat poised on the edge of the helo's synthleather seat. Grids tasted mint and the faintest hint of garlic left over from Tamara's dinner. It amazed Grids how fit she was, how good it felt to be able to move with grace and dexterity without strain or effort. She rode professionally for the L.A. Sabers combat biker squad; she was broad-shouldered for an elf and strong for her size, though Grids knew she was acting the role of the female consort this evening.

Cool wind blew her long hair back and tugged at the hem of her long black evening dress as the door breathed open. The beast opening the door for her was a troll of considerable size. Horns jutted from the top of his head, curling up and back like the rack on a huge mountain goat. The ends had been filed to a point and tipped with engraved silver caps. The troll wore a black tuxedo, mirror shades, and he smiled at Tamara as she stepped out.

Behind her came a large man, easily as tall as Tamara, with a barrel chest and a graying brown beard. His name was Andreas Michaelson, and Grids knew he was an exec of some rank at Saeder-Krupp. He'd been seeing Tamara since before Grids had come into the picture.

Michaelson wore an extremely expensive and fashionable suit of shark-skin gray, and a datajack gleamed gold on his temple. He took Tamara's outstretched hand, his palms rough against hers, and he escorted her through the blustering wind of the helicopter to the set of double doors.

The troll took up a position behind them as they reached the edge of the helo pad and passed through the doors, flanked by two Saeder-Krupp security guards. Tamara flashed them a coy smile as they passed, all the while cozying up against Michaelson's shoulder.

She was really turning it on.

"I've missed you so much," she said when the high whine of the helicopter's motor faded enough to hear. "L.A. is hardly bearable when you're gone." Her voice was breathy, a harsh rasp in the back of her throat. "And, of course, I can't come to Essen."

Michaelson laughed. "Yes, well, I'm sorry that my wife is such a traditionalist."

Tamara smiled at him. "Is she?"

Michaelson nodded. "But soon, my sweet, soon I should be spending more time here." He pulled her close and put his mouth over hers.

She reacted in kind, pressing her breasts against his chest and parting her lips slightly in the embrace.

Grids recoiled instinctively as the softness of Michaelson's moustache and beard scratched against the edges of her mouth and the warmth of his tongue pushed past her lips. It tasted of cigar and beer. He was glad when Tamara pulled back and pecked Michaelson on the side of his mouth. She jerked her head in the direction of the troll with the mirror shades who walked behind them, simultaneously pulling at Michaelson's arm. "Let's get inside first," she said.

The hall led to another set of double doors adorned with antique-looking silver door knockers in the shape of lions' heads. A print-scanner maglock hung on the wall next to the doors. Michaelson pressed his hand against the scanner's matte black surface.

A second later, the maglock released the doors with a sliding click and Michaelson escorted Tamara into the plush chamber of the suite. She kicked off her shoes and rubbed her stocking-covered toes into the thick gray carpet as she pulled from his grasp and danced away from him. Playing.

"Ruger," Michaelson said, addressing the troll, "please have my aide bring up some chilled champagne and a sushi tray."

Ruger inclined his horned head. "As you wish, sir."

"And nothing local. The champagne should be French, and the sushi from either Japan or San Francisco."

A slight frown touched Ruger's face. "Of course," he said. "I'll tell Claudio right away." Then the troll closed the double doors, leaving Tamara alone with Michaelson.

Grids took in the hotel suite through Tamara's eyes as she looked around. The place was massive and luxurious with a full kitchen, dining room, sunken living room, and a large bedroom. The walls were adorned with paintings of beach or desert scenes represented in Southwest impressionist style—lots of brown and gray-blue colors, blurry images and such. A wall-sized trideo filled one side of the living room and adjacent was a bay window offering a fantastic view of the ocean.

Tamara walked to the window and watched the blazing half-circle of the disappearing sun. "Grids," she whispered, "I hope you're getting this. I'm sure you'll enjoy it as much as I do."

Michaelson came up behind her and put his arms around her in a bear hug. His beard nestled up against her neck.

She moved her head against his, nuzzling him.

Shivers of the heebie-jeebies shook Grids, but he fought them and stayed locked into the sim.

Michaelson kissed her neck, and she responded by granting him access. His kisses were warm and wet, leaving a trail of cooling saliva on her neck and up to the point of her ear.

Grids fought down the urge to yarf up his soykaf.

But Tamara's physical body was responding to Michaelson's attentions. Her breathing grew deeper. Her mouth slightly parted, her eyes closed.

Michaelson moved his hands over her body. One pressed low on her stomach, crushing the black silk of her dress against the sensitive skin of her abdomen. His other hand traced tiny circles over her breasts, causing her nipples to harden.

A knock at the door brought Michaelson's advances to a halt.

Grids breathed a sigh of relief.

"Yes?" Michaelson said.

"It's Claudio, sir. Here to serve you." Even through the electronic modulation of the intercom, Grids could hear Claudio's affected, fake British accent.

"Come in."

The door clicked open and Claudio entered with a silver cart. Claudio was a fat dwarf, plump and aging; the stark white hair on his head had mostly migrated to his chin. He wore a traditional black tuxedo. "Ah, my dear lady, Tamara Ny," Claudio said, parking the cart near the dining table. "How good it is to see you again."

"Likewise, Claudio."

"I must say I was impressed with my lady's performance last week against Atlanta. I particularly enjoyed the goal you scored on that hand-off from Jonathon Winger. That was—"

"Claudio!" Michaelson broke in. "This is not the time. And would you please put the cart by the couch. And go."

"Yes. So sorry."

Tamara burst out laughing, rich and full. And after a slight pause, Michaelson joined her.

"I will expect your assistance with the Magenics visit tomorrow," Michaelson said.

"Yes, of course," Claudio said. "I will be ready." The dwarf bowed slightly and retreated through the doors.

As Tamara glanced after the dwarf, Grids caught a glimpse of Ruger standing alertly just outside the door, and with him stood several other security personnel including a human woman who Grids took for a security mage—a potential problem if the simlink signal was discovered and decoded.

"Now, where were we?" Michaelson said, "before we were so rudely interrupted."

"Right about here." Tamara put her arms around his neck and kissed him.

He reacted by lifting her into his arms. She laughed as he carried her into the bedroom, and lay her on the king-size bed. Grids tried to get a sense of the room while Michaelson covered Tamara's body with caresses and slowly undressed her. Anything to avoid concentrating on what was about to happen. He thought briefly about jacking out for this next part, but Tamara would kill him if anything went wrong. So he clenched his teeth and tried to keep his attention on the periphery of Tamara's vision, on the decor and the layout of the bed chamber.

The room was huge, with a desk along one all, presumably where Michaelson worked late into the evening. Executive VPs were supposed to have to work long hours, or at least that's what Grids knew from his friends at Amalgamated Studios. On the desk was a cyberdeck and a small telecom unit as well as an open briefcase.

Tamara's vision was filled by Michaelson's hairy chest now. She was naked down to her black silk bra and panties. Her body, when Grids could catch a glimpse of it, was fantastic. Muscles as hard as stone, cut into her abdomen, arms, legs. Michaelson's, by contrast, was soft and pliable. She kissed one of his nipples, then the other, working her way down.

Grids knew what was about to happen and he cringed. She removed his pants slowly, teasing him. Driving him wild. Grids faded his senses out as she reached to brush Michaelson's groin. Grids couldn't take any more. He dulled the input to where he could know what was happening, but he didn't have to experience it.

The fact that she seemed to enjoy it was bad enough.

Thirty-three minutes later, the two of them had finished

and Tamara fell asleep. The Truman simrecorder recognized it and paused itself. Grids had faded himself in once or twice to make sure the signals were clear and strong. After the initial act, to which he had a particular aversion, the sex was more bearable. He even found himself having fun. Michaelson was no porn star, but Tamara knew how to enjoy herself.

By the time the Truman shut off, Grids himself was ready for sleep. But he didn't; he reviewed the chip. Tamara would be pleased; for a wet record, the chip was excellent and it would serve her purpose well. If Michaelson's wife was as traditional as the exec implied, Tamara now had a perfect tool for blackmail.

Grids fell into a deep sleep on the bed, and didn't wake until 09:28:43 a.m. the next morning. He went to pack up the Truman and he noticed that another 58 minutes had been recorded after the sex. The Truman had detected Tamara's signal in the morning and started recording again.

Grids prepared some instant soykaf, then jacked in to sim it. And as he experienced Tamara's morning, a sinking feeling took hold of him. She had done something stupid. Dangerously stupid.

Something that could easily cost them their lives.

THE WORLD OF SHADOWRUN®

YOUR OPINION CAN MAKE A DIFFERENCE!

LET US KNOW WHAT *YOU* THINK.

Send this completed survey to us and enter a weekly drawing to win a special prize!

1.) Do you play any of the following role-playing games?
Shadowrun ______ Earthdawn ______ BattleTech ______

2.) Did you play any of the games before you read the novels?
Yes __________ No __________

3.) How many novels have you read in each of the following series?
Shadowrun ______ Earthdawn ______ BattleTech ______

4.) What other game novel lines do you read?
TSR ______ White Wolf ______ Other (Specify) ______

5.) Who is your favorite FASA author?
____

6.) Which book did you take this survey from?
____

7.) Where did you buy this book?
Bookstore ______ Game Store ______ Comic Store ______
FASA Mail Order ________ Other (Specify) ______

8.) Your opinion of the book (please print)
____
____
____

Name ____________________ Age ______ Gender ______
Address ______________________________________
City ____________ State ____ Country ______ Zip ______

Send this page or a photocopy of it to:

FASA Corporation
Editorial/Novels
1100 W. Cermak Suite B-305
Chicago, IL 60608